EVALENE'S NUMBER

The Number Series

*Danielle —
Thank you for
supporting my debut
novel! ♡ Bethany
Atazadeh*

BETHANY ATAZADEH

Grace House Press

EVALENE'S NUMBER

Copyright © 2017 Bethany Atazadeh.

For information contact:

Grace House Press

https://www.gracehousepress.com

Bethany Atazadeh

https://www.bethanyatazadeh.com

Cover design by Jessica Lindell, Aquila Watercolor © 2017 Grace House Press

Cover art by Erin Miller, Lustruous Elements © 2017 Grace House Press

ISBN: 978-0-9995368-0-3 (paperback)

First Paperback Edition, 2017

10 9 8 7 6 5 4 3 2 1

1

Numbering Day

EVALENE LAY IN BED with the warmth of the sun on her face and the sound of a bird chirping happily outside her window. It looked like a textbook robin, though she couldn't be sure, having never seen one before. The Grid shot down any objects, man-made or animal, that flew above 100 meters. That made the rare bird an especially good omen for today. Her thirteenth birthday. More importantly, her Numbering Day. Finally.

Lola crept into the room quietly with the breakfast tray, expecting Evalene to be sleeping. But how could she, on such a glorious day?

Hopping out of bed, Evalene impulsively gave her nanny a hug. She'd never admit it, but she was going to miss Lola. After today, Evalene officially no longer needed a nanny – hadn't for years really – but the idea of the older woman working in the kitchen from now on put a tiny damper on an otherwise long-awaited moment.

Lola allowed the hug to last a few seconds, though it was against the rules, as if she too might be a bit nostalgic. Then the tiny woman unwrapped Evalene's arms and patted Evalene's soft white hands with her own frail, sun-darkened ones as she let go. "Let's get you dressed, Miss Evie," she said. "First, eat your breakfast."

Ignoring Lola and the breakfast tray, Evalene untied her long silk robe and dropped it on the ornamental rug. She was too nervous to eat a single bite. Running over to her grand mirror along the far wall, where her beautiful ceremonial dress hung on the wall beside it, Evalene stroked the elaborate beading and lace, admiring the stunning, floor-length dress. It was white like the priests wore.

Lola picked up her discarded night robe and placed it in the laundry chute. The older woman then held out Evalene's undergarments, and while Evalene donned them, Lola carefully lifted the layers of the white dress up high so Evalene could dive under the skirt and into the stunning lace-covered fabric.

While Lola moved to the windows to pull back the floor-to-ceiling velvet curtains, letting sunlight pour into the large room, Evalene turned towards her wall-length mirror once more to admire the expensive dress. She remained standing while Lola brushed, and then curled, Evalene's long brown hair.

The dress was soft, but heavy. She wiggled impatiently. Anticipation made it impossible to stand still, much less sit.

When Lola pronounced her done, Evalene hardly recognized the grown up thirteen-year-old in the mirror. She touched her cheek. She didn't feel any different. Maybe the change would come once she got her Number.

Lola shyly tapped her on the shoulder. Evalene turned to find the tiny woman was holding out a gift, plainly-wrapped in yesterday's newspaper. Evalene ripped it open gleefully. Inside was a beautiful baby blue cashmere scarf.

"Lola," she gasped, "You shouldn't have!" With the little allowance the woman was given, it had to have cost at least six months' wages.

The wrinkled old woman smiled, showing all the gaps where teeth were missing. Her slanted brown eyes nearly disappeared as they always did when she was happy. "Presents on Numbering Day is good luck, Miss Evie."

Sighing in happiness, Evalene stroked the soft fabric. She smiled and held it against her cheek, feeling its touch like a sign from God.

Lola clasped her hands over her own deep-brown dress. Glowing with an almost maternal pride, she told Evalene, "It covers your tattoo, like a proper lady."

Evalene touched the unbroken skin on the left side of her neck. She grimaced at the thought of a needle there. But it would be worth it. Though children were automatically considered a part of their parents' class, Evalene was dying to lay claim to her own Number.

While Lola bent to pick up the pieces of the shredded wrapping paper scattered around their feet, Evalene lifted her hair to avoid crushing her curls and carefully wrapped the short scarf loosely around her neck once, tucking the tails under so it looked like a thick necklace.

She admired the beautiful scarf that matched her eyes perfectly, emphasizing the brightest blues, drawing attention to them. Her future color, the color of the highest class of Numbers.

Lola finished tidying and stood. She saw Evalene admiring the gift in the mirror and gasped.

"Miss Evie, no!" she yelled, yanking the scarf off Evalene's neck so roughly a few hairs were caught in it and pulled from Evalene's head.

Sucking in a sharp breath at the twinge of pain, Evalene frowned, too surprised to be angry. "What in the Number One's name was that for? Are you taking it back?"

Cringing, Lola ducked her head, but she didn't apologize. "Miss Evie," she told the floor, "it is very, very bad luck to wear a color before your Number is given to you. We must never assume…" She crossed herself and muttered a prayer.

Evalene rolled her eyes. "We know I'll be in blue… Everyone knows that. Honestly Lola, you're so superstitious."

But she didn't put the scarf back on.

2

The Ceremony

EVALENE RODE WITH HER father in the backseat of his favorite car. The scarf was tucked safely into one of her dress's hidden pockets. For good luck. And because she couldn't wait to put it on the moment the ceremony ended and show it off to all her school friends.

None of the household servants were invited to the ceremony. Mixing the classes was frowned upon in Eden. So Lola had stayed home, waving from the front door until they were out of sight.

Their driver took them through the oldest parts of town, where the streets were almost entirely made up of buildings that had survived World War III.

Evalene loved all of Eden, but she loved this city the most. Delmare was one of the few cities left in the world that still had buildings standing from before the bombs.

Most other cities in Eden were built in valleys, against rock formations and canyons formed by the bombs, still as arid and dry as a desert, with only the sturdiest plants able to survive since the last war.

Yet Delmare had remnants of the old-style buildings left, as well as some of the old-world trees. Those ancient trees were scarred and sometimes off-tilt, yet their roots had held through even the worst explosions. Delmare held the Vandereth household's largest home, one of three mansions, but more importantly, it was where the Number One lived along the coast. His grand home surpassed theirs and every other high-class Number's the way it rose five stories on the edge of the cliffs with its turrets, guard walls, and elaborate gardens and pools surrounding it, like a fairytale castle.

Evalene fought the urge to tug on her father's sleeve as he talked on his cell phone. She was a grown lady; time to start acting like it. Her chest puffed up with pride as she considered her father's phone now. Only a few of the other girls at school had a cell phone in their family. And none of them could claim theirs had Internet on it like Byron Vandereth's did.

Obviously, his work in the government was extremely valuable. This is what she told her classmates when they asked why he didn't show up for her presentations or recitals. The truth was he hadn't been the same since her mother died in the Bloom Rebellion four years ago. But they didn't speak of that. Evalene didn't want anyone reminded of the possibility that her own mother had been involved in the shameful rebellion. Even someone as young as Evalene, theoretically even someone in her own class, could potentially be an informant.

Her classmates had nearly all graduated to their Numbers at this point. Evalene had watched over the last few months as one by one her friends moved on.

Nina Leven and Vonda Lyse had both promised to keep in

touch when they graduated near the beginning of the year. But Evalene wasn't surprised when they didn't. Sophie Ette at least managed one short letter from her boarding school.

No one was surprised when Pha Min was Numbered 12, and joined the priesthood. But when both Calham Itte and Kha Munest were Numbered 11, future Regulators, rumors flew. So many were Numbered 11 these days. Some said the Regulator forces were beginning to look like an army. But these were just whispers.

Evalene's birthday was near the end of the school year, so she was one of the last to leave. The only students left were Osh Witt, Mazz Aker, and herself. She hoped to see all her friends at her ceremony today, although to be fair, some of their schools were too far away.

Walking into the cathedral, the priests had already lit the candles, giving the silent, old building a magical quality. The large sanctuary was eerily quiet. Any noise Evalene or her father made in the connecting entryway echoed across the room and back. Shortly after they arrived, the other guests began to appear, standing outside the sanctuary in the common room, mingling around the food and drink tables. Their chatter bouncing off the walls made the noise level grow louder and louder. Evalene carefully wrapped a huge brownie in a napkin and pocketed it when no one was looking. She would give it to Lola later.

She wandered around looking for her friends while the adults congratulated her father in advance. Glancing nervously towards the sanctuary, where the ceremony would be held, Evalene wished it were time already. Her father proudly placed his hand on her shoulder and Evalene's heart beat hopefully faster.

After today, he would have more time for her. Maybe she could go with him on his business trips now that she was old enough, and had a Number. Anyone could travel if they were Numbered 1 through 16. There was no way her Number and color-class could be worse than that!

Everyone was talking and laughing so loud, her head was starting to hurt.

"Congratulations!"

"May God grant you a good Number."

"How exciting, dear!"

"May your Numbering be blessed."

"Thank you," Evalene murmured to the blue fabric on their chests. "Many thanks. Yes. May it be so. Thank you."

Though Evalene spied a few school friends, she suddenly felt nervous, wanting to be alone. The large coat closet offered her a safe refuge from all the watching eyes in the main room, and after checking that she was alone, Evalene buried into the far back behind the fluffiest coats. The furs tickled her nose.

Eyes closed, she pictured what was coming. The short walk from the back of the room to the altar, like when the brides met their grooms on every first of the month's Wedding Day. But unlike those brides, who had to share the glory with each other, this day was all hers. Another large difference would be the man at the front: not her future husband, just short, balding Father Alfred. He would read on and on in his deep baritone voice, sharing the history of Eden for the millionth time.

As if everyone didn't already know. As if they didn't hear it multiple times a year at other Numbering Ceremonies. Evalene had heard it four times already just this month. And for families who went to services regularly, like the Vandereths, they heard a shortened version every single Sunday as well.

"We endured great trials and tribulations," Father Alfred always began, using all his favorite tragic words, enunciating like a television broadcaster. "Our world was falling apart. The disasters of World War III, worse than anyone could have predicted. The terror and the fighting escalated. We faced money shortages. Paper money became worthless. So many deaths over the simplest things. Food. Water. The bombs, impossible to survive without underground shelter, killing those that starvation did not. The entire surface of our world, destroyed before our eyes. So few people left, yet still we fought each other. Until one day our great leader rose up with a message from the Lord that would save us all."

Just like a politician, Evalene's mother had said once, shortly before she died, *to use God as a tool so no one could argue.* She slid down the wall until she was sitting on the floor. On and on, Father Alfred would drone about the man now known as Number One. How God had revealed to this man that He'd created every human being with a Number. A Number that declared their place and the impact they could have on the world.

It was so simple. Evalene absently stroked the tassels on the bottom of a sky-blue coat in front of her. She couldn't even imagine how the old world had functioned before people knew their Numbers. Her father was so obviously a Number Four, with his grasp of politics, math, sciences, history, literature, economics, and the old languages.

The most talented and genius minds were naturally given the superior numbers of the higher classes, like the Number One, while those meant to serve and support were given lower numbers, not out of lesser value, but as subordinates. Dependents. It just made sense.

Father Alfred often reminded everyone that, "Every Number is valuable, if they know their place. While the rest of the world fights among themselves, starving, unable to make any progress or advance in the world, we in Eden have no fear of war. When Numbers know their place, they do not go hungry or worry for their safety. Everyone is protected. Everyone is fed. Everyone is happy. We are proud of our Number, proud to serve, wherever we are!"

As she heard the crowds moving into the sanctuary, the ceremony minutes from starting, Evalene's fingers itched to do something. She braided the different strands of the blue tassels together as she pictured Daeva, the Number 24 housekeeper who ran their current Vandereth household staff.

The woman's voice was so deep and strangled, it sounded like a dog's growl. With lines permanently etched in her forehead from constant scowling, Daeva always yanked her prematurely grayed hair back in a tight bun, displaying her Number tattoo, obeying the law to keep lower Numbers visible when in public, though she rarely went out. Daeva was an awful woman. It made sense to Evalene that her Number was low.

Evalene cringed. Her mother would have chastised her immediately for such a thought.

But it was true!

Dropping the strings altogether, Evalene clenched her fists. She would never forget the day Daeva had appeared on the news to be publicly rewarded as an informant shortly after the Bloom Rebellion. Though the idea of an informant made sense to Evalene in theory, as she wanted the country to reach its full potential just like everyone else, she'd stared at the television in shock, trying to hide her reaction in case they were observing through the screens, as Daeva spoke out against her own family, her husband and two teenage sons.

She'd reported them with not one, but two treasonous Bibles in their possession, and when questioned, they'd admitted to being heathens, or in their words, true believers. This cult believed they could actually read and understand the Bible on their own, as well as pray to God by themselves, without the help of a Priest or the Number One.

Though Daeva had assumed they would spend a month or two in jail, instead of hanging, Evalene still couldn't believe Daeva's passionate belief in the Number system led her to expose her own family. Staring at the television screen, Evalene had tried not to wonder what she would've done if she'd known her mother was a traitor. Would she have informed on her family as well? This always led her to wonder if her father had known. They'd never discussed it.

But of course, Evalene thought as she stood up in the closet, it was irrelevant now. Her mother was gone, and the future awaited her. Scurrying out of the coat room into the hallway, she worried she was late for her own ceremony. She bumped into one of the priests who worked with Father Alfred as he shuffled towards her.

"Miss Vandereth," he spoke softly, bowing slightly to show respect in the formal atmosphere, his white robes revealing the tips of his shoes as he bent, "the Ceremony is about to start, we must get you to your place."

But Evalene ruined the somber mood by clapping excitedly. "Oh yes, Father Benjamin! This is the best day of my life!" She grinned, then grabbed his arm in a panic, looking into his eyes. "What if I'm Numbered as low as an 8 or a 9? Or worst of all, a 10! How will I ever live it down?"

His wise eyes smiled even though his mouth barely moved. "Miss Vandereth, I very much doubt you need to concern yourself with that."

She smiled back at him, nodding. He tucked her hand under his arm, briskly turning them both to walk back towards the sanctuary, where the ceremony music trickled out.

As they stepped through the tall doorway into the back of the sanctuary, the priest let go of her arm, moving to stand along the back wall with the other clergy. The sun shone brightly through the stained-glass windows as it began to set. The mix of the candles and the sun created a warm, golden glow. The high ceilings made the sound of her footsteps echo, causing the guests from the party, who now filled in the many rows between Evalene and the front of the room, to twist in their seats to stare at her.

The out-of-tune piano stopped briefly, transitioning, before the first notes of Eden's National Anthem started to play, and everyone began to sing along. Evalene lip-synched the words along with them, her mouth too dry and her breathing to shallow to sing a note.

As Evalene moved forward on her own, all eyes followed her progress down the long aisle towards the front of the room. The short walkway seemed to go on forever. All her excitement leading up to this day hadn't prepared her for the weight of it. Her entire future would be decided in the next two hours. She was at the mercy of God and His priests. She suddenly felt small.

Reaching the steps that led to the stage, Evalene felt the room spin. Father Alfred's pudgy hands twitched like he was ready to catch her. Evalene gave him a quick, nervous smile to reassure him before taking the steps and carefully kneeling at the altar in the position of humility. She would stay in this posture until the last portion of the ceremony.

Everything passed in a blur.

The long history of Eden, over before she remembered to start blinking again. The call and response between Father Alfred and the audience, barely registered in the corner of her mind, as she felt her back beginning to sweat and tried to focus on making her breathing less erratic.

The personal testimony to her Value and Worth, given by her Father, caught her attention. Though no one quite knew how much this influenced their given Number, if at all, it was traditionally the longest portion of the ceremony. Evalene glanced at her father out of the side of her eye, where he stood at the podium. He was talking about her mother? He hadn't spoken of his wife once since she'd died.

Her breath caught.

But he only mentioned Pearl Vandereth to bring up her high Number, a Six, and then moved on. Evalene sighed. Her father focused on Evalene's skills in basic school, her talent and creativity and ability to learn quickly. Her passion for reading. She knew Lola was the source of his information. Even so, Evalene glowed with pride.

Finally, they reached the last portion of the service.

The real reason they were all there.

Walking ceremoniously with Father Alfred, Evalene entered the room built into the front of the chapel, which held a mirror, two chairs, a needle and a small pot of black ink on a table. Another member of the clergy sat in the first chair. He held the needle ready. Evalene sat in the chair that tilted, and lay back.

The tattoo artist had thin graying hair and a blank expression. A pair of spectacles rested on the tip of his nose. As he brought the needle to her neck, he pulled a second pair of lenses off the top of his head, resting them on the bridge of his nose. He peered through both frames, utterly focused. Evalene didn't dare laugh.

She lay still, tense, waiting for the sharp pain of the needle on her neck.

It wasn't bad. After the first poke, she relaxed a little, although she still had to fight the urge to pull away.

Though she watched his face intently, he gave no hint what he was etching onto the left side of her neck. She wiggled her fingers nervously. Wished she could see the mirror from where she sat. She listened to the soloist on the other side of the door, singing on stage while they were out of sight, an overdone song about the glory of Eden and the Number One.

Finally, it was done.

Her neck tingled.

The tattoo artist wiped a bit of blood away with a napkin. Some of the black ink smeared onto it as well. He didn't say a word, just nodded towards the mirror, bowed to Father Alfred, and exited the room.

Father Alfred's face was oddly pale.

Evalene opened her mouth to speak, but he put a finger to his lips, and she stopped. He cleared his throat. "Take a moment to compose yourself, and then you *must* come out and present your Number." He emphasized must, like he was worried she wouldn't come out.

Evalene squinted at him in confusion, but nodded.

"You have two minutes, child," he said, and reached out as if to touch her shoulder, but then stopped short of actually touching her. He left without another word. Evalene slowly turned toward the mirror, afraid now, for some reason.

Her clear blue eyes stared back at her. Brown curls gracing the delicate white dress, at first glance picture perfect. She saw herself bite her lower lip, the color draining out of her face and neck until she nearly matched the ceremonial dress. She sank to the ground, unable to stand. Her whole body started shaking. Her hands reached up to touch the wet tears streaming down her face as it crumpled into a tight, painful, silent cry.

She rocked herself back and forth as the clock ticked by the seconds so fast. Too fast. How had this happened? Somehow she found the strength in her shaking hands to reach toward the table with all the colored ribbons. She picked up the appropriate color ribbon, pulling her hair back with shaking fingers, nearly dropping it. She tied her hair back behind her neck, to make sure her

Number showed. Because that was what she would have to do now.

Evalene felt like she'd been snapped into a million pieces, but she clenched her fist. She would not cry in front of them! It had to be a mistake. But there were no mistakes...

Stop.

Stop, she repeated to herself. Father would know what to do. Father – she had to go out now. She stood, still shaking, and wiped the flow of tears.

Wiped them again.

She touched the mark on the left side of her neck, watching herself in the mirror. Tilting her neck as far as she could while still able to see the mirror, she stared.

Small, black numbers stared back at her.

Her Number.

29.

3

So Many Questions

EVALENE'S FINGERS KEPT INCHING up to the left side of her neck. Her new Number. She felt numb. A bandage blocked her fingers where it covered her new tattoo, though only allowed today while it healed.

She stood in the foyer of the Vandereth's large home, barely blinking, watching the swirl of activity around her.

The moment they'd arrived back at the estate, the staff had been informed, and the entire household had leapt into action. They worked to remove her from her old bedroom – her old life – faster than she'd ever seen them move before, as if this in-between stage where her old life touched the new was not to be tolerated.

Her father disappeared into his study after only a few words to the staff. Lola had tearily listened to the news before clapping her hands over her mouth and stumbling out of the room. Evalene hoped her reaction wouldn't be seen as treasonous.

Daeva, the family's housekeeper, hesitated only a moment before she began hollering orders. Evalene watched from the front entryway, looking up the grand staircase that stretched as wide as a dozen people all the way to the second floor, where the servants gathered in a large circle in the foyer at the top of the stairs, waiting for instructions.

The large master bedrooms were down the second-floor hallway to the right. Where her room had been. The servants' rooms were down the hallway to the left, where Evalene expected to be placed.

But as she listened to their harsh whispers float down the stairs, she made out the words "no room" and "attic." Her forehead wrinkled in concern. There were spiders in the attic. She hated it up there. Frowning she kept her mouth shut. It didn't matter what she wanted.

Evalene touched the bandage again, flinching. The tape along the edges made her skin itch, and she was dying to rip it off, while at the same time wishing it would stay on forever so no one would see what was underneath.

But soon everyone would know if they didn't already.

She winced as she thought of the announcement cards, prepped to go out to friends and family. They didn't have much left in the way of family, just some distant relatives on the other side of Eden. But even if her father threw all the cards away, the family would find out eventually. Everyone would.

Numbly, Evalene watched the servants scurry back and forth from her old room to the attic, disappearing up the stairs to the third floor. A tiny door on the third floor led to a dark, narrow staircase, barely wide enough to carry anything larger than a chair. This led to the attic. Evalene hadn't been to the attic in years, and could barely picture it besides remembering it was packed full of odds and ends. There would barely be enough room for a bed and amenities.

Swallowing hard, Evalene finally moved to the grand staircase through air as thick and heavy as water. Breathing hard, she climbed to the top, wanting to yell at them to stop. Her mind screamed, *Don't touch that! Leave it be!*

Instead she pulled back from the chaos surrounding the master bedrooms, leaning against the hallway leading to the servant's rooms. She tried to be invisible, unnoticed. It wasn't hard. The servants, desperately focused on getting this awful task completed, looked as shell-shocked as Evalene felt.

Daeva hadn't seen her yet, her back to Evalene as she concentrated on directing traffic, saying yes or no to different items. She didn't say yes to much.

"There's a trundle bed already in the attic," Evalene overheard Fleur say to the housekeeper.

"That will do." Daeva replied.

Evalene watched what they carried up from where she stood to the side. A wash stand. One of her larger mirrors. Daeva sent the mirror back. Only a hand mirror made it up the stairs. The housekeeper didn't do any of the work, just stood with her hands on her hips, swiveling back and forth to monitor each item's progress.

Daeva turned and saw Evalene, pursing her lips and frowning for a long moment, looking ready to make Evalene join the work. But then someone asked a question, followed by another, and thankfully Daeva seemed to forget about her.

Stepping backwards, Evalene moved further down the dark servant's hallway, hiding behind a heavy floor-length curtain. A tiny dresser went up the stairs next. From her hiding place, Evalene couldn't tell what clothes were in there, if any.

All her old clothes would have to be thrown out. She felt only a small flutter of sadness at the removal of her childhood clothing, multi-colored to indicate a child pre-Numbering. She'd had years to detach herself from those.

But her brand-new clothes, all lovely, fashionable styles in a dozen different shades of blue, a gift from her father, were much harder to think about the servants removing. Glassy eyed, Evalene shook her head, blinking to clear her vision.

Everything she wore was now required to be a shade of brown. The Number One had created a strict policy on this many years ago. His reasoning, that a person's Number class needed to be easily distinguishable if the Number system were to work, had always made sense to Evalene before. His policy was quite simple:

"PREPARED AT THE DIRECTION AND REQUEST OF THE NUMBER REVIEW ORGANIZATION: STATUTE 146.38: ATTIRE FOR SEMI-RESTRICTED AND RESTRICTED AREAS.

BLUE – 1-10 (PARTY MEMBER ELIGIBLE)

BLACK – 11 (REGULATORS)

WHITE – 12 (CLERGY)

RED – 13-16 (MERCHANTS/TRADERS)

GRAY – 17-23 (HIGH LEVEL EMPLOYEE)

BROWN – 24-30 (LOW LEVEL EMPLOYEE)

The color classes had never bothered Evalene before. After all, the higher classes followed them more loosely, allowed to wear hints of other colors as long as their own was most prevalent. They weren't even required to display their tattoo, and as a result most found stylish ways to cover it up. These were just a few of a million little exceptions to the rules that Evalene had taken for granted.

She sank down to sit on the floor behind the curtain, hugging her knees. Why was she thinking about such a stupid insignificant thing as the colors she would wear? From her hiding place, she watched as they emptied the last few belongings out of her old room, carrying them through the door to other parts of the house. Every personal belonging or gift, every childhood memento such as her books or drawings she'd done–

Evalene jumped up and ran towards the assembly line, suddenly worried they would throw away the few items she had left from her mother. Frantic, she clenched and unclenched her fists, looking around for Lola, for a friend in one of the servants, someone she could ask for help.

No one would meet her eye. None would risk Daeva witnessing their sympathy. Once an informant, always an informant. And there could always be a first time for any of the others.

Thankfully Daeva had departed to the kitchen. Evalene wouldn't have asked her for aid under any circumstances, much less now.

Touching her bandage again, Evalene was grateful that Father Alfred had allowed her this one temporary breach of etiquette, even if only for the night.

Evalene thought of her mother. The last four years had dimmed the memory of her; she couldn't quite picture her smile anymore. She tried to imagine how Pearl would've reacted to this day. But that made Evalene think of her father, who was still noticeably absent. A small part of her remembered the hour following the Numbering Ceremony, and understood.

While everyone in the audience who had come to celebrate slunk out of the church in small, whispering groups or pairs, pretending not to see her family's disgrace, Evalene and her father had been sent to the Priest's office for a stern discussion. "You will never speak to a higher Number unless spoken to first," he began, staring at Evalene. She shut her mouth.

"You will not touch a higher Number without permission, or hold conversations outside the frame of your work. You will be permitted to stay on as a lower-level employee in the Vandereth household, if your father so wishes. However, if he terminates your employment at any time, he is within his full rights to do so, and you will need to find work elsewhere."

Evalene had listened obediently, overwhelmed, standing to the side while her father sat in the chair across from the priest. "If any rules are broken, any other Number is within their full rights to report you, which will result in severe punishment." Thorough and painstaking, the lengthy list of directives took over an hour.

As they left the church, Evalene had immediately felt the distance between her and her father, already a wide chasm since her mother's death, now growing rapidly larger. But she hadn't expected Lola to leave her too. The elderly woman had always been there for her. Until today.

Yet here Evalene stood, alone in the busy hallway as the staff flowed around her, abandoning her.

Returning to her hiding place, Evalene huddled in the corner, knees pulled in, back pressed against the wall, resting her head on her arms. She didn't want anyone to see her like this. Pulling the heavy curtain around so it covered her completely, she held a fist to her mouth, fighting tears.

The noises in the hallway began to die down. As the bustle slowed and the last few items were moved, the voices moved away to other tasks.

After a while, Evalene stood. How much time had passed? The hallway lights remained on, but the entire floor was empty. It was late. Everyone had gone to bed.

As she walked down the empty hallway and reached the doorway of her old room to view the changes, she couldn't quite swallow past the lump in her throat. It might as well have been a stranger's room. Though the dark room still held her old furniture, not a hint of its previous owner remained. Not a single picture, ornament, or decoration. Her favorite childhood blanket, made by her mother, was gone.

She felt afraid to stand this close to her old room, already feeling the weight of her Number. It settled onto her shoulders and chest, making it hard to breathe. She was not a high Number. She was one of the lowest. A 29. Her mind fought against the thought, her years of training for a high-class Number struggling to accept it. But it was true.

She felt tears threatening again, and desperately turned towards the stairs. Taking them two at a time, she reached the third floor and pulled open the little door leading to the attic. Climbing the narrow wooden steps to her new room on the fourth floor, she resisted the urge to cry.

Evalene burst into the tiny attic and swung the door closed behind her. Turning around she gasped at the sight of Lola sitting on the bed. Through blurry vision, she saw Lola held the blanket her mother had made. Evalene ran towards her, falling into the tiny woman's outstretched arms.

"Why did this happen?" Evalene couldn't help asking. Fear caught in her throat at the traitorous words, not to mention Lola was a higher Number now – everyone was – and yet Evalene had spoken first. But Lola wasn't an informant. She just couldn't be.

Lola held her tight, breaking the rules as well. "Shhh, shhh," she said, rocking Evalene in comfort, just like she always had when Evalene was young and nightmares came. "It'll be alright," she said over and over. "You'll be alright."

Evalene's eyes were swollen and ached from held-back tears. She stared at the shoulder of Lola's scratchy brown dress. Both their legs hung off the little bed, Evalene's still wrapped in her Numbering day dress, white for purity and the religious ceremony, and Lola's in her creased skirt, brown for the service class. Evalene sat up finally, rubbing her eyes, and meeting Lola's cloudy brown ones, she whispered, "Lola, what do I do now?"

Rubbing Evalene's arms gently, Lola sighed. Evalene thought she saw her eyes water, but then her nanny smiled at her. She searched for the right words. "Miss Evie, my mama always told me you can choose your real Number for yourself."

Evalene's eyes grew huge. "I thought that was up to God?"

Lola patted her hand and her eyes crinkled, disappearing into her cheeks as she smiled for real this time. "Sometimes I wonder if God would rather not get the credit for things like this." Evalene was perplexed. That sounded like something a true believer would say. Complete heresy. The Number One said God chose everyone's Number, and to disagree was intolerable, traitorous, direct opposition of the Number system.

"But," Evalene risked whispering, glancing around for an eavesdropping television out of habit, though of course, her new room didn't have one, "if God didn't choose my Number, then who did?"

Lola took both of Evalene's hands in her own, cupping her thin, calloused hands around Evalene's younger ones. She glanced at the door reflexively as well before answering in a whisper, "Be very careful, Miss Evie. We can wonder these things, but we must never ask them out loud." She shook her head, struck by one of her coughing attacks before Evalene could ask more.

Pulling the handkerchief away from her mouth finally, Lola spoke again, "There's nothing we can do now, Miss Evie. Just remember, this is not who you are." Lola folded up the handkerchief, but not before Evalene noticed a tiny spot of red on it.

After Lola went to bed, Evalene tossed and turned on the thin, lumpy mattress, unable to sleep. Lola said she wasn't a Number 29, not really. *But then,* Evalene kept coming back to the same question, feeling the bandage on her neck covering her tattoo, *who am I?*

4

Jeremiah, Age 15

JEREMIAH GAVE THE ELDERLY woman his most charming smile. It was unclear why she stood in the orphanage, studying the line of children. Mr. Meyers hadn't told them anything, only slapped them into place, glaring if they slouched or argued. It was even more unclear why this woman was looking at the older, already-Numbered children, like himself, instead of the young ones down the street. One thing was certain: a high Numbered lady such as herself was not here, looking at low Numbers, to adopt.

Though he'd like to irritate Mr. Meyers, Jeremiah wanted out of this miserable hole even more. The old lady probably needed someone to work for her, and though he had no intentions of doing so long term, it could be his ticket out from under the orphanage's watchful eyes.

He smiled even wider, making sure his dimples showed. He had his parents' perfect caramel complexion, his mother's big brown eyes which almost made his brown clothing look good if not for the holes and poor fit, and his father's silky black hair, roughly cut by Mr. Meyers in a bowl shape, but still thick and full.

The last time a female Regulator had caught him stealing, this smile had gotten him off with just a warning.

Sure enough, the older lady stopped in front of him. Everything about her was soft. Her white hair waved in curls to her shoulders, a gentle contrast against her light chocolate colored skin. But it was her brown eyes that struck him most. They were kind. And sad.

The two years since his parents had died in the Bloom Rebellion had shown him just how poorly a lower Number could be treated. The last time someone had truly looked at him like this was right before his mother hugged him goodbye, left him with the neighbors for the weekend, and never returned home. It was unnerving. He stood taller, forcing himself to keep smiling, trying to appear strong, capable of heavy labor.

He was 15 years old. More than old enough to live on his own. A plan began forming in his mind.

"What's your name, dear?" The older woman startled him by speaking directly to him instead of to Mr. Meyers.

"Jeremiah," his voice, deepening this last month, squeaked at the end, and he coughed a little to cover it. That wouldn't help his case.

"A Christian name," she said, her eyes widening; whether in approval or not, Jeremiah couldn't tell. His parents had been true believers, ignoring the ridiculous current trends in Eden to name children after disasters or minerals, and naming him after one of their favorite bible heroes. But he couldn't tell her that. The stories they'd told him about his biblical namesake were just that, foolish stories to make people feel better about God. Since his parents' death and his own Numbering ceremony, Jeremiah had formed his own opinions about God.

The woman nodded once to herself, and turned away, continuing down the line. Jeremiah deflated a little.

He allowed his mind to wander. He would sneak out that night. Maybe he would pinch a fresh loaf of bread from one of the vendors, or some fruit if it was less guarded, something to take the edge off since he was still going without dinner as punishment for last week's crimes.

Mr. Meyer's bark to go with the elderly woman's driver startled him out of his daydreams. While she disappeared out the door, the chauffeur stood impatiently in front of him, beckoning for Jeremiah to follow. She'd chosen him after all?

He shadowed the driver into the vehicle, admiring the luxury car as he climbed into the front seat next to the chauffeur. It was an old-world model he'd never even seen before, expensive.

Her home was equally expensive, lavishly furnished, four levels, more rooms than she would ever need, and more of those fancy cars in the garage. Jeremiah didn't want to get sent back to the orphanage until he had time to lay the foundation for his plan, so he obediently worked on the chores they gave him, but avoided the older lady.

The fact that she'd adopted him, instead of simply hiring him on to work chafed at him. It was as if she made a lifetime claim on him instead of just offering a job. Who did she think she was?

Though she invited him to come to dinner every day, he used his chores as an excuse to miss it, disappearing when necessary. He was good at hiding. He'd done it often in the orphanage, and her vast estate only made it easier.

When no one was looking, he stole supplies, stockpiling as many treasures as he could find in the room he'd been given, with plans to run away, sell everything, and live off the income. The first month proved he could gather quite a lot if he played his hand right. He held off leaving a bit longer, just one more week, two weeks, three.

But then he was caught.

In the middle of pocketing some of the household's expensive silverware, this sighting led to a search of his room and the discovery of the rest of his stash. Angrily dragged into Lady Beryl's parlor by two servants, he knew the beating he'd expected since his arrival was finally coming.

Instead, the older woman studied him from where she sat in a parlor chair, waving the servants out.

"Come sit with me, Jeremiah," she said with a small smile, and gestured towards the tall flowery chair opposite her. She held some multi-colored yarn, busily knitting something long and thin, not stopping for a moment as he hesitated, then sat.

They sat like this in a silence that stretched uncomfortably long. Jeremiah stared at her in defiance, but slowly, as she didn't react, or even look up, he lost his confidence.

Confused, he watched the knitting needles fly back and forth, wrapping around and repeating, again and again. Glancing around the room, he noticed dozens of framed family pictures covering the walls of her sitting room. Jeremiah didn't have a single photo of his family, but this woman's walls were covered with them. Some of the frames held just one or two individuals; others were filled to the brim with people. A few looked extremely old, with the subjects wearing extremely out of date clothing and sporting strange hairstyles.

There were more modern frames as well. More than one held photos of a young boy, capturing him on camera as he grew up. They stopped around the same age as Jeremiah was now.

Sprinkled in the middle of the oldest and the newest, were a few photos of a young girl who looked a lot like Lady Beryl. Same face shape, same mouth, same eyes, same chocolate colored skin... Jeremiah glanced back and forth, between the elderly woman and the girl in the photo, mulling over the possibility it might actually be the Lady Beryl when she was younger. She'd been pretty, with a joyful smile that touched her eyes. The older woman looked at him just then and caught him staring. That same wide smile that made her eyes crinkle at the corners crossed her face.

"I hear you've been keeping a few household odds and ends in your room," she said, still smiling, as if they were sharing a secret.

Turning away, he crossed his arms and leaned back deep into the chair, even going so far as to put one of his feet up on the chair where he knew the dirty shoe would soil it. When she didn't immediately yell, he snuck a glance out of the corner of his eye, and found her staring at him, not in fury but something he couldn't quite name, almost a sadness. Guilt niggled at him, and he found himself putting his foot back on the floor and wiping at the dirt, trying to get it off.

"Jeremiah," she said after it was clear he wasn't going to answer unless it was a direct question, "What were you planning to do with all of the items you've been saving?" He stopped rubbing at the dirt, which wasn't coming out, and crossed his arms defiantly again. He could pretend he didn't know what she was talking about, but no doubt the servants would rat him out if he did. He hadn't made any friends with his behavior these last couple months. She wanted the truth? Fine, he would tell her.

"I'm going to sell them," he said, lifting his chin and looking straight at her.

Lady Beryl's brow wrinkled in concern. "Why ever so?" she asked, sounding surprised. "Are you going hungry?"

"No," Jeremiah mumbled sullenly, brushing invisible lint off the shoulder of his brown vest and dropping his eyes, not quite able to meet hers.

"Is something wrong?" she asked, and he noticed she'd put down her knitting in concern. "Do you need money?"

He didn't answer. He wasn't lacking anything at the moment, but that wouldn't last. "I have plans," he said, and cut off. No way he was going to explain the details to her. He wasn't an idiot.

She sighed softly. "You're planning to run away." It was a statement, not a question.

Jolting in surprise, Jeremiah immediately wanted to kick himself for reacting and confirming her suspicions.

Still she didn't yell. Her conduct was such unfamiliar terrain, every inch of the conversation so unexpected, he didn't know what would happen next.

Lady Beryl sighed again, and put her unfinished knitting into a basket beside her chair, freeing her hands to massage her eyelids. When she looked up again, Jeremiah was shocked at the tears in her eyes. His own eyes widened in fear. He hadn't meant to make her cry. What punishment would he receive now?

She blinked and dabbed at the tears, as if embarrassed, and then, amazingly, she gave him a small, sad smile. *She's lost it,* he thought to himself, jaw dropping open just slightly in astonishment. Up until now, she'd never seemed crazy. She handled the estates with intelligence, clearly, as she was extremely wealthy. And she had kind eyes. Jeremiah was confused.

Sniffing, the lady put her used tissue down, and when she spoke her voice cracked a little. "I must confess to you, my dear. You remind me of my son, Jacob. He was around your age when he died, nearly 20 years ago now."

Digesting this information, Jeremiah was tempted to play on her sympathy. A long pause stretched between them until finally, staring back into her eyes, he said quietly. "I doubt I'm anything like him."

"It's true," she replied, winking at him and laughing at his bemused expression. "Jacob would've been discovered within a week! I gather from the things that have turned up missing, you've been at it quite a bit longer." Again, a shrewd conclusion. He would have to rethink his previous assessment of her mental state. She was peculiar, for sure, but her intelligence was razor sharp.

At a loss for words, Jeremiah just blinked at her. She didn't seem offended at his silence, just regarded at him thoughtfully, without malice.

"I'll tell you what," she said with another smile, and Jeremiah found himself listening respectfully, something he hadn't done in years, "let's make a deal."

Lady Beryl ignored his raised eyebrows. "I would like it very much if you would stay with me a little bit longer." She met his eyes as she said this, and he couldn't find a hint of deceit in her face. "But if, after... oh, let's say, a month... yes. If after a month you still wish to leave, I promise I will help you financially and even send you wherever you would like to go myself."

She met his gaze evenly, not once looking away or stirring in her seat.

When he spoke, his voice was laced with skepticism, "Why would you do that." He tried to imitate the way she turned a question into a statement.

"Because my dear, I like you," she said simply. "You remind me of my son. And I want you to be able to trust me."

He found himself wanting to do just that. Admiring her ability to be straightforward, he lifted one eyebrow cockily, and responded in the same way by challenging her. "What's the catch?"

Jeremiah expected denial, but instead the Lady Beryl grinned mischievously and clapped her hands like a giddy schoolgirl. "Ah yes, we need a catch don't we?" Once again, he was caught off guard, but he found himself grinning back at her.

He shook the smile off.

Clearing her throat, Lady Beryl also became solemn. "If I agree to do this, then you must give me your word you will cooperate while you are here. No more skipping your lessons. You will attend every reading and writing lesson, and do whatever homework Master Edward tells you to do."

Jeremiah groaned, but she wasn't done. "You must also eat dinner with me instead of pretending to be ill or busy." As she proved once again that she was far cleverer than he'd assumed, Jeremiah felt his cheeks growing red. He nodded.

"And finally, Jeremiah," she said, waiting patiently for him to meet her eyes before finishing, "you must, *must* talk to me if you need something. I mean it," she said, rapping a finger on the table between them to emphasize her point. "There is no sense in you stealing what I would gladly give to you. Do you understand?"

Blinking, Jeremiah tried to figure out what the real catch would be. Maybe she was just lonely. He supposed it wouldn't hurt anything to stick around a couple more weeks. If the old bird didn't come through on her end, he could still sneak away with a couple easy scores left out in plain sight. He nodded, more to himself than to her, but she smiled at him, eyes crinkling again.

"Wonderful. So we have a deal?" she asked, and then did the most shocking thing of all. She held her hand out to him to shake, as if he were an equal. He couldn't stop his mouth from falling wide open this time, eyes wide.

"Shake on it," she insisted, and he swallowed, mouth dry, before reaching out.

He barely touched her hand enough to shake it once, then whipped his hand back and choked out one word. "Deal."

Jeremiah attended every lesson and showed up for every dinner, per their agreement. It felt odd, almost as if he really were adopted. But a deal was a deal.

Reading and writing came naturally to him; he enjoyed the chance to share his opinion. Master Edward brought his essays to Lady Beryl on multiple occasions, concerned, yet she chuckled as she read them over dinner, not offended in the slightest.

"I knew your parents were true believers," she said one night, peeking up from the page. He hadn't said so straight out, yet Jeremiah belatedly remembered how well she read between the lines.

"I'm not, though." He was careful to enunciate in case anyone was listening. Though Beryl reminded him of his parents, slowly gaining his trust as time went on with her honesty and integrity, that didn't mean he trusted the rest of her household staff.

"That's alright. But you should know that I am." Beryl surprised him as she often did by confiding in him. If she wanted to risk being reported, so be it, but he wasn't going to join her in talking about it. Yet, he respected her enough to listen.

At the end of their month-long deal, they were eating dinner when Lady Beryl asked Jeremiah about his family. He found himself telling her, staring at his uneaten peas as they grew cold.

Lady Beryl sniffed, making him look up. Her eyes were filled with tears. "We have both lost family, dear one, but I can't imagine losing both parents in such a way."

He remembered she'd lost her son, and nodded. Dropping his gaze to his plate, he moved pieces of food around with his fork.

What he did not expect was to suddenly feel her hugging him, frail arms holding him tightly. After a second, he slowly lifted his hands to her arm wrapped around him and hugged her back.

He'd cried that day.

The following day when she'd asked him if he needed help getting ready for his journey or if he'd like to stay, he'd swallowed hard, trying not to cry again, and asked if he could stay.

5

Five Years Later

IT **HAD BEEN NEARLY** five years since Evalene's numbering. Lola had fallen ill that same year, passing away only a few months after the Numbering ceremony. Evalene's thirteenth year had been painful in more ways than one.

After spending her entire childhood prepping for a high-ranking Number, groomed for perfection, importance… the shame of her Number had suffocated their household, driving them out of the city. They'd moved to their countryside home. Permanently.

The beautiful country house was almost as large as the one back in Delmare, but more quaint, with a huge wrap-around porch, striking white pillars, and a large garden filled with flowers, bushes, and even a few trees, that covered the entire five acres surrounding the house. This was especially impressive considering they were out in the dry, arid desert.

Inside the household, the servant's quarters were almost an exact duplicate of the previous household, although all servants' rooms tended to look alike. Evalene had been given the attic room once again, though in this house there'd been enough room for her downstairs. Daeva's eyes had dared her to argue. No matter how hard Evalene tried to remember her place, and act accordingly, Daeva still watched her like a hawk for insolence towards the Number system, which could not be tolerated.

As Evalene cleaned the mirror in one of the bathrooms on the second level of the house, her tanned, freckled face stared back at her. Big blue eyes, long brown hair pulled back into a loose bun with pieces falling out, and a high-necked brown dress in the shape of a potato sack. So much brown. The mirror didn't show the bottom of her dress, but she preferred not to see how out of fashion it was. How it brushed her ankles.

She smiled at the mirror and pretended she was wearing blue instead. Would she be considered pretty? Boys didn't pay her any attention since her Numbering, so it was hard to know for sure, but she'd been popular back in basic school.

Out in the countryside, with fewer neighbors, she rarely saw anyone outside the household staff anyway, unless she was sent on an errand to town. It was good they'd moved. There were less people to judge them, less high Numbers to call on her father, out of curiosity, to see his low Numbered daughter.

Although Byron Vandereth still traveled for business on behalf of the Number One, they no longer took family vacations. Low Numbers weren't allowed to travel between cities without permission. Regulators stood at watchtowers near every city wall, checking Identity Cards at every gate. Evalene couldn't travel for pleasure anymore. She couldn't go anywhere, period.

She finished her morning chores early and raced down the back stairwell on silent slippered feet, taking them two at a time. She had about ten minutes until it was time to start breakfast.

Reaching the back door, she glanced around, then snuck out into the backyard. Behind the homestead's gardens were another twenty-acres of rock formations, twisting desert ravines, and sharp cliff walls.

Hurrying through the cultivated gardens, she reached the end of the green grass and entered the dry, brown desert, stepping into a small rift between cliff walls. As she rounded a corner and the path faded away, she knew without looking back that she was out of sight of the main house now. Thankful as always for the cover of the rocky hills, Evalene raced along the bottom of the valley towards the one small crooked tree ahead.

Kevra Greene was already waiting under the tree, their designated meeting place before breakfast, if they had time. Kevra always had time. She didn't start work until nearly an hour after Evalene's morning chores. As a higher-level employee working in the local television factory, she had the privilege of leaving work behind in the evenings, and even had her weekends off, unlike Evalene, whose entire life was devoted to the household, all day, every day, for the rest of her life.

Kevra grinned when she saw Evalene. Her crooked teeth made her look impish, and her red hair and sparkling green eyes added to the effect. Her gray clothes marked her as a lower Number, but in the class above Evalene's. Her tattoo was highly visible, of course, with her red hair pulled back per the law, showing her Number 23 tattoo.

Kevra's parents had been hired on shortly after the household moved from the city. Her mother worked in the garden and her father in the garage. When Kevra showed up to eat in the kitchen with Evalene on that first day, it was as if she'd been there all along.

Unlike everyone else, even though Kevra had full authority over Evalene as a superior Number, she didn't act more important or abuse her power, the way Daeva and some of the other staff did. Sure, she could be bossy, but she was that way with everyone. Her friendship over the last five years was the only thing keeping Evalene sane.

Kevra didn't even wait for Evalene to reach her. "I've been dying to talk to you since I picked up the milk this morning. But I'm scared you'll feel you have to turn me in because it's, well, it's disloyal..." Kevra's words tumbled out on top of each other as Evalene approached. "But of course, I know you won't turn me in, because no one would believe a lower Number, so there'd be no point –"

"Kevra!" Evalene stopped short in front her friend, crossing her arms and shaking her head. "Talk about what? What's disloyal?"

Kevra squinted at her, frowning. "Wait, you don't know?"

"Know what?"

Turning, Kevra reached behind her to pick up the milk delivery carton from where it sat on a tall rock. Her little apartment above the garage where she lived with her parents received two jars of milk a week while the Vandereth household received six. Evalene hadn't noticed the small containers until Kevra pulled them forward. Why had she brought her household's milk jars all the way out here?

Kevra reached underneath the jars and pulled out what looked like a small poster or flier. She waved it in excitement so that Evalene couldn't make out any of the words written on it. "This. This bulletin came in the bottom of the milk delivery this morning."

"I haven't picked up the milk yet –" Evalene tensed, trying to think if anyone might be in the kitchen right now waiting for it. "What is it? I only have a few minutes. Show me quickly!"

Kevra held out the tiny paper and Evalene snatched it from her hand. The top of the little bulletin had huge bold font and Evalene read it aloud, "OUR WORLD CANNOT EXIST HALF SLAVE AND HALF FREE!"

She gasped. This was treason!

Glancing at Kevra, Evalene saw her friends jaw tighten in response, hands clenching at her sides.

Returning her gaze to the bulletin, Evalene stared at the six boxes they'd drawn beneath the words. Each box held a simple caricature of a person from a different Number category. A woman in an expensive blue dress, and just above her elaborate sapphire necklace, the Number 2. The second box held a man wearing the stern black uniform of the Regulators, not bothering to cover the Number 11 on his neck. The third held a priest, Numbered 12, wearing the traditional white robes. Next a curly-haired woman wearing a fierce red, a Number 15 tattooed on her neck.

The last two boxes resonated deeply with Evalene. They held a woman in gray who frowned just like Kevra was now, Numbered

20, and a man wearing a shade of brown identical to Evalene's skirt, Numbered 28. Both of them without any neck covering, following the laws that Grays and Browns always reveal their Number in public. Both looked haunted.

Evalene shook herself. She had less than a minute before she needed to return to the house. Below the six people was fine print. She began to read out loud again, feeling her skin grow cold and clammy at the words.

"107 low Numbers executed last year alone... 792 known low Number suicides or disappearances... Approximately 28,000 'given' the Number 11 over the last ten years," Evalene stumbled over the word *given* as she realized it was mocking the idea. She paused to glance at Kevra, whose face was hard.

Swallowing, Evalene read on, "The Grid shoots down any plane trying to enter or exit Eden... Not even the birds are safe... None of us can leave... Life expectancy for low Numbers: 38 years... Civil rights for a lower Number: None."

Taking a deep breath, Evalene let the words sink in, staring at the final thought written across the bottom of the bulletin, in the biggest font yet.

THIS IS NOT RIGHT.

Softly, she repeated the treasonous statement in a whisper, "This is not right."

The words transported her to a moment in her childhood. She'd come in from playing outside and found her parents arguing on the other side of the study door. Pearl's voice whispered, "It just isn't right!" And Byron's softer, more feeble reply, "I know. But what can we do about it? What can anyone do?" As little Evalene had cracked the door open wider to see her parents, the hinges squeaked. Pearl had picked her up with a smile that didn't quite reach her eyes, and they were off to the kitchen. Evalene had completely forgotten the conversation until now.

Kevra didn't say a word, just took the bulletin when Evalene handed it back to her. They stood next to the small tree in silence, afraid to say anything beyond what the bulletin said, anything personal. They both knew what happened to someone who was turned in as a traitor. Staring at the ground, Evalene whispered, "I think my mother was involved in the Bloom Rebellion."

She was surprised when Kevra nodded. "That's what most people say." They'd never talked about Pearl before. The rumors must still be circulating, if Kevra had heard. Evalene hated herself for being cowardly, but chose the safe response. "I don't know what to think."

Kevra didn't say anything back for a beat, but when she did, her voice was firm, confident. "I do." Standing, she put the bulletin safely back inside the metal container under the milk jar. "I agree with it. And you can turn me in if you want to, but I'll just say you're lying and who will they believe?"

Grabbing Kevra's arm to stop her from walking away, Evalene said, "Kevra, I would never turn you in!" Glancing around to make sure no one was near, Evalene lowered her voice. "I promise you don't have to worry about that. And... I agree too." This was her friend. The one person in the whole world she could trust. She knew Kevra would never betray her.

Kevra stretched her lips in a thin smile. "Good. I'm not going to turn you in either. But you should probably get the milk. If the household got a bulletin too, Daeva's going to kill you."

Racing away from Kevra towards the house, Evalene only had one thought. The milk delivery was her job. She panicked imagining Daeva asking if she'd written those words. No one else could see that pamphlet.

Evalene cracked open the back door, snuck down the hallway and worked her way through the rooms most likely to be empty until she reached the front door. She stepped onto the porch, pulling the front door closed behind her, and making sure she was alone before she knelt to lift the freshly delivered jars of milk, one by one. There it was.

She pulled the paper out to read it again, much quicker. The last phrase echoed in her mind the entire time. This is not right.

Scanning the front yard and drive for any prying eyes, Evalene discretely folded the bulletin in half twice before burying it deep in her dress pocket. Picking up the milk carton, the jars jostled together noisily as she entered the house. She took a few deep breaths to slow her heart rate.

The bulletin stayed in Evalene's pocket while serving breakfast, feeling like it weighed 10 pounds. After the meal, while she was supposed to be dusting, she snuck away and hid the scandalous thing in her sock drawer. Daeva would never see it.

Breathing a sigh of relief, Evalene returned to her chores until after dinner, when the household gathered as usual to watch the nightly news. She stood in the back of the room with the servants.

Within moments of the show's start, the station declared a state of emergency.

"We have a villain on the loose," the first newscaster said, frowning deeply and leaning forward in his seat in a way that formed wrinkles all over his heavy blue suit. "Opal, tell them the story." It was their usual banter, performed nightly, and was supposed to come across conversationally, but his words came out sharp and angry instead.

"Ah, yes, thank you Sterling," said his fellow newswoman, smiling even as she shot him a look of annoyance. "We have breaking news. Today, just this morning in fact, a prankster exposed a small portion of our great country to false propaganda."

A photo of the bulletin replaced the two newscasters on the screen, but the station blurred out all the words, and held it under a pulsing red light, making the page seem angry and aggressive. Evalene barely held back a gasp of recognition. She regretted hiding it from Daeva now. She schooled her face to be as surprised as everyone else in the room, although no one was looking at her. No one knew when someone might be watching on the other side of the screen.

The woman on the television continued, "These false advertisements were found in the bottom of some of the population's milk delivery just this morning. It is unknown how many were distributed, but we suspect the jokester will be apprehended very soon." She smiled as if she were talking about a small child, shaking her head at the newsman, who smiled back and nodded. As she went on with the report, her voice became more conspiratorial, leaning in towards the camera with a smile, "Although we know the citizens of Eden are all loyal to the Number One, we want to emphasize that the facts listed on the bulletin have no concrete proof, and confirm that they are completely inaccurate. We cannot believe everything we read. Right, Sterling?"

The newsman smiled too, visibly relaxed now, as they wrapped up the emergency announcement. "That's right, Opal. It sounds like a bunch of nonsense to me. Some people just want to scare others. But as always, the Number One keeps us safe. Our Number system guarantees it!"

They moved on to news about the Number One's annual festival celebrating the success of the Number System, but Evalene couldn't pay attention. Everyone in the room was sneaking glances in her direction. When she was younger, she would've spoken up immediately, said something about their household not getting the bulletin. But lower Numbers must wait to be spoken to. She forced herself to wait. And wait. Someone would ask her soon enough.

By the time the program ended, Evalene was wound so tight she ducked out of the room before anyone could say a word, hurrying to the kitchen to finish cleaning. Instantly she regretted leaving. It made her look guilty. But she didn't have time to agonize over it. Daeva burst into the room.

"Where did you put it?" Daeva demanded, marching across the room towards her.

Evalene tensed, retreating automatically. She hurried to answer, "I never got it, I swear!" She put both hands up in front of her. "You heard the news. 'Some' households got it! Not all!" Daeva continued to advance, balling her hand into a fist. Evalene backed up, knocking over a chair, and cried out, "I promise you, Daeva, please believe me. I would have brought it to you immediately if I had!"

Daeva stopped less than a foot from her and stared into her face, so close Evalene was scared to breathe. "Is that so?"

"Yes, ma'am," Evalene nodded, biting her lip and looking down. Catching herself acting guilty, she tried to meet Daeva's glare instead.

"Hmmm," was all Daeva said in response. She turned sharply and left the kitchen. Evalene felt tremors of anxiety. This could mean the subject was closed, or it could mean Daeva didn't believe her.

Creeping up to the swinging door of the kitchen, Evalene cracked it open. Daeva was speaking with one of the maids. "Tell Master Byron it appears we did not receive a bulletin," she was saying to Violet.

Evalene sighed in relief, gently closing the kitchen door. After a moment's thought, she decided to commit the bulletin to memory, then tear it into shreds and burn it in the wood stove. Picking up a broom, she began sweeping so Daeva wouldn't catch her standing idle.

6

Bulletins

THE ATTIC WINDOW WAS the only place in the house where someone could see past the backyard gardens full of trees and rock formations to the crooked little tree on the other side of the rocky hill where Kevra waited. Her friend was pacing, probably having been there a while. But thanks to extra chores from Daeva, Evalene didn't have time to meet her. It was two long days before they were able to speak again.

Rushing towards their meeting place on the third morning, Evalene arrived at the tree at the same time as Kevra. She impulsively hugged her friend.

Kevra laughed, pushing Evalene's arms off and stepping back. "What was that for?"

Evalene tried to laugh too, but her chest was too tight. "The house has been tense lately." An understatement.

Settling onto one of the larger rocks, Kevra patted the bumpy surface, inviting Evalene to join her. "Come sit. If you think the household is upset, you should see the factory!"

Evalene shook her head, too nervous to sit. "After watching the news, I can imagine."

"The news only tells you what they want you to hear," Kevra shook her head, standing to pace, "but work is buzzing with rumors. You know, I only work in the Circuit Board Department, but my friend Jade in Cables says they're lying through their teeth. Every one of those statistics is true. I guarantee you this isn't just some prankster." Kevra stopped pacing abruptly. "And it wasn't just a small area that got the bulletins by the way. The whole country got them!"

"You're kidding," Evalene breathed, suddenly needing to sit after all. "Do you think it's leading to another rebellion?"

Kevra lowered her voice in a whisper, "That's what everyone's wondering. They're saying the people disappearing aren't random. That the Regulators are part of it, taking anyone they observe with insubordinate tendencies."

"What do you think it means?"

Kevra shrugged. "Well, don't talk in front of your TV, obviously. Or in front of anyone you don't trust. Anyone could be an informant. But I'll tell you one thing for sure: this isn't going to die down this time."

This time. Last time it'd been this bad, Evalene had been just nine years old. The daughter of a Number Four and Six, whose mother was still alive. A foolish child who had wanted the rebels to lose. She didn't feel that way anymore.

Every morning for the next three weeks, Evalene checked the milk delivery at the crack of dawn, before meeting Kevra, sometimes waiting on the doorstep for it to arrive.

Every morning, nothing.

Then one day, as she lifted the milk jars one by one, there it was. Another bulletin.

Pulling it out slowly, heart beating fast, Evalene saw it was even more straightforward than the last. A banner across the top screamed in bold block letters, "NO MORE NUMBERS!"

Evalene choked.

Coughing, she glanced around, worried someone would hear her. She hurriedly read the rest of the flyer.

There was a cartoon sketch again, but this time the artist simply put one man in the middle, faceless except for an angry mouth. His neck was noticeably bare, Number-free. This man was standing with hands outspread, defiantly holding back a swarm of Numbers, swirling all around him in the air like a cloud of flies, shouting just one word, "NO!"

It was such a simple image, but the idea of saying "no" to her Number fascinated Evalene. Something small and fragile blossomed in her chest. Something she hadn't felt in five years. It felt light and hopeful.

Below the image were three simple phrases.

"FREEDOM. EQUALITY. It's TIME to be NUMBER-FREE!"

Frightened, Evalene instinctively reached both hands to the top of the bulletin to rip it in half like the last one. She caught herself just in time. The household would expect to see this.

Undoubtedly the Regulators would find out, and it would be on the news again, probably tonight. If it didn't show up a second time, Daeva would assume she was somehow a part of it, maybe even report her. It wouldn't even matter that it would be false information. As a higher Number, Daeva's word was the only one that counted.

Against all her impulses, Evalene jammed the bulletin back in the bottom of the milk container, under the same jar where she'd found it. Slowly, anxiously, she walked the jars with the offensive piece of paper through the house and into the kitchen. Finding the room still empty, she sighed in relief. She set the entire upsetting package on the table and raced out of the room.

It only took her thirty seconds to reach the tree. Kevra was already there waiting, bulletin in her hand.

Clapping her hands in excitement, Kevra squealed the moment she saw Evalene, "Tell me you saw it!" She held the bulletin out to Evalene anyway.

"I did!" Evalene said, wide-eyed, coming to sit by her friend. She rubbed her face in disbelief, taking the small piece of paper. Holding it, just like holding the first one before she'd burned it, made her feel closer to her mother. The undeniably rebellious language, so similar to her mother's words in private, felt exciting, familiar, hopeful. Evalene held it carefully in both hands. "I never expected this... Number-free? What would that even look like?"

Kevra shook her head and frowned. "Are you kidding? Think about the textbooks we used to read in school." Pulling out a peach to munch on for breakfast, Kevra took a bite. She continued talking around a mouthful, "They had hints of what the world used to be like all over them, if you paid attention. Do you realize our grandparents' parents were, very likely, Number-less?"

Kevra talked with her hands, her wild gestures dripping peach juice all over her dress. "Probably only into their twenties, but still!"

Evalene couldn't picture it. She tried to imagine not having a Number, high or low, but it made her head hurt. She didn't want to give the bulletin back. The longer she held it, the more memories came back to her of her mother.

Pearl used to give money to homeless low Numbers on the street whenever they went out shopping. One particular memory hit Evalene as she held this new bulletin, of Pearl buying a poor low-Number girl in dirty rags some ice cream. The girl couldn't have been more than a few years older than Evalene at the time, newly Numbered. Pearl and Evalene had finished their cones only to turn and find the shopkeeper beating the girl. Pearl had swung between outrage and tears the rest of that day.

With one last squeeze, Evalene gave the bulletin back to Kevra. Before they parted ways, Kevra dropped one more bomb on Evalene, "I have a friend in the Keyboard department who owns a map. She says there's at least one other country besides Eden that survived the war. People call it the FreeLands. Because they don't have any Numbers."

7

The Proposition

FLEUR SHRIEKED WHEN SHE discovered the second bulletin. Her reaction seemed overly dramatic, probably for Daeva's sake, who confiscated it immediately, delivering it to Evalene's father. No one seemed to wonder if Evalene had seen it first. She breathed a soft sigh of relief as she served breakfast.

The staff was all whispers and side conversations. Evalene was used to being excluded. She tried not to wonder what they were saying about the bulletins, but found it harder than usual. Even her father's girlfriend, Ruby, broke off whispering to him whenever Evalene entered the room.

By dinner, Evalene couldn't stand it. She risked Daeva's wrath and dropped the basket with the last few eggs meant for tomorrow's breakfast. Furious, Daeva demanded to know how she could be so stupid.

Though it was rhetorical, Evalene took the question as an invitation to speak, "I can borrow eggs from the Greene's household?" Daeva yelled to hurry. As Evalene rushed out of the kitchen with a spare basket, Daeva was screaming at Violet to clean up the mess.

Racing along the carefully kept up path leading to the Greene's apartment over the detached garage, Evalene went around to their door on the side. Knocking on the door felt odd. She never had reason to be here. She hoped Kevra would be sent to answer.

When she saw her friend's red hair and smiling green eyes, she breathed an audible sigh of relief. "Hello," she said in a loud voice, "the Household has run out of eggs. We need to borrow what you have for tomorrow's breakfast." It wasn't a question. The Vandereth household came first. The Greenes knew that, and would make do with toast in the morning. Evalene mouthed silently, *Can we talk?*

Kevra, nodding in understanding, replied to both, "Of course." She waved Evalene into the tiny entry and the girls started up the stairs, "Come with me to the kitchen. I'll give you what we have."

Once there, Kevra whispered as she pulled out their egg basket, "Tell me quickly. My father is in the other room and my mother is resting. What's going on?"

"Nothing happened," Evalene reassured her, "I just couldn't wait until tomorrow morning. I know you have news from the factory, tell me everything!"

Kevra nodded solemnly. "It turns out, the first time they distributed the bulletins, they used the farms," she began, placing six eggs in a smaller basket as she spoke, wrapping them carefully in a soft towel. "Some of the lowest Numbers work on farmsteads. It's such constant, heavy duty work, I heard they found a lot of sympathizers."

Just the fact that Kevra called them sympathizers instead of traitors shook Evalene's entire worldview. She nearly dropped the eggs for real this time as Kevra handed the basket to her. Evalene hugged the basket close to her chest as Kevra continued, "So the last few weeks, the Regulators had been watching the farms, but this second bulletin was handed out to the delivery boys. It happened right under their noses because they weren't watching the right people!"

Evalene smiled too, but couldn't help asking, "Aren't most of the delivery boys un-Numbered? Wouldn't some of them report it instead of delivering it, hoping to receive a higher Number?"

"Well their parents are all low Numbers, so it's not like theirs could raise much higher. I don't know for sure, but I heard rumors the bulletins went to the parents first, right before dawn, asking them to help their kids with the delivery!"

"Wow," Evalene breathed. She hadn't realized so many people were willing to take that risk. "What do you think is going to happen?"

Kevra took a deep breath and let it out slowly for dramatic effect. "There's going to be a revolution. I'm sure now. Bigger than the Bloom Rebellion..." Evalene opened her mouth in surprise, but Kevra didn't give her time to speak. She rushed to continue, "Evie," she said, using Evalene's nickname. She only did that when she was asking for something, "I can't stay here. We could be executed or disappear one day, never to be found again, or worse. Work is unbearable. I don't know if I can handle one more day..."

A few months ago, Kevra had hinted that her boss was forcing her to touch him, and it was making her uncomfortable. There was nothing she could do about it; he was a higher Number. The more time went on, the less Kevra was willing to talk about the situation. The haunted look on her face now told Evalene it must've gotten worse. Much worse.

Kevra whispered so quietly, Evalene strained to hear her, "I just can't stay here any longer." Grabbing Evalene's hand over the egg basket handle, Kevra squeezed it in both of hers tightly, as if to force her to pay attention. She glanced over at the door to the living room and the rest of the house, before she lowered her voice to an even softer whisper, "Evie, listen. I think we should run."

Evalene stepped back, "Run. You want to leave? Where would we even go?"

"Shhh!!" Kevra's hands flew to her hair and she grabbed at the red strands as if to pull them out, then closed her eyes quickly and blew out a deep breath. Her eyes flew open. "Evie, look," she said Evalene's name a third time, smiling with thin lips, "You've been my friend for years now. I know you, and you know me. We don't deserve this. I mean, how in the Number One's name did you even get the Number 29? Your father is a FOUR. There is no way that's legitimate, or what 'God' wants." She made quotation marks in the air when she said God's name, another rebellious move, though she glanced around to make sure no one else saw.

This argument always swayed Evalene. Everyone knew when they had children, their Numbers would be within a few of their own. The fact that Evalene was twenty-five Numbers apart from her own father was still gossiped about, years later.

If the rumors could be believed, Evalene's Number was the consequence of her family's actions. To shame them. To take away their credibility. A punishment for her mother and father, for disappointing the Number One.

Pearl's involvement in the Bloom Rebellion, and maybe even beforehand, helping low Number refugees escape, was unacceptable. And Byron, married to a traitor, was equally unacceptable. His authority as a Number Four didn't change in theory, yet the higher Number circles began to ignore him. As time passed, he was often snubbed entirely.

Since Evalene's Numbering, he'd shrunk even further into himself. He fulfilled his duties as a Number Four and a party member quietly. Resigned. A few years ago, he'd met Ruby. The little woman had moved into their home practically minutes after becoming his girlfriend. It was odd for Evalene to think of her father having a girlfriend, but so was everything else she'd heard about him. He was a stranger to her.

Shrugging, Evalene shifted the egg basket in her arms. "I don't know what to say." She was luckier than most, sheltered in the Vandereth household. But Kevra was not so fortunate. Evalene hated to see her friend in pain.

Kevra was quiet, but she put on a small smile as she shooed Evalene out. "At least think about it. I can't do it without you."

Evalene held the railing as she took the narrow stairs down, with Kevra on her heels. It was tempting. But she knew what Regulators did to runaways. Everyone knew. Running was considered treason. And treason was the worst crime. They put fugitive's bodies on display in the town center after they were done with them, to discourage others attempts.

Reaching the tiny landing, Evalene opened the door and

paused. "I'll think about it okay? Please don't be mad…"

"I'm not mad, I swear!" Kevra said, putting on a big smile and giving Evalene a quick hug before she swept her through the door. "See you tomorrow. I'll bring you a present for your birthday!" she hollered as the door shut in Evalene's face.

8

18th Birthday

EVALENE DIDN'T HAVE A clock in her little room, but she was up before the sun, even earlier than normal. Today was her 18th birthday. The trundle bed was lumpy but warm, keeping her protected from the cool spring morning air that snuck into the room.

She burrowed deeper under the blankets to savor a few extra minutes. It wouldn't be long before she was supposed to meet Kevra by the tree. Normally it was the highlight of her day, but she still didn't have an answer for her friend, and Evalene knew Kevra would ask.

Maybe today she would 'miss' the meeting. She wanted some time to herself before Daeva began hollering for her to get to work. Birthdays were for high Numbers, Daeva would say.

But Evalene had gotten herself a little present.

Reaching under her bed frame, between the broken metal slats where there was enough space to hide a small object, she pulled out a book she'd borrowed from her father's library.

Happy birthday, she thought to herself, opening to the first page. In the five years since her Numbering, she'd missed being allowed time to read, more than almost anything else in the world, except her mother. When she was young, she'd spent hours reading – anything from novels to history books to "how to" books on things like gardening or cooking.

She settled in to read, turning the pages, sucked into the story, a romance between a lesser Number girl and a high-class Number boy whose family disapproved. Well, relatively low. They were both still in the top 10, but Evalene could use her imagination. She lost track of time, savoring the novel.

"Twenty Nine!" Daeva's harsh voice bounced off the walls of the stairwell, scaring Evalene out of her daydreams. "Time to work!"

Evalene jumped. She folded a corner of the book to save her page, shoving the book under the bed in a hurry. Daeva did not ask twice. Once the book was stashed, she quickly rolled to face her tiny drawer on the other side of the bed and pulled out light brown stockings, the last step to getting dressed.

Brown hair, brown dress, brown socks, brown shoes… such an ugly color! Evalene smiled at the hiding place under her bed. Her tiny rebellion. Such a small thing. But if not for the temporary escapes, and Kevra, how would she survive a single day?

Working hard all morning and afternoon, Evalene pushed herself to be faster than ever, cleaning the upstairs master bedrooms in record time. No one would expect her to report to the kitchen until 5pm. She had a full, glorious 45 minutes all to herself to read.

She pulled out the hidden book again, curling up on her bed, holding the book at a tilt towards the light coming in the attic window.

As the light faded, it got harder to make out the words until Evalene startled, pulling herself out of the daydreams. What time was it? The sun was low on the horizon.

She clenched her hands nervously. Throwing the book under the covers, she didn't waste time storing it properly, but ran down the narrow attic staircase. She sprinted down the hallway on tiptoes to the mansion's grand staircase and tore down the steps, two at a time.

Peering around corners, she raced to the swinging door that led to the kitchen and slipped in, completely out of breath.

When she entered the kitchen, Daeva was screaming at Violet, "You knew about the bulletins all along - I knew you were a traitor!"

"No, I didn't know! I believe in the Number System!" Violet cried, backing away from Daeva toward the door where Evalene stood. "Numbers are the only way, I know that!"

"But how can we know you didn't plant the filthy thing in the milk delivery yourself?" Daeva accused, stepping towards Violet.

"She didn't," Evalene broke the rules and spoke without thinking, stepping forward to stand next to Violet. They weren't close friends, but she was kind to Evalene and looked out for her when she could. It was the least Evalene could do to stand up for her now. "I found the bulletin myself, right after the milk was delivered."

The silence in the room was deafening. Daeva's face was turning a deep purple.

"You're telling me you saw the bulletin first and *didn't say anything.*" It was not a question. "Do you realize what you're confessing?"

The three other people in the room, the chef, and the two maids, Violet and Fleur, all stared at her with anxious, raised brows.

Evalene tried not to react, tried to keep her face still, voice calm, eyes directed towards Daeva's feet. "I only picked it up," she said. "I had nothing else to do with it. Please don't inform on me."

"TWENTY-NINE," Daeva growled, stepping closer. Evalene flinched at the title. Only Daeva called her that. "Do not lie to me, girl."

"I'm sorry I didn't tell you earlier, I –" The hand came at Evalene so suddenly she didn't have time to duck or even flinch. The sound of the slap cracking across her face echoed loudly in the high-ceilinged room. Fleur, who had been studiously looking away, startled and dropped the whole stack of porcelain plates she'd been holding. They crashed and shattered into a million pieces on the tile floor.

Evalene gasped from the pain. The left side of her face burned red hot and she felt something wet trickling down her cheek. Touching it, she found blood. Daeva's ring had cut the skin by her eye.

"Look what you've done now," Daeva snarled, pointing at the shattered pieces of the plates on the floor.

Evalene pursed her lips tightly, trying not to let her anger show, and blinked back tears from the slap. Of course she would be blamed for that.

"I'm sorry," she ground out through gritted teeth.

But speaking out of turn just made Daeva more upset.

She lifted her hand as if to slap her again, which made Evalene duck.

"Hold still!" Daeva shrieked, and grabbed her by the hair. She shook Evalene as hard as she could, and with once last shake, she heaved Evalene at the wall, letting go. Evalene's right eye connected soundly with the pantry door knob.

Evalene yelped and crumpled on the floor, covering her face. Both sides throbbed. She felt her face swelling.

Huddled on the floor, she didn't dare risk looking up in case Daeva still wanted to lash out. The old woman's growl floated down to her, a frightening whisper, "You still don't know your place. It's because of people like you that the Number System can't flourish. If you can't comprehend your true worth, I will be forced to do my duty for my country and report you."

Evalene panicked as she watched Daeva's slippered feet turn towards the others in the kitchen through blurry, burning eyes. She couldn't apologize, or beg Daeva not to inform, or promise that she knew her place, without breaking the rules and proving herself false. So she stayed silent.

"She will not be given dinner tonight as punishment for her lies and rebellious behavior," Daeva said. "Neither will she receive any breakfast or lunch tomorrow." Evalene's stomach growled as if it heard the news.

Daeva's feet shifted back towards Evalene, who kept her head down. "This is the most merciful thing I can do for you. You will suffer until you learn your place. You will not come out of your room until it is time to begin the evening meal tomorrow."

She clapped her hands together, making everyone jump, before she left the room. Evalene felt her body sag in relief. Violet hurried over with a bag of ice, and a quick, comforting hand on her shoulder. But they couldn't sit with her in case Daeva came back. They had to finish preparing and serving the meal.

Evalene picked herself up off the floor, humiliated, beaten. She wanted to fight back, but the punishment would only be more severe. She turned toward those in the room, the only ones who would see her on her birthday. No one met her gaze.

She held the ice to one black eye and then the other. Her only gift today. Pressure built behind her eyes from holding back tears.

Stepping into the dark servant's hallway, she slowly climbed the two flights of stairs back to her little attic room. Without bothering to undress or assess the damage done to her face, she crawled into bed under the covers, pushing the book aside, laying her tender face on the pillow, and closing her eyes.

A knock on her door startled Evalene awake. She was confused. No one came up to her room. It took her a moment to remember what happened, but as she rolled over her face stung where it touched the pillow, reminding her. "One second," she croaked. Dragging herself out of bed, she flipped on the light switch and opened the door.

Violet was standing on the other side, wringing her hands. Her eyes widened at the sight of Evalene's face. Eyes swollen half shut, Evalene could only imagine how bad it looked.

"Thank you," she whispered. And Evalene nodded. That was all that needed to be said.

"Your father noticed your absence at dinner, and during the

news when they talked about the second... bulletin..." Violet stumbled over the word nervously, as if it were a crime to even say it. "He asked for you when the broadcast ended." Had he remembered Evalene's birthday?

Violet smiled a little in encouragement, "Do you think you could make it downstairs to serve tea if we give you a few minutes to clean up first?" Violet whispered the last few words. "Daeva told him you were being punished, but he still asked to have you sent down."

Clean up? How did someone clean up two black eyes? Violet shifted her weight back and forth, one foot turned towards the stairs. "Lady Ruby retired for the night," she offered after a moment's pause, and Evalene appreciated the girl's thoughtfulness. One less person to see her like this.

"Thanks," Evalene said, her voice coming out raspy. She cleared her throat and tried again, "I'll be right down."

Violet nodded and disappeared down the narrow staircase. Evalene closed her door softly. She wasn't sure what to do about her face. She didn't own make up.

Peering into her hazy little hand mirror, Evalene understood what Violet meant. Her eyes were red and puffy, the skin around them already bruising shades of purple and blue that would only get darker, and her hair was all over the place. That at least could be fixed. She pulled a brush through it a few times, and quickly tied it back.

There was crusted blood by her left eye from where Daeva's ring had cracked the skin. Evalene picked up a small cloth, dipped it into a water bowl on her dressing table, and squeezed the water out. She brought the damp cloth to her face and gently held it to her eyelids, and then around them, trying to wash away tears and blood without opening the cut again. Wincing, she pulled it away and took another peel. A small improvement.

Evalene's natural rebellious spirit rose. *Let him see,* she thought, *maybe he'll be shocked into doing something for once.* But she doubted it.

She lifted her chin, wrapping her frail dignity around her like a shield. Trudging slowly downstairs, she stepped into the doorway of the dining room, where her father sipped his tea and read the newspaper. Moving around the table, she came to stand against the wall next to Violet, crossing her hands to clasp them in front of her.

She cleared her throat. Not allowed to speak first, she waited.

He dragged his eyes from the paper, distracted. His brows rose high and forehead wrinkled when he saw her, and he adjusted his glasses, face registering surprise and confusion. Or maybe concern? Evalene wished she could read him better.

"Ah, yes," he said, and coughed. "Ah, Violet, dear, could you fetch me another cup of tea from the kitchen please?" He let the girl come and take his half-empty teacup away, waiting until she left the room to continue.

"Come sit, Evie," he said and patted the chair next to him. Evalene's heart softened at the childhood nickname. Obediently she came and sat next to him, turning in the chair to face her father. It felt for a moment as if they were family again, having a meal together, until she glanced down at her hands where they rested on her brown dress, a forceful reminder that this wasn't the case.

Byron patted his pockets as she sat, searching for something. "Ah, here it is," he mumbled, pulling out a tiny velvet box.

He briefly startled again at the sight of her face and frowned. Yet he still said nothing about her injuries. Though Daeva was a lower Number, her history as an informant seemed to weigh heavily on him. Did he feel as helpless as she did?

He cleared his throat, taking her hand without a word and placing the little box in her palm, wrapping her fingers around it. "Just a little something for your birthday." Patting her hand once, he let go. "You can open it later."

Evalene put the little box in her pocket, understanding the underlying message. It would be their secret.

"Thank you, I will." Evalene didn't know what else to say.

Her father nodded and opened his mouth as if to say more, but Violet's footsteps sounded on the hardwood floor coming back from the kitchen. Her father picked up the paper and shook it out. Evalene stood on cue.

As she moved back to her place against the wall, he frowned at the front page. The article held a blurry photo of the morning's second bulletin. She wanted to ask him what the article said, what she'd missed on the news, what he thought about it all? He wouldn't mind her speaking out of turn.

But Violet appeared in the doorway with a fresh cup of tea, and Evalene kept silent. If Daeva heard about it, she would mind very much.

The girls stood quietly, waiting to be needed, waiting for the night to end. The little box felt like it was burning a hole in Evalene's pocket.

Finally, Bryon stood and moved towards the library, his favorite room in the house. As he left, Evalene felt her throat close up, making it hard to swallow. He'd never once said a word about her face.

As she moved to pick up his dirty cup and saucer, Violet waved her off, "I'll handle it." Gesturing towards the door leading away from the kitchen, Violet indicated she should go back to her room. "It'd be better if Daeva didn't see you..."

Evalene pursed her lips, but didn't disagree. Making her way up to her little attic room, Evalene's stomach growled in protest at leaving the food behind. Her whole face flamed from the swelling. But she clung to one small piece of joy: she still had the stolen book hidden away in her room. And without meaning to, Daeva had provided her an entire day alone to read.

Softly shutting the door to her room, Evalene took the two steps to her bed in the dark, dropping onto the mattress. A lump under her hip reminded her of the little box in her pocket. She hurried to flip on the light switch, pulling out the tiny velvet box and lifting the lid.

It held a circle pendant on a thin chain. The round jewelry might have been a small coin, but the old markings had been melted away and around the edges was an inscription, written in a language she couldn't read and didn't recognize, that encircled the design in the middle of the coin. On top of this lay a second charm of a simple, beautiful tree surrounded by a circle.

It was not expensive or feminine. Lady Ruby would have scoffed at it and demanded to know where her father hid the real present. But for Evalene, it was beautiful.

She gently pulled it out of the box, undid the clasp, and fastened it around her neck. The chain was long, making it easy to hide under the collar of her dress, and the charm was so light, she barely felt it. Picking up her hand mirror to admire it, she touched the gift affectionately, trying to smile. Trying to be happy her father had remembered her.

It was a tiny bright spot in her world, like a candle burning in a huge dark forest. She tried to focus on it, keep it burning, but her injuries and his response doused it. How was one cheap necklace going to help her? It was all she could do to turn out the light and crawl under the covers, with one thought taking form in her mind as she fell asleep.

As she slowly woke the next morning, an overwhelming thought was on her mind: *escape*. Her dreams had been filled with failed attempts, everything that could possibly go wrong taking place, making her anxious. Yet the longer she thought about it, the more certain she was that she had to try, needed to try, in spite of her fear. How had she been foolish enough to think adulthood would be different? Age didn't change anything. Her future would look exactly like her present if she stayed here.

She rolled over, wincing when her black eye hit the pillow. She sucked in a breath at the pain, and closed her eyes. Rolling away from the sunlight streaming in, she considered sleeping through the whole day. But as the little room flooded with warm, yellow light, thoughts of escape kept her awake, her chest tight with anxiety.

Her book made a lump under the mattress where she'd tucked it back in the safe place, but she couldn't summon the energy or the desire to read it now. Such bad timing to be on house arrest when she needed to talk to Kevra more than ever. But she couldn't risk getting caught.

She played absently with the little necklace her father had given her. Thinking of his reaction last night led to wondering how her mother would have reacted. If Pearl really had been involved in the Bloom Rebellion, then Evalene doubted she would've taken it sitting down.

No, in her mind, Evalene imagined her mother standing up to Daeva, maybe even firing her. She tried to envision her mother, but couldn't quite picture her anymore. Just a memory of kind blue eyes and soft arms hugging her tight. Ruby had demanded to have all photos removed years back. Her father hadn't even noticed. He probably wouldn't notice when Evalene was gone either.

Rolling back to the front, Evalene pulled her book out and cradled it half under the covers, in case anyone burst into her room unannounced. She would endure today's punishment. If possible, she would even enjoy it. Grimly, she opened to the last page she'd read. For now, this was her escape.

9

Can It Be Done?

WAITING UNDER THE TREE two days later, Evalene heard Kevra's footsteps on the hard-packed earth before she was even in sight. As her friend rounded the corner, her mouth was already half open, ready to begin a conversation when she glimpsed Evalene's two black eyes. Kevra gasped, stopping where she stood. "What in the name of the Number One happened to you?"

"It was Daeva," Evalene shrugged. "You know how she gets." Trying to ignore the tightening in her gut, she took a deep breath to speak the words that would change everything. "Kevra, I'm ready." It was harder than she thought it would be to say it out loud. "We have to leave."

Kevra lit up and started dancing around, squealing in excitement, but Evalene was unable to join her. She'd never made such a drastic decision in her life. The consequences of getting caught weighed heavily on her.

Interrupting Kevra's celebration dance, Evalene leaned on the rock. "You told me you had a plan? Were you being serious?"

Kevra grinned, and pranced over, plopping down to sit next to

Evalene. "Of course I have a plan!" She laughed. "You're going to love it."

"Tell me quickly," Evalene said. Glancing at the path back to the house, and then towards the sun, trying to gage how much time she had, Evalene bit her lip. "I want to leave as soon as possible."

But Kevra's plan was full of holes.

"How will we get through the Regulator checkpoints? That's at least…" Evalene tried to picture the road to Delmare, how many cities there were along the way, "five or six cities. Which means at least that many check points." And it had been five years since she'd traveled those roads. In that amount of time, a lot could have changed.

Kevra shrugged, "We'll steal Ruby's ID. You could pass as her if they don't look too close."

"But won't she list it as stolen?" Evalene frowned, imagining the Regs arresting them at a checkpoint when Ruby reported the missing ID.

"We'll have to wait until the last minute. If we leave at night, and she sleeps until noon like she usually does, that'll give us almost 12 hours head start." Kevra smiled as if that resolved everything.

But Evalene shook her head. "No, it's a two-day drive. Even if we drive through the night and don't stop, it'd still be at least 24 hours. That's too risky." She needed to get back to the house. "I'll see if I can sneak a peek at Ruby's calendar. If we can find a day where she doesn't have any commitments… we could slip her an extra sleeping pill at dinner." Ruby loved her sleeping pills.

"Or two or three," Kevra grinned, "That's perfect!" It was far from perfect, Evalene chewed her lip at everything they'd need to decide. How would their absence go unnoticed by the staff? Especially Daeva? And if they did get reported, which they probably would, how long could they avoid the Regs catching up to them?

"I wish we could fly," Kevra said, sighing, interrupting Evalene's thoughts. Thanks to the Number One's Grid, no planes could come anywhere near Eden by air without being shot down instantly. But neither could anyone leave that way.

Evalene stood. Their only option was the coast, and finding a ship. Kevra knew that as well as she did, so Evalene only replied, "I hate heights. And I'd probably get motion sickness." She moved to walk back towards the house and Kevra followed.

"Oh yeah," Kevra rolled her eyes, "and a boat is so much better." She had a point. But they couldn't afford to be picky. They made plans to meet late that night to plan further, but Evalene could already tell the majority of the details would fall on her shoulders. Kevra thought big picture. She hadn't even considered they'd need to get gas!

Evalene's bruises were still present, making her look a bit like a raccoon the way they surrounded her eyes and cheek. Daeva seemed content that Evalene knew her place with this evidence, but the temporary calm didn't slow Evalene's plans in the slightest. It was short-lived. She wanted to leave in the next few days if possible.

By nightfall, Evalene felt better about their plan, having spent the day filling in most of the holes. Waiting for everyone to go to bed so she could meet Kevra was agonizing, but finally, she snuck outside, racing down the short path to the detached garage. No need to meet out by the tree when it was dark.

"We have three days," she whispered to Kevra the moment her friend's face appeared in the shadows.

As Evalene explained each step, Kevra stopped her with a hand on her arm. "I have an idea for that," she said, and her teeth flashed in the moonlight as she smiled, "Come with me."

Entering the huge garage from a side door, Kevra flipped a switch to turn on a small lamp, reaching into a bin, and pulling out car keys. Shaking her head, Evalene backed up, "No, it's too soon to go tonight."

"No silly," Kevra laughed softly, "We're not going anywhere, just trust me. Get in the driver's seat." She pointed to the closest car.

Frowning, Evalene did as directed, watching Kevra climb in on the passenger side.

"Okay," Kevra twisted in her seat to face Evalene, "I've never told you this, because it's not legal, but I've known how to drive since I was a kid. My dad taught me. By the time I was Numbered, we'd gone out driving on country roads so many times I could've been a professional driver like him. If I'd been Numbered higher." Kevra's mouth twisted sourly. "But the good news is, now I can teach you!"

Evalene smiled for the first time since she'd agreed to run. This was the one problem she hadn't found a solution to. It was perfect.

Kevra spent nearly an hour explaining the car to her, making her repeat each step back. The dim lighting of the lamp made it more difficult. It was hard to see the pedals and buttons clearly. But they didn't dare turn on more lights in case the main house noticed.

"We can meet tomorrow night and the next. By the time we leave you'll be a pro," Kevra reassured her, and Evalene agreed.

The next day, when it was time to clean the master bedroom suites, Evalene quietly locked the door when she reached Ruby's room. Ruby liked to try on dozens of outfits before deciding, leaving the discarded options strewn across the floor. A few extra minutes cleaning here should go unnoticed.

Opening Ruby's closet, Evalene stared into it, blinking, wondering where to start. It was the size of her entire room in the attic. Sorting through the tops, skirts, and dresses, the different accessories, and the shoes, she tried to pick quickly.

Ruby wore sky blue as her main color, just like her father, although Evalene couldn't understand how the woman had been Numbered Six when she didn't seem to have a brain at all.

Donning a top and a skirt, Evalene then pulled her own dress back on over them. The neckline of the brown dress was severely high compared to Ruby's and the hemline much longer, so she wasn't concerned about anything showing.

She placed some accessories – leggings, boots, and a jacket – into the bag she'd brought. Leaning out one of the windows, Evalene searched the entire yard for any sign of movement, before carefully dropping the bag straight down.

It dropped perfectly into the hole she had dug between the bushes last night. She hoped it was deep enough. Since it was below ground, no one should notice it. She would pick it up tonight after meeting Kevra. Tomorrow she would repeat the process once more with an outfit for Kevra.

In a flurry of activity, Evalene raced around the room, putting everything back in its place, tidying up in half the time.

When she got a chance to stop at her room later, she would remove the sky-blue layers underneath that felt like layers of white hot lies burning her skin. They would go in the hollow space under her loose floorboard, next to her most valuable possession, the blue scarf from Lola. The day after her Numbering she'd found it in her pocket, but instead of turning it in, she'd kept it, hidden. Now, after all these years, Lola's gift would finally be worn.

10

Escape

WHEN THE DAY ARRIVED, Evalene still didn't feel ready. Holding her hand mirror in front of her, she tried on Ruby's huge dark sunglasses. Thankfully, the borrowed frames covered her bruises completely. The black and blue around her eyes had faded to a sickly yellowish green, but they would still give her away if anyone noticed.

The timing tonight had to be impeccable.

At dinner, she crushed the extra sleeping pill into Ruby's nightly glass of wine. As soon as she saw Ruby take a sip, Evalene advanced her complaints of stomach pain to actual retching. Daeva couldn't stand the sound and ordered Evalene to bed, which she was counting on.

While everyone else watched the nightly news, Evalene snuck into her father's study and stole a pair of scissors. In the safety of her attic bedroom, she propped the hand mirror up against the bed and wall the best she could. Pulling the tie from her hair, allowing it to fall unhindered almost to her waist, she tried to picture Ruby's fashionable shoulder-length hairstyle, and cut.

Locks of hair fell to the floor like wounded soldiers until she was finally done. Her hair just brushed her shoulders, longer in the front, and shorter in the back. It wasn't as chic as Ruby's, but the guards at the gate were men. Hopefully they wouldn't spot the difference.

Last night, Kevra had gripped her arm so tightly it hurt. "We can do this, Evie, I swear. Promise me you won't hesitate?"

Evalene had bit her lip, and nodded. The moment had felt more solemn than a Numbering Ceremony. "I promise."

Now, pulling up the loose floorboard in her room with the hollow space beneath, Evalene took out her bag full of Ruby's stylish, high-Numbered clothing and the scarf from Lola. She swept the long, chopped off pieces of her hair into the empty hole in the floor before closing it back up.

While her own brown dresses were as formless as potato sacks, this light blue outfit had been carefully tailored exactly to Ruby's form. Since Ruby was smaller than Evalene, the top was tiny, but thankfully the fabric had quite a bit of stretch to it. It was the most natural blue, the color of a bright, cloudless sky, with pretty lace accents.

Next she pulled on leggings. Again, the fit was off, since she was taller than Ruby. The boots came up just past her ankles to meet them. It would do. Finally, a short blue skirt with a dozen layers of a stiff, uncomfortable fabric, almost like the old-world ballerinas, sewn together, creating a stiff bubble around her.

Picking up a short leather jacket, she added it to her ensemble. The boots, leggings, and jacket were all black, but this was acceptable for a high Number. They often got away with wearing splashes of other colors, even some of the other classes did so occasionally. As long as the colors were beneath a person's station and not above, the Regulators didn't seem to care.

Finally, Evalene added the sapphire scarf from Lola. It was lightweight, decorative, for the exact purpose of covering a Number. Evalene tied it carefully. Her outfit was complete.

She wished she had a full-length mirror to see the results. Despite Kevra's confidence, Evalene knew the disguise wouldn't hold up in front of anyone who knew Ruby well.

A knock sounded at the door. Evalene's whole body flashed ice cold before she started sweating. For a second, she couldn't move, couldn't even breathe. She choked trying speak, cleared her throat and tried again. "Just a minute!" she said trying not to sound frantic, panicked eyes darting around the room.

There wasn't a lock on the door. If the person outside wanted to come in, she couldn't stop them. Her feet came unstuck from the floor and she hurled herself into the unmade bed, pulling the covers over her boots and the sky-blue dress, lifting it all the way up to her neck.

Her hair! She gasped, not knowing what to do… Without any other options, she pulled the blankets completely over her head in desperation. *God, why?* She cried out in her mind, tears forming uninvited, *You've always been out to get me!* She railed at Him, angry now. *What did I ever do to you to deserve this?!*

Then she flinched, certain if God did exist, He definitely wasn't going to help her now. She couldn't make them wait any longer. "Who is it?" she called out, voice muffled by the blankets.

The door creaked open, and Evalene worried her thunderous heartbeat might give her away, it felt so loud in her ears. The blankets were suffocating, but she only tightened her grip where she clasped them over her head.

"It's me." It was Violet's voice, but Evalene felt no relief. The girl would expect Evalene to lower the blanket. They may not be close friends, but neither were they enemies.

Please... Evalene prayed desperately. *I know I don't deserve it... but please, save me...* She groaned out loud. Remembering she was supposed to be sick, she turned the groans into gagging as if about to throw up. If Violet didn't leave soon, it could very well be true.

"Evalene, are you okay? I –" Violet cut off as a yell sounded from downstairs.

"Violet! Kitchen, now!" Daeva's growl could make anyone flinch, even when someone else's name was being called. Evalene held her breath.

"I'll tell Daeva you're still not feeling well," Violet said. "Don't worry about work tomorrow."

"Thanks Violet," Evalene mumbled through the layers of blankets.

The door clicked closed on top of her words. Violet hadn't even waited for her response. Daeva had that effect.

Cautiously, Evalene pulled down the covers enough to peek out. The door was closed. The timing had been incredible. The stress of near discovery was compiling in her muscles, giving her a headache. Every inch of her body was tight with worry.

Evalene forced herself to climb out of bed, stiff with fear. She molded the pillows and blankets into the shape of a person, a decoy that might buy them a bit more time.

Then she sat on the edge of the bed, counting the seconds, waiting until the house was still and quiet, and even longer after that. She scanned the room once more, before pulling the door shut behind her.

She had to hurry.

Slipping down the stairs in the dark, Evalene headed for the master bedrooms. This part of the plan scared her out of her mind. But it had to wait until the last minute, until now. Because if Ruby realized her ID was gone days before they planned to leave she would have sounded the alarm. And her Identity Card was vital to their plans.

Slowly twisting the doorknob, Evalene softly opened the door to Ruby's bedroom. It took a second for her eyes to adjust to the dark. The small lump in the middle of the bed showed Ruby was alone, and Evalene breathed a sigh of relief that her father slept in his own room tonight. She'd refused to drug him earlier, but once dinner was past and it was too late, she'd regretted it.

Quietly sneaking in, she left the door cracked, hoping to find the ID quickly. Ruby didn't stir as Evalene dug through the dark piles on the floor. The pills were working. Searching through three different purses scattered across the room, Evalene found nothing but bits of lipstick and small coins. She pocketed the copper, wincing when they clinked in her pocket, but Ruby slept through it.

Finally, underneath a pile of clothes on the dressing table, Evalene felt a tiny wallet. Bringing it to the window, she opened the curtain slightly and held it up to the light of the moon. There was the Identity Card, along with some larger coins. She started to empty the wallet, then thought of a better idea. It would take Ruby longer to notice the ID was missing if she thought she'd misplaced her entire wallet. She put it in her jacket pocket.

Glancing at the door leading to her father's bedroom, Evalene touched the necklace she still wore – had worn every day since he'd given it to her. She considered leaving it behind for him, as a sort of goodbye. But after a moment, she tucked it back in instead. Better for her to keep a memory of the nice thing he'd done than leave him with a memory of the daughter he'd rather forget.

The next few minutes were a blur as Evalene stole out of the bedroom and crept down the stairs in terror, taking the back hallways, utilizing the less traveled areas in the house. There was no reason for anyone to be awake, yet every second ticking by felt like an hour, and by the time she reached the back door she was shaking from head to toe in a full-on panic attack.

Not pausing to think or even let out a sigh of relief, she whipped the door open and crossed the threshold, pulling it tightly shut behind her. *Relax*, she told herself. *Be Ruby*.

Strutting towards the garage, she hit a crack in the sidewalk and nearly toppled over right there. Wobbling, she caught herself. She tried to walk more carefully. How anyone could walk normally in heels was beyond her. She was more grateful than ever they'd chosen to escape during the night. If anyone had seen that during the day, her cover would've been blown.

Tottering to the garage's side door, Evalene opened it like she owned it, channeling Ruby's swagger.

But it wasn't necessary.

No one was inside.

It took forever to find the keys for the car they'd chosen. One by one, she pressed the buttons for each set, watching for flashing lights, listening for the sound of doors clicking unlocked.

They'd picked one of the older cars, rarely used by her father. The interior was fabric instead of leather, and it didn't have as many gadgets across the dash as the others, although the convertible top still came down and it had a high-tech GPS system they hoped to use if one of them could figure out the technology.

Shutting the door quietly, Evalene took a moment to study the car, running through the steps Kevra had taught her once more. It was time to test them out.

Nervously placing the keys in the ignition, she paused. She patted the sun visor on her side and then on the passenger side, searching for the garage door opener. Opening the glove box, she found it resting inside. The door roared to life and began rising in front of her with the press of a button. Evalene put her hand on the key in the ignition once more, and started the car.

Testing the gas pedal, she tried to roll smoothly out of the garage just like Kevra had described. The car began moving too fast, making her nervous, and she pushed hard on the brake. She quickly learned, after her chest slammed into the seatbelt, that it only needed a light touch.

She stepped on the gas again, and the car jerked out of the garage and onto the long driveway. Gripping the wheel tightly, Evalene's knuckles were white as the car slowly ambled down the dirt drive. It stretched a quarter mile long, weaving back and forth around the rocky terrain. As she took the first curve, the house disappeared from the rear-view mirror. Evalene let out a shallow breath. That was one hurdle. Now the guard station.

As she rounded the last bend, and the little hut appeared at the end of the driveway. Evalene pressed the brakes lightly, gliding to a stop in front of it so slowly the guard leaned out in impatience.

Rolling down the car's tinted window, Evalene adopted Ruby's careless attitude again, holding the open wallet with the Identity Card out the window in their general direction, while staring straight ahead.

As soon as the guard saw her in Ruby's clothes, he waved her on, pressing the button to open the big metal gate, not even glancing at the ID. The gate swung open inch by inch while Evalene rolled the window back up, tossing the little wallet into the passenger seat next to her. Putting all her energy into a smooth take off, she carefully increased pressure on the pedal, just like Kevra had described. She turned left out of the gate, taking off towards the intersection.

A person stood at the far end of the road, a shadowy, shapeless silhouette in the moonlight, stepping out into the street in front of the vehicle. It forced Evalene to stop, which she did, abruptly, slamming on the brakes as her heart stopped with it.

11

Roadtrip

THE DARK FIGURE APPROACHED the car. As it drew closer, Evalene let out a huge sigh of relief. It was Kevra. They'd agreed she would sneak past the guard station and wait on the road, but Evalene had been thrown off by her friend's hair, which was much darker than her original shade of red. In the moonlight, it was hard to tell, but it almost looked brown? And she'd cut it as short as Evalene's!

They didn't say a word to each other, per their previous agreement, as Kevra climbed into the passenger side and carefully shut the door. But Evalene frowned at her, confused.

Pulling away from the intersection, Evalene drove on. In just a few minutes, they reached the on-ramp to the main highway, and both girls breathed a huge sigh of relief. Kevra laughed loudly, startling Evalene, who giggled a second later. Pretty soon both were laughing so hard they had tears running down their faces.

Evalene relaxed her hold on the wheel, glancing over at Kevra. "What in the Number One's name did you do to your hair?" She flipped on the overhead light in the car to be sure. The gorgeous shades of red were all gone. From the back, the girls could easily be mistaken as twins now, although Kevra's hair had a hint of red peeking through.

"I needed to look like the Identity Card," Kevra said, shrugging. "I might need to use it too. Plus, now if they put out an alert for us, they'll be watching for a brunette and a redhead, right? This will throw them off our trail."

It made sense. But Evalene frowned. "Why didn't you tell me?"

Kevra laughed. "I didn't think of it until last minute, or I would have told you. I promise!" She mimed crossing her heart and smiled at Evalene. "Seriously. I had the time, and it's so much better this way. Now either of us can be Ruby if we need to!"

It still felt odd to Evalene. Kevra usually talked everything through with her. But the stress had messed with Evalene's mind too. It could make anyone forgetful. "It's actually brilliant," she said, giving in, and Kevra grinned back, proud of herself. Kevra wore the other outfit stolen from Ruby's closet, a navy-blue dress with a white-speckled pattern like stars in a night sky, growing gradually lighter as it reached the top, as if dawn was coming. It would've been Evalene's first choice, if the dress hadn't been too small for her. But Kevra, being more petite like Ruby, fit into it perfectly. A thicker scarf, also blue, wrapped around Kevra's neck over her tattoo.

Kevra's green eyes flashed in excitement, "Wow. This feels amazing, right?" She grinned widely as she put her feet up on the dash, relaxed now. "I honestly didn't know if this would work."

Evalene stared at her friend, forgetting for a moment to watch the road. "What? I hope you're kidding. I only agreed to your plan because you were so sure!"

Kevra shrugged, a simple gesture that didn't match the pain in her voice. "I couldn't stay another second. It was now or never." Evalene was gathering the courage to ask her what exactly had happened with her boss when Kevra laughed loudly, throwing her head back, lightening the mood again. "We're free! We made it!"

Evalene couldn't help smiling. "It's not over yet." She shook her head at Kevra – the weightless sensation of her short hair swishing over her shoulders felt strange. "We still have to get to the coast and onto a ship."

But she felt a tiny spark of hope for the first time since her Numbering.

Since Evalene was already driving, she took the first shift. They would take turns driving through the night and all day tomorrow, hopefully reaching the coast by nightfall. Kevra was far too excited to sleep, chattering excitedly about the FreeLands and how the first thing she would do when she got there was get her tattoo removed or eat a steak like high Numbers did. Maybe both at the same time. Evalene laughed. She couldn't picture anything past the next day and a half.

The night sky was filled with stars and they stared out at the little bit of road visible in the headlights. The road curved around the desert terrain, winding through valleys. Kevra played with the high-tech GPS system. Thanks to her position in the television factory, she had a better grasp of technology than most low Numbers in Eden. After fifteen minutes of Kevra cursing at the machine, a robotic voice squawked on and began chirping directions.

A few hours later, Evalene's leg ached from holding down the gas pedal. "You drive so slow," Kevra complained for the third time. "Let's switch. It's my turn."

Pulling over, they changed places. Kevra settled comfortably into the driver's seat, immediately flipping a switch, "No wonder your leg hurts. You never turned on the cruise control."

Evalene groaned, "I wish I'd known that a few hours ago."

Kevra glanced over and sympathetically patted her leg, but didn't say much. After the initial burst of conversation during the first couple hours, she'd grown quiet. Besides telling Evalene there were sandwiches in the bag she'd brought, Kevra stayed silent.

"Evalene, I was thinking," Kevra broke the silence a few hours later, "we're coming up on the first city border here in about 20 minutes. Since we only have the one ID, I think you should get in the trunk until we're passed. Just to be safe. And of course," Kevra added, "I'll get in the trunk the next time. We can take turns!"

She made it sound like a game, such a Kevra thing to do. But Evalene didn't argue. She welcomed the chance to avoid pretending. She always said the wrong thing. Anxiety gave her a headache from clenching every muscle in her body, and just the idea of facing the Regulators made her start sweating. The trunk would be a pleasant relief.

They pulled over, and Evalene climbed out as Kevra searched for the button to open the trunk. "I'll let you out as soon as it's safe," she promised Evalene, who nodded. Nerves fluttered once again. Evalene wondered how much anxiety a person could take before they simply stopped functioning.

Climbing into the open trunk, Evalene reached up to find a grip on the inside and pulled down hard, pulling her hand back a split second before the lid crashed over her and clicked closed. It was as dark as a cave without the moonlight. She should've expected that. But the fears preying on her mind grew ten times the size they'd been in the front seat.

Lying there in the dark, Evalene felt the car pull out onto the open road again, and regretted being so willing to take the trunk spot. The rocking, bumping, swaying motion of the trunk made her carsick, and the confined space made it hard to breathe.

Twenty minutes passed painfully slow. When the car slowed to a halt, time stopped. Evalene took a big gulp of air and another, focusing on not hyperventilating. She picked up a male voice, and possibly a second, but it was only mumbling from her vantage point.

Kevra must have been acceptable to the Regulators on border patrol, because they didn't detain her more than a few minutes before the car jerked forward. About a block or so further down the road she heard Kevra give a little squeal of delight. A small smile briefly crossed Evalene's face. Another five minutes passed, then ten. Twenty minutes. Longer.

Finally, Evalene heard the crunch of gravel and felt the car slow to a stop. Kevra was already apologizing as the hood popped open and the light of the moon poured into the trunk. "I didn't see a good place to stop. I'm sorry. This was the first spot that looked safe. I didn't want to risk it, just in case, you know?"

Evalene climbed out and tried to shake off the waves of stress. She stretched her hands up high and stood on tiptoe, enjoying the relief it brought to her muscles. "It's okay. It was nice to sit in a slightly different position for a couple minutes," she tried to joke, but it fell a little flat.

"Well, get back in the car, because the luxury seating is over and this little party is overdue to get back on the road." Kevra tapped her wrist where a watch would be if she had one.

"Okay. But I get to drive now." Evalene held out her hand for the keys. She wasn't nearly as smooth a driver as Kevra, but she didn't care. It was a taste of freedom, and she loved it.

Back on the open road, the black pavement no longer curved, but stretched out in front of them for miles and miles. Evalene felt a deep sense of relief sweep over her as the sun began to rise. The flat desert sand stretched out in front of them on both sides, not a single tree or even a bush to be seen, and mountains off in the distance.

Munching on a sandwich for breakfast, Evalene started to hum along with the radio, tapping the steering wheel happily as they passed the halfway point in their journey. Even though they still took precautions, keeping their sunglasses and scarves on, only stopping in deserted areas, and avoiding towns and checkpoints wherever possible, Evalene still felt more free than she had in years.

Kevra had packed so much food they could've lasted a week, and they'd made great time. Hours flew by, although it was hard to sleep in the car and they were both exhausted. That, plus the uncomfortable feeling of dirty clothes, that itched and smelled like sweat and dust, had put Kevra in a lousy mood. But Evalene ignored her because they were only a few hours away from

Delmare. She turned the radio up even louder, much to Kevra's dismay.

Beaming over at her friend who frowned out the window at the blue skies and wide open spaces, Evalene reached out and lightly punched Kevra's arm. "What's got you so gloomy?" she demanded. "This isn't like you, especially now - I feel like I'm coming more alive every mile!" But Kevra just shrugged. In exasperation, Evalene turned down the music. "What happened to my friend and all her plans for when we get to the FreeLands, hmm?"

Kevra stretched sleepily and drooped back into her seat with an exaggerated yawn. "I'm just sick of this car, that's all," she said. "It's hard to be cooped up so long, you know?"

When she didn't say anything further, Evalene took her eyes off the road to squint at her. But Kevra closed her eyes, blocking her out. Shrugging, Evalene turned the radio back up and shook her head. She tried to tune back into her mood from a few minutes prior.

If Kevra was homesick, Evalene refused to join her. Considering the home Evalene had grown up in before her Numbering, as well as Lola, her freedom, her father the way he used to be, her mother when she'd been alive – Evalene had been homesick for years. And she was sick of it. Enough mourning. She was ready to start fresh. Bobbing her head along to the music, catching onto the chorus, she sang along.

The late afternoon sun shone down on them like a warm, golden hug, and the fresh breeze coming in the windows cooled off her toasting skin. The day felt like perfection. Evalene was gloriously happy. She felt like she could conquer anything. Even knowing the Regulators might have been alerted to their absence by now didn't bother her. They were almost out of Eden.

Time passed without notice, while Kevra slept against the window, and Evalene drove until the gas light dinged.

She'd known it had to happen, but her anxiety returned anyway. Here was the next test. On the lookout for a discreet place to pull over, Evalene quickly hopped out to let Kevra drive again, climbing back into the trunk once more. So far, Kevra had handled every checkpoint, and they would have to go through another to get into town for gas. Evalene was more than happy to let her handle both.

They'd been gone all night and half a day. If either girl was reported missing, or more importantly, if Ruby realized they'd taken her Identity Card, this next checkpoint could go horribly wrong.

12

Delmare

VOICES SOUNDED OUTSIDE THE car as it slowed, one in particular barking at the car impatiently. Kevra's flirtatious laugh floated back to where Evalene lay in the dark trunk. She could easily picture her friend flipping her now-brown hair and winking at one of the Regulators. But would it work?

They mumbled for what felt like ages, but was probably just five minutes. From her vantage point, Evalene couldn't make out a single word, just muffled chuckles from a deep, male voice and high-pitched trills as Kevra joined him.

Finally, the car shifted into gear and crossed through the checkpoint into town without a hitch. Now they just needed gas. Evalene felt the car turn frequently, as Kevra searched the town for a pump. She didn't stop to let Evalene out, but that wasn't surprising. There were probably too many people around. A girl climbing out of a trunk would be suspicious.

So Evalene waited it out, feeling claustrophobic in the tight space. The air was musty and the way the sun beat down on the car without any breeze to cool her off had her sweating heavily.

The car stopped and shut off. Metal hit metal as Kevra placed the pump in the car and began filling up. Other voices sounded, faint in the background. The pump stopped. A long period of time passed, making Evalene nervous that Kevra was getting arrested inside the store right then. Evalene would have to live out her last few days in the trunk of a car. Or her last few hours, the way she was roasting. But then she heard the front door click open and felt Kevra climb in.

Just one last checkpoint before they arrived in Delmare. Kevra seemed determined to get to it as fast as possible, even though it meant leaving Evalene in the trunk another 30 minutes. She tried to sleep, but it was too hot.

Annoyed at Kevra for not asking her if this was okay, Evalene was agitated and wide awake by the time they reached the last checkpoint; the wall surrounding the city of Delmare. Though she was trapped in the trunk, she knew from growing up in this city that the wall encircled it like a half moon, all the way up to the coast on both sides. It was where the Number One lived, and so it was the most protected.

Kevra was flirting heavily now. Evalene could tell from the way her voice rose a full octave and she laughed at everything the Regulator said. She held her breath.

They were moving. Then the car stopped again. Kevra's laugh sounded strained. Evalene pressed her ear to the roof, trying to make out what they were saying. All she could hear was her pulse thundering in her ears, drowning them out.

But a miracle must have happened – they were pulling away! This time, after they'd gone for about five minutes, Evalene thought she'd spent more than enough time in the trunk and kicked the hood a few times to make herself known. Only three times though. She had no idea where they were and didn't want to risk a stranger noticing. A couple minutes passed and Evalene was getting ready for a few more kicks, harder this time, when Kevra pulled the car to a stop.

"Alright, alright," Kevra said, lifting the hood. "Relax, geez. It was already past five, and I didn't know how much time we had before a report might reach the last checkpoint. Every minute counts, I figured you'd understand!"

Clenching her teeth at the argument, Evalene climbed out. She did understand. But that didn't mean she liked it. But she nodded. "What happened at that last stop? You were leaving, and then they held you back?"

"Oh, ha!" Kevra rolled her eyes. "He was asking to call me on my cell phone." She acted like she was used to men hitting on her. Maybe she was. "I told him I dropped it in a toilet!" Now she was laughing for real, and Evalene had to grin as she shook her head. Quick thinking. She was thankful it had been Kevra who talked to them. But she never wanted to see the inside of a trunk again.

"My turn." Evalene held out her hand for the keys, and Kevra reluctantly handed them over. Climbing into the driver's seat, Evalene looked around for the first time. They were in a part of town she didn't recognize. Most of the houses in Delmare were squat and tough, made of cement and other bomb-shelter materials, a product of all the wars before the Number One took over. The streets were dirty.

Since her family had lived on the other side of the city near the coast, Evalene felt a little lost, but after Kevra pressed a few buttons, the GPS snapped back on to guide them to the coast.

As the sun dropped lower in the sky, Evalene soaked up another new song, cheering quickly as she drove through the hills leading to the coast. She navigated carefully around the outskirts of Delmare, staying away from where the Regulator Station rested in the heart of the city. Evalene gasped as they rounded a corner and came up right next to the ocean, at the top of a cliff.

"Look at that view!" Pulling the car onto the shoulder of a lookout point Evalene jumped out of the car, leaving her door open. The fresh air felt good. She could almost taste salt in the gusts of wind. The ocean stretched as far as her eyes could see to the left and the right. She hadn't seen it since she was a little girl. It was so heartbreakingly beautiful.

Kevra grudgingly climbed out of the passenger seat and shuffled over to the stone wall of the outlook to join her. Evalene hoped the view would cheer her. "Isn't it incredible?" She smiled at Kevra. "We just need to get on a ship now." Kevra smiled back slightly, moving to rest her elbows on the stone barrier.

They stared out at the beautiful, clean water, ignoring the dirty, gray city behind them, where the buildings crowded each other out and left no room for yards or trees, only sidewalks and streets. "We've still got a lot to figure out before we're on the water," Kevra murmured.

In the distance, the Number One's home rose like a fortress on the cliffs, its white pillars, turrets, and guard stations making it look like a modern, well-guarded castle. The house and grounds took over an entire hillside and the surrounding area, and Evalene remembered from visits with her father as a child that it was even bigger and more intimidating in person.

Kevra's gaze though, was on the Regulator Station, another imposing tall, gray building in the heart of the city, and much closer. "What will we do if they check our Identity Card and find an alert? And how will we get on a ship without – " Kevra cut off, frowning, without finishing her thought.

Evalene didn't pursue the question, letting it fade off into the valley below them, into the frothy white foam where the waves crashed against rocks. She knew full well the questions they both had were all just versions of the same root question: How?

Getting back in the car, they drove the last hour in silence until they reached the pier. They pulled up to the docks, where the ships stretched out for many city blocks, barring their view of the ocean almost completely. The water here was deep. The pier was a huge platform built to stretch far out over the water so that the ships rested right next to it. A few people walked along the pier in various directions, and most of them wore red, for the merchant class, since they were allowed to travel for their trade, and their vocations depended on successful commerce.

Kevra perked up, whipping off her seatbelt. "Now we can finally get some answers." Her door swung open before the car even came to a full stop.

Evalene threw the car into park, moving to unbuckle her seat belt. "Wait for me!"

"No!" Kevra said sharply, grabbing Evalene's hand before she could press the button. "We only have the one Identity Card. If anyone needs to see one and I'm alone, it'll be fine. But if you're there, they'll want to see two cards." With wallet and ID in hand, she leapt out of the car, shut the door and was gone before Evalene could respond.

Dazed, Evalene tried to process the range of emotions she'd just witnessed. At first glance, Kevra's argument made sense, but what if a Regulator stopped at the car instead? What was Evalene supposed to do without an ID?

She waited, chewing her fingernails to the quick until they bled, jumping at every sound, shrinking into her seat whenever someone walked too close to where she'd parked. At one point, she even started the car and drove it a block down the pier, further away. Kevra would still see it, but this way she was out of the way of foot traffic. Her chest felt tight.

The passenger door handle clicked and swung open when Evalene was staring out the drivers' side window. She yelped before Kevra's face appeared. Blowing out the breath she'd been holding, Evalene scowled at Kevra. "For Number One's sake! What happened?"

Kevra smiled, buckling back into her seat, but somehow her smile seemed a bit crooked. "Sorry it took so long," she said. "I wanted to make sure I did my research. Let's go." She gestured for Evalene to start driving.

But Evalene shook her head in exasperation. "Kevra, tell me what happened? Aren't there any ships? Why aren't we getting ready to board?"

"Oh – no there aren't any ships leaving until tomorrow." Kevra's face was unreadable with the dark sunglasses. "First things first, we need to find a place to stay tonight, and then I'll tell you, I promise!"

No more ships? That was strange. But it was getting late, and the sun was setting. They must not leave at night. She vaguely remembered sailors using the tides somehow. Evalene sighed in disappointment, starting the car. If they had to stay the night, Kevra was right, it would be good to get off the road.

They drove away from the pier into the nearby suburbs of Delmare. Inspecting the houses on both sides, they concealed their scrutiny behind their sunglasses. They needed something uninhabited, whether an abandoned factory or warehouse of some kind, or a vacant home.

As they crept along side roads, they travelled further and further away from the pier. "Maybe we should focus on finding something in this area." Evalene itched a spot on the bridge of her nose where the sunglasses were beginning to bother her. "I don't want to go too far from the docks, it's already going to be at least an hour walk from here."

"But I don't want to walk," Kevra argued. "We already bent the license plates – what if we just took them off altogether?"

"And risk getting pulled over for not having a license?" Evalene shook her head. "No. We need to ditch the car completely. The sooner, the better. Even if Ruby didn't report her ID missing yet, I'm sure Daeva's informed on us by now."

Kevra grimaced and nodded. "Then we need to find a place to park that isn't visible from the road."

"And hopefully a place with a roof," Evalene agreed. If worse came to worst, they could try to sleep in the woods, but neither of the girls knew anything about camping.

Kevra didn't reply. When Evalene glanced over, Kevra was biting her lip, staring absently out the window. "Don't worry," Evalene tried to cheer her up, feeling as if their roles were reversed, and she was the optimistic one, "we'll find the perfect place to hide for the night." Driving in a zigzag pattern, Evalene made her way up and down the nearby streets.

Her stomach growled audibly. Without a word, Kevra opened their small bag of food, rationing out their dinner. Evalene was taking the last bite of her sandwich when they both saw it. At the end of the street, right next to some trees, was a building that was without a doubt completely abandoned.

A few windows were boarded up, and shattered glass littered the sidewalk in front of the brick building. Dingy, shadowy letters spelled out G—O-C-E-R——S, missing letters fallen off and never replaced. There was garbage strewn across the sidewalk on both sides of the street. It was perfect. The only trick would be getting inside.

Evalene drove into the parking lot, discovering the store was shaped like an L. If they parked the car in the corner, right up against the building, it couldn't be seen from the road. The perfect hiding spot. But would the inside of the building be as accommodating?

Kevra got out the moment Evalene put the car in park. With a quick glance around for watching eyes, she trotted up to the door and knelt to peer at the lock. Evalene turned off the engine and climbed out of the car, shutting both her door and Kevra's. She pulled the license plates off the front of the car, just for good measure before walking up to the door to join Kevra.

They stared at the old-fashioned sliding door. Neither of them had experience picking locks, but this one looked complicated. Kevra whipped a couple of the pins from her hair, shoving them into the latch. She squinted, face stiffening in concentration.

Evalene stood in front of Kevra, acting as lookout, though not sure what she would do if someone actually appeared.

Five minutes later, after Kevra had poked the pins into the tiny lock every way imaginable without success, she threw them on the ground in frustration and smacked the door with both hands, "Ahh!"

Evalene jerked around in surprise. "Maybe there's a back door that would be easier," she tried to pacify her. "I'll go look."

But Kevra grabbed her arm to stop her. "No, I'll go." She picked up the pins from the ground, heading past Evalene around the side of the building.

Evalene shrugged, feeling helpless. She could circle the building in the opposite direction, she supposed. But instead she stepped up to the glass sliding door, cupping her hands above her eyes to shade from the sun, trying to see inside.

Without thinking, she casually pushed on the door. It shifted! Evalene put her whole weight into an intentional shove, and the door immediately began sliding open! Evalene grinned to herself as she pushed the door wide enough to enter, stepping inside the store.

Glancing around the dimly lit room filled with empty shelves and small, high windows, Evalene's eyes caught on the back door on the opposite side of the room. She laughed. Kevra was undoubtedly on the other side of that door, struggling and failing to pick the lock again.

Evalene scanned the road. It was empty. She shoved the sliding the door closed, just in case someone did drive by. Then she skipped across the room to the huge black door on the other side. Flipping the big deadbolt on top and unlocking the lock on the doorknob, she flung the door open.

"Ta-da!" she sang, and burst out laughing at the expression on Kevra's face. Startled at the sound of the door unlocking, Kevra had jumped up to run, but had tripped and fallen backwards onto her rear end.

"Oooh, Number One save me," Kevra said, her words muddled as she clapped her hands over her mouth. She said something else, but it was blocked by her fingers and came out mangled.

"What?" Evalene shook her head at her friend, smiling. "You don't want to come in?" she teased, and held out a hand to help Kevra stand.

"Not cool." Kevra spoke more clearly now as she grabbed onto Evalene's hand and pulled herself up. "You could've come around to get me. Or at least yelled so I knew it was you before you opened the door." She crossed her arms and marched past Evalene into the store.

Evalene rolled her eyes and followed her inside, slamming the door shut.

Crossing her arms as well, she watched Kevra investigate each aisle of the store, exploring their hideout, and double-checking they were the only ones there.

Evalene moved to lock the front sliding door, only to find the latch was broken, which explained why she'd been able to open it so easily. She wandered back into the middle of the room.

The store, just one big square, didn't have too many corners to search before Kevra was satisfied it was empty. She came back to the center, glancing at Evalene, then away, hands on her hips. "Where's the bag with our food?"

"I don't know," Evalene said. "Probably still in the car."

Kevra's eyes flashed at Evalene. "Well, go get it."

Evalene raised her eyebrows and said, "Excuse me?" She felt conflicted. Standing up to a higher Number was wrong, yet her pre-Numbered self surfaced. She hated being bossed around.

They were both silent for a beat, stubborn.

"Nevermind, I've got it," Kevra said abruptly, right as Evalene was about to give in. Evalene's jaw dropped. Technically Kevra was right to tell her what to do, and if not for the fact that they were hiding from the law, she could've reported Evalene.

But Kevra rushed towards the back door and swung it open. Pausing, she picked up a roll of duct tape from a shelf, carefully placing it in the crack so the door wouldn't lock behind her.

Evalene's stiff spine wilted. That didn't feel like a win. Sighing, she spun around, deciding to explore while she waited.

As she wandered down the closest aisle, she turned the corner and meandered through the next row and the next, taking in the details of the room now as she went. The ceiling was high, with mirrors all around the edges of the room, so you could see what someone was doing from one end of the room to the other, no matter what row they were in.

Since the lights were off, and only a handful of tiny windows placed sparsely around the room allowed light in, the room was dimming quickly as the sunset. As tempting as it would be to test the lights for electricity, Evalene wasn't willing to risk it.

Moving towards what would've been the cashier's counter when the store was open, Evalene walked around behind the long counter and began opening the cabinets underneath it, one at a time, exploring.

She felt the hairs lift on the back of her neck and a tingly sensation of dread hit her, right before she felt it. A loud crack sounded as something hit her, heavy metal smashing into the back of her skull, sending sharp spikes of pain through her head before the room faded quickly into black.

13

The Betrayal

WAKING UP SLOWLY, EVALENE'S head felt like it was splitting open. She felt numb. What had just happened?

She tried blinking, squinting, trying to see, and felt her eyes tear up from the pain. She was sitting in a chair against a wall. Her head hurt. Eyes watering, she tried to touch the back of her head, but both hands were stuck behind her back.

Straining, she felt around her wrists and discovered a scratchy, thin rope. Evalene moved her fingers along the rough edges of the rope, feeling where it was tied around her wrists and to the base of the chair.

The muffled sound of footsteps came from her right. As she turned her head to look, she groaned and was forced to close her eyes. It felt like someone was hammering sharp nails into her skull.

What's going on? Her thoughts were groggy but getting clearer. *Where am I? Where's Kevra?* She blinked and looked to the right, more carefully this time. The first thing to catch her eye was the puddle of something dark red near the corner of the cashier's counter in front of her. Blood. Her blood.

Someone was making noise out of sight behind the shelves. There was movement in the mirrors above her. Evalene looked up and made out a dim reflection. Her attacker.

Evalene felt icy cold as her eyes took it in. Her mind refused to comprehend what was happening. This didn't make sense. A sharp stab of pain registered on her forehead, overpowering the pounding coming from the back of her skull. She sensed something wet trickling down the right side of her face. She must have hit something sharp when she fell.

Kevra appeared around the corner of the shelves, walking towards Evalene. Her face had an odd calm, not smiling, not frowning. Just an emptiness in her eyes when she stared at Evalene, except for a flicker of something Evalene couldn't name before she looked away. She stopped a few feet from where Evalene sat.

"I never wanted to do this." Kevra crossed her arms, sighing. "I didn't have a choice." She stepped closer, and knelt on one knee, grasping an arm of the chair as if desperate to connect and be understood. "Evie, I found every ship headed to the FreeLands. I talked to every captain. They all said the same thing. Passage requires proof of ID. They confiscate your Identity Card when you board, and keep it until you land. I spent weeks trying to think of a way around this if we ran into it, but I've come up empty."

Evalene was having trouble concentrating. Her head throbbed and she felt overwhelmed. "Did you say... weeks?"

For the first time since she'd woken up, Evalene thought she saw remorse flash across Kevra's face. "I had to plan for the possibility," she whispered, expressionless.

"Is that..." Evalene felt the words forming in her mind, but could barely speak them, not wanting to believe it, "the real reason you dyed your hair before we left?" Then an even worse thought came to her. "Is that why you needed me?" Her voice broke. She felt tears come to her eyes again, but not from the pain in her head this time. "You needed me to steal Ruby's Identity Card," she whispered the last words, "because that was the one thing you couldn't get by yourself..."

"Well, not exactly," Kevra defended herself. "I mean, I hoped we wouldn't run into this problem. The ID was just supposed to be a backup. In case we ran into trouble and needed proof. But Evie, it's not like it's over for you. I'm not turning you in or anything." Kevra took a deep breath, stood and continued, "In fact, I think you can still make it. We just can't go together."

Evalene gave a short laugh without any humor, then winced at the pain it caused her head. "How do you imagine I'm going to *make it*?" she snapped, ignoring the pain that made lights dance in front of her eyes. "You just told me passage on a ship requires an Identity Card, and you're taking the only one we have. Across the sea. It's not like you can mail it back to me."

Kevra started to pace back and forth in front of Evalene, waving a finger back and forth. "No, listen. You could steal someone's purse, use another high Number's Identity Card." She gestured wildly, the way she always did when she was trying to emphasize her point. "You could be just a day or two behind me!"

"With. What. Money," Evalene said through clenched teeth.

Kevra spun to reach into her pocket. She'd been carrying the wallet since the harbor. Everything made sense now. Counting out a few coins, Kevra tucked them into the pocket of Evalene's jacket. "This is how much it costs. And," she sounded almost cheerful as she pulled out a couple more coins and added them to the pile in Evalene's pocket, "here's a little extra for food, in case it takes you a couple days to get the right ID. Ruby was loaded."

Evalene gritted her teeth so hard the ache in her head turned into a piercing pain. She tried to relax her jaw. "Thanks so much for the advice," she snapped sarcastically. "Could you please also give me some directions on how to get to the nearest Regulator Station and turn myself in?" She bit out the last words, "I think that'd be faster."

Kevra had the nerve to act like they were still back home at their tree, planning. "You could also go back home, if you'd rather. I know your father would keep you safe, make up some reason you'd disappeared... You could go right back to the way things were. But Evie, I can't." Her voice broke a little, and she shook her head. "I can't live like that anymore, you don't understand. I couldn't say no... I couldn't report him... I couldn't do anything."

Kevra took two steps to the back door. When she turned back she'd wiped her face of all emotion. She pointed to the duct tape where it sat, jammed between the door and the wall, "I'm going to block the door open with this. I haven't tied your feet on purpose. Once I'm gone, you can wedge your foot in the crack to get it open and get outside. You'll still be tied to your chair, but I'm sure someone will drive by and see you."

"Sure." Evalene glared at her. "And they definitely won't call the Regulators. Or have me arrested."

But Kevra acted as if she hadn't heard. "All you'll have to do is be your pretend high-Numbered self, and tell them you were robbed." She took two steps back to Evalene and gently rearranged her scarf. "There," she said softly, "no one will be the wiser."

Speechless, for a moment Evalene just stared at her, feeling as helpless and alone as she had back home. Maybe freedom had never been in her grasp.

She found her voice. "You honestly think someone will not only NOT check my tattoo while I'm tied up," she grew louder as she spoke, "but they will also NOT report to the Regulators that they found me?" By this point she was yelling, something she hadn't dared to do since she was 12 years old. "And you believe I've somehow developed the skills to steal a high Number's purse, right from under their nose in the middle of a crowded public space?" The tears poured out of her eyes now, unbidden, as she cried out, "You can't honestly expect me to believe this is a legitimate plan!"

Kevra wasn't quite meeting her eyes anymore. That was answer enough for Evalene. She stared at her supposed friend with tears flowing freely down her cheeks, watching Kevra turn and walk towards the door, where she paused, holding the door knob. The fading light made the red tints in her hair shine, and she spoke quietly to the floor. "I really am sorry. You have to believe me, I never wanted this to be the case… it was just supposed to be a backup plan… just in case."

Repeated apologies meant nothing to Evalene, and they didn't seem to reassure Kevra either, although she kept trying as if she hoped they would. "I have to look out for myself, you know," she tried one last time. "It was between you and me, and I had to make a choice." The last part came out so quietly Evalene almost didn't hear it. "But I really do hope you make it..."

And then the door swung shut and she was gone.

In the fading light of twilight, as the sun set and the last bit of golden light started to disappear, Evalene sat tied to the chair, unable to move.

She turned her face to the wall, rested her head against it, and wept bitterly.

14

Jeremiah, Age 22

JEREMIAH STOLE INTO THE gazebo as the sun set over the lake behind him. The little building sat just a few dozen feet from Lady Beryl's main home, and was just a roof over a porch with some comfortable chairs. But it was the perfect place to meet because it was surrounded on all sides by the lake, except where the path led to it from the house. No one could eavesdrop without them knowing. He was early, so he settled in to wait.

If not for Beryl, Jeremiah couldn't imagine where he might be today. Dead probably. Instead, she'd changed him by being the family he'd so desperately needed, making sure he got an education far past his Number level, and dragging him to her house church every Sunday during the five years he'd lived in her home, and even in the two years after, when he was around.

There were Numbers across the entire range of classes at her house church, mingling and actually enjoying each other's company without imposing their will on each other. This was the first time Jeremiah had truly seen past the Number system and understood what his parents had been fighting for. Equality and freedom could exist, and did exist, right there under the Number

One's nose.

The house church was highly illegal for this reason. But also because each person had their own Bible, or pieces of one, and they read it themselves without the help of a priest, even *praying* to God by themselves. Jeremiah's parents had only ever done so in the safety of their own home. But these people did so *together.*

Beryl attended faithfully and insisted on Jeremiah joining her. "But I could inform on you," Jeremiah said once, testing her.

"You won't, child," Beryl replied, shaking her head at him.

It took him a few months after that to realize he trusted her too. He was not so quick to let his guard down with the others in the church, although one in particular struck him as highly interesting, an older man, around the same age as Beryl, named Welder. A Number 11 Regulator, yet he broke just about every law to attend the little church with them on Sundays. Jeremiah was especially fascinated when he learned that Welder worked in the Number One's navy.

Welder humored him, describing the many ships and submarines in the navy, and how they worked. Beryl sat with them as Welder taught Jeremiah everything he wanted to know about how to captain a ship. He hinted at his work often, but Jeremiah was nearly 18 years old before he truly grasped the role Welder held in leadership. That was when the first seed of an idea began to form in Jeremiah's mind. He read every book he could get his hands on, studying geography, armies and battles, politics, dictatorships versus voting systems, learning about leadership and planning. His confidence in the idea grew gradually over a year before he brought it to Beryl.

"Welder says there are a lot of outdated submarines from countries before the war, just sitting there collecting dust," he'd told her. His idea felt far-fetched when he said it out loud. But Beryl had surprised him as she always did by adding to it. Many in the house church would be willing to join them, she was sure of it. And if they were to operate one of those old vessels safely, they would need everyone's help.

Not everyone in the house church liked the plan, feeling the risks were too many, but most agreed to help, and one even told them stories of a large island that had formed during the war, about two days off the coast of Eden, which was now inhabited by a new country entirely separate from Eden. Jeremiah and Welder talked of making a trip there, a practice run with whoever would join them, but for a long time it was just talk.

It wasn't until Beryl created the first draft of the Lower Level Employee Work Rule document that Jeremiah truly began to believe their plan could work. The document requested all available lower Numbers report for duty on a vague assignment at various times, dates, and locations, indefinitely. Between Beryl's connections with the different diplomats and politicians and her knowledge of the Number One's policies, the Work Rule sounded real. She was a genius. But Jeremiah had known that for years.

And Welder had seen enough policies cross his desk through the years to forge the Number One's signature on the bottom of their work rule. This small rebellion took place in Welder's basement. Yet copies went out across the country. They sweated for weeks afterward, certain they'd be found out. But no one dared question the Number One, and the man himself had no clue. And that's how they'd managed to create an army of revolutionaries over the last two years.

The sun had fully set by the time Beryl's heels echoed on the wooden deck, alerting Jeremiah to her arrival. Most 62-year-olds in Eden would need a cane or someone to help them walk, but Beryl was an active woman and still as energetic and spry as when Jeremiah had first met her. Instead of a cane, she carried a tray. From where he sat in the back, in the deepest shadows, he doubted she'd noticed him, so he spoke as she reached the gazebo entrance, "How are you going to explain a dinner tray if someone sees you?"

Lady Beryl gasped. "Jeremiah!" Her white hair gleamed in the moonlight. "I thought I'd beaten you here," she chuckled, placing the dinner tray on the bench beside him, settling onto a seat nearby.

He shook his head at the evasion, but in the gloom, she didn't see it. "You can't keep taking risks like this."

"Pshh," she said. "Can't an old lady have dinner outside occasionally? I'm eccentric. They expect me to behave strangely. Would be more suspicious if I didn't. Besides, who's going to inform on a little old lady?" Darkness had fallen completely now, but in the moonlight, her teeth flashed white in a grin. Sighing, he dropped the subject. The household staff loved her. If they hadn't informed on her by now, they probably wouldn't, but it still made him nervous. He felt for the plate.

Finding a large sandwich, he took a bite. Delicious. He hadn't eaten all day. Relaxing a little, he inhaled the food, speaking around a mouthful, "I'm sorry I haven't had a chance to come back for a visit since last month. I've been working with the newest recruits."

Every fresh batch of low Numbers to arrive on the island knew nothing about fighting. But Jeremiah hadn't either when he started. Teaching that was easy. The hard part was instilling confidence – removing the brainwashing of the Number system. Many needed months on the island before the truth even began to sink in. He enjoyed that work, but had missed his visits with Beryl. "Any news since last month?"

"Oh, yes," she exclaimed, but a shuffling followed the response instead of her news. "This is ridiculous. It's so dark my old eyes can't even see you." A match hissed, lighting up a small circle of space around them as Beryl lit one of the gazebo candles. Even as Jeremiah opened his mouth to object, she shook a finger at him. "I have Ingrid and Ibo keeping the staff busy, don't worry. No one's going to spot us."

Again, Jeremiah sighed. Ingrid and Ibo were true believers. He'd attended the house church with them for years – they weren't informants. He didn't trust the rest of the household staff nearly as much, but dropped it. He'd learned early on not to argue when she had that tone. "This is the last run, anyway," he told her. "Thank God you can't get yourself in too much trouble before we're back in a week."

"Just a week?" Her voice rose. The candlelight lit up her face as her forehead wrinkled in surprise. "I suppose I knew the time was coming." It had been nearly three years since they'd begun planning this venture, two since they'd begun helping refugees escape. "It just feels so sudden."

Jeremiah nodded his agreement. "I know. But it's time. We need to keep the element of surprise. If someone ever questioned the work rule…" he trailed off. It didn't need saying that all their work would be for nothing. "It'll be two days back to the island, as always, and we'll stay there for three to let the last group consider joining us, and then two days back. One week. It's past time really."

"Well then."

They sat in silence for a moment, the weight of their carefully-laid plans draining the light-natured conversation out of them.

"Oh, my news," Lady Beryl perked up. "I held an Abandoned Kittens Fund for the high Numbers a few days ago. It was a huge success. Almost as many donations as last month's Whale Relief event." She grinned wickedly, winking as if she were just twenty-two years old like him, instead of nearing her sixty-third birthday. "I already sent all the donations ahead with Luc when he stopped by yesterday. Enough to keep the camp going for nearly a month."

Jeremiah smiled his thanks. Luc had been his closest friend at the orphanage all those years ago. Two years older than Jeremiah, Luc had taught him how to steal food when Mr. Meyers withheld it, how to run away from the Regulators, and how to survive as an orphaned low Number. Leaving his best friend behind at age 15 had eaten at him. When he'd mentioned Luc to Lady Beryl, in the hopes of convincing her to hire 17-year-old Luc on as a gardener or butler or driver, somewhere he could make himself useful, he tried not to expect much. But despite the fact that Luc was just months away from turning 18, Beryl had adopted him as well.

Though Luc had refused to attend the house church with them, he felt indebted to Beryl. They had found a comfortable understanding. And Luc had leapt at the chance to join their plans.

Now, as one of the twelve members of the council Jeremiah had formed from the refugees on the island, Luc was Jeremiah's second in command whenever they made trips back and forth between Eden and the island, collecting unwitting refugees via the work rule. Jeremiah trusted his friend and adopted brother with his life.

"I realize now that's more than you needed," Beryl continued when he was quiet.

"Don't worry, Welder will find a use for the money," he said, smiling. The older man was also one of his council members now, though he was often gone, overseeing missions to Eden. He was still the most experienced at running their ships. "He said to tell you hello, by the way," he teased Beryl. "I think he misses you." That was an understatement. The quiet man had been in love with Beryl for as long as Jeremiah had been around, and everyone could see it, except Beryl.

"He's a good friend, that's all," Beryl tsked. "I've had two husbands already. I'm too old to have a boyfriend."

"If you say so," Jeremiah said, trying not to smile. If their plans next week were successful, he intended to bring it up again, but for now, he dropped it. He had a more important request tonight. "Beryl, listen. I need you to go to your summer home. Delmare won't be safe next week."

"Oh, goodness." Beryl flung a hand over her shoulder as if the idea was just one of the weeds in her garden. "I've lived a full life. If anyone is going to attack me, let them. I'll be fine."

But Jeremiah shook his head, not yielding this time. "I'm not talking about avoiding gossips. I'm talking about Regulators knocking down your door and arresting you. Or worse. I know you think your Number protects you, but they won't pay any attention to it if you're a suspected traitor. Please, Beryl. For me? Please go."

She dropped her cavalier attitude, and met his eyes solemnly. After a moment's pause, she nodded once. "Alright."

"Thank you."

"You worry for nothing," she argued anyway, despite her agreement. "There won't be time for them to search out traitors and put them through trial. When you arrive, they won't know what hit them. By the time they get their act together, you'll have won."

"We'll see." Jeremiah didn't want to put ideas in her head. But he didn't think it would be that easy.

15

A Surprise Discovery

I T WAS NEARLY TWO in the morning when he left Lady Beryl's with a full stomach and a fresh change of clothes. The blue high-Number clothing disguise felt like second nature to him now, after the last two-plus years of wearing it, but he still kept an eye out for Regulator vehicles and skirted around them when he could. No matter how many forged papers he carried that said he worked for a Number 2, and gave him the right to wear the blue when it didn't match his Number, it would be far better if he didn't have to use them.

The walk to the pier took about three hours, and he wanted to make a stop on the way. He and Luc used a little store as a semi-regular hideout to leave messages for each other and catch a few hours of sleep if they had time. He'd left Beryl's home too late for that nap, but he would still swing through in case Luc had left any info or supplies for him.

Jeremiah was thankful for the full moon, allowing him to see when the night would've otherwise been pitch black. Exhaustion made his eyes burn, and he wished for the millionth time that he had a car. But though Lady Beryl would've been happy to borrow him one of hers, he couldn't leave it abandoned at the store when he was out at sea. At least, not without arousing suspicion.

Reaching the front of the little abandoned grocery store, he moved silently, out of habit, opening the sliding glass door without a sound. Stepping noiselessly into the room, he froze.

Someone was there.

There was a dark shadow against the far wall. Keeping still, Jeremiah scanned the room, looking for others. The light of the moon was strong, but the windows of the store were small, and his eyes needed a moment to adjust to the lack of light.

Every muscle in his body drew tight, as he feared the worst. If he ever ran into a Regulator, he was prepared to do whatever he had to do. Hopefully the papers would work, but if it came to a fight, he'd also gained some skills in that area.

But nothing happened.

From where he stood in the doorway, he only saw the one person, and they weren't moving. Confused, he moved inside, slowly. The shadow on the other side of the room began to take shape. The person was sitting in a chair at an odd angle, facing sideways, leaning against the wall. They seemed unaware of him. He could barely make them out, but as he crept closer he saw it was a woman, and it looked as if her hands were tied.

All his instincts screamed caution. This could be a trap.

On silent feet, he backed outside, prepared to run if necessary. If it was a trap, he wasn't going to get stuck inside. Closing the sliding door, he ran a quick lap around the building, checking the parking lot first. No hidden Regulator vehicle, but there was a strange car. That could mean anything. He reached the back door without encountering anyone.

It was propped open. Uneasy, he almost turned to leave. Through the opening, the person inside was more visible now. Something about the person's posture, slumped over, too still, stopped him.

He stepped inside. Keeping a prudent distance away from the girl, he moved to the left, circling the inside of the store next on silent feet, pausing to glance down every aisle, making sure they were empty. Keeping an eye on her, he watched the mirrors along the top of the walls where they met the ceiling, and made it to the opposite side of the store without meeting anyone.

Checking the supply closet and finding it empty, he was finally satisfied no one else was there. The dim light made it difficult to tell any details of the girl in the chair until he drew up next to her. She leaned against the wall, fast asleep, not even stirring as he came to stand in front of her.

To be fair, he had yet to make any noise. She was young and pretty, looking vulnerable as she slept. Studying the chair confirmed his guess that she was tied up. A messy cut on her forehead had bled heavily, leaving a trail of blood down her face that was dry now.

A desire to help her rose uninvited. He wished he'd had the good sense to leave when he first spotted her. Now that he was just a few feet away, her light blue clothing was visible, and he wanted to groan. *Why now, Lord?*

Just what he needed, a run in with a high Number who would ask too many questions. But his inner voice, always curious, immediately began to wonder what a high Number would be doing out here, in this section of town especially. Alone. Visibly beaten. Most likely robbed.

He had a sudden hunch, and couldn't help himself. Reaching out with the light touch of a practiced thief, thanks to the years spent in the orphanage, he lifted the scarf around her neck carefully. Softly, so softly, he manipulated the fabric to loosen without her feeling his touch, until he could see the tattoo underneath.

29. He read, confirming his suspicion. She was a low Number. Very, very low. *A runaway,* he thought, feeling a pang of sympathy, as he pulled the scarf back up over the tattoo.

What to do now? Frustrated, he ran his hands through his short hair. He couldn't just leave her here.

He studied her. Numbers 29 were viewed by most people as cursed by God. No one wanted to hire them into their homes. Only offered the most severe jobs, they were usually paid too little to afford living on their own, often starving or dying of abuse and mistreatment. He rarely met a 29.

But this girl appeared oddly well-fed. Except for some faded bruises on her face, she looked fairly healthy. Her hair fell soft and straight, just brushing her shoulders, and it had fallen across her face where she leaned against the wall, partially covering her lips. He found himself wanting to push the hair back to see the rest of her face. He wondered who had attacked her and why? He couldn't piece together a clear background, but overall she appeared markedly better off than any 29 he'd ever met before.

Her arms were thin though, and she looked weak, vulnerable. The fact that she was tied up added to the effect. He couldn't leave her on her own.

But her light skin was much more visible in the moonlight compared to his dark golden-brown skin, and the shades of blue she wore lighter than his, meaning she would be more noticeable on the streets. He sat in the silence, listening to the distant sound of traffic, picturing the two of them ducking down side streets in the dark.

He kept still, standing in a dark shadow out of the light of the moon, not wanting to wake her. Jeremiah trusted his disguise, and had answers prepared for any questions, with his papers and his carefully crafted story. The issue was wasting time he didn't have.

Folding his arms, he tapped a finger to his jaw, feeling the stubble forming where he hadn't shaved since the previous day. He contemplated taking her to Lady Beryl's. The older woman would instantly take the girl in. But he shook his head. Not enough time to trudge all the way back to her estate, which he had left hours ago, and still make it back to the pier before sunrise. Going back simply wasn't an option.

One thing was clear from her disguise: she was obviously running away from something, hoping to escape whatever life she currently had. He'd bet his entire savings she planned to board a boat. What she likely didn't know, however, was that the Regulators hounded the ships that came through this port. Every captain was expected to not only collect his passengers Identity Cards, but to physically check them against the owner's tattoo.

Jeremiah sighed. If he was right about her goal, he could help her. He was the only ship's captain in Delmare who didn't answer to the Regs, and probably the only person who both understood exactly what she was running from, yet also had the power to rescue her from it. He knew Luc would roll his eyes at him for thinking it, but he considered the possibility that God may have put her in his path exactly for that reason.

Keeping silent, he crouched on bent knees, sitting on his heels and resting his head on his hands, knowing he'd made his decision. Without him, she would be caught and imprisoned. Or worse. But how could he make her think coming with him was her idea? There was no guarantee she would want to board his ship. If Jeremiah told her about the work rule, and its purpose, and she said no, he risked exposing their entire mission.

Glancing out the window, he was aware of the time. He stood and took a couple steps back before bending down once more to remain at her eye level. He had no idea how she would react. Better to give her some space.

Hopefully she would be easy to manipulate because he didn't have a lot of time. Removing all emotion from his face, he cleared his throat.

16

The Rescue

EVALENE DRIFTED AWAKE, BLINKING away the crusty feeling of sleepiness and tears. It was dark. What had woken her? Easing her head away from the wall, she turned to find herself staring into dark brown eyes just a few feet away from her. She gasped.

Evalene jerked back instinctively, causing her injured head to throb in pain. The stranger blinked calmly at her as her heart pounded. Who was he? He crouched on the ground in front of her, and she squinted in the poor lighting to make out details. His dark hair was cut stylishly short, his clothing tailored and rich, and even in the moonlight she could tell the color. Her heart sank. He was dressed in blue.

"Hi there," he said casually, offering her a smile as if they were old friends.

She swallowed. That's right, she was also in blue. Remembering Kevra's suggestion to play a high Number in distress, she managed a weak, "Hello."

Head full of cobwebs, she tried to sit taller. The sharp headache attacked her skull with renewed force. The adrenaline rushing through her body made her muscles tense, but her brain struggled to keep up, to formulate a plan, or even a full sentence.

He spoke first. "My name is Jeremiah. I won't hurt you." He set down his bag and started digging through its pockets. Pulling out a small knife, he stepped towards her. Evalene found it hard to swallow as she stared at the knife and wished she could run.

He paused and held his hands out, palms facing her in a gesture of peace. "It probably doesn't mean much coming from a stranger, but I'm just here to help. I saw you through the door." He pointed to where Kevra had left the door cracked. He stepped toward her again, moving slowly as if she was a frightened animal, kneeling beside her. "You looked hurt. I thought you could use some help."

Evalene didn't know what to say. Her head ached. This man – Jeremiah – reached behind her to take hold of the rope holding her to the chair, and began sawing at it with the knife.

A dark blue bandana circled his neck, hiding his exact Number just like her scarf hid hers, but she feared a true high Number would recognize an imposter in an instant. Trying to channel Ruby once more, she lifted her chin, feigning arrogance, and opened her mouth to speak, to say something in response, but fear paralyzed her and her mind went blank.

She turned her head carefully to where he knelt at her right, working on the ropes, and watched in fascination. His caramel-colored skin was darker than her own even when she was her most tan, and while his hands worked deftly to set her free, she was caught up in noticing how calm he was. What must it be like to have the confidence and fearlessness of a high Number?

When the restraints fell off her wrists, Evalene ripped her hands out in front of her, jumping up. The room spun. She worried she might throw up. Reaching out blindly, her hand connected with the wall and she leaned into it gratefully.

She felt him touch her elbow, and jerked away, frightened, groaning as the awful ride of pain started all over again. The helping hand let go and gave her space, but the room continued to spin. Giving up, she leaned further into the wall and sank down until she was sitting on the floor.

"I'm sorry," she breathed. "It's – been a rough night." She rubbed her eyes, feeling awfully scattered, and tried to focus. Jeremiah stood a few steps away, where he'd backed up to give her room. "Thank you for rescuing me. I should get going." She moved to brace her hands against the floor as if to push off.

Jeremiah knelt in front of her, blocking her path. "You won't get far in your condition. Why don't you let me look at that head injury first?" Moving as if she'd already said yes, he reached to gently push her hair back to examine the cut on her forehead. As he did, Evalene touched the back of her head, where the worst of the pain was located, and found a huge, raised bump where she'd been hit. It felt wet. Pulling her hand around, she stared at the blood on her fingers.

Jeremiah frowned when he saw it, gently turning her head to the side. Lightly touching the bump, he pursed his lips, then stood, and walked away without a word in the direction of the cashier's closet.

Confused, Evalene stared at the fresh, bright red blood on her fingertips, scarlet evidence of Kevra's betrayal. She couldn't picture her escape now. She couldn't even picture the next five minutes. She stared numbly at the boots of her rescuer as he walked back towards her. He walked so gracefully, without making a sound.

Jeremiah knelt in front of her again, holding a simple med kit. Evalene let him tend to her wound, wondering vaguely how he'd known where to find a med kit. Why was a high Number wandering the city late at night, and in this part of town especially? The fog in her head spread like a thick blanket over the unanswered questions.

He wiped up the blood on her forehead first, then an even softer touch on the back of her head gently cleaned the wound, although she still winced. A cool sensation came next. It stung at first, but then brought relief.

"What's a nice girl like you doing out here?" He asked what any curious stranger would have, what she should've expected.

All Kevra's ideas whispered in the back of her mind, but Evalene couldn't quite grasp any of them and she swallowed hard as he waited. "I could ask you the same thing," she said finally.

He chuckled and let it go. The sounds of the first aid kit closing made Evalene turn to study him. His lashes were so long. "Thank you," she said.

"No problem," he nodded back at her, acting as if this was normal, like they were at a party exchanging pleasantries instead of an abandoned store cleaning an unexplained head wound.

Evalene forced herself to stand, more carefully this time, with the help of the wall. Standing as well, Jeremiah was just a few inches taller than her. He offered his hand in support, but she didn't take it. He leaned down to pick up the small med kit, shoving it into his pack and pulling the ties closed. "Are you going to be alright?"

"Yes, thank you." Evalene moved towards the door, stepping backwards, keeping him in front of her just to be safe. She was free. She just needed to get somewhere alone by herself so she could think, and she would figure out what to do next. "I appreciate your help," she faltered, not sure how to exit gracefully. "I'm sorry to have kept you."

"That's alright. I was just heading to my ship," Jeremiah said calmly from where he stood, hoisting the bag over his shoulder.

Evalene paused at the word *ship*, her hand on the doorknob, "Your ship?" Had she heard him right? "Are you a captain?"

Jeremiah nodded and calmly replied, "I am. The HMS Victorious travels on trade routes. Our next port is a large island outside of Eden."

Evalene stopped breathing for a moment. Outside of Eden. Was it possible she'd found a way? She let go of the doorknob. "Any chance you have room for one more passenger?" Her voice came out breathless. She cleared her throat, trying to imitate Ruby. "I've recently been robbed of my Identity Card. I had hoped to leave as soon as possible, and this delay –" she cut off, fearing her desperation showed as she rambled on.

Crossing his arms, Jeremiah put one hand to his chin in thought, studying her. He didn't say no right away, but he didn't say yes either.

Wringing her hands subconsciously, Evalene caught herself and clasped them together, trying to be still. Her hand brushed the lump in her pocket where Kevra had placed the coins, and she whipped the money out to show him. "I have enough for passage." That wouldn't make sense to him when he thought she'd just been robbed. She tried to think quickly. "They… didn't search my pockets…" she added lamely.

Trailing off, she regretted showing him the money. But Jeremiah was gazing at the moon as if to judge the time, and didn't notice her faltering. He spoke slowly, considering, "Well, since you've obviously been stripped of your ID against your will, and you are clearly a Number…" he waited.

"Six," Evalene answered, giving him Ruby's Number, clearing her throat nervously. She fidgeted with the coins for a moment. They clinked loudly in the quiet room. Trying to be discreet, she awkwardly placed them back in her jacket pocket.

"Yes, of course, a Number Six." Jeremiah nodded. "I think, in this instance, we could make an exception." With one final nod, he dropped his arms, relaxing. "Most captains are fairly strict about this, mind you," he said, eyebrows raised for emphasis, then smiled to take the edge off his words, "but I don't see any reason to stand on ceremony when we have this particular history. Of course, you'll have to be willing to board before dawn, due to the tides. Will that be a problem?"

"No, not at all!" Evalene agreed immediately, hoping she didn't seem too eager. She didn't have any other option.

Jeremiah smiled, and Evalene found herself smiling back. He stepped towards the door, turning the knob, and held it open for her to go first. "We'd better get going. It's a long walk to the docks."

Evalene stepped outside onto the pavement. "Thank you."

Though it was still the middle of the night, the full moon felt like daylight compared to the darkness of the store. He followed her out, and the heavy door locked shut behind him with a solid thud.

He led her along the dark city streets in the direction of the docks. Though Evalene tried to walk quickly, she could tell he slowed his pace for her. Each step hitting the pavement felt like a fist hitting her head. The brisk spring night air was cold, but in spite of that, Evalene was sweating.

As they walked, he glanced over and in his direct way, he said, "You haven't told me your name yet."

"Oh, it's Evie," she responded as abruptly as he'd asked, then winced.

"Nice to meet you, Evie," he replied.

At least she'd only given him her nickname instead of her full name or the name that was supposed to match a high Number ID. Maybe it didn't matter now. Once she made it onto his ship and got out of Eden, she'd never need an Identity Card again, high or low. She peeked over at him out of the corner of her eye. He was facing the road, staring straight ahead.

Evalene followed his lead, ducking down dark alleyways wherever he guided her. She ignored the tightness in her chest.

Soon she would be on a ship. Ahead of Kevra, no less! Soon she would be free. Tensing, she wondered if Kevra would be on this ship, or if multiple ships left at dawn? But this ship was on a trade route to some island, not the FreeLands. Deep in thought, she put all her energy into walking smoothly in a way that didn't jar her head so much, not paying much attention to where they were headed.

A fishy smell wafted towards them, signaling the nearness of the ocean before it came into sight. Rounding the corner, they reached the docks. With the sun not yet risen, their only light was the full moon, but now Evalene saw a building lit up ahead. The small Regulator station office on the corner was open. Jeremiah passed by it, continuing down the pier, which was a little odd, but Evalene had no desire to see a Regulator and reasoned that he must have checked in with them earlier.

The sound of the waves lapping against the docks filled the air. They walked along the shore, passing ship after ship, looming above them in all different sizes. Evalene checked the side of each vessel for the name he had told her, "HMS Victorious." The name was a good omen.

But they didn't stop until they reached the far end of the marina, turning onto an empty dock, no ship in sight.

Evalene's steps slowed.

As Jeremiah stepped onto the long wooden pier, Evalene saw a small group of men standing next to a short, small building built onto the far end of the dock.

She tensed.

"Who are they?" She stopped at the foot of the dock, refusing to go any further.

Jeremiah paused, glancing at the men at the end, then back over his shoulder at Evalene. "Who? You mean the other passengers?"

Other passengers. Slowly Evalene stepped onto the wooden dock, but her instincts still screamed at her to run. "Then where is your ship?"

Waiting for her to catch up to him, Jeremiah said, "The HMS Victorious is a submarine. She's mostly underneath the surface, but if you look closely at the end of the dock, you'll see the top of her a few dozen feet above the water. That's the conning tower."

He gestured towards the little structure she'd taken to be a building. It still looked like an odd-shaped hut built onto the end of the dock. Thin and tall, it was only as wide as two or three people. But as she watched, six men stepped up to this "conning tower" as he'd called it, and all but one of them disappeared inside. There really was an underwater ship then. They'd gone into the belly of the beast. Her hands started to sweat at the idea.

Frowning at Jeremiah's back as he continued down the dock, Evalene couldn't tell from his laidback attitude if this was normal. She'd never spent time at the pier and knew next to nothing about the marina. A ripple of concern went through her. But she didn't know what else to do, so she shuffled after Jeremiah, feeling like a cow on the way to the slaughterhouse.

17

The Submarine

THEIR FOOTSTEPS ECHOED LOUDLY on the wooden dock in the early pre-dawn, silence reigning on the shore while the city slept. The waves crashing against the coastline seemed louder, more aggressive.

Reaching the far end of the dock, Evalene could make out the top of the submarine more clearly now, though the black metal merged seamlessly into the deep, black shadows of the water. It had appeared small from shore, but the way it rounded on both sides before disappearing into the water hinted at a huge mass under the surface.

Jeremiah had stopped to talk to the only man left on the dock. This stranger had dark skin and wore dark blue clothing as well, made of such deep hues, that between them and his ebony skin, he almost completely blended into the darkness of the night.

Turning toward Evalene, Jeremiah beckoned her forward to join them, nodding his head towards the other gentleman. "Evie, this is my first mate, Luc." He made the introductions quickly.

This second high-Numbered fellow flashed her an easy going smile with perfect white teeth, ignoring Jeremiah's hurry and reaching in front of him to hold out a hand towards Evalene. "Welcome aboard."

Evalene hesitantly took the hand he held out and let him shake hers for a brief second before she pulled it back. She lowered her eyes to a button in the middle of his blue coat and mumbled, "Hello."

"Come with me," Luc said with a smile, waving his hand toward the tower. He stepped onto the gangplank. Evalene reminded herself this was her best shot to get out of Eden. Possibly her only shot. She followed him.

Luc crossed the couple feet to the small dome that Jeremiah had called a conning tower. "Let me get the hatch for you." As he spoke, he spun a wheel connected to the door, and it opened smoothly.

He held it wide so Evalene could enter first. She moved towards the door, glancing back at Jeremiah. She caught him doing a quick scan of the harbor before he stepped up behind her.

The tower immediately forced her to descend a circular metal staircase with a cold, metal railing. Dim orange lights glowed all along the staircase, illuminating the steps, which were metal grates filled with holes. The lapping of the waves faded in her ears as she went lower and Luc entered last, letting the door slam shut behind them.

What had she been thinking, trusting a man she'd just met hours ago? What kind of captain piloted a submarine instead of a regular ship? And needed to leave before dawn? *The kind that has something to hide,* she thought, feeling her heart beat faster and faster, blood rushing to her head.

Halfway down the stairs, she turned sharply without thinking, to go back up. But she immediately ran into Jeremiah's torso, unable to step even one stair higher, with Luc just two steps behind him and the hatch tightly closed at the top, all blocking her escape.

Jeremiah caught her by the shoulders to steady her, forehead creasing, and peered into her face. "You alright?"

Evalene gave a jerky nod, whipping back around in the tight space, tripping slightly. She felt her face growing red.

"Are you sure?" he asked again.

Evalene waved a hand at him. "I'm fine, really." She began to descend again, more carefully this time, gripping the slender railings on both sides. She was not fine. Her head spun and she was terrified she'd made the wrong decision, but she couldn't tell him that.

It was dizzying to circle so many times in such a small space, and by the time she reached the bottom, she felt disoriented. The other men from the docks a few minutes prior all stood here in the small compartment.

Her eyes registered the size of the room first, barely larger than her attic room back home, before her attention came back to the men. She took in their brown clothing in confusion. The other passengers were low Numbers? But low Numbers weren't allowed to travel. What kind of trade ship was this?

Jeremiah and Luc stepped down after her, and Evalene backed up until she was against the metal wall, not wanting anyone behind her. The back of her head throbbed at the thought. When Luc and Jeremiah faced the group in the dim orange light of the ship, Evalene was able to get a good look at them for the first time.

Both men wore blue clothes made of fine silk and cut to fit them, meaning they were well made and expensive. Jeremiah's golden tan seemed paler now next to Luc's dark brown skin, and her rescuer's solemn expression and hint of a beard was a stark contrast to Luc's wide smile and clean-shaven face.

Jeremiah leaned in to speak quietly so only she and Luc could hear. "Luc will take care of your fare and give you a tour with the others." Stepping back, he raised his voice to speak to the whole group as he moved away. "We'll hold a meeting in the mess deck in fifteen minutes."

Evalene started to follow Jeremiah without thinking, but stopped when he didn't wait for her. The hatch door swung shut behind him with a clang of metal hitting metal. She wished the ache in her head would go away.

She thought back to what he'd said. Mess deck? Tour? There was more to the ship? Luc was staring at her expectantly. Fare. Yes, that's right. She needed to pay. Digging into her jacket pocket, she tried to be discreet in front of the group of men as she counted out the number of coins a voyage cost that Kevra had told her what felt like weeks ago now instead of mere hours.

Handing the chunk of change to Luc, she was surprised he didn't bother to count it. The men were staring her down. One in particular eyed her blue clothing and sneered at it, turning away to his friend. Though her passage was bought and paid for, Evalene's worries only increased.

Luc moved towards the door on the opposite side of the little room, pulling off his blue jacket to reveal a gray shirt underneath. That, along with the black and gray bandana tied around his neck to hide his tattoo, left Evalene confused as to whether he was actually a high Number or not.

"This way, everyone." Luc opened the hatch with another friendly smile, revealing a second compartment. "That was our captain, Jeremiah. We'll let him do his job while we take a little jaunt around the ship and get all of you settled."

The men followed Luc, stepping through the hatch over the threshold, which was nearly a foot tall. They also looked a little uncertain, although Evalene might've just imagined it. She tagged along at the back of the group, the last one through.

This compartment was still tube shaped and confining like the last, but it was twice as wide and better lit. The air was musty. Bright bulbs all along the ceiling cast a white fluorescent light that filled the room. The black metal walls of the submarine had been painted white, which also helped lift a bit of the gloom.

The room was extremely full. Cluttered even. Jam-packed with at least a dozen tables with checkered tablecloths and chairs all around them, as well as various items all bolted down along the walls, including a radio, a couple refrigerators, and even a television hanging on the far wall, although it was so old fashioned Evalene wondered if it even worked. About two dozen people sat throughout the room at the tables, which were also bolted down. Mostly men, but also a few women, which made Evalene relax a little. There were even a couple teenagers. Every single person wore brown.

Luc waved a hand expressively at the room and spoke to the whole group. "This is where we will meet in a short while, like the captain said," he began the tour, moving through the room slowly towards the other side, gesturing to those already seated. "And you'll have time to get to know your fellow passengers." He waved at them as he said this, adding, "As you can see, it's not just for meals. There's not a ton of common areas on a sub so we tend to hang out here in the mess deck or downstairs, but I'll get to that."

On the far side of the room was another door, and Luc strode towards it, Evalene and the others in the group following automatically. The same man who'd stared at her before cut in front of her rudely. He was easily six feet tall. Evalene stared at the back of his balding head. Had she done something to upset him or was he just ill-mannered?

As Luc pulled the round hatch open to the next section of the ship, he smiled and spoke in the cadence of a tour guide as he explained, "Everything is separated into compartments on a sub, in case of a leak. That way the captain can seal them off if need be and avoid flooding the whole ship. But don't worry," he swung back around to soothe their fears before they even had time to form, "Big V has been fully operational since 1993, and she's never had a problem yet."

Evalene's eyes grew huge at the date. It was nearly two centuries old? Questions rose up in her, but she was too shy to speak. The bald man entered the next compartment first, and Evalene gave him as much distance as possible, waiting until everyone had gone before she crossed into the next room. Luc nodded to each of them as they passed. "Remind me to show you the ship's manifest and captain's log from when she first became active. Her first voyage was years before World War III was even a threat."

The excitement in his eyes was contagious. He smiled at Evalene, the last to go through the door, and followed her into the compartment. It held rows of bunk beds on both sides of the long hallway. The beds stretched the length of the compartment. Each bunk was made out of a beautiful stained wood, instead of the metal ship walls, making this room feel more cozy. Every bunk had a little red curtain that could slide across the front of it to block out the light. The curtain was pulled back on the nearest one, and Evalene peeked in out of curiosity to find the sleeping unit had a thick mattress, a cozy blanket, and a pillow.

"These are the racks," Luc said, pointing at the sleeping compartments. "If we were at capacity, some people would end up having to share bunks and take turns sleeping while the others in the crew were on duty, but as it is, we're sailing light, so you all get your own bunks. Go ahead and stash your belongings now while we're here."

Evalene didn't have anything to leave behind. Everything she possessed she was either wearing or carried in her pockets. She waited while the others chose their bunks, staring at the backs of their brown shirts as they stored their bags, and then the group moved on. Luc angled his body to talk to them as he walked down the narrow passageway. "Next I'll show you the Head – that's the sub name for our showers and toilets – so you can find it later if things get urgent."

As Luc reached the other end of the hallway, he raised his voice to reach everyone in the compartment. "We'll do introductions once we get back. You'll meet everyone else on board soon enough, and we'll all get to know each other real well by the end of the trip." Evalene cringed and averted her eyes as the group of men looked around at each other, and at her. Maybe she could sneak away and hide in a bunk when they weren't paying attention.

Luc didn't take them into the next compartment, though. He just opened the hatch so they could peer into it. The black metal ceilings, floors, and walls of the initial compartment were here again, with a door on the left and on the right. The left door had a stick figure man painted onto it, a universal symbol that Evalene recognized right away for a restroom, and the door on the right just like it but with the stick figure wearing a skirt.

Evalene breathed in and her nose wrinkled at the smell. It wasn't strong, but it was clear what this section was even if she hadn't seen the symbols. Luc plugged his nose, miming a stomachache.

"Women didn't used to be allowed on subs back when V was first built," Luc continued, clearly enjoying his tour guide role as he waved expressively to the right side with the stick figure in a skirt. "So maybe 10-20 years or so after she was commissioned, they had to dry dock her and do a bit of maintenance to overhaul this one Head into two separate Heads. One for the gentleman and one for the ladies."

Closing the door on the smell, Luc pointed to the door. "Past the Head is the Auxiliary Machinery Room. It takes care of Atmosphere Control, has an emergency generator, and so on."

Luc paused to point back the way they'd come. "And in the opposite direction, where our captain went, is Operations. The control room, sonar – you name it. All the instruments we need to keep us going are in that room."

Smiling easily at the group, Luc leaned back comfortably against a bunk. The men stood in a semi-circle around him, but Evalene hung back, trying to be invisible.

"The battery compartment, missile room, reactor room, engine room, and maneuvering room are all off limits. Just keep an eye out for the signs. But if we have time before the meeting, I'll take you to the lower level of the sub, where we have a few more compartments you're free to use."

Just how big was this ship? The huge, bald man voiced the same thoughts in his deep voice. "It didn't look that big from the docks." Evalene stared at the rolls on his neck. She studied the other men with him, trying to figure out if they knew each other. They were all different ages, and most of them stood apart from each other, but one smaller man stood next to the bald man, nodding at his observation.

Luc threw his head back and belly laughed. "You can say that again!" Chuckling, he gestured generally at both sides of the sub. "She's narrow, but she's long. From the bottom of the hull to the top fin, she's roughly 60 feet. Ol' Victorious is definitely one of the larger subs they built, although very few are built anymore."

Evalene felt a shift in the floor and her stomach started to feel queasy. She put her hand against one of the top bunks to steady herself, fighting the sudden urge to throw up. The smaller man bumped into the bald man, also clutching his stomach, looking dizzy and a little green. "The sea sickness will pass," Luc told them. "After we get to a certain depth, you'll barely feel the movement of the sea at all."

But Evalene found that hard to believe as she continued to feel off-balance, and her already throbbing head started to spin. She sat abruptly in the nearest lower bunk, feeling faint. The smaller man sat too, making Evalene feel a little better that she wasn't alone. The others widened their stance a bit, but otherwise seemed fine.

"You all are lucky," Luc encouraged them, putting on his tour guide voice again. "We have Officer Welder with us for this voyage. A sub is naturally smoother sailing, especially underwater, but when he's at the helm, you often won't even feel the turns."

As Luc moved back down the hallway, he waved for them to follow. "Let's head back towards the mess deck. I'll wrap up our tour with some comforting facts that should help you all relax. Let's see..." As he ambled past Evalene, she worried she might empty her stomach on his shoes.

"Everyone on the crew knows how to drive a sub, work the sonar, contact tracking, damage control, you name it." As the other men in the group shuffled past, they gave Evalene a wide berth. Staring down at her blue skirt and leggings, it was easy to figure out why. They thought she was a high Number. Luc, with his good-natured attitude and multi-colored clothes, didn't bother them nearly as much as her presence.

Luc was nearing the other end of the hallway. Forcing herself to stand, Evalene leaned heavily on the bunks, trailing after the group. "Everyone on board is trained to fight flooding," Luc continued. "And we're all trained on the basics of every system on board. Even the cook knows a bit about navigation." Evalene lifted her eyes from her feet briefly to peek at him and found he was grinning widely at his own joke as he paused by the hatch back to the mess deck.

"How fast is it going?" The bald man spoke up again, near the front of the group. He was by far the most vocal, though he wore brown like everyone else. Evalene's focus had been on the floor and avoiding their gazes, but she guessed if she glimpsed their tattoos, his Number would be the highest.

"We typically travel at about 25 knots once we're on the ocean floor, which means it'll take us about two days to get to the island. But I'm getting ahead of myself. I'll let the captain tell you all about our destination. Don't worry," he added, directing his words to Evalene and the smaller man, "in just a few minutes, it'll smooth out a lot more. You'll be ready for breakfast and introductions."

Nodding to each man as they passed through the hatch into the mess deck, Luc told them, "Looks like it's time for the meeting, so we'll pick up the rest of the tour afterwards. Go ahead and get comfortable."

At the back of the group, Evalene's heart sped up again at the mention of meeting the other passengers. This small group was bad enough, and now he reminded her of just how many people on board could find out her true Number. She was not going to let that happen, no matter what. Her new status and the clothes on her back were all she would have in her new life outside of Eden. If someone found out she was inferior to them, there was no telling what they might do. And she would be lower than all of them. She always was.

Mind racing, Evalene tried to decline as she reached the door, the last one to go through. "If it's alright with you, I… was thinking of taking a nap." That was true. She'd only slept a few hours the night before, and combined with the emotions of the past couple days, she was exhausted.

"Oh absolutely," he said with a nod as he ushered her through the hatch door into the mess deck, "as soon as the meeting is over, you can go sleep in the racks or relax in the mess hall, you name it. You're a paying customer, so this is your chance to put your feet up and take it easy. We even put on a movie every night after dinner." He said this proudly as she stepped over the threshold and into the mess deck.

At his words, the full magnitude of her escape began to sink in. It felt oddly distressing.

Now, instead of knowing what her days would look like for the rest of her life, the future was a big blank nothingness. She felt almost a twinge of regret realizing she could never go back. That was stupid. Yet, she found herself missing her old life – the bed in the attic suddenly seemed safe and comforting. What would she do when she got to this island they talked about? What if she couldn't afford to go on to the FreeLands? What had looked like opportunity from inside Eden had swiftly transformed into an enormous risk.

Luc moved forward to greet a group of what Evalene assumed were crew members, since they all wore similar blue, black, and gray uniforms, and seemed to know each other. The room was loud, filled with their conversation and laughter, and the quieter tones of the passengers getting to know each other. The bald man and the rest of her tour group all moved into the room to sit.

Evalene bit her lip, feeling out of place. The room was filled with people in brown. She didn't want to irk anyone else the way she had the little tour group. Spotting a chair in the corner where she could fade into the background, she crept over to it and sat.

Someone at the table in front of her elbowed his friend and pointed to the glass of water in front of him. It was slanted in the cup. The ship was turning. It took a few more seconds before Evalene even felt it. Her stomach was calming as well. Luc had been right, it was smoothing out after all.

Surveying the room filled with people, it struck Evalene as odd once again, that the passengers were all low Numbers. Jeremiah had said this was a trade ship. Maybe high Numbers avoided traveling on those? The women she'd spotted earlier sat at some tables on the far side. Most wore brown, but there was a blonde girl at the table on the far side who wore a shocking flower print dress that didn't fit anywhere within the color laws. Not only was it covered with all kinds of blue, purple, pink, and white flowers, but the dress itself was yellow!

The girl met her eyes. She gave Evalene a friendly smile, and waved for her to come join them. Ducking her head, Evalene acted like she didn't see. She didn't want to sit with anyone. They would want to know her story. Where she came from, where she was going, and why.

She directed her gaze to Jeremiah as he entered the compartment from the other side, the only person in this room she knew even remotely. What had she gotten herself into?

18

Jeremiah's Speech

JEREMIAH STRODE INTO THE mess deck where everyone waited for him. He made his way through the cramped room, circling tables until he reached the middle. He could hear the cooks behind the metal window on the side as they prepared breakfast. They would start serving shortly after he finished speaking.

New faces mixed in with the familiar faces of his crew. He was impressed they had so many recruits this trip. Almost three dozen. The last few trips hadn't even come close to that. Though the Lower Level Employee Work Rule still worked in their favor, with no one the wiser, most members of the council had voted for this to be the last pickup.

"Welcome everyone," Jeremiah spoke loudly to reach the entire room, his voice projecting easily. "I'm the captain of the HMS Victorious, but if you're not part of the crew, you can just call me Jeremiah." He left out his last name intentionally. "Luc, over there," he pointed towards where Luc sat on the other side of the room and heads swung around to look at him, "is my second in command, the ship's chief officer."

The new recruits had the same furrowed brows of those who had gone before them. The girl, Evie, sat in the back corner. Her eyes were huge and her skin pale, like she might throw up. Distracted for a moment, he made a mental note to check on her once they were done.

"Most of you are here because of the Lower Level Employee Work Rule." Everyone, in fact, except Evie, but he didn't say that. There were nods around the room at the mention of the policy. But the way Beryl had written the work rule was so vague that none of the people in this room knew exactly what they'd signed up for, just showing up because they needed the job.

He elaborated as he always did for that reason, and for Evie's sake, "The work rule was instated about two years ago now. It requested every available low Number to respond to the call for workers on a specific, but classified operation. Over the last two years, we've utilized the schedule posted with the Work Rule to periodically pick up low Numbers across the country. You all are the last group to be picked up."

Their reactions were muted. Years of being under the thumb of higher Numbers had trained them to hide their feelings. But he caught raised eyebrows, some shifting in their seats, the way the room grew even quieter. "What you don't know is that we're headed toward a large island called Hofyn. It's a country all its own, and the closest land mass near Eden, formed during one of the worst bombings of World War III." The day he and Lady Beryl had discovered it had been the day they'd started planning in earnest, finally believing a revolution might be possible.

"It's about a two-day trip. The people who live on this island are not part of Eden. They are Number-free." Jeremiah studied the faces around him as he spoke. They were soaking up every scrap of information, just like he had when he'd first discovered the island. He smiled. Opening the refugees' eyes to the rest of the world never got old.

"Tomorrow, when we get close to port, I'll reveal the full scope of the assignment. But for now, settle in, get comfortable, and get to know each other." The moment he dismissed them, Evie leapt out of her seat, already on her way to the racks before anyone else had finished standing. Jeremiah held his place, though he would've liked to follow her out to make sure she was alright. After suffering a blow to the head like she had, it wasn't wise for her to be alone. But he was needed here.

Keeping an eye on the clock, he stayed and answered questions while breakfast began. After a half hour or so, he asked Luc, who was deep in discussion with another crew member, to take over.

"No problem, man," Luc said with his signature grin. He never called Jeremiah Captain even though the rest of the crew did. Years of habit. His best friend probably wouldn't call him Captain even if he told him to, not that he ever would.

Luc entered the circle and took over smoothly. Before Jeremiah had taken two steps, Luc was already joking with them. "You look like *you* wanna know where the toilet is. I see that jittery dance. If you're ever lost on good old V, just check the map near the door in each compartment," He heard Luc good-naturedly tease the poor passenger. "Go on man, hurry! It looks urgent!"

Jeremiah chuckled under his breath as the passenger ducked

past him, running in the direction of the Head. Following at a more leisurely pace, Jeremiah wove around tables. Luc's voice reached him loud and clear, even from the other side of the room, "And I'll bet *you* wanna know if you can ask those lovely ladies out. Well, try to hold your horses for two days until we get to the island, my friend. There's not a lot of privacy on good old V, and things can get kind of awkward for the rest of us, if you know what I mean. We got a saying, 'don't fraternize on a boat this size.'"

Laughing out loud as he reached the door, Jeremiah opened the hatch and passed into the racks, hearing Luc's roaring laugh until the door closed and the seal cut off all noise from the mess deck.

The racks were still, a peaceful quiet compared to the previous room, although that wasn't always the case. Jeremiah moved past each bunk, listening, wondering where Evie had gone. If not for his habit of walking on silent feet, he might not have heard her. A soft sigh came from one of the bunks behind him, and he turned to go back. One of the lower bunks sniffed.

Casually, Jeremiah knocked on the wood outside the box bed. There was shuffling inside. "Who is it?"

"It's Jeremiah," he said.

A hand tucked the red curtain back on its hook, and he saw Evie sitting inside, wrapped up in the blankets.

"Hi there," he said, with a smile. Keeping himself as non-threatening as possible, he turned his back and moved across the narrow aisle to the opposite side, bending to sit in the doorway across from her.

Even with her calm front, her white knuckles and wide,

unblinking eyes gave her anxiety away. She lowered her gaze. Years of low Number habits didn't break easily.

Despite the fact that her disguise was meant to declare her high-Number status, her posture and behavior would give away the truth to a Regulator immediately. Jeremiah tried to think of the right words to make her relax.

But she surprised him by speaking first, soft and tentative. "That thing you said about the people on the island being Number-free?" He nodded, but didn't interrupt. "It sounded just like this bulletin that came out in my town recently…"

Smiling, Jeremiah nodded again. He lightly rested his arms on his knees, keeping his stance open and inviting, trying to be as non-threatening as possible. "That's probably because I wrote it."

Startled, she stared directly at him, forgetting her usual habits. In the back of his mind, Jeremiah noted her ability to break from the rules so quickly. She was already far surpassing any other low Number he had ever met in boldness. He was intrigued.

"Did you write the first one also?" she breathed, and then ducked her head. "I'm sorry."

Bold one moment, timid the next, yet both seemed natural. "You can ask whatever you want, Evie," Jeremiah tried to catch her eye. "I won't be offended." He smiled at her and was rewarded with a tiny smile back. Twisting to reach into his back pocket, he pulled out a piece of paper as he said, "I wrote both of them. And also a third that was just distributed yesterday morning. Would you like to see?"

Her eyes widened as she nodded and accepted the bulletin he offered. He knew what she would see. Hours had been poured into each pamphlet, wanting them to appeal to high Numbers just as much as low Numbers. There had to be more people like Lady Beryl out there, who saw the injustice even if they didn't feel it personally.

This latest bulletin had two parts. On the top half, Jeremiah had asked the artist to draw two people, a low Number and a high Number, each tied to a post, as well as a Regulator swinging a whip, inflicting punishment, while a crowd looked on. He'd asked for detail on the faces in the crowd, reflecting fear and anger at the sentence. Below this first picture were the words, "SOMEONE NEEDS TO STOP THIS."

On the bottom half, the artist had rendered the same image, but changed a few important details so that it told a vastly different story. The low Number and high Number were still tied to their posts, and the Regulator still had his whip. But now the crowd stood with arms locked together, making a barrier between the victims and their abuser. Their faces were no longer afraid, but determined. Keeping the wording as simple as possible, since the majority of the population never finished school, Jeremiah wrote just three words across the bottom, "TOGETHER WE CAN."

Watching Evie's face as she took it in, he watched her bite her lip, her eyebrows knitting together. Her eyes widened in surprise at the second half, the idea of others standing up to a Regulator, especially for a low Number. She blinked, not looking up right away, just staring at the piece of paper. He was beginning to wonder if she would speak at all when she whispered, "This reminds me so much of my mother."

His eyebrows surged upwards as curiosity sparked in him. "Is that a good thing?"

She met his gaze then, serious, haunted by some memory. "Very good," she said softly, and looked back at the pamphlet. "I wish I was more like her. And you."

The hatch squeaked as it opened. Someone was coming in from the mess deck. He didn't want to be interrupted by other passengers now, not after she'd just begun to share her story. Standing impulsively, he said, "Come with me." He held out his hand, and then, realizing his tone was commanding, he added, "We can talk somewhere more private. If you'd like."

Evie took his hand and let him pull her to her feet. He let go when she tugged her hand away, turning to lead the way back through the mess deck. Meekly, she followed him without a word as they wove through the crowded room. He'd probably scared her. He held in a sigh. Opening the door to the bridge, he tried to be a gentleman like Luc and wave her through first. As they entered the dim orange lighting of the bridge and he pulled the door closed, it again became quiet. With everyone in Operations still setting the course, and Luc busy getting the passengers settled in the mess deck and racks, this was one of the rare times the bridge was completely empty.

He stopped. This was the best place they would find to talk privately. "Evie, listen," he began, stepping towards her to close the gap, but stilled when she stepped back. Struggling with his words, he spoke over the distance between them, "I'm sure you can guess from the bulletins that we're involved in an uprising, but I haven't told the rest of the passengers yet. I need you to keep that a secret until the meeting tomorrow. Can you do that?"

She nodded. "Thank you," Jeremiah accepted her promise. Sometimes people still guessed, but from his experience, if the group of refugees were told outright, they tended to let their emotions get the better of them. Sometimes it got out of hand. The ship was too small for such outbursts, and he and the council had learned to save that disclosure until they neared the end of the trip. But Jeremiah trusted Evie with this secret. Maybe because he knew one of hers. That brought him to the second part of their conversation, which was much harder.

He rubbed a hand across his face. After a moment, he forced himself to begin before someone came in and interrupted them. "Evie, when I first found you in the store, you were unconscious." He scratched the back of his neck, searching for the words. "I need you to know… I looked at your Number before you woke up."

Her hands flew up to her neck and touched the scarf there, and she looked small, scared, like a dog in a cage.

Jeremiah moved towards her, and she stood frozen this time. Standing in front of her, just a couple inches taller, he held her gaze. "I won't tell anyone. But I wanted you to know that it doesn't mean *anything* to me." He stressed the word anything, wishing there was a stronger word that could convey how he felt. "Honestly, Numbers are not who we are. This Number that they gave you – it's not *you*." He softened his voice, trying not to scare her. "You are safe here. You're not your Number anymore. From this point on, you are *free*. Do you understand?"

Slowly she nodded at his hands, then after a moment, she dared to look up at him and shook her head a little. He frowned. "What don't you understand? I'll try to help."

"It's not," she said, "that I don't get it... I just... I can't imagine it." She bit her lip.

That was normal. It often took refugees weeks or even months to adjust to the idea. He wanted to comfort her, but he didn't know what else to say. The idea of telling her his Number sprung to mind.

As the leader of the revolution, he kept his real Number carefully guarded. People were still so easily influenced by the system. Only Luc and Lady Beryl knew. Because if no one knew his true Number, then he could be the first to prove to the world that they were not necessary.

Jeremiah's mouth was open, the words on his tongue, wanting to be set free, when the metal door's hatch twisted and scraped open. Luc walked in, noting Jeremiah alone with the girl. Though he put on a clueless smile as he approached, when Evie wasn't looking, he raised a brow at Jeremiah.

"Evie," Luc said, nodding to the girl, then to Jeremiah, "Jer." He cleared his throat, putting his hands behind his back and becoming serious as he gave an account of the ship. "Everyone is settling in now. I was on my way to find you and check on Operations."

Jeremiah nodded his approval, glad his friend had caught him. He barely knew this girl. If he had revealed his Number to her, she could have told others until the entire ship knew. And once they landed, it would've spread to the people on the island. He hated to think that their revolution was still weak, but he had to admit the news could hugely undermine his authority.

Luc relaxed his stance now that he'd given his report, and

turned to the girl. "Didn't you say you'd wanted a nap? I believe the racks are quieting down now."

As if her feet were un-glued, Evie nodded and darted around them, not meeting their eyes, disappearing through the door. Before Jeremiah even had a chance to say anything, she was gone.

Luc crossed his arms. "What happened to not getting attached until after the war?"

"I'm not getting attached. Nobody's getting attached," Jeremiah waved off his concerns. Luc misunderstood his intentions. He was simply helping the girl get her footing after everything she'd gone through.

Jeremiah frowned at the closing door. He wouldn't really have told her his Number. He knew better. But he wished he could. She would immediately feel safer. Maybe even relax completely.

After all, he was only one Number higher than she.

He was a 28.

19

An Olive Branch

EVALENE ARRIVED AT THE bunks in a haze, overwhelmed. Her emotions over Kevra, the past few days, the pounding in her head from her wounds, and her fears of the future all took a back burner to this new revelation.

He knows.

He'd seen her Number. He knew. He saw through the blue clothing disguise every time he looked at her. He knew the Number didn't match.

But he also said he wouldn't tell anyone. This reaction was unexpected. It didn't make sense. Crawling into an empty floor-level bunk, she pulled the little red curtain across the bar until the light was blocked out. The darkness and quiet provided a much-needed sanctuary. Not one to enjoy crowds and loud noises anyway, her senses were screaming in exhaustion.

She lay down to sleep, feeling drained. Her head still ached from her injuries. But her mind refused to stop thinking about him and what he'd said. He was a high Number, but how high, she didn't know. Party member eligible for sure. Yet he planned to fight on behalf of low Numbers like herself. He even seemed like he meant it when he said that her Number didn't define her.

But she knew it did.

Curling up in a ball on her side, Evalene ripped the blue scarf off her neck in the safety of the private bunk, tossing it in the corner. She dropped her head back on the pillow with a sigh and cocooned herself in the blanket. Though her muscles were tightly strung, she tried to relax.

Closing her eyes, Evalene saw her mother's face the way it had been the day that Evalene came home from school, eight years old, sobbing. "Tavis said let's play Numbers, and then he gave me a 19!"

Her mother had pulled her into her lap and held her while she wept, rubbing her back. "Shhh, Evie. You're not a 19, and you know it."

"But he drew it on my neck with permanent marker, look!" she'd cried, scratching at her neck as if to rip off the skin along with the ink. "He says I'm garbage!"

"Well he's wrong," Pearl had told her, catching her hand and standing to bring Evalene to the sink. She'd wet a rag and gently washed the side of Evalene's neck. "You don't need him or anyone else to give you a Number, because I already know," she'd told Evalene as she scrubbed, "you are priceless."

Those words from ten years ago melded with Jeremiah's words just a few minutes ago. Had Pearl really believed the same as Jeremiah, that the Numbers weren't real?

She was so tired. A day and a half of driving followed by a mostly sleepless night left her eyelids feeling heavy and her body drugged. Finally, she felt herself begin to doze off as her mind relaxed its iron grip, and she slept a dreamless sleep.

An hour or two later, maybe more, Evalene groggily pulled back the soft curtain and poked her head out of her bunk.

"Good afternoon!" A cheerful voice sang out, coming from somewhere above her head. "Or at least I think it's afternoon. Time of day is hard to tell on a sub. Are you hungry? I'm starving. It's got to be time for dinner soon."

The voice came from the blonde girl wearing the illegally colored flower-print dress who had waved earlier. She looked like she was around the same age as Evalene. Sitting in one of the bunks on the second level with her feet dangling out, swinging idly, her blue eyes crinkled almost closed as she laughed, and her smile was wide and genuine. Afternoon? Almost time for dinner? Had Evalene really slept the entire day?

Blinking at the bright lights, Evalene felt her eyes adjust, taking in the long hallway of bunks on both sides. The girl hopped down from the bunk to come closer. "I work with the female recruits, and there are hardly any this trip. I've had breakfast and lunch with all the women except you! My name's Olive, what's yours?"

Evalene felt thrown off balance by the abrupt beginning of the conversation. She gave her nickname, like she'd done for Jeremiah. "Evie."

Not wanting to engage the girl, she began to pull the red curtain closed again, but that didn't deter her new acquaintance in the slightest. "Evie, I have *got* to tell you. I *love* your hair." Olive plucked at her long blonde hair flowing over her shoulders as smooth as silk as if it were pieces of smelly straw. "Mine is so much work, but you just wake up naturally fresh. I'm *so* jealous."

"Um… thanks," Evalene mumbled. She touched her hair subconsciously, and as she did her hand brushed her bare throat – she'd taken off her scarf before sleeping!

Jerking back out of sight, Evalene frantically tore at the blankets until she uncovered the blue scarf and quickly tied it around her neck so tight it nearly choked her. She spread the edges of the fabric up towards her chin and down towards her collarbone, making it as wide as she possibly could. Then she sat, unsure what to do now, berating herself. How could she have let someone else see her tattoo? With her hair down, what were the odds that the blonde girl had seen the full Number?

Evalene crawled back to the entrance of her bunk. Reaching the opening, she tentatively poked her head out.

She almost had a heart attack when she found Olive sitting in the bunk directly across from her. Just a couple feet away now, she eyed Evalene's neck, "That's a pretty necklace."

Evalene frowned. Did she mean her scarf? She lifted a hand to her neck and felt the jewelry from her father. Usually tucked underneath her shirt, it must have fallen out in her scrambles. It now rested in plain sight, just below her collarbone.

Evalene breathed a sigh of relief that this was all the girl had noticed. "Thanks, it was a gift," she said as she slipped it back under her shirt.

"I love the tree. It's so unique," Olive replied. Leaning forward, she rested her elbows on her knees, still staring at Evalene. "So is your tattoo."

Evalene blinked in surprise, then squeezed her eyes shut in

frustration, but Olive said, "Hey, don't be mad! I'm sorry. I don't care about your number, I swear."

"That's what everyone keeps saying," Evalene muttered, not believing it for a second.

But Olive shook her head violently. "No, I promise! I was born on the island and I've lived there my whole life. I've never even stepped foot in Eden. I've only heard stories about your 'numbers.' Okay, look, I'll prove it!" She sat up straight, dragging her thick hair back so her neck was visible, twisting her head to show Evalene. Her skin was smooth, unbroken. There wasn't a tattoo. Not even a hint of a tattoo that might've been erased.

Could it be true?

"See?" The girl's voice came out high pitched in sincerity. "I don't even have a Number!" She faced forward again, letting her hair fall back around her shoulders. "I know what you're thinking, but it's not removed." Evalene had barely considered that. It was illegal in Eden. But now her hand touched the left side of her neck as she imagined her own skin without the offensive ink.

Leaning forward on her knees again, Olive grinned. "Yeah, they can be removed. It's a bit expensive since new skin is pricey. And you'd have a bit of a scar, just to forewarn you. But I see refugees do it all the time. Anyway," she flipped her hair back over her shoulder, not noticing when it fell right back down, "I never had a tattoo, so the fact that you're a 29 doesn't mean anything to me."

"Shhh!" Evalene shushed her, tensing. She glanced down the hallway at the other sleeping compartments to see if anyone was near enough to have heard. With most of the red curtains closed, it was difficult to tell how many people, if any, were in the room, and equally impossible to know if they were awake.

Evalene pulled herself forward to sit on the edge of her bunk as well, and spoke in a stern whisper. "Don't you dare tell anyone my Number, do you understand? Don't even say it aloud again," she repeated for emphasis, staring the girl down until she nodded back. "Nobody can know!" First Jeremiah and now this girl? The chances of having a successful life outside of Eden without anyone knowing she wasn't good enough seemed less and less likely.

Number-free Olive surprised Evalene by tearing up as she reached across the aisle to touch Evalene's hands lightly, "I'm so sorry. I really am." When Evalene pulled away, Olive waved her hands wildly in the air instead. "I know better. I wasn't thinking. I won't do it again, I swear!"

Evalene ignored her promise. Pulling on her boots and lacing them up with sharp jerks, she tied them at the top and mumbled, "Nothing you can do about it now."

Olive stiffened. "Well, maybe no one heard! I'll check every bunk!" She hopped to her feet and began whipping curtains aside to peer into each bunk.

"No, no!" Evalene tried not to yell, jumping up.

"Are you sure?" Olive's hand was gripping a curtain as she looked back over her shoulder.

Evalene moved down the hallway towards the hatch in a hurry as she said, "I'm sure, thank you." If anyone had overheard Olive speak her Number, at least they hadn't seen Evalene's face yet. She wanted to keep it that way. "Did you say something about food?" Her stomach growled as she brought up the distraction; she was starving. She hadn't eaten since yesterday afternoon. Since Kevra.

"Oh yeah!" Olive lit up at the idea, smiling widely again. "I'm sure it's dinner time by now! Let's go see if they have the food laid out yet. I want to get to know you, and it's my job to answer any questions you might have about the island."

She surprised Evalene by hooking her elbow with her own, linking them together as they walked. "Submarines are known for having the best food ever. Did you know that?" Olive told her as they went. "Not many people do, but you'll love it!"

She let go of Evalene's arm to go through the hatch, but she was still talking as they passed into the mess deck, full of people eating and socializing, and continued as she led the way towards the dinner line.

Following Olive's lead as they went through the short line, Evalene piled food on her plate, and the girls sat at an open table to eat. Evalene resigned herself to listening to Olive's chatter through the meal. The one upside was that Olive didn't ask many questions.

Taking another bite, Evalene glanced around the room. Most of the tables were full. On the far side, Jeremiah sat with Luc and a few others wearing blue, black, and gray uniforms. The illegal mix of colors intrigued her. Averting her eyes, she tried to ignore him, but couldn't help glancing over again in curiosity.

He was in serious conversation with his chief officer, Luc, from her tour. She wondered what they were talking about. The uprising he'd mentioned? She wasn't supposed to tell anyone about that, although with Olive's commentary, Evalene couldn't get a word in even if she wanted to.

But Olive didn't miss Evalene's third glance in his direction. "Isn't he *cute?*" she exclaimed, lowering her volume slightly, but still loud enough for the tables around them to hear.

Evalene whispered, "Excuse me?"

Olive misunderstood. She lowered her voice in imitation of Evalene, but responded with excitement, "I think he's cute too. I've never been in love before, but I think I might be…"

Gritting her teeth, Evalene glanced around. No one was paying them any attention. She took a deep breath, trying to be reasonable as she whispered back, "It's not that I don't think the captain is handsome," she tried to be diplomatic, reminding herself this was the second person on this ship who now knew her Number. She adjusted her scarf at the thought, "…I just don't think of him that way."

Olive's eyes lit up as she spoke, and she barely let Evalene finish, "Wait! I was talking about Luc – you have a crush on the captain?"

"No!" Evalene exclaimed, throwing her hands up in exasperation. "I just said I don't!"

"But, you think he's handsome," Olive said, squinting in confusion.

"I—I just—It's none of your business! None of my life is your business!" Evalene hissed, and Olive's face fell. "No, aghh! I'm sorry!" Evalene clenched her fists. "I just don't want to talk, okay?"

Olive stared at her plate. "Why not?"

"Because how do I know you won't go tell my personal

history to everyone?" Evalene blurted out, all her frustration from the past few days directed at Olive. "How do I know you can even keep a secret?" A not-so-veiled reference to Olive's recent mistake. Eyeing the door to the racks longingly, Evalene wished she'd stayed in her bunk and suffered through her hunger.

But Olive shook her head fiercely. "I wouldn't tell anyone, I swear!" She tugged Evalene's arm. "Here, come with me, I'll prove it!" Letting go, she picked up her tray in one hand, beckoning for Evalene to follow with the other. "This way!"

Rolling her eyes, Evalene trailed after her towards the kitchen window, copying Olive and dumping her tray with the other dirty dishes. She spotted the bald man from earlier at the table right next to her, eating dinner with the small man and a few others. She veered away from him, but felt his eyes boring into her back.

As she passed, he muttered, "Stupid high Numbers." Whether he was speaking to his friend or wanted her to overhear, she wasn't sure. She stayed close on Olive's heels as they wove through the tables, moving towards the bridge.

They passed through the hatch and out of the mess deck, the hair tingling on the back of Evalene's neck at the idea of the big man watching them. She sighed in relief when the door closed.

She nearly ran into Olive when the girl stopped. "Wait here. I'll be right back." She darted away, leaving Evalene to stand in the middle of the bridge.

As Olive disappeared into the opposite compartment, a few crew members came out of it, deep in conversation. They stopped before parting ways, deep in conversation, not paying her any attention. Evalene felt out of place standing there, worried that she was breaking the rules.

The hatch opened and shut behind her and the metal door barely registered in her mind until a male voice growled. "It's the high Number brat." Evalene spun to face the man, heart pounding. She swallowed at the sight of the huge bald man and tried to stand taller, to act like the high Number he thought she was, hoping it would deter him and he would leave her alone. But that just aggravated him more.

He approached, leaning over her, close enough that Evalene felt the stink of his breath on her face as he growled, "What makes you think you're better than me?"

Wide-eyed, Evalene backed away, shaking her head at the accusation. She almost blurted out that she wasn't, but caught herself. If he knew that, he could make her life miserable. She was so frightened she couldn't speak, couldn't think.

"Captain says this 'island' doesn't have any Numbers." He loomed over her, following her step for step. "We're going to be equals soon. And when we are—" he cut off as Olive appeared through the hatch coming towards them. Evalene appreciated Olive far more than she had a few minutes ago. Because she knew if the man ever did find out her true Number, they would never be equals.

"Is everything okay?" Olive's nose scrunched up in concern. Though she hadn't heard the bald man's words, the seething hatred rolling off of him was obvious enough to catch even her attention.

"Everything's fine," he growled at Olive without looking at her, pinning Evalene in place with his glare.

"What's your name, sir?" Olive asked him. Her etiquette

soothed him somewhat, and as he turned to her, he grew more civil.

"Talc," the big man replied.

"Nice to meet you, Talc." Olive smiled, genuine and open, disarming him the way only she could. His return smile appeared uncomfortable and out of place on his surly face, but he ceased to loom over them, settling back into a less threatening pose. "Are you exploring the ship? Or have you already seen everything?"

"Just been here and the food, mostly," Talc mumbled, his face returning to its naturally sullen state.

Nodding, Olive spoke up so that the two crew members nearby could hear. "These are my friends, Clay and Larimar." When the two men looked up, Olive waved for them to come over. "This is Talc," she told them. "He hasn't had a tour yet."

The words seemed to have an underlying meaning between the girl and the crew members. Something shifted in their relaxed posture that suddenly made them more alert, watchful. "Is that so?" the lighter haired man said, clapping a hand on broad Talc's back. "We'd be delighted to show you around." The second man, whose long, dark hair hung down his back, neatly held in place with a cord, nodded and angled to face the bald man in such a way that he ended up between Talc and the girls. The two crew members' light prodding was all it took to lead Talc away, and the three men moved back towards the mess deck, leaving Evalene and Olive alone.

Olive waited until the men were out of sight and the metal hatch noisily latched shut before she said, "You okay?"

And Evalene nodded, although she felt far from it.

"That happens sometimes," Olive said, moving behind the spiral staircase that Evalene recognized from first entering the submarine. "People are excited to get out of Eden, sometimes they handle it poorly. Just let the crew know if you ever have any trouble." Her calm demeanor eased some of Evalene's fears. As long as she stayed in areas with crew members, she would be safe enough. Spending time with Olive didn't seem like such a bad idea now, and she willingly followed the girl towards the metal wall of the submarine.

Olive spread her hands out along the sheet of metal behind the spiral stairs. The wall was smooth except for nail heads every few feet attaching each sheet of metal to the next. She was feeling for something.

Out of nowhere, the wall opened. First a crack, then, as Olive pushed the slab to the side, it widened into a makeshift doorway.

"Hurry, hurry!" Olive squealed, grabbing her by the arm and yanking her through the door into the dark space. Sliding the wall closed behind them, Olive shut them into pitch-black darkness.

Heart beating fast, Evalene panicked. She swung her arms wildly, trying to find Olive, who had let go. Her right arm smacked hard into something solid and unyielding with a thunk, and she yelped in pain.

"Shhh!" Olive's voice came from somewhere a few feet in front of her. A second later a crackling sound came from the same direction. Olive held two plastic sticks. They were thin, clear tubes full of some kind of liquid that lit up as she cracked the outer shell. The light grew wider and brighter as she continued to bend them until the two sticks lit up the area surrounding them.

Evalene rubbed her hand where she'd smacked it on a large wooden crate next to her, feeling foolish for panicking now. They were surrounded by miscellaneous crates and containers in all different sizes. It was just a storage room.

Olive moved towards one of the shorter crates and sat on it, leaning back against the taller crate behind her, and setting the glowing sticks on a table-height box nearby. "Welcome to my lair," she said with a grin. "Have a seat."

Evalene moved to sit on the edge of a short box on the opposite side of the light, as close to the sticks glow as she could be.

Olive gestured to the room and smiled at Evalene. "This is one of my secrets," she said.

"Ahh," Evalene said, understanding now why they were there.

Crossing her legs under her skirt, Olive settled in comfortably on the wooden bin. "I've been helping Captain Jeremiah and Luc bring refugees to the island for over a year now. I help all the women adjust to life on the island, including trips back from Eden. And I love meeting new people," she smiled, talking with her hands, full of exuberance. "*But*, I've never shown anyone else this room. I know it's just storage, but this is where I come when I want to be alone."

Raising an eyebrow at the idea of Olive wanting to be alone, Evalene bit her lip to keep from smiling. She took in the storage room, observing how it was narrow but stretched the length of the bridge. That explained why the bridge appeared smaller than the other rooms – it was split in two. "Why are you showing it to me then?"

"Don't you see?" Olive grinned, making dimples on her cheeks. "I can keep a secret. You can trust me."

Evalene felt herself warming up to the girl. She sighed and gave in, "What do you want to know?"

Olive swiveled to face Evalene eagerly. She tapped her chin in thought, studying Evalene. "How about what happened to your face?

Crossing her arms, Evalene leaned back into the wall. Did the girl mean the newest cut on her forehead, or the fading yellowish-green bruises around her eyes from Daeva? She tried to decide where to start. She didn't want to talk about Kevra. Touching one of the bruises, she felt the lump under her skin, and said, "This happened about a week ago."

"Did you trip and fall?"

"No."

Olive was persistent. "Someone did that to you?"

Evalene just nodded.

Shaking her head, Olive said, "I hope you gave them just as good as you got! I know how to fight as good as any boy, I could give you some lessons if you want!"

Squinting at her, Evalene wondered just how different life was on the island. "You really don't get it," she said, more a statement than a question.

"Get what?" Olive's eyebrows bunched together in confusion.

"I'm a Number 29. I'm not *allowed* to fight back. They can do whatever –" Evalene voice was hard and cold as ice, as she slowly repeated the word, "*whatever* they want."

Olive's face paled, even in the dark candle-lit room. She grew smaller as she comprehended Evalene's words. "Anything at all?" she whispered.

"Anything," Evalene confirmed.

Not meeting her eyes, Olive stared into space and whispered, "What if they steal something from you?"

"It's theirs," Evalene answered simply.

"So they can hit you and you can't even fight back?"

Evalene nodded.

Olive looked like she wanted to ask more questions, but Evalene didn't want to talk about Daeva. Or anyone back home. She took a deep breath and let it out. "You don't want to know about my life."

Olive nodded thoughtfully. "I promise I'll be more careful. But I do want to know about your life. You're my friend. You have to be able to trust your friends."

But that just made Evalene think of Kevra.

Olive hopped off the crate, moving to the false wall that she'd used as a door. "Dinner's probably ending," she said, cracking it open to peer out into the bridge. "I need to check on the other women. Let's go back to the mess deck. They'll be putting on a movie soon. Maybe they'll play one of the old-world ones they found on the sub – those are always a hit!"

Evalene wasn't interested in a movie. She'd slept the whole day. Now, though it was late, she was wide awake. As they snuck back out onto the bridge, Evalene stood lookout in the dim orange light while Olive pulled the wall back into alignment. Evalene waited until it was closed, amazed at how the opening was undetectable once shut, before she said, "Thanks, but I think I'll stay here for a bit. Or maybe explore, if that's alright..." The mess deck was where Talc had disappeared. She wanted to go the opposite direction.

"Sure, I remember my first day on Vicky, lots to see," Olive said with a grin, circling around the stairs towards the door to the mess deck. Evalene realized she meant the HMS Victorious and decided this was her favorite nickname for the old sub yet. On the other side of the stairs, Olive stopped. "You want me to come with you?"

Evalene shook her head. Talc was probably watching the movie that Olive mentioned. She'd rather explore in the other direction and avoid him. "No, thanks... I'll be okay. Talk to you later?" she finished lamely.

Olive nodded and moved to open the mess deck hatch. She twisted to look back at Evalene as she did. "You're going to *love* the island! We'll hang out again tomorrow and I'll tell you *all* about it. I'll wake you up for breakfast!" And with that, she disappeared through the door before Evalene had a chance to argue.

Standing still for a moment, Evalene turned towards the opposite door in the bridge, where Jeremiah had disappeared earlier that day.

She couldn't picture where Luc had said this door led. Her hands started sweating. What was the worst that could happen? They couldn't kick her off the ship. She'd paid for passage. Well, she supposed they could. But they were heading away from Eden. If they did kick her out it would be onto the island, which was fine with her.

Breathing shallowly, Evalene cracked open the door and peeked inside the unknown compartment. Noise assaulted her senses.

20

Jeremiah's Offer

STANDING IN OPERATIONS AT the instrument panel, Jeremiah ran his crew through a routine check, supervising as one of his officers gave the crew commands. He stood against the back wall. The soft whirring of the machines was a constant background noise.

"Reverse course to the right using a twenty-five-degree rotor angle," Welder ordered. As Officer of the Deck, he was in charge of this room and all the men in it, standing in the middle. Panels covered every surface of the room, all with different equipment. Three men sat at the monitors near the front wall with two more standing behind them, and all devoted their full attention to the indicators on the screens. The sound of the high-pitched sonar bouncing off the ocean bottom and echoing back to the ship pulsed regularly.

Clay sat at one of the monitors. He repeated the order back to Welder, word for word with one addition, "Reverse course to the right using twenty-five-degree rotor angle, *Sir*." On Jeremiah's left were more panels, also covered with buttons, levers, dials, and more monitors. To a passenger, it might appear overwhelming, but each crew member knew exactly what they were doing, well-trained and comfortable after the last two years, working together in unison.

Jeremiah trusted them completely. This drill, just like the others they did daily, were mostly for muscle memory. But also to keep them sharp for battle stations and evasive maneuvering, if they ever were detected. It was unlikely anything other than another submarine could detect them while submerged, but if they did come under attack, his men would be fully prepared.

He simply observed while Welder continued to give orders. The hatch clicked softly behind him, and Jeremiah turned to find the door cracked open just a few inches, just enough for him to recognize Evie's face, staring with wide eyes at the mass of panels and screens. The moment he saw her, she ducked back and the hatch began to close.

"Evie, wait," Jeremiah whispered, hoping the crew wouldn't notice. "Come in, please."

The door paused an inch before closing, then slowly swung back open. Evie stepped up to the threshold, but stayed outside.

"You've found the control room," Jeremiah said.

She blinked, nodding, and copied Clay. "Yes, Sir."

A hint of a smile lifted the corners of his mouth. Angling his body sideways, he leaned toward her and kept his voice low. "I'm putting the crew through their paces. Give me one moment." She nodded again.

Jeremiah wanted to catch Welder's eye to let him know he was leaving, but didn't want to draw attention to Evie's presence, for her sake. Welder was focused on the screens. "Steady course one eight zero."

This time Flint repeated the order back to him. "Steady course one eight zero, Sir."

Out of the corner of his eye, Jeremiah noticed Evie watching closely, so he leaned over again to explain, "They're doing a check to see that everything is functioning properly." A second later something metallic shifted and fell to the ground, making a huge racket. "And also to make sure everything is stored correctly." His lip twitched, holding back a smile.

His men argued with each other over whose fault the loose item was, looking to their captain as they did and spotting Evie for the first time.

Welder finally glanced back and Jeremiah tilted his head toward the exit. "Let's leave them to it," he said to Evie.

She backed up as he stepped over the threshold out into the bridge, letting the door to Operations close behind him. Strolling through the bridge towards the mess deck, he asked, "Did Luc give you a tour of the lower level yet?" Evie shook her head shyly.

As they entered the mess deck, he moved past the chow line, the microwaves, and the TV, to the opposite corner where a railing stuck out over an empty corner of the room. He knelt to grasp the handle on the floor and pulled up a hatch to reveal a set of stairs going down. "This leads to the lower deck," he said, holding onto the railing as he made his way down the narrow, steep rungs, more like a ladder than an actual staircase.

For a second, he thought she wouldn't follow, but then her feet began to descend after him. She modestly held her skirt close, which left her with only one hand to hold the railing for balance, slowing her down.

He waited in the wide-open compartment below, which served as a gym. It stretched the width of the mess deck and the racks combined, and since the compartments on the lower decks were larger, the ceiling was higher as well. After the claustrophobic spaces on the upper deck, this room always helped newcomers breathe easier. He smiled as Evie reached the landing and took it in, her shoulders visibly relaxing.

He took in the room with her eyes. How strange it must look from her perspective. Old-fashioned workout machines were carefully spaced throughout the room, bolted down. A remnant of the past. Jeremiah had left them not only because they were too bulky to be removed easily, but also because they still served their purpose of keeping bored off-duty crew members busy.

A couple of his officers were using the treadmills on the far side of the room, as well as a new passenger, in brown attire from head to toe, trying out one of the rowing machines.

"At the front end of this level, there's a small sauna," Jeremiah told Evie, pointing in that direction. She gasped in surprise. But he turned towards the aft of the ship, away from the sauna, walking down the wide aisle between machines as he told her, "My favorite compartment is this way. We call it the 'living room' because it's where we like to relax and hang out when we're not on duty. It's technically called the rec room, but we like the reminder of home."

This smaller compartment was his favorite because it was filled with couches and chairs, also bolted to the floor, that smelled old and musty, their hideous puke green and neon orange colors reminded him of his childhood home.

Entering the room, he paused in the middle and glanced over his shoulder to find that Evie hung back. He studied the room, trying to find what upset her. Maybe that there weren't any other passengers? He still didn't know who'd attacked her back in Eden, but he understood her not wanting to be alone with him. "You can leave the door open," he suggested, not sure how else to put her at ease.

That helped a little. Enough that she crossed the threshold.

Jeremiah settled into his favorite chair while he watched Evie slowly step further into the room, taking it all in. "This is my favorite place on the ship," he told her, hoping she would relax a little and sit. "Reminds me of my parents' house. Small but cozy." Resting his elbows on the soft arms of the chair, he clasped his hands loosely on top of his stomach, slouching to get even more comfortable.

Walking around to take a seat on the couch at least half a dozen feet away and leaving multiple chairs open between them, Evie's eyes examined him as she settled into the cushions. Jeremiah realized a tiny house would be odd for a high Number. But he didn't want to lie to her outright.

"Do your parents live on the island?" she asked, interrupting his thoughts.

He brought his hands up to his mouth, taking a deep breath, and sighed. "No." Staring at the opposite wall, he spoke more to himself than to her. "I don't usually talk about my parents. Not sure why I brought them up... They both died in the Bloom Rebellion."

He was aware this tidbit about his past was revealing. Any intelligent person would immediately assume that his parents had somehow been involved in the unrest. And in his case, they would be right.

"I'm sorry," she said, and he saw her lean forward a little out of the corner of his eye. "My mother died during that time as well."

Jeremiah turned his head to look at her directly. "Really?" Remembering how she'd compared him to her mother before, he hazarded a guess that the woman had died in the same way as his parents. "I'm sorry to hear that," he said softly.

Itching to get up and move to a chair closer to her rather than have so much distance between them, Jeremiah lifted his feet and propped them up on the coffee table instead. He forced himself to speak casually, as if there weren't nearly ten feet of space separating them. "It was a hard time for both of us then." He winced at the understatement of the year. "Is your father still alive?"

"He is," Evie nodded, averting her eyes again.

Touchy subject. He didn't pursue it. "My father was one of the leaders in the Bloom Rebellion," he said instead, enjoying her reaction. She'd probably guessed it, but it still surprised people when he was so straightforward about it. "My mother too. I'm proud of both my parents," he continued. "They stood up for people who couldn't fight for themselves."

Jeremiah rested his chin in his hand, staring into space as the memories came back to him. "My dad argued with his coworkers that our country needed to change. He didn't think he said anything that would get him into trouble with the Regulators, but he said enough. People started to suspect him." He risked a glance at her face. She'd put a hand over her mouth, and her eyes were glued to his own as he half-smiled. "My mom was more stealthy. She whispered to the women at the market that she'd 'heard from a friend of a friend' that an uprising was coming. That's how she'd determine who was interested and who might report them."

Evie lowered her hand and her lips were parted in amazement. Jeremiah admired her. She seemed unaware of how beautiful she was, and clearly intelligent as well. Why she thought she deserved such an awful Number was beyond him.

Leaning his head back to rest against the cushion, he stared up at the ceiling. "My mom would drop me off with the neighbors, even though I was nearly Numbered. Old enough to stay home by myself. Just so I would get fed and go to bed on time, she would say." He smiled slightly, recalling how she'd kiss him on the cheek goodbye, and hug him so hard, even as he protested that his friends would see.

He felt his smile disappear. Still gazing at the ceiling, he swallowed but kept his voice light, as if discussing a regular weekday. "My dad disappeared a few weeks before my mom. One day he just never came home. Didn't show up for work. We guessed someone had informed on him, but without a trial or any official notice, we had no way of knowing." It had been some of the worst weeks of his life.

"A few weeks later, my mom left me with the neighbors and never came back either." He crossed his legs, sinking deeper into the chair. Despite his casual body language, he'd never told anyone else the full story besides Luc and Lady Beryl. He blew out a breath of air.

"When we finally realized they weren't coming back…" That day would haunt him forever. It had taken years to get over his bitterness at everyone involved. They had all done the best they could for a poor 12-year-old boy who'd just lost his parents. "The neighbors were good people. But they could barely afford to feed their own family."

He saw Evie frown at that. Why did he keep hinting at his real Number?

He chose his words more carefully, to mislead her. "The neighbors were low Numbers." That was true. "They helped out my parents by watching me." Also true. "My parents would pay them." The lie at the end soured his mouth.

He moved on. "When we saw my parents' bodies displayed on TV by the Regulators, the neighbors told me they needed to bring me to – to someone else who could take care of me." He had been about to say orphanage, but only low Numbers went there. A high Number orphan would've been taken in by a family member or friend of the family. Even without her knowing that last detail of his story, it still sat heavy in the air between them. Evie pulled her knees to her chest and wrapped her arms around them, hugging herself.

He was about to apologize for sharing too much when she spoke up. Her voice was just a faint whisper. "You saw their bodies?"

Jeremiah nodded. Evie didn't say anything for a moment, then she met his eyes and he saw the glint of unshed tears. She licked her lips and said softly, "I never saw my mother's. We buried an empty casket. I never knew what happened to her body."

Jeremiah received the little bit of information, honored that she would tell him that. He was certain now that Evie's mother had been involved in the uprising.

Evie didn't cry once, but her voice was thick with tears. "I wish I was more like her. Brave. Fearless. She didn't run away..." She trailed off, but he knew she was referring to herself.

Jeremiah pulled his feet off the table, sitting up to lean towards her. "Evie, I know I've hinted at our plans for a revolution..." He waited for her to nod before continuing. "I don't want to lose anyone in this war, man or woman. But no matter how peaceful I plan to be, the Number One has no problem with bloodshed. He isn't going to let us win without a fight."

He leaned forward earnestly. "I'm planning to bring a small group of volunteers with me, separate from those who will fight. Men, women, even children, who won't *ever* be in the line of fire. We have an entire company of men dedicated to protecting them. Each person volunteered to come, to share their story with everyone in Eden."

He waved his arm towards the door even though no one was there. "Luc is going to tell his story. I'm going to tell mine." But she thought both of them were high Numbers. "Many of the low-Number refugees we've rescued will tell their stories. We're going to broadcast the truth to every television in every home. We are going to expose the Number system for what it really is and demand that people take a stand!"

In an effort not to stand and pace, and risk making her nervous again, Jeremiah gripped his hands together until his fingers grew numb. "Once we prove to everyone that the world is not right, that we should *not* have Numbers, we will have the support of the people as we remove the Number One from power."

Evie's brows rose in interest. "Remove him?"

"Yes," Jeremiah said simply. "He claims God called him to rule this country, but he's the exact opposite of who God is."

That sparked her curiosity. "Are you one of those..." She paused and he knew she'd been about to say heretics. That was the official title in Eden for those who believed as he did. "...true believers?" she finished, hesitantly, using the word that the underground house churches preferred to call themselves.

He appreciated her kind choice of words. "I am." Beryl had prayed unceasingly until he gave God a chance again as a teenager.

"I don't think God exists," Evie whispered the heretical statement, checking out of habit for a television that might be recording, though of course, there were none here. She bit her lip and added, "I think the Number One made him up." A brave declaration. It held even more weight because she trusted Jeremiah enough to say it out loud.

He sat forward, trying to remember how Beryl had spoken to him when he was young. His natural tendency was to state his beliefs confidently, as facts, but he tried to hold back, framing his words as a question instead. "Haven't you ever wondered if maybe God is real, but He isn't who the church or the Number One says He is?"

Shaking her head, Evie frowned at him doubtfully. "Not really."

The Number One had people so convinced of who they were and who God was. Why couldn't she understand that both came from the same deceitful source? Jeremiah tried a different tactic. "We're no longer in Eden. You can be honest with me. Do you believe everything the Number One tells you?"

"No," Evie answered, but she was hesitant. "But what about the church?"

"The church is filled with people who say whatever the Number One tells them to," Jeremiah argued. "Just because the Number One and the church tell you who God is, and give you a Number, doesn't make it true."

Her eyes squinted at him as she took that in. Jeremiah sensed that he should stop, but pushed her just a little bit further. "Have you considered getting to know God for yourself?"

She stared at him thoughtfully. "I wouldn't know where to start."

"Just ask Him."

Evie looked completely mystified by that idea. "So you're going to start a revolution because you think God is different than the Number One says?"

"No, that's only part of it," Jeremiah shook his head, laughing. "Yes, I believe God is very different from what the Number One says, but we need to remove the Number One from power for so many reasons. Everything about him and his leadership is corrupt. People should be allowed to decide for themselves who they are and what they believe. We want to incorporate a new government where people have rights, like they used to in the old world."

He crossed his legs again, leaning back, his casual movements clashing with the gravity of his words. "We can't win the fight or make changes without the support of the people. That's why we need both high and low Numbers, like yourself," she flinched at the reminder that he knew her Number, "to tell everyone else why it's wrong. People all over Eden are kept in the dark. They only hear what the Number One chooses to tell them on the nightly news. They *need* to know the injustice going on all over the country. Every story – no, every *truth* – will make it that much harder for them to go on blindly the way things are now."

Jeremiah felt a sudden certainty that her presence would have more of an impact than he even knew. Maybe it was an impression from God or possibly just his own personal response to her, but he always listened to that quiet voice when he heard it. "Evie, we need you."

She started shaking her head, but he held up a hand. "Not to fight, but to tell your story. You can stay safe while making a real difference in the world by telling people the truth. And when we succeed, you could live in a world where your family and friends are free. Without Numbers. You wouldn't have to start over, or be alone. You could go back to your home."

But she was already shaking her head. Pulling back against the couch, she said, "I can't."

Jeremiah took a breath to speak, but she didn't let him.

"Listen… Jeremiah," she said his name for the first time. She stood, pacing in front of the couch. Her voice trembled. "You have no idea what you're asking. As much as I want to help – and I do – I can't go back."

"I have some idea." He understood the hardships of a low

Number life more than she knew, but he couldn't say that. "My parents fought because they wanted the world to be a better place. And I think your mother did as well."

Evie's eyes widened at the mention of her mother. "I know she did," she whispered, stopping in front of a chair a few feet away from him. "And I want to help." The desperation in her face said she'd give anything to go back home. "But what if it fails again?"

She meant like the Bloom Rebellion. A valid question. One Jeremiah asked himself privately often. He didn't have an honest answer for her, except to say, "We'll do everything in our power to make sure it doesn't."

Nodding, she stared at a spot on the floor in thought. "I know. But you don't understand. As a high Number, they'd probably let you go after a few months. But I'd be arrested and executed for treason. Or, if they somehow let me go, I'd be a slave again, probably forced into an arranged marriage, or just... alone. Forever." She backed away from him towards the open door. "I'm sorry. I want to, but I can't." She whispered, "I can't go back."

Jeremiah let her go, wanting to go after her, but holding himself back. He brought his hands to his face and rubbed his eyes.

He wished she knew just how well he understood.

21

Exploring

EVALENE WOKE UP TO the sound of Olive's voice singing slightly off-key, something about a sailor drowning at sea, which felt at odds with the bouncy tune.

Groggy, she blinked the sleep out of her eyes, and shook her head a little to wake up. As soon as her blankets started rustling, her curtain swung open wildly. Olive's head popped in and she grinned at Evalene, unabashed, the corners of her eyes wrinkling in amusement.

"Good morning, good morning!" Olive said with a playful flourish of her hand. "The other ladies all went to breakfast already, but I've been waiting for you! The smell of eggs and bacon and especially the maple syrup have been tickling my nose for hours!"

"Hours?" Evalene blinked.

"Well, probably just a half hour. But c'mon, hurry up!" Olive's head vanished as fast as it had appeared. Evalene sighed and pulled herself up out of the bunk to sit on the edge, still wearing her clothes from the escape, feeling grubby and uncomfortable.

Olive danced up and down the narrow hallway, not discouraged at all by the confined space or the fact that she might be waking people up. Pulling her boots on as Olive pranced towards her, Evalene whispered, "Aren't people sleeping? You're going to wake them up."

"No I'm not, sleepyhead," Olive protested, smiling undeterred. "Everyone is in the mess deck for breakfast or below decks. It's almost 10 o'clock!" That shocked Evalene. She couldn't remember the last time she'd slept past seven. It must be due to the lack of sunlight, confusing her body into thinking it was still night.

Moving towards the door, dancing backwards now, Olive said in a sing-song voice to go along with her dancing, "If you don't hurry up they're going to put the food away. Do you want to starve?"

"No," Evalene mumbled. She *was* hungry. Evalene ignored Olive frolicking back up the aisle toward her again as she fought with the laces on her boots. The girl was humming a lively tune under her breath as she spun in circles.

Finishing the laces, Evalene sat for a moment, still waking up, taking in her surroundings more closely as she did. No one else seemed to be in the racks, like Olive said, but even so, Evalene would keep an eye out in case Talc appeared.

Olive was still twirling around. The blonde girl wore a soft, green tunic, which was shocking enough on its own, but instead of a skirt, she wore pants like a man! They were black like Evalene's leggings. None of the women would dare to wear pants back home. Was it just Olive or did all the women on the island dress this way? "I like your outfit," she offered as she stood.

"Thank you!" Olive beamed, coming to a stop. "I like yours too, it's so different from what I usually see women from Eden wearing."

Evalene's stiff blue skirt, leggings, boots, and jacket were different then her usual clothing too. The high Numbers were much more fashionable than she'd ever been allowed to be. But if this ship only carried lower Numbers, maybe Olive had only seen the drab browns. "Don't you ever watch the rest of Eden on TV?"

"Are you kidding?" Olive shook her head, laughing. "Eden's broadcasts are blocked. Before the captain, we only knew what the Number One wanted us to." No longer dancing, she reached out to touch the unique outer layer of Evalene's skirt, a rough fabric that was more abrasive and stiff than the rest of the dress, making it stick out a bit like an old-fashioned ballerina. "Let's trade clothes!"

"What?" Evalene blinked in confusion.

"Let's switch!" Olive repeated, tugging at the sleeve of Evalene's jacket. "I can tell you have bad memories of the color rules." She smiled and pulled at Evalene's coat, waving towards the Head. "Come on, let's go change!"

Evalene balked. "No, I couldn't!" She'd never worn pants in her life, "Besides, I've worn these clothes for..." she calculated how long it had been since the escape. It felt like years. "This will be the fourth day. They're dirty and smelly. You don't want to wear them."

Raising her brows, Olive let go but cocked her head in thought, spinning towards a nearby bunk and hollering over her shoulder, "I know just the thing!" The girl darted inside, her feet hanging out as she dug around within her bunk. A few seconds later, she popped back out, holding a pile of fabric.

It was another patterned dress, this one made of priestly white fabric, but with red, orange, and yellow flowers with beautiful green ivy and leaves twining them together. It looked soft and flowed prettily as Olive unfurled it to show her. The length was modest, yet it broke all the color rules. Evalene loved it immediately.

"I always bring options," Olive grinned, coming back to Evalene. She thrust the dress into Evalene's hands. "Put this on, and we can wash your clothes. You probably want a shower too. I showed the other women where everything was yesterday."

Evalene hesitated to accept the offering. What was the catch? "Thank you, but I couldn't."

"Yes you can," Olive disagreed cheerfully, grabbing Evalene's arm. She dragged her towards the Head, storming into the women's restroom at full steam. Ignoring Evalene's protests, Olive smacked Evalene's hand away when she tried to give the dress back. She showed her how the showers worked, where the towels and soaps were, and then left her alone with a repeated, "Hurry up! We're still on a deadline if we want to eat!"

By the time Evalene was finished, she was sure they'd missed breakfast, but the shower and the new dress felt so refreshing. The last time she'd worn this many colors was before her Numbering Day. She found herself smiling as she stepped out of the shower stall, holding the stolen blue-clothing disguise in a bundle. She ran her fingers through her wet hair and left it to air dry, dropping the towel into a bolted-down hamper.

The dress flowed just to her knees in front, and longer in the back. She loved it. And the neckline was a simple bowl shape, wonderfully higher and more modest than the outfit she'd borrowed from Ruby, with simple cap-sleeves. Loose and relaxed compared to the tight layers of her previous ensemble. She felt like a new person.

Olive clapped her hands together, "Much better, huh?" Look in the mirror!"

Taking a step towards it, Evalene felt fifty pounds lighter. Even though the neckline was modest, it still showed more skin than she was used to, so she pulled out the soft leather jacket from her pile of old clothes and put it back on. That, along with the black boots and leggings, made for an extremely colorful outfit. Olive's grin was contagious, and Evalene smiled back at her. "Thank you."

"No problem," Olive shrugged off the thanks. "Here –" she took the bundle of clothes, carrying it to the sinks. "Let's wash these quick before we go." She filled a sink with hot water and soap, scrubbing the clothes underneath and rinsing them off. "This is the best we can do until we're back on dry land. We'll let them air dry. C'mon, let's go eat!" Everything was always in a hurry with her.

Rushing with Olive to the mess deck, they paused to hang the clothes from the ceiling of Evalene's bunk on their way. When they arrived, Evalene discovered Olive was just being dramatic. Breakfast was served all the way up until lunch, with only an hour or so break between meals.

She followed Olive through the breakfast line, the soft fabric of the dress flowing around her legs elegantly, making her feel graceful. She hated being indebted to the girl, but she loved the dress so much she didn't want to give it back.

She filled up her entire plate with pancakes, eggs, bacon, and a sampling of everything else available whether she recognized it or not. They headed towards an open table, a smile still on Evalene's face, when she saw the man from yesterday, Talc.

He was seated with other familiar faces. Weaving through the tables after Olive, Evalene avoided eye contact, thankful when they sat on the other side of the room with a couple other women, but she could feel his eyes on her back. The blood pounding in her ears made it hard to hear Olive's introductions. She ducked her head, hoping they wouldn't talk to her. She wished she could disappear.

"Grandma Mae makes the best eggs in the entire world," Olive was saying. "And I mean the *best*! Chef Peridot's are good, but hers are better." Olive took a huge bite, continuing to speak around the mouthful. "The eggs come from the chickens on our farm." She swallowed and scooped up another bite, as she said, "You *can't* beat fresh eggs."

Nodding, Evalene risked a glance around, looking for Jeremiah, wishing she hadn't left so abruptly last night. Maybe she could go apologize now. He was nowhere to be found, but two tables down she spied a few crew members enjoying their breakfast. They were close enough to provide her some relief from Talc's presence. Evalene swallowed a few times, trying to get rid of the lump in her throat before finally picking up her fork to eat.

The food was savory. Despite her worries, she inhaled her food, listening to Olive's stories with half her attention, the other half focused on the bald man and his friends. She was careful to sit in such a way that she could always see Talc's table out of the corner of her eye. They hadn't left yet.

"She also puts tiny pieces of ham in it," Olive was saying, and Evalene tried to remember what the girl was talking about. The crew members nearby stood to leave, scattering Evalene's thoughts as Olive continued. "The ham is also from our farm, because we raise a pig or two each year, but I try not to think about Edgar or Louise or Henry or the others, because it ruins breakfast a little."

When Olive paused for a reaction, Evalene searched her brain for what the girl had just said. Only a few words had stuck, but she ventured a question, "You have pigs?"

"Yes, on our farm! I told you!" Olive threw her hands up, fork swinging in the air. Evalene opened her mouth to apologize as she watched her potential rescuers dump their breakfast trays and leave the room. But Olive's offense lasted only a moment and then she happily chattered on. "It's technically Grandma Mae's farm. My parents and I have our own house on her land. But we all help. Someday I'll build my own house right next to theirs. Settle down with a husband and kids..." She trailed off for a moment, looking over at a table on the other side of the room near Talc's.

Olive wanted a husband and kids. On the island. Evalene followed her line of sight, to find Jeremiah and Luc eating at the table next to Talc's. How long had they been there? After yesterday's conversation, it was clear who Olive's choice was for the role of husband. Evalene tried to imagine having a husband. She couldn't picture it.

Playing with the crumbs on her plate, scooping them one way

and then the other with her fork, Evalene snuck one more glance at Talc's table where they still sat, considering her options. She could apologize to Jeremiah, and maybe if the big man saw her with the captain, he would leave her alone. But that was a big maybe. Or she and Olive could just leave since they were done eating. "Olive, do you want to go to the lower level? I was there yesterday when I was... exploring," she finished weakly to avoid mentioning Jeremiah.

"Yeah! Let's go!" Olive jumped up and grabbed her tray. They dropped off their dirty dishes in bins by the kitchen before heading to the lower level.

Entering the makeshift gymnasium and the wide-open room immediately boosted Evalene's spirits. Olive ignored the exercise equipment, walking towards the back of the ship where Evalene had sat with Jeremiah last night.

"Have you been to the living room yet?" Olive asked over her shoulder. She wilted for a moment when Evalene nodded, then perked up. "But did you see all the games and the music area?"

Olive skipped into the cozy compartment ahead of Evalene without waiting for an answer. "We have so many games – you'll love them!"

Evalene wandered inside, over to the chair Jeremiah had sat in, and tried it. It enveloped her like a hug. She wished she was brave enough to help him.

Olive dug through a closet full of different boxes, pulling out one at a time and shaking her head until she found the one she wanted. "Have you played chess before?" she asked, coming over to set the thin box on the table in front of Evalene.

"My father had a set," Evalene said, smiling a little at the memory of them playing when she was young. His set had been made of marble, but these pieces rattled in the box. One game was enough to trigger her memory, and she could've played five more times, but Olive dug out another box instead.

"Let's play Rutabaga instead!" She dumped the contents onto the table, setting up a new board with figurines of plants and animals and two little stick figures with bows.

Evalene had never heard of it. "How do you play?"

"What?" Olive threw her hands up, "You've never played? It's like… kind of an economical version of chess, where you see who will survive, and if you can gather enough plants and shoot enough food."

"Sounds like it was invented after the war," Evalene laughed, then cut off, catching herself. It was easy to let her guard down with this girl.

But Olive laughed too. "I bet you're right!"

The day passed in a blur as they went up for lunch with the other girls, and then came back downstairs to the living room again. This time Olive pulled out a guitar to show Evalene, playing a tune and offering to teach her how to play. This was the life Evalene had always dreamed of – the ability to choose how she spent her day, having fun, learning new things. Olive taught her chords and Evalene practiced until blisters began to form on the ends of her fingers.

"We should probably take a break. You don't want your fingers to bleed," Olive told her. "Plus it's almost dinner time and I'm starving."

But Evalene was enjoying herself for the first time since Kevra's betrayal. "Just a couple more minutes." She placed her fingers on each string in the order Olive had shown her and strummed. It sounded clearer. She was getting the hang of this.

"Alright," Olive smiled. "You keep practicing. I need to go to the bathroom. I'll come back to get you when dinner's ready." She skipped out of the room, leaving the door open.

Alone in the living room, Evalene tried to put the chords together, pushing herself to switch the position of her fingers faster. Olive had to go all the way upstairs and down the long hallway to get to the Head. By the time she got back, Evalene was determined to have smooth transitions.

She was starting to get the hang of it when a shadow filled the doorway. "That was fast," Evalene said to Olive without looking up from her fingers, placing them in the next chord.

"Well, look who it is," a voice growled, and it wasn't Olive's. Evalene's head jerked up. Talc stood in the doorway, his smaller friend behind him as well as another younger man with long hair, all wearing brown.

22

Running into Talc

THE GUITAR DROPPED ONTO the floor with a loud crash of hollow wood and clashing notes as the strings vibrated from hitting the ground. Evalene stood, heart pounding. They stood between her and the only way out of the room. She tried to gauge how soon Olive would be back, but it was impossible to say, if she got caught up talking to someone or side tracked by dinner.

Evalene straightened her spine and lifted her chin, forcing herself to stare directly into the big man's eyes. He thought she was a high Number, and she was determined to keep it that way. She knew his type. If he found out she was a lower Number, he'd still be a bully, but he'd be far less likely to take it easy, since no one cared what happened to a 29. If she stood tall and proud like Ruby, they would back off and leave her alone. Wouldn't they?

"Excuse me." She took a few steps towards them. "I'll be on my way."

But they didn't budge. "Schorl," Talc said over his shoulder, cracking his knuckles, "guard the door."

The long-haired man nodded, stepping outside and pulling the door closed behind him. It clicked shut. "There's no lock," the smaller man said, but Talc waved him off, stepping towards Evalene.

"I know a brat just like you back home," he told her, advancing. She backed up until her legs ran into the sofa behind her. "She thought she was better than me too. Had the Regs give me a couple beatings over nothin' and now I'm thinkin' why don't we get a little payback?" This last part he said over his shoulder to the smaller man.

Evalene took advantage of his momentary distraction to move around behind the couch into the next circle of chairs and sofas. Now if he wanted to come after her, he had to chase her around. Her mind raced, trying to think of a way that she could make both men chase her, instead of just Talc. If she could get them both to come to this side, then her path to the door would open and she could make a run for it.

But as Talc turned back with a sneer, she remembered the third man on the other side of the door. She backed up further, glancing around the room for some sort of weapon to defend herself against his huge hands, but the only objects close at hand were the couches and chairs with their soft cushions and pillows. Desperate, she continued to back up, moving towards a picture that hung on the wall.

The men were enjoying their position of power, not in a hurry, and as Talc rounded the corner of the couch with a sinister grin, Evalene reached up to yank the frame off the wall. She would throw it at him, in hopes that it would hit or trip him, so that she could round the couch and try to get past the others.

But the picture was anchored to the wall. With the frequency that the sub dove and resurfaced, it made sense that everything was bolted down, yet Evalene pulled harder, frantic.

Talc laughed, a deep, menacing sound that gave her shivers. She gave up, turning to face him, crouching to run or fight as the smaller man rounded the couch from the other side. Despite being terrified, Evalene clenched her fists, preparing to swing when they got closer and take them by surprise. She refused to take a beating the way she'd had to back home.

"Let me in right now!" Olive's voice demanded from outside the door. "This room is for everyone to use—" The door knob turned. "If your friend wanted privacy he should've gone to his bunk. Excuse me!" As the door burst open, Talc and the smaller man both moved away from Evalene, leaving her to stand trembling against the back wall while they dropped into the nearest chairs. Olive appeared in the entrance, scowling.

"Evie, hurry up, it's time for dinner and the meeting," Olive said, as if Evalene should've known. She waved vehemently for Evalene to come, and Evalene didn't dawdle. Almost running past the smaller man, where he sat in his chair, she hurried to Olive's side.

Evalene didn't look back until she was standing with Olive. The men's faces held barely veiled resentment, but they stayed seated. Though two girls wouldn't be any more difficult for three men to detain than one, something about Olive's confidence, or maybe her connections with the crew, made them hold back. "Let's go," Olive said to Evalene, and to the men in a louder voice, almost like a mother chastising naughty children, she said, "I'm glad everyone is behaving. Wouldn't want anyone kicked off the mission and sent back to Eden." With that threat in the air, the girls exited the room.

Passing the long-haired man named Schorl as they left and crossed the gym, Olive spoke to him sternly, "Tell your friends to come to the mess deck for the meeting. It's mandatory." She spun on her heel towards the ladder and Evalene followed closely.

When Olive waved her up first, Evalene stepped onto the rungs and began climbing. Reaching the mess deck, Evalene didn't stop moving until she was on the other side of the room by the door to the bridge, her back against the wall. Her heart still raced, but as her flushed skin cooled, it was replaced with a cold sweat that made her palms feel clammy.

The room was packed. All the tables were full, standing room only, and the crowd reminded Evalene that Olive had mentioned a meeting. Evalene had thought that was just an excuse. She stayed planted in the corner. Though she'd rather be alone in her bunk, this was by far the safer place to be right now. Talc wouldn't touch her in this crowd.

Jeremiah stood comfortably in the center of the group, waiting for the last few stragglers before he began. Olive caught up to where Evalene stood against the far wall, "Are you okay?"

Evalene shook her head once, slightly. She didn't speak. What could she say?

At that moment, Talc's head appeared as he climbed the ladder, followed by the other two men. Did Olive have to tell them to come? Even in the midst of all these people, Evalene felt herself shiver. She tried to angle behind those in front of her so that Talc wouldn't see her.

Olive caught on and moved to stand in front of her as well. Her sensitivity surprised Evalene. "Thank you," Evalene whispered, and Olive nodded in response.

Impressed by this new serious side of the girl, Evalene was thankful. Kevra certainly wouldn't have protected her like that. A new appreciation for Olive rose up at that thought.

In the middle of the room, Jeremiah turned to Luc and spoke over the quiet conversation around the room. "Is everyone here?" When Luc nodded, he began without preamble. The chatter died down naturally as people stopped talking to listen.

"Yesterday, I promised I would elaborate on the Low Level Employee Work Rule. Our mission. Are you ready to hear the assignment?" Jeremiah swung around, directing the question to each corner of the room.

Everyone's eyes were riveted on his face. Some lit up with excitement for the long-awaited mystery while others, older and more experienced, looked on anxiously. But there were nods all around the room, and even a soft call of "Yes, please!" from a teen and "I am!" from his friend sitting next to him. They immediately hunched down into the crowd to hide where the voices came from.

But Jeremiah smiled slightly and nodded in their direction as if to praise them for speaking up. "What I'm about to tell you about the Work Rule is something almost no one in Eden, including the Number One, knows." Evalene frowned at the idea of the Number One not knowing one of his own policies. She saw similar frowns across the room. Jeremiah clasped his hands in front of him and touched his fingers to his lips, as if choosing his words carefully.

"The Work Rule has only two purposes. First, we are helping all of you… to *escape from Eden*."

Everyone gasped.

Jeremiah spoke over the murmurs that rose all around the room, "Without the Number One, or the Regulators knowing it, we have helped you leave the country. You are now officially in free waters. And you will arrive on free land."

The whispers grew to outright conversation as everyone voiced their excitement, shock, disbelief. Jeremiah let it sink in for a moment.

Swiveling to look at different people around the room as he spoke, his eyes met Evalene's briefly, then moved on, "When we land on the island, I want you to understand that Numbers don't exist there at all."

Instead of whipping the talkers into a frenzy, the room froze, as everyone held their breath. It sounded too good to be true, and Evalene could tell she wasn't the only one who thought so.

Jeremiah repeated himself, driving the point home. "From this point on, you no longer have a Number either." Though he had said similar words to Evalene the day before, it still didn't feel real to her.

"Now, you can stay and live the rest of your life on the island. Or travel to another country altogether. Or," he paused, "you can be a part of something greater."

He gazed at those in front of him, then swung back in Evalene's direction, and she watched the fire in his eyes as he told them, "The second purpose of the Work Rule is to gather an army and fight to take our country back." He emphasized each word as he spoke, enunciating so that no one misunderstood. "Our hope is that you will stand with us against the Number system – against the Number One himself – and fight until Eden is free!"

Jeremiah's voice and charisma were captivating. Evalene liked how he talked with his hands. The room was so still that the only sound was the cooks in the kitchen banging pans together as they prepared dinner behind the metal window. But Jeremiah ignored it, continuing, "Over the last two years, we have gathered a small army. Using the Work Rule, we sailed back and forth between Eden and the island, rescuing people just like you." Someone whooped at that, although quietly, and cut off quickly. Jeremiah nodded to them, again praising bravery.

"But there are thousands more who still need us." The cheers died down at the sobering thought. His voice rose again, challenging them. "Do you see anyone else standing up for us? Who will fight for our friends and our family if we don't?"

His questions hung in the air. The room was silent, quiet. The crowd shifted at the challenge, uneasy. To offer freedom and then ask them to give it up? His speech wasn't earning him any cheers now.

In a soft voice, almost a whisper, Jeremiah pleaded with them. "Think of those who have been disciplined with death row by the Regulators. Or what about those who simply disappeared?" Evalene thought of her mother. She tried to imagine how Pearl would have responded to Jeremiah's words. She blinked back tears as she pictured someone just like Jeremiah saying these things to her mother years ago. He spread his hands wide as he stared into their faces. "Who will be next?"

Around the room, faces hardened. A couple people sniffed, and hands tightened into fists, men, women, and teenagers alike. Jeremiah's voice grew hard as well. "Eden cannot afford to be a land of Numbers any longer. Your friends, your family, everyone back home needs us. We have to fight for them!" A few soft murmurs of agreement rose around the room, but Evalene took a shuddering breath. What if he was right?

"I am extending this invitation to all of you, just as I have to those who came before you," Jeremiah continued with his hands outstretched, and everyone hushed immediately, hanging on his words. Through the crowd, Evalene caught a glimpse of Talc and his friends, as angry as ever, but now their eyes were trained on Jeremiah and his words.

"Join us."

Just two words, but they hit Evalene in the chest as if she'd been punched.

Jeremiah stepped back, dropping his hands to his sides. "I won't tell anyone what to do. I'm not the Number One and I never want to be."

He pointed towards the front of the ship, in the direction it was going. "Tomorrow we reach the island. We will spend three days there while we rest and finalize our plans. Please take those three days to consider my invitation. You are welcome to stay in the tents with us while you decide. If you have any questions between now and then, please come talk to me or Luc."

Evalene studied the faces around her as he spoke, trying to gauge who was moved by his plea. Everyone looked riled up to some extent, but she couldn't tell by their frowns if they wanted to fight or flee. Maybe they were as conflicted as she was.

Jeremiah spread his hands expansively. "On the fourth day, we will return to Eden. And we will fight!" A few people shouted in agreement at that, including Talc, who moved forward as if to volunteer right then and there. The volume was so loud, Jeremiah yelled his final statement: "It's time to be Number-free!"

Everyone burst into applause, shouting approval, thrilled that someone was taking their side. Amid the chaos and cheering, when Evalene was sure that Talc wasn't looking, she snuck through the hatch that led to the bridge.

She made her way to the secret panel that Olive had showed her the day before. Testing the wall, she glanced back over her shoulder to make sure she was alone before she pushed, hard. It slid open.

Grateful, she sighed in relief and snuck inside, immediately sliding the door closed behind her. Without the glow sticks, her heart pounded anxiously in the darkness, but she didn't care. Talc couldn't find her here. That's all that mattered.

She crept blindly towards the back of the storage, as far from the entrance as possible. This was where she would stay until they arrived at the island tomorrow. She was tired enough that she could sleep anywhere. And she'd gone without food much longer than this. It wouldn't be hard. That fate didn't bother her nearly as much as her conscience did after Jeremiah's speech.

She'd only had her freedom for a few days, and now she was considering giving it up?

23

Jeremiah's Dream

JEREMIAH NOTICED RIGHT AWAY when Evie left. It was odd that she'd disappeared so abruptly. Maybe she felt judged. But he couldn't follow her out; the faces around him were full of questions.

Luc joined him in the middle of the room without needing to be asked. They had this whole speech and the aftermath down to a science. Though the crowd was still shy of acting above their Number, some would undoubtedly turn from talking to each other and move to talk to them. He and Luc would be there a long time.

Sure enough, a few people from several groups stood and began moving towards him and Luc. A large, hostile man approached first. "If we join you, can we do whatever we want to the high Numbers after?" he asked without bothering to introduce himself.

This was always the most difficult question to answer, and it came up on almost every mission. Jeremiah tried to side step it. "We are planning to change the entire country of Eden, to do away with Numbers entirely." He made sure to pitch his voice so that his answers could be heard by everyone in the room who might be listening. "There will be new leadership, a new government run by the people, and new laws that will protect everyone equally."

Jeremiah was unsurprised when this didn't satisfy the big man, who scowled, "Where is the justice in that?"

But Jeremiah stayed firm, crossing his arms. "There will be justice to *all* who cause harm, including those who try to take revenge afterward."

This was enough to make the man back down, at least for the moment. Jeremiah wasn't foolish enough to think he wouldn't try something down the road. But he would still allow the man to fight with them. They needed all the help they could get. As he thought this, he noted a few people slipping out of the room towards the racks. But most stayed, even if just out of curiosity.

Another shy face stepped forward, a young man who held the girl's hand next to him. "What if we," he swallowed, hard, "we want to help, but we also want to start a family…"

Jeremiah held his hands up. "You don't need to make any excuses to me," he said, cutting the young man off, again he spoke to the room as a whole. "No one needs my permission to stay. The offer to join us is just that – an offer. Not a requirement." As soon as he said it, another five or six people stole out of the room.

But others stayed.

These were the people he needed to convince.

A third person, an older woman who looked thin but had strong, wiry muscles built up from years of hard work. "Can we ask how you plan to do it?"

Nodding, Jeremiah began to explain his goals for taking over the news stations across the country. To have the Regulator stations surrounded. To have as many rebels in the fight as there were Regulators, if not more. How they would storm the Number One's home and remove him as leader.

Jeremiah knew the more time he spent helping them understand, explaining his hopes for a peaceful transition, the time frame for the takeover, and the adjustment period, the more comfortable they would be joining the cause. So he stayed. And explained. And repeated himself.

They needed every volunteer they could get when they shipped out in just a few short days. As the kitchen began to serve dinner, he and Luc continued to field questions until his voice grew hoarse. Luc went to work with the crew while Jeremiah remained with the group as it slowly dwindled. Many left to eat and then returned. Having missed questions while eating, they would ask the same ones as those before them. The dinner hour ended, and they continued late into the evening.

Stomach growling as he finished speaking with yet another anxious passenger, he eyed the closed meal station in disappointment. He sighed in relief as Luc came back to relieve him. Jeremiah stood and left the job of winning over the last few concerned individuals to Luc before moving towards Operations to check in with his crew. Though he'd told the passengers they'd arrive at the island tomorrow, they would actually reach it sometime around two or three that morning.

He clapped a hand on Welder's shoulder as he entered Operations. The older man had been with him since the beginning. As one of the few people who'd known how to run a submarine prior to their plans, he'd been instrumental in training the crew.

Equally important, he was a good leader, and a member of the council Jeremiah had formed on the island.

Exhausted from the hours of conversation, persuading, and empathizing, Jeremiah slipped away to the captain's quarters, to his private bunk.

It was late. He needed sleep. But he was wide awake.

After hours tossing and turning, he finally dozed off. He dreamed of his mother. She smiled at him and he clapped in excitement, a five-year-old boy again, grinning back at her. They were in his childhood home, and as she worked, he followed her around like a puppy at her heels.

She turned from the little stove to smile and ask him what he wanted to eat for lunch. A second later, they were sitting at the table enjoying his favorite dish of noodles that his mother had always made. She smiled and asked him what he wanted to do that day. They played jacks in his childhood bedroom for what seemed to him like hours. Then she smiled and asked, *Why do you have to lead the revolution?*

He stared at her in confusion. But she just repeated herself, asking him again and again why he had to lead the revolution? Why? She started to cry. *Why?* She screamed at him. In a heartbeat, she morphed into a 12-year-old version of Jeremiah himself. *Why?* His own voice screamed back at him now, high pitched and childish.

When he looked in the mirror, he found that he was now his father. His 12-year-old self continued to scream at him, *Why did you leave me?*

Turning away from the mirror and the image of his father, he found that it was the girl Evie who now stood next to him. She fluttered her lashes at him, moving to sit on his small bed. *Tell me, why do you need to lead this revolution?*

Frowning in confusion, Jeremiah opened his mouth to repeat what he'd told people for years. But nothing came out. His mind was empty. What were his reasons?

That's what I thought, she said, sighing and averting her eyes. *You're going to die.* So matter of fact. Was that what she thought of him? He felt a noose around his neck. Lifting his hands to it, his fingers felt the coarse threads of a rope, tightening.

It's too bad you won't stay. It would've been nice to get to know you better. Standing, Evie came to stand in front of him, just inches away, so close he could see the flecks of gray in her blue eyes. *But why would I be friends with a dead man?*

She brushed past him, out of the room, leaving him alone.

Jeremiah woke up in a sweat. He hadn't had that dream about his mother in months. And now he dreamed of Evie as well?

24

Day One: The Island

EVALENE STEPPED THROUGH THE hatch, out onto the flat, narrow surface of the black metal submarine deck, blinking in the bright sunlight. After spending the night in the pitch-black storage room, she felt like she'd been buried alive. The night had gone on forever, but Olive had found her there in the morning.

"Evie, I've been looking for you everywhere. Have you been here all night?" the girl had said the moment she found Evalene in the back of the room. Evalene's nod wasn't enough explanation though. "What's going on? Is it that Talc fellow? I can talk to the crew –"

"No, no, that's okay," Evalene told her friend, standing stiffly and feeling the consequences of sleeping on the metal ground. "I don't want to do anything. Just leave it."

"Why not?" Olive asked as they made their way into the bridge, her forehead furrowed. "We could remove him from the rebellion. Causing conflict is taken seriously in camp."

But Evalene shook her head as Olive slid the storage door closed and led the way up the spiraling staircase in the bridge towards the conning tower. "If the camp and the island are as big as you say, I won't run into him again. But if he's removed from fighting, he'll find me and blame me for it. I've known people like him my whole life. Please, I just want to drop it."

Frowning, Olive clearly didn't like it, but before she could argue further, they'd reached the top of the sub and the tail end of the group as they disembarked.

The rays nearly blinded Evalene. The submarine was docked in deep waters against a long cement wall that curved out from the shore and across the mouth of the bay, keeping the crashing waves of the surf out and the inside of the bay calm and still, with just one small opening on the far side for smaller ships and boats to sneak into the bay.

Stepping onto the gangplank between the submarine and the thick levee wall, Evalene crossed carefully. Her first step onto the smooth, dry cement felt momentous, like a band should be welcoming her with a song of celebration. She had escaped.

But instead there was only the roar of the wind and the waves crashing rhythmically onto the sea side of the thick wall, drowning out most of the conversation between the other passengers as they walked along the long, cement wall in clumps of twos and threes ahead of her. Evalene stared in awe at the shore, drinking in the wide-open spaces of the harbor.

Only a few tall buildings rose in the distance, too far to make out any details, and the rest of the landscape was covered in green trees and smaller, colorful buildings with mountains in the background. Just a quarter mile down, the levee gave way to sandy beaches all along the waterfront on the other side of the bay, a stark contrast from the crowded, manmade Delmare harbor.

As they walked along the cement embankment, they passed docks inside the bay where smaller boats anchored, floating and bouncing cheerfully in clear blue water. Evalene's nose crinkled a little at the fishy smell floating towards them on the wind as they passed, mixing with the salty ocean air. Seagulls called to each other as the waves lapped at the boats and the docks. Staring at the birds in awe, she stopped in her tracks to admire them. The island had so many birds! Out of the corner of her eye, she saw a few others stop to gawk at the birds as well.

It felt like a dream, but the sun was too bright and the smells too powerful to be imagined. Trailing after the group, Evalene picked up her feet as they neared the beach. Once she reached the sand, she picked up a handful and felt the soft grainy pieces pour out of the cracks between her fingers until she let it spill back to the ground.

A memory of when she was a little girl and her family travelled to a beach struck her. Instantly, she craved that feeling of her bare feet in the sand. She'd taken to leaving her boot laces mostly untied. Just needed to undo the knot at the top, and with a quick tug they slipped right off. She wiggled her toes in the warmth, closed her eyes, and inhaled deeply.

"Have you never been on a beach before?" Olive's voice floated across the wind to reach her ears. "The sand is hot – your feet are going to burn."

Opening her eyes, Evalene felt the heat Olive mentioned, but she didn't care. Burrowing her toes deeper into the sand, she found cool grains untouched by the sun underneath and stayed put, admiring the wide-open spaces. The salty ocean air on her tongue tasted like freedom.

The small harbor was filled with all sizes of ships and small boats. The largest ones, like their submarine, were forced to anchor out in deeper waters on the other side of the levee wall. Fishermen sailed through the small opening on the side of the bay out into vast ocean while others stood or sat along the wall as they tossed their lines out into the sea.

Now that they were closer to the city, it stretched out in front of her. She'd never seen a city like it. Perfectly rounded buildings on the outskirts made out of a shiny metal she didn't recognize gave way to skyscrapers in the middle, taller than any back home. Their spires stretched up and up towards the clouds, with a few of the tallest disappearing into the mist. Odd angles, steep roofs, and the way the tips sloped inward as if tapering off only to angle out again all gave the impression that the grand buildings were almost a form of art. Most were silver or gold, and some the same blue as the sky. When she caught sight of a cloud on one of them mirroring the one above it, she realized they were made of a reflective material. The strange glassy architecture gleamed bright in the sunlight, making her eyes water.

Evalene stopped at the edge of the beach as it changed to grass, keeping her toes in the sand. She soaked in the warmth of the sun, studying the city. When Jeremiah had described an island, she'd pictured something tiny. But that closest city was as huge as Delmare, if not larger. She could definitely get a job as a maid or a nanny... Or possibly a cook, if they weren't too picky about what they ate.

As the group left the beach, Evalene continued to carry her boots. She wanted to stay barefoot as long as she could.

Olive chimed in beside her. "Whatcha thinking about?"

"Ah... the city... It's beautiful." Safe answer. She stepped off the beach, reveling in the feeling of fresh grass between her toes. It felt like freedom. The sun touched her face gently.

"That's Hofyn," Olive said. "Grandma Mae and my parents and I live right on the other side. Well, a few miles past technically."

"I thought the island was called Hofyn?" Evalene squinted in confusion.

"It is," Olive nodded. "They named the island after the city because it used to be the only one here."

"But it's still just an island," Evalene felt comfortable enough with Olive to speak her thoughts out loud. "Why didn't Eden conquer it?"

Olive's laugh startled Evalene. "Island is kind of a loose term," Olive told her. "Hofyn is really more of a small continent. And our technology here is far more advanced than Eden's. We're perfectly capable of fighting back, if it ever came to that. From what I understand, the only machinery Eden has that surpasses ours is that Grid that shoots down flying objects."

Was Eden not as powerful as the Number One let on? Who would win if it came to a war between the two countries? Evalene didn't have time to ponder it long. As they topped the hill, the camp stretched out before her, capturing her attention.

A mass of white tents sprawled from the edge of the harbor out into the distance across the hills and valleys in organized rows.

This must be the camp that Jeremiah had referred to in his speech. Hundreds, if not thousands, of people milled about, all on their way to different destinations, preparing for the fight. Larger tents, the size of five or six put together, were also sprinkled throughout the camp, though she couldn't tell what they were from the distance.

Most fascinating of all, there were various squares of green grass throughout the camp, about the size of an acre each, where men and women seemed to be training. At first glance, the people in one square looked as if they were in actual fist fights, but at a signal that Evalene couldn't hear from the man watching on the side, they broke apart, clapping each other on the backs. In another square, on the opposite side of the camp, Evalene could just make out targets and soft, sporadic pops in the distance that she realized were gunshots. In yet another square, she was surprised to find that people were actually shooting at each other, popping out from behind haystacks and makeshift wooden obstacles. She stopped as the scene gripped her, her nerves tingling in anxiety when one of the shooters was hit, but instead of blood, a big spot of green splattered on their vest, followed by another shot, which sprayed the vest with yellow. It was just a game, a simulation of a battle. She breathed a sigh of relief.

As they drew closer to the camp entrance, they caught up to the group finally. Evalene searched for Jeremiah among the passengers or the crew, but didn't spot him. Had he stayed behind? Why did she keep thinking about him?

She spotted Talc's bald head towering above those with him, near the front of the group, talking to Luc. Reminded of his promises of "payback," Evalene made sure to keep her distance. She felt safe enough in the group. Now that they were on the island, maybe he would take the Number-free idea seriously. Either way, it didn't matter much. She didn't plan to stay here long.

Luc's voice boomed from the front of the group, easily projecting to where Evalene and Olive stood at the back. "Listen up! We're guests on the island. They've welcomed refugees from Eden into their homes, and have allowed those who plan to fight to set up camp here in preparation for almost two years now. If you choose to stay, we have people who can help you find work, and you are all welcome to stay here in camp until you find a place to live. We have enough food and shelter for everyone. Our only expectation is that you'll pitch in and work. There's a lot that needs doing. So let's all work together and have a good time, huh?"

Luc grinned and slapped the man Evalene recognized from the day before, Schorl, on the back. "Follow me. I'll be assigning everyone to available tents."

The group followed as Luc dropped off a few people at each tent, giving them instructions before moving on. Evalene sighed in relief when Talc was one of the first to be assigned.

"C'mon," Olive whispered as Luc took a turn to the left and she turned to the right instead. "I have an extra bunk in my tent for when Grandma Mae visits – you can stay with me!"

"Don't I need to sign up to help out?"

Olive waved a hand, leading Evalene further away. "Don't worry about that. You can help set up the training grounds with me. Or there's always rotations available for cleaning the bathrooms." She pointed towards the only two solid structures in camp, one on each side, made of cement. "We have running water. It's not like they're still holes in the ground, but you'd be surprised how disgusting they can get."

Evalene doubted she'd be at all surprised, after her years cleaning bathrooms back home, but she nodded, following Olive down row after row. How Olive found "her" tent amidst the identical white tents surrounding it, Evalene had no idea. But she followed her inside. If she was lost, no doubt Talc would be too, which made her feel safer.

As Olive set her suitcase on top of the cot on the left, chattering away, Evalene tested the cot on the right, laying her head on the soft pillow and letting the tension drain out of her. She was so tired. Spending the night in the storage area, afraid of being found and terrified of running into Talc, meant she'd barely slept. She closed her eyes to rest for just a minute.

Salty ocean air jolted her awake. The tent was quiet. Olive's small bag was tucked under her cot on the other side of the tent, but the girl was gone. How long had she slept?

Swinging her feet over the side of the cot, Evalene picked up her boots from where she'd dropped them at the entrance, lacing them at the top and tying a quick knot. Opening the flap of the tent, she peered out. The sun was curving in the sky, beginning to make its way back down. The time on the submarine had confused her sleeping schedule. She'd slept all morning and a bit of the afternoon.

Her stomach growled in confirmation. Evalene stepped

cautiously out of the tent, glancing around, not sure what to do. She turned to the swinging, fabric door behind her. Discovering a zipper hidden in a pocket of fabric at the top, she pulled it carefully down to the bottom.

She took a step back, surveying her work. Not much of a deterrent to intruders. But it would keep out bugs. What did she have to steal at this point anyway?

"What do you think of the island so far?"

Evalene whirled around at the voice. It was Jeremiah. He stood smiling slightly at her efforts to lock the tent. She brushed off her hands briskly and moved into the makeshift road between the tents. "I haven't seen much of it yet," she told him, turning to walk away from him without a clue where she was going. Better not to spend time with him. It just added to her guilt about not joining the revolution. "Have a nice day," she called over her shoulder.

But he jogged the couple steps it took to catch up with her, walking alongside as she strode down the dirt lane in the general direction of the ocean. "I was actually on my way to help with supper," he said, keeping pace with her. Evalene's stomach growled again at the word. "Would you like to join me? Or did Luc already assign you to a rotation?"

Slowing to a stop, Evalene cleared her throat. "He didn't," she admitted, giving in. She was hungry, and supper rotation sounded far better than cleaning bathrooms. "Which way is the kitchen?"

"Follow me." He turned, leading her in the opposite direction that she'd been walking. She followed a step behind, but he slowed to walk beside her. "Did you enjoy the submarine?"

She wanted to tell him that the little bunks were surprisingly soothing, the way they blocked out noise and light. That if her nerves hadn't been wound so tight, she might've slept as peacefully as she had pre-Numbering. She especially wanted to tell him about Talc. But what could he do? Nothing, except reveal her true Number or remove the man from the rebellion. Neither of those things helped her at all. Both would just lead to the big man hunting her down. No. This was a fresh start. No one here knew she was a Number 29, and if she kept to herself, it could stay that way.

So she just said a quiet, "Yes, thank you," and they walked in awkward silence, dirt and bits of gravel crunching under their feet. A lot of the people they passed still wore brown, but they'd covered their tattoos with their hair or a scarf or a patch, and almost all of them wore some other spot of mutinous color, whether a jacket, or new shirt, or shoes, or even hair pieces, making the crowd a vibrant rainbow of rebellious colors.

Jeremiah spoke after a minute or so of silence. "Now that you're here, have you decided what you're going to do next?"

"I'm not sure…" All of her questions about the city poured out of her, unbidden. "How many people live in town? The houses are all so small – do they all have their own individual homes? How would I get a job working in a home? Or could I work outside of a home here? How do people know what jobs they should be doing without a Number? Do they just pick at random or do they get to try things to find out what they like first? And –" Jeremiah started laughing and Evalene caught herself.

"I could help you find work," Jeremiah chuckled, answering

the most urgent question, "if you'd like?"

"That's okay, you have more important things to do," Evalene shook her head. She couldn't tell him that she was avoiding him and his revolution. She changed the subject. "Do you know what we'll be making for dinner?"

"Honestly, I'm not sure yet," Jeremiah replied. "But in a group this size there are only so many options. Nothing too fancy when you're feeding nearly ten thousand. Whatever it is, we'll divide it up. We serve meals in three shifts." Evalene nodded gravely.

They came to a stop in front of a huge tent that could've held two dozen of the smaller tents inside it easily. Pulling back the flap, Jeremiah gestured for her to go first, and they entered the portable kitchen. The heat of the ovens hit her right away, beads of sweat starting to form on her back. A dozen or more people stood at different stations throughout the tent, hard at work.

"Jeremiah, open those blasted flaps for us," a larger, big-boned woman yelled from a half dozen feet away. "We're sweating to death in here!" Without waiting for him to do as she'd asked, she marched over to them and whipped the folds of the tent door up, yanking the ties around to keep them open. Her face was bright red from the heat. She walked right past them to the opposite side of the tent, where she whisked the flaps up and out of the way there as well, talking as she worked. "About time you showed up. Sanidine's already working on the mix, so now you get to do the bread. Start by slicing it and spreading them out on that table, you hear me?"

Jeremiah winked at Evalene behind the woman's back,

unfazed by her yelling at him. He moved towards the table the cook had pointed out. Wide-eyed, Evalene regretted agreeing to come.

"New girl!" the woman's voice hollered from the table where she worked.

Evalene's shoulders tensed. She stared at the ground, turning towards the cook. "Yes, ma'am." She responded the way she always did to Daeva.

The woman paused for a beat, then said in a calmer tone of voice, "See all that tuna?"

Evalene followed the direction of the cook's finger and saw a dozen huge tin cans with blue and white labels. Biting her lip, she nodded.

"Open each tin and add the contents to Sanidine's mix, understand?" The cook pointed towards another younger woman in the tent nearby, who waved a few fingers covered in a white paste in their direction at her name.

Nodding again, Evalene was careful to be on her best behavior that even Daeva wouldn't have been able to find fault with. "Yes, ma'am. I will, ma'am." She didn't meet the woman's eye, just curtseyed to the edge of the cook's pale yellow dress and worn gray slippers. Evalene moved towards her assigned station, next to Jeremiah's table.

Jeremiah cleared his throat once, then a second time more loudly from where he stood a few feet away. When Evalene didn't respond right away, he appeared at her side.

"Hey relax," he whispered, bumping her arm with his elbow teasingly. "Don't take Trona too seriously. She's all talk."

Evalene risked a peek over her shoulder in Trona's direction. The cook was busy holding a spatula next to the woman she'd called Sanidine. Taking a bite, Trona smacked her lips together in distaste. "Needs more salt."

Looking back at Jeremiah, Evalene caught a slice of bread disappearing under the table, in his hand one second and gone the next. He looked up and smiled. Still whispering he told her, "This is Juno." He wiggled his fingers near the edge of the table and a black nose appeared, sniffing and stretching up towards them. Evalene caught a glimpse of white fur that looked like a mop before the huge dog pulled back under the table.

"Oh!" she exclaimed, more loudly than she'd intended.

Trona overheard. The big woman marched over to them. Evalene kept her eyes on the table, picking up one of the tins and beginning to twist it open with the can opener.

The woman's face was still flushed and sweaty, despite the cool air coming in. "What's so exciting over here? I'd like to think it's my fine cooking, but with the captain in our kitchen," she gave him an exaggerated glare, "I'm afraid I know better."

Evalene shrunk under her gaze. Gluing her eyes to the floor, she didn't say a word, just waited for her punishment. But then out of the corner of her eye, she saw the dog's black nose peek out from under the table. It had made its way from Jeremiah's end of the table to where she stood, and now it stretched out slowly in curiosity towards her hands where they were clasped in front of her. Its pink tongue flicked out towards her and in a panic, Evalene swung her hands behind her back, trying to shoo the dog discreetly before it was spotted.

Too late.

"Captain!" the cook bellowed. "How many times have I told you this filthy animal is not allowed in my kitchen?" She shrieked as the dog stepped out from under the table, almost as if it knew that it had been caught, and began to wag its tail at the cook so fast its body wiggled. "Its hair! It's getting dog hair everywhere! Oh Lord almighty, we might as well toss all the food and start over!" she cried, fanning herself and swatting at the dog all at once.

Juno backed away from the hands swatting at her face, but when Jeremiah came to take her by the collar, she hopped away from him as well, tongue hanging out, and dropped into a play bow with her paws along the ground and her rear in the air. Hopping up, she danced back and away from them all, wiggling with happiness.

"Juno!" Jeremiah snapped in a stern voice. "Out." The dog's joyful dance stopped at the command, as if she couldn't believe her ears. "Out of the tent, right now," he told her again, and, head lowered, Juno slunk over to the tent exit and out onto the grass outside. Spinning around, she dropped to the ground with an audible huff right outside the door.

Evalene wanted to laugh as Juno lowered her head to the ground, depressed and mournful, to stare at them all. But when the dog saw her smile, her tail started to slap against the ground. Quickly, Evalene turned away, covering her grin with her hand and a cough. One glance at Trona was enough to sober her. Could she be punished for laughing?

But Jeremiah just smiled at Trona, completely unfazed by her hysterics. "Don't worry. Juno knows where the line is. She'll stay outside."

Trona crossed her arms, unamused. Raising her eyebrows at him, she surprised Evalene by moving back to her table, though she muttered loudly as she went. "Sure. That makes sense. How could anyone ever doubt it? There's no way she could get in now." Before she'd even reached her work table, she yelled, "Sanidine, close the tent doors! It's unsanitary!"

Evalene squinted at Jeremiah, who was laying out the bread as if nothing had happened. Picking up the can opener once more, she watched Sanidine pass her on her way to close the tent flaps. Though Sanidine was quick to obey, her blue eyes sparkled kindly as she smiled at Evalene, also calm and unconcerned. Trona was still muttering to herself, but since Sanidine and Jeremiah weren't taking it too seriously, Evalene began to relax.

The familiar routine of working in the kitchen, even one in a tent, helped Evalene find her comfort zone and soon she had her usual rhythm, working and sneaking small bites of food when no one was looking. She wished she had access to something besides tuna, but once it was blended with the soupy mixture it was surprisingly delicious.

The cooking flowed smoothly into serving dinner, and before she knew it, they'd finished the third shift. In the down time, she'd eaten not just one, but two sandwiches. Leaning against her assigned table as the last few dinner stragglers came through, Evalene considered the best way to wolf down another half without anyone noticing.

She was still assessing the options when Jeremiah appeared at her right shoulder. "Someone has been dying to meet you," he said in a soft voice, and tilted his head towards the tent flap on the far side of the room. Those with full plates were exiting through it, and Juno's nose was cheerfully inspecting the air as each one passed, although she stayed faithfully seated by the door outside the tent.

The corners of Evalene's mouth lifted as she met Juno's eyes and immediately the dog's fluffy white tail started tapping the ground. "Is this a stray?" she whispered back.

Jeremiah shook his head. "No, she's mine." No one had pets in Eden, making this yet another glimpse of the island's freedom.

She turned to face Jeremiah and found he was much closer than she'd anticipated. Only a few inches separated them. Staring into his eyes, she hiccupped. Retreating to a safer distance, she flushed bright red and hiccupped again. How embarrassing!

"Excuse me, sorry," she managed to say before another hiccup. She drew in a deep breath and held it, shaking her head in frustration and covering her cheeks with her hands to hide the heat that was spreading.

"No problem." Jeremiah shrugged. "You know what you do for the hiccups?" Without asking, he stepped close to her and grasped her arms, lifting them up above her head. "Trust me, this works."

He directed her arms towards the ceiling, "Stretch them out as high as you can." He let go, throwing his arms up as well to demonstrate. "Like this, see?"

Evalene giggled at the sight they made, both standing with their arms in the air. A hiccup snuck into the middle of it, making her laugh harder. Jeremiah grinned back at her, but took her hands which had come down to hold her stomach, and pulled them up high again. "Laugh all you want, but it works." He held both palms out, motioning for her to hold the pose this time.

She kept her hands up this time, trying to stretch like he was. "Good," he said. "Now take deep breaths. Just like that. You feel it stretching your lungs?" She nodded, inhaling deeply. "There you go. They'll be gone in no time."

And sure enough, as soon as she stopped giggling and focused on taking deep breaths, the hiccups were gone. She lowered her arms.

"I'd better get going," Evalene said, tucking her hair behind her ear and glancing at the tent door, where Juno still waited. "I haven't seen Olive all day. I'm sure she's wondering where I am."

Jeremiah rested against the table next to him. "Don't worry. She's the one who told me where to find you."

"You were looking for me?" Evalene eyes darted back to Jeremiah's face.

He ducked his head, scratching the back of his neck. "I feel a certain responsibility for you," he told her, and when he met her gaze, his was unreadable. "All the others signed up for the work order of their own free will, but you didn't really get a choice..." He shrugged. "I just wanted to make sure you were okay."

For some reason Evalene couldn't fathom, finding out she was a charity case to him stung. She blinked rapidly. Lifting her chin, she put on the emotionless mask she'd grown used to wearing back home. "I'm great."

She strode to the opposite side of the tent, away from Juno, ignoring the dog. "Thanks for checking on me," she spoke over her shoulder as she reached the exit. Sanidine or Trona must have closed the tent flaps on this side to signal the end of dinner. As Evalene pulled the flaps up to duck through the door, she told the dirt floor near Jeremiah's feet, "I'll make sure to check in with Luc for my next shift. Goodnight."

She dropped the flap without waiting for his response. Stepping forward into the dark night, Evalene labored down the path between the tent rows in the darkness, waiting for her eyes to adjust. How was she going to find her tent?

In the moonlight, the white, slanted roofs of thousands of tents stretched out into the distance all around her. She walked down one row, then the next, trying to get her bearings, staring at the cheerful lights of the town as she caught one or two blink out and others turn on. She hadn't paid attention to where her tent was in relation to town, so it didn't help now.

Crossing her arms, she shivered. Without the sun, the temperature had plummeted, and the difference was noticeable after standing near stoves all night. She rubbed her arms for warmth.

She was lost.

25

Day One: Scheming

THE MOONLIGHT SHONE BRIGHTLY on the paths, but without a lantern or flashlight, Evalene squinted at the ground, moving at a snail's pace to avoid tripping over tent pegs or debris. The idea of being alone when Talc lurked somewhere nearby made her shiver harder.

A cold, wet nose touch her wrist. She yelped as she jumped and pulled her hands away. A white blur danced around her in the dark. "Juno?" she whispered, and the dog whined back happily, coming up to lean into her leg in greeting, begging to be pet.

"Juno was worried about you." Jeremiah's deep voice came from behind her, and she recognized it right away. Evalene turned around, relaxing. She made out his shape in the darkness as he bent down and beckoned the dog. Juno moved to her master, tail wagging and hitting Evalene's shins. "She made me come look for you to make sure you got to your tent safely."

Evalene bit her lip, wanting to trust him. "Is that so?" she said finally. "I guess if she's that worried…" she trailed off and admitted the truth. "Okay, yes please help me. I have no idea where I'm going…"

Juno scampered back to Evalene, wet nose catching her hand again, bumping it persistently until she gave in and pet the dog.

Instead of rubbing it in, Jeremiah just straightened. "You were pretty close. Come on Juno, let's show her the way." The dog bounded after him, and Evalene followed.

They proceeded to backtrack, finally reaching a little white tent that looked just like all the others around it. She hadn't been close at all. Annoyed with herself, Evalene simply said, "Thanks."

"Sure," he said. His form backed away in the dark, and Juno's white shape followed. "In the morning you'll notice each row is marked, and each tent has a number. That should help. But don't worry. It's easy to get lost here in the beginning."

"Thanks," Evalene said again, wondering why he spent so much time helping her if she was just a charity case. "You don't have to worry about me. I've been on my own for a long time." She winced at the sharp words.

But he didn't seem put off. "And now you're not alone anymore," he said, and she could hear the smile that made it hard to dislike him. "By the way, Olive told me about Talc."

Anxiety spiked. Evalene opened her mouth, about to beg him not to talk to Talc or do anything, the way she had with Olive. But he spoke first. "Don't worry about him anymore. I have my men keeping him extremely busy between now and when we leave. He won't have time to bother you." He said it like it was nothing. But Evalene's entire body flooded with relief at the knowledge that someone was protecting her.

"Thank you," she whispered softly.

"No problem. Good night," he said, and whistled for Juno who took off after him like a shot. His shadow rounded a corner and was gone.

Turning to her tent, Evalene smiled at his kindness. Fumbling around in the darkness of the tent, she found her bed and sank onto it. The only breathing in the tent was her own. She was alone.

Though she felt a candle on the small table between the beds, her fingers couldn't find matches anywhere. She gave up and lay down to sleep. Besides taking her boots off, she didn't have anything else to do anyway. With the tent flaps closed, not even much moonlight could get in.

Despite having napped earlier, Evalene found herself drifting off to sleep with the sound of frogs croaking and crickets humming in her ears. But she kept picturing Jeremiah stepping onto Eden's shores, and getting shot by Regulators. The idea shook her.

Rolling over to escape it, Evalene tried to ignore the direction her mind was going, but there was no stopping the flood of thoughts now. All the ways the Number One might stop the rebels, specifically Jeremiah, hammered her mind. The Number One had more men. He controlled the citizens. More importantly, he controlled the Regulators, who outnumbered even the many rebels in this camp who had stayed to fight. Ten thousand, Jeremiah had said earlier? The past few years since the rebellion, so many had been Numbered 11 as Regulators, their forces were easily twice that many, if not more.

Evalene vividly remembered the news during the Bloom Rebellion. Especially the day they'd found out about her mother's death. The camera had panned across a long line of bodies hanging from the executioner's ropes.

And now it was going to happen again. The sight of those men and women hanging lifeless, forever burned into Evalene's memory, played across her vision again, but this time when the camera zoomed in on one of the victims, it was Jeremiah's face.

Evalene blinked furiously, trying to erase the image. She stared aimlessly at the shadows by the tent wall rather than close her eyes and risk seeing the vision again.

The sound of footsteps crunching in the dirt and gravel signaled Olive at the entrance of their tent what felt like ages later, though it was probably only an hour, two at the most.

"Evie! You're here!" the shadow of the blonde girl chirped from the doorway. Evalene rolled back towards the inside of the tent and lifted herself up to rest on her elbows as Olive entered, grateful at the interruption from her thoughts.

"What're you doing in the dark?" the girl asked. The sound of a match sizzled as a tiny flame appeared. Olive held the match to the candle and the room lit up.

"Oh, sorry, I didn't mean to wake you," Olive said as soon as the light showed Evalene in bed under the blankets. Olive's apologetic face was illuminated by the dim light and her hair glowed golden-orange.

"Don't worry, I wasn't sleeping" Evalene told her, sitting up on her elbow to prove it was fine. "What did you do today?"

Olive hopped up onto her bed across from Evalene and sighed, biting her lip and starting to smile. "I was helping Luc go over details. Get organized." She brushed her wavy blonde hair off her shoulders, then leaned forward towards Evalene, not noticing this made the golden locks fall back in front again. She whispered confidentially, "I think he likes me."

"Oh?" Evalene propped her head on her hand, smiling. "Did he say something?"

Olive grinned like a school girl. "Well... no, he hasn't said it straight out yet, but I'm pretty sure. I wish he followed me around like the captain shadows you." She kicked off her flats and they flew haphazardly, one in the direction of the door and the other under Evalene's bed.

Sitting up, Evalene ignored the shoes. "You're talking about... Jeremiah? And... me?" Pointing a finger to herself, she laughed a little in confusion.

Olive was taking off the many layers of Evalene's dress, which she loved to borrow, giving Evalene an excuse to keep wearing her dresses. In the middle of stepping out of the skirt, one foot in and one foot out Olive paused. "Yeah, you! He was looking all over for you earlier."

Evalene rolled her eyes as Olive dropped the skirt on the ground. Taking two steps to Evalene's cot, Olive hopped up onto it, forcing Evalene to move her legs or be sat on. "I'm not joking!"

"I've only known him a few days," Evalene reminded her, eyebrows raised.

Olive shrugged, pulling her bare feet under the blankets to get comfortable and sitting cross-legged. "A few days is all it takes."

Evalene squinted at Olive as the girl wiggled her eyebrows suggestively. "What takes? What are you talking about?"

"I can tell you like him," Olive said, ignoring Evalene's questions. "You stare at him when he's not looking." The girl was a born romantic. But it didn't matter, even if Evalene did think

Jeremiah was kind, or thoughtful, or handsome. He'd made it clear how he felt about her.

"Olive, no." Evalene lightly kicked her through the blankets to get her attention. "Stop."

"You really expect me to believe you don't like him?"

"It's not important." Evalene rolled her eyes. "He's leading a revolution. And he's not interested. He made that extremely clear. He feels responsible for me." Evalene spread her fingers out across the faded pattern of her quilt, pressing it down until it was flat and smooth.

"What? When did he say that?" Olive asked.

A sigh slipped out. "Tonight in the kitchen."

"Oh."

They sat in silence.

Olive spoke up. "That's a shame because I just spoke to him on my way back. We made plans to take you job hunting in Hofyn in the morning." Olive hopped down from Evalene's bed and moved to her own, climbing in under the blankets.

"What?" Evalene blurted, sitting up now. "What do you mean you 'made plans?'"

Olive flopped her head onto the pillow dramatically. "I'm sorry." She fiddled with a tiny string that had unraveled from her blanket and mumbled, "I just wanted to be a matchmaker. I thought you liked him, and he liked you…"

"Mmm-hmm." Evalene sighed, rubbing her eyes as she lay back down, rolling onto her back to stare at the slanted ceiling, mulling it over. "I guess it would be nice to see what jobs are available in the city…"

"Perfect!" Olive snuffed the candle out and the tent returned to blackness. In the dark, Evalene heard rustling as Olive got comfortable. "I'll wake you in the morning. Goodnight!"

"Goodnight, Olive. Sweet dreams."

Evalene pulled her own blankets up to her chin to cocoon herself in their warmth, exhausted. She squeezed her eyes shut against the images of Jeremiah and the revolutionaries against the rebels, tossing and turning, unable to escape them until finally, sleep came.

26

Day Two: Hofyn

EVALENE AND OLIVE SWUNG through the cook tent in the morning, picking up breakfast to go. The pastry melted in Evalene's mouth, soft and sweet. If not for the daunting job search, this day would have been perfect.

"We should get you some new clothes and shoes too," Olive said as they passed one of the training squares, already in full swing. This square was working on assembling their firearms, which were unusually sleek and lightweight, with some kind of technology attached that pinpointed their targets for them with amazing accuracy.

"I don't have enough money to buy anything," Evalene said. What was she going to do about that? She didn't even have enough money to buy food for a week, much less clothes. She'd spent most of what Kevra had left her on boarding the ship.

"Don't worry, you'll get a job in no time," Olive reassured her. She clapped her hands excitedly. "You could come work on the farm with me!"

"Maybe," Evalene agreed, just to get Olive to breathe again. "I've never worked on a farm…"

"Oh it's easy!" Olive grinned. "The machines do most of the work for us. We have chickens, pigs, and cows, but mostly crops. We plant in the spring, work the fields all summer, and harvest in the fall. Our best crop is potatoes."

The farm sounded much more advanced than those on Eden. "I like potatoes," Evalene offered, trying to be open to the idea. After all, this was her one and only friend in the world. Might be nice to stay on the island for a while before taking another ship to the FreeLands. One thing was for sure: either way, she needed a job.

"Me too," Olive smiled contentedly. Evalene found she admired that about the girl. Living in the moment instead of in constant fear of the future. But the quiet only lasted a few moments.

They met up with Jeremiah at the edge of camp. "Shall we?" he said, and they set off towards the city. A soft, orange mulch covered the path and paved the way. The carrot colored dust of the mulch settled onto Evalene's black boots as they walked.

From the camp, the smaller homes and buildings on the outskirts looked like bubbles with their glass dome ceilings. The bright sun shone through openings between skyscrapers where pieces of the buildings would branch away from each other, only to weave back in and meld together at the top, like a work of art.

"We need to take her shopping first," Olive said, walking in the middle of the path between Evalene and Jeremiah. Evalene tried to catch her eye to shake her head no, but Olive was distracted. "Have any refugees from the last trip decided to stay with us?"

"Yes, ten people so far," Jeremiah told her, leaning past Olive to wink at Evalene as they walked, "eleven if I can convince one more."

"Did the captain tell you about the broadcasts?" Olive chimed in, swinging around to face Evalene as they walked, not waiting for an answer. "We're going to use live TV, take it over, and convince the entire country to stand up and fight with us. Everything the Number One says on the news is full of lies, so we're going to tell the truth!"

"Ahh…" Evalene said, then risked asking, "What truth?"

"So many truths!" Olive spoke again before Jeremiah had a chance. "For one thing, there's still dozens of other surviving countries. I'm pretty sure Eden doesn't want anyone to know that."

Evalene's jaw dropped. In basic school, she and her classmates had watched a program on other nations. As they watched blurry footage of a people shooting at each other in a countryside, falling and dying on both sides, a voice had narrated the scene. "Out of just a few countries left after the bombing, Eden is the only country that isn't plagued by war and disease. These other nations constantly fight over their place in the world and their possessions. Each day is a struggle to survive." But Hofyn wasn't like that, at least not so far. And now Olive was saying it wasn't the only one?

Evalene was distracted from Olive's conversation by the city. She held back a gasp as they drew closer. The towers were built out of an unusual clear metal, allowing light to pour into every corner of the city, which was made up of layers. People walked along avenues in the sky as well as on the ground. As they reached the paved road into the city, near enough now to get a better picture, it looked like glass, but it couldn't be. The translucent paths in the sky from one building to the next appeared so fragile from this vantage point on the ground, some so high up they looked like the neck of a wine glass, yet they held up under the weight of multiple cars as well as people, all crossing from one building to the next above them. The cars made box-shaped shadows on the ground below, and tinier ant-sized shadows indicated people.

Not a single citizen looked down out of fear; all strode confidently towards their goals. All the women in Hofyn wore pants. It made sense with those paths. But the thought of traveling those dizzying heights without anything to block her view was enough to cause panic without the added concern of passersby looking up her dress. She wished she'd worn her leggings today.

The city came to life as they moved further into it. A sidewalk began on the next street, which widened to allow for more traffic. Surrounded by strangely designed stores with harsh music blaring out onto the street, Evalene watched strangers push past them on both sides, all confident like high Numbers, but wearing the strangest mix of bright colors and patterns, with sheer cut outs, or beading, or feathers on their clothing. Something felt off about them, but Evalene couldn't put her finger on it.

Unusually short cars, barely large enough to hold two people, lined both sides of the street, rocketing past them on silent engines, slowing and swerving around each other. Soft whooshing sounds and conversation filled the air until a honk startled her. Jeremiah let Olive go ahead, staying next to Evalene as she took it all in.

"The city can be a bit much your first time. I remember when I came here a few years back. You'll get used to it."

Evalene nodded, blinking. A roar sounded in the sky above, growing louder like thunder. She flinched and looked up in time to glimpse a huge machine between two skyscrapers above them as it flew past. Its huge shadow passed over them in an instant. "Was that –?"

"A plane," Jeremiah confirmed, smiling openly at her now. They'd stopped moving, but he didn't seem to mind.

She swallowed, clearing her throat, trying not to appear as shocked as she felt. "It looked like it was going to crash into the city!"

"They do fly pretty low when they're landing, but they don't hit anything," he reassured her with a calm shake of his head, resuming their walk. "The airstrip is just on the other side of Hofyn."

Evalene nodded again, wide-eyed. Olive danced back towards them. "Come on, I know the perfect place to start!" She waved for them to follow, and took off again. The deeper into the city they went, the taller the buildings became until Evalene thought if it wasn't for the glass architecture allowing sunlight to filter down to the street, they'd be walking in deep shadows. Advertisements covered every wall that wasn't clear, as well as every sign post, bench, and bus that passed. *New Skin! Why look your age if you don't have to?*

Olive stopped at a storefront with human-sized dolls in the window wearing vivid colors and pants, even on the women. She disappeared inside. When they caught up, Jeremiah held open the door for Evalene to go inside first.

The fluorescent lights in the store lit up any nook and cranny that the sun didn't. As they crossed the threshold, a bell chimed, alerting the rest of the store to their arrival. Joy swelled up in Evalene at the simple fact that she was shopping. She hadn't gone out to buy clothes or anything else, besides household supplies for Daeva, since her mother died.

She reached out to touch a bright yellow pantsuit made of leather. Out of the corner of her eye, she saw a woman march towards her. Evalene tore her hands off the material, wishing they hadn't come in. She kept her eyes on the ground and felt her shoulders hunch forward.

"My, my, what a beautiful dress!" the woman chirped. "Welcome to my store! Are we here for a special occasion? Or just browsing?"

Evalene waited for Jeremiah to answer as the higher Number, but he didn't speak. She risked a glance at the shopkeeper and found the woman was smiling kindly, waiting for her to answer. Evalene said the first thing that came to her mind, half-whispering, "Pants?"

"Oh, creative freedom, I love it!" the woman exclaimed, whirling towards the closest rack. "So many different styles and colors to choose from – where to even start?" Evalene found herself hustled into a dressing room as the shopkeeper hung over a dozen full outfits on the wall inside, including shoes, leaving with a breezy, "Get started with those – don't worry, I can bring more!" The door swung shut.

Overwhelmed, Evalene touched the fabrics hanging on the

wall. She didn't know where to start. She passed over the rougher materials and the ones with strange straps that didn't make sense, pulling the softest out from under the rest. She tried it on and immediately fell in love. The pantsuit was a soft material that rippled around her like a dress but accentuated her legs instead of hiding them, making her feel daring. The sleeveless top was attached, making the whole outfit one piece, and it had a modest turtleneck for a neckline. Best of all, it was purple. She'd never worn purple in her entire life.

Next, Evalene tried on the different shoes, finding that the second pair of sandals were just her size. The woman had a talent for guessing correctly. She ignored the rest of the options on the wall, tucking the necklace from her father underneath the top and stepping out of the dressing room still wearing the outfit and sandals. She held her old boots and Olive's dress in her hand. A huge mirror stretched from floor to ceiling directly outside her dressing room. She barely recognized the girl in the mirror. Brown hair hung daringly around her shoulders, covering the left side of neck completely and framing her face. She'd transformed into a different person in the purple pantsuit. The blue scarf wasn't even needed – the neckline of the pantsuit rose halfway up her neck, covering her tattoo on its own. She pulled the scarf off. It felt like another step towards freedom.

She smiled at the stranger in the mirror. Olive stopped flipping through hangers, coming over to the mirror to swoon over the outfit. "Oh Evie, it's perfect!"

Jeremiah pointed towards Evalene from where he stood by the register talking to the shopkeeper. She replied, and he nodded, handing a few pieces of paper to her before he came over to join the girls.

"Doesn't she look amazing?" Olive asked him, grinning between the two of them.

"It looks good on you. You'll fit right in," Jeremiah agreed, although Evalene wished Olive hadn't prompted him so she could know if he meant it.

Pulling out all the coins she had left, Evalene asked, "How much is it?"

"I took care of it," Jeremiah told her. "Hofyn uses paper currency, so coins from Eden aren't always accepted, but you can pay me back later."

Evalene took a deep breath, wanting to push until she found out the cost, but not wanting to argue in front of the shopkeeper. If she couldn't afford to pay him back, she would have to return it.

"Oh wow, I'm late for my appointment!" Olive said, distracting her as she hugged Evalene and waved to Jeremiah, hurrying towards the exit. The bell chimed as she opened the door. "I'm sorry I can't stay, but I'll meet you back at camp!" And with that she was gone. Very subtle. Leaving her alone with Jeremiah. Evalene kept her eyes lowered, avoiding his gaze.

The shopkeeper rounded the counter, holding a plastic bag for Evalene to put her dress and boots inside. She walked with them to the front door. Jeremiah held it open again, but before Evalene could pass through, the shopkeeper stopped her with a hand on her arm, whispering confidentially, "I hope I'm not being too forward, but where did you go for your New Skin? I've been looking everywhere for a place that can do a BioGrade as nicely as yours!"

Evalene glanced at the woman and then Jeremiah, confused. "I'm sorry?"

"Psshh, no need to be coy with me!" the shopkeeper chuckled. "I passed my 150th birthday a few years back myself." Evalene stared at the woman who still grasped her arm, studying her face. Her skin was nearly wrinkle-free, her dark hair didn't show a single gray, and her teeth were white and straight. She couldn't possibly be over 40, much less over a hundred.

Jeremiah subtly nodded. Was that a hint to go along with the fantasy? "Congratulations, that's... an accomplishment," Evalene stuttered, "but I'm... I'm only 18."

"That's not possible!" The woman shook her head so violently that she shook Evalene's arm a little as well. "I saw wisdom in your eyes the moment you walked in the door. You can pretend with me," she winked, "but I know better."

Jeremiah cleared his throat, finally jumping in. "Actually, Evie is from Eden. Most of the population has never heard of BioGrading. You know how strained the political relationships are there." He shrugged. "If anyone does use it, it's a well-kept secret."

"You're kidding." The woman gasped, turning to Evalene. "You're only 18-years-old?" At Evalene's nod, she sung out, "Oh bless your heart, sweet thing. I've heard about what goes on in that God-forsaken country. Shameful. Treating people like that. It's inhuman!" She pulled Evalene into her arms, squeezing her in an emotional hug.

Smothered in the woman's sweater, Evalene just nodded. Thankfully, that was enough to satisfy her. "You two have a wonderful day. You take her to see everything, you hear?" The shopkeeper shook a finger at Jeremiah as she moved to begin tidying up the dressing room. "Come back anytime!" she hollered after them as Jeremiah led the way outside, the bell chiming again as they left.

"A hundred and fifty?" Evalene waited until the door closed and they'd walked a dozen feet down the block before she spoke. "That's almost as old as World War III, can you imagine?"

But Jeremiah grinned at her, watching her face as he said, "It's true."

"You're kidding!" Evalene stopped where she stood in the middle of the sidewalk, forcing people to go around them.

"No, she's probably even older than that but won't admit it." Jeremiah stopped too. "Most of the people on the island are her age or older. When the scientists here realized the chemical warfare made most women sterile, they threw all their energy into 'living forever.' BioGrading is done by almost everyone."

"BioGrading," Evalene repeated, ignoring the sound of another plane going past.

"Sorry, yes," Jeremiah gestured to the advertisements she'd noticed earlier but hadn't paid any attention. "Biological Upgrading. It's a bit like the old-world botox."

When Evalene shook her head, not recognizing the term, he scratched his neck again, searching for the right explanation. "It's something to do with cloning. They can replicate just about any organ now, except the brain." He shrugged. "It's expensive, but most people say it's worth it. Right now, life expectancy is a few hundred years."

He began walking again, and Evalene jumped to keep up. "That's crazy!"

"I know," Jeremiah smiled as he agreed. "The scientists who created BioGrading say life could go on forever in theory if they could find a way to clone the brain. But once dementia sets in, no amount of new skin or organs can save anyone."

Suddenly the strangeness Evalene hadn't been able to pinpoint earlier hit her. Every single person who passed them was young. She didn't spot a single gray hair in the crowd. They paid for biological enhancements?

"Why didn't she ask Olive how old she was?" Evalene asked.

Jeremiah chuckled. "Olive is pretty well known around here. She's sort of a prodigy, one of the few children to have been born on Hofyn. That's why she left for her appointment with the fertility clinic." He pointed to the left, towards the heart of the city, where the buildings were so tall they were lost in the clouds. "She goes there at least once a week for tests. The fertility issue is also a huge part of why they're so welcoming to our refugees, because I think they hope we'll bring some new blood and somehow resolve the problem."

He stopped outside a building that Evalene guessed to be a restaurant, since it had dozens of tables and chairs with place settings neatly made up, but the entire inside wall was an enormous tank filled with water, sand, coral, and multi-colored fish swimming about, as if you were sitting in the middle of an ocean. "This would be a fun place to work. Want to start here?" Jeremiah asked. "Or we could visit some of the nearby clothing stores or hotels if you'd prefer to apply there—"

Evalene forced herself to cut in and ask, "Luc said there are teams set up to help people find jobs here. Why are you helping me?

Rubbing the stubble on his jaw, the rough hairs against Jeremiah's fingers made a chafing sound. "That's true," he admitted, "but it's my fault that you're tangled up with revolutionaries instead of on your way to the FreeLands. When Olive asked, I thought it was a good idea."

Evalene felt her shoulders hunch at the reminder. That's right, it wasn't his idea. It was Olive's attempt at matchmaking. He was just being kind. She cleared her throat, wishing she hadn't said anything, and dropped the subject, gesturing to the fish diner. "This will work."

They sat at a vacant table and Jeremiah picked up a miniature computer resting on the table, showing her how to create an account, typing her answers to questions on the keyboard and using other buttons she didn't understand. White spots danced in front of her eyes and she tried to hide her anxiety. She'd never used a computer in her life.

"Okay Hiccups," he said when her breath hitched a third time and she didn't catch it in time to hide the peep. He winked at her. "Deep breaths. Try to relax."

The corners of Evalene's mouth twitched. She tried to follow his advice, taking a few shallow, shaky breaths. It took the two of them nearly an hour to fill out that first application, listing Jeremiah as her reference and the camp as her temporary address. But once it was turned in she breathed a sigh of relief. This was possible. Hard, but possible.

After that, they walked in and out of store after store, faster each time. Hotels, gift shops, restaurants, and anything else she showed a hint of interest in, he took her inside for an application. Each time they left, he reminded her of a street marker or another easy way to find the business, so she could find her way back in the future. That more than anything else caused the pressure building in her chest.

"Alright." He stopped on a street corner under another blaring advertisement. A sing-song voice in the background sang a jingle reminding people they weren't getting any younger. "Let's take a break. I'm sure all these places would love to hire you. They all know Eden refugees are hard workers. You won't have a problem getting a job. But what do *you* want to do for work?"

Evalene bit her lip and shrugged. She didn't have any talents or skills besides low Number jobs. "This is fine. I'll do anything."

"Evie," he raised an eyebrow at her, crossing his arms, "I can't help you if don't at least try. Just tell me some things that you enjoy doing. Anything."

She glanced around them for inspiration. The men and women walking by scared her. All so confident, so certain of themselves. The clothing was bizarre. She knew how to sew, a little bit. Maybe she would enjoy working with clothes? She studied the woman walking by specifically. One wore a pantsuit covered in feathers that formed wings on her shoulders, all of which swayed in the wind as she walked. Another wore a similar costume with stripes instead of feathers, but the outfit ended in shorts, with a half skirt attached to the back, making it look like a jumper from the front, and a dress from the back. A third woman strode by going the other way in a creamy sheer ensemble with sequins making a wild pattern across it, so see-through that the sequins only just barely covered her up. Averting her eyes, Evalene shook her head at the idea. Not fashion.

Jeremiah waited. He wasn't going to budge without an answer. Back home, there was only one thing Evalene truly enjoyed, and she knew it wasn't what he wanted to hear. But she didn't know what else to say. "I like to read…" she finally told the sidewalk.

When he didn't say anything, she risked looking up at him, expecting disappointment. But he had a small smile on his face. "Come with me." He waited for traffic to pass before crossing the street, waving for her to follow. He kept a brisk pace, and they walked side by side, taking twists and turns until Evalene was completely lost. The thought of navigating this city on her own was daunting.

When she didn't keep up, Jeremiah slowed and tugged at her hand. She felt a flutter at the warmth. Her whole hand tingled and the heat spread up her arm. But he didn't hold on, simply got her attention to turn down a different street and let go as if it was nothing. She wiggled her fingers to shake off the feeling.

They walked until blisters began to form on her feet from the new sandals. The bag holding her dress and boots grew heavier. Jeremiah offered to hold it, but she politely declined. When they rounded a corner on a quieter street, he stopped so abruptly she almost ran into him. The building was made of that same shiny clear metal, so much like a mirror that she could see her reflection in the exterior. Instead of a tall, angled roof, they'd built the top of the building completely flat and cultivated a garden on top, the tallest plants peeking out above the edge. The lettering across the doorway read Hofyn Library.

He'd brought her to a building full of books.

A more perfect job had never crossed her mind. Jeremiah smiled at the expression on her face. Eyes wide, she took in the walls upon walls of books, the different couches and chairs lining the walls and dotted across the room, and the curved staircase in the center of the building that led to the garden on top. Elated, Evalene raced ahead of Jeremiah up the stairs into the building. Though it took twice as long, she insisted on filling out the application herself. It needed to be just right. She asked Jeremiah to check it for errors not just once, but twice.

When Jeremiah pulled the front door of the library open afterward, the bright sun hit Evalene's eyes, making her blink out of her daze. She must have looked overwhelmed because he took her hand and squeezed once before letting go, causing her heart to beat a new and different panic rhythm. And this time, when Jeremiah let go, Evalene wished he hadn't. The warmth of his palm in hers was a comforting distraction.

Without needing to talk about it, they made their way out of the city, knowing this was the last application. Nothing else came close. He made sure to point out the nearby landmarks and roads once again so that she'd have no trouble finding her way back to the huge building.

Evalene felt as if she were walking two feet taller on the way back. Finally something she was good at. Not just something any person could be good at, but specifically her. As they travelled out of the city and its suburbs, reaching the orange gravel path back to camp, she got up the nerve to speak. "Thank you. For all your help."

"No problem." Jeremiah brushed it off with the wave of his hand. "Make sure to go back a few times with Olive to get familiar with the city before you explore it alone. It's easy to get lost. And make sure Olive shows you some boarding houses too. You can stay in the camp as long as it's open," he added for the second time that day. "The tents will stay up at least another month after we're gone. But it's good to be prepared."

Evalene nodded. Her chest felt tight and heavy, as if something heavier than Jeremiah's submarine sat on it.

"Don't worry, Hiccups." He smiled reassuringly, as if reading her mind. "Deep breaths, remember?" Evalene felt the nickname almost as much as she heard it, like a warm blanket wrapped around her snugly, comforting.

Neither of them said a word until they reached the camp. As they crested the last hill and the tents came into sight, Evalene frowned. "Hey, don't worry, I'm not going anywhere," Jeremiah said, bumping her arm lightly as he stepped towards the camp. But then he stopped, shook his head, and half turned toward her. "Well, I mean, I am going *somewhere*…"

She knew she was supposed to laugh at the bad joke. But she pictured the hangings from the Bloom Rebellion, and she couldn't.

They stopped where tent paths crossed, Evalene standing on the one that led to her tent, and Jeremiah at the beginning of the path towards the council tent. "We may not run into each other again before I go," he said. "But if you change your mind about joining us, let me know, okay?"

Evalene nodded. "Thank you again." What else could she say? *Don't go?*

"No problem, Hiccups." He grinned at her, turned, and strode away. Evalene stood in the middle of the path, not moving, staring at the man she hadn't even known a week ago as he disappeared around a corner. Why did the idea of never seeing him again make her so miserable?

27

Day Two: The Dream

AFTER JEREMIAH WAS OUT of sight, Evalene wandered aimlessly for a while, watching the training squares out of curiosity. She saw a few women fighting. The desire to learn how to fight and take control of her life was overwhelming. But the thought of the bookstore also beckoned her. She stopped at the cook tent and passed through the lunch line on her own, not sure if Olive was back yet, and afterwards she made her way back to her tent. Only when she stepped inside and set down her bag with the old clothes and boots did it occur to her that she'd never paid Jeremiah back for her new clothing.

Outside the tent, Olive's voice yelled, growing louder as she drew up to it. "Evie! Evie guess what? Grandma Mae's here!" A second later, the flap busted open with a loud slap. "Evie, guess what?"

Evalene laughed. "I heard you. Your grandma is here in camp?"

Olive spun around, flipping the tent door open. "C'mon, I want you to meet her!" Olive disappeared from the tent as quickly as she'd entered.

"Sure," Evalene said to the empty tent, "I'll meet your grandmother."

They strolled towards the front of the camp where Evalene had first entered it by the docks. Or rather, Evalene strolled, despite Olive's urging, while Olive skipped ahead and back again like Jeremiah's dog, chattering excitedly. The sun was shining and the birds were singing. The sound would forever remind her of freedom. Evalene could've watched the birds soar and dip through the sky for hours.

Olive took her to an enormous tent, almost as large as the cook tent. A sign post out front read Council Chambers. They reached it just as people began flowing out the tent flaps, signaling the end of a meeting. The council members travelled around the girls where they stood in the middle of the packed dirt between the tents until a white-haired lady appeared and made her way towards them, holding her arms out towards Olive.

"Hello, lovey," the elderly woman said, hugging Olive affectionately. Her voice was warm. "Who's your friend?" The wrinkles around her eyes deepened as she smiled kindly at Evalene. Her neck was bare of any decoration or scarf, and her snowy white hair swept over her shoulders and all the way down her back, revealing bare skin on the left side of her neck, completely whole and unscarred by any tattoo, just like Olive's.

Olive stepped back cheerfully, swinging around to wave an arm towards Evalene. "This is my friend, Evie. She came over on this last mission. Evie, this is my Grandma Mae who I've been telling you about!"

Evalene lowered her eyes in respect and murmured, "Nice to

meet you, ma'am."

But Mae reached out her hands to take Evalene's, holding them between her own. Her brown eyes were sharp and intelligent, and her strong gaze held Evalene's as she said, "Evie. Wonderful to meet you." Warming to the older woman, Evalene managed to squeeze back slightly before she pulled her hands away.

Olive tugged on both her grandmother's and Evalene's arms. "C'mon, let's go to the beach!" She let go and took off ahead of them towards the ocean.

Evalene was surprised that Mae tolerated Olive's behavior, but the older woman just smiled over at Evalene as they followed. "Olive's always been quick to make friends," Mae told her, "but she's really taken to you. I'm glad."

Though Evalene smiled her thanks, she doubted that. Olive barely knew her. They walked in silence down the packed sand that led to the beach. As they went the sand softened, making it harder to continue the swift pace, until Evalene was breathing hard to keep up with the elderly woman. Out of the corner of her eye, Evalene studied Mae's muscled arms and deeply tanned skin from spending her days working in the sun. That, plus her dark brown eyes, only made her long, white hair stand out more. She didn't look like the people in town with the BioGrading that Jeremiah talked about, but neither did she seem slowed by age.

Olive sat on a log on the beach right next to the water, each wave that came in licking her toes before receding back again. Her long blonde hair blew in the wind, wild and free. Evalene felt her own hair waving as well, though it felt far less majestic, whipping across her face and eyes.

Mae settled onto the log next to Olive, and Evalene stood to the side, feeling a bit like she was intruding.

"Grandma," Olive was frowning at the water, "where are mom and dad? Did something happen?"

"No, love," Mae said, leaning on a thick branch sticking up near her end of the log. Her hair was so long, the wind lifted only the last few inches. "Your parents went to New Haven for supplies. They're fine. Everyone is fine."

Olive breathed out and visibly relaxed. But a moment later her forehead wrinkled in a frown again. "Well then, why are you here? You never come to camp unless you need help – are you here to make me come home?" Her words turned into a whine at the end of her question. "Please don't make me come home."

But Mae shook her head. "Not just yet, love. Don't worry. I came with a message for Jeremiah and the council."

At that, Evalene perked up where she'd stood staring out at the ocean pretending not to eavesdrop on a family conversation. Olive's eyes widened as well and she grinned. "What kind of message?"

"It's a secret until the council makes their decision," Mae said, and her calm demeanor changed into a frown for the first time.

"Oh please tell us, Grandma Mae," Olive begged, "Please? We won't tell anyone, will we, Evie?"

Evalene nodded agreement, coming to sit on the log on the other side of Olive. But Mae's mind was made up. "You will have to wait and hear like everyone else."

"When will the council decide?" Olive asked after a moment of silence.

Mae raised a brow at her granddaughter, and Olive surprised Evalene by dropping it. But after a moment, Mae answered her question. "They'll need to make their decision by tomorrow at the latest, so I'm sure you'll hear then. Jeremiah called for the council to take a break when I left. It's likely they're meeting again now."

With curiosity swimming in her head, Evalene went to dinner with Olive and her grandmother. They sat outside, able to find a few seats open on a bench with a simple wooden table.

"Olive, why don't you come with me to the farm tomorrow instead of waiting until they leave on Sunday?" The older woman dipped her spoon into the hot soup and took a bite.

"But Grandma, I was hoping to stay here for..." she glanced over where Luc sat at another table nearby, "For Evie, and... others..." she trailed off.

Grandma Mae shook her head firmly. "You've been gone long enough. There is too much to do for one old woman, especially with your parents gone for a few days. Chores are falling behind. We'll sleep here tonight and leave in the morning."

Olive bowed her head, uncharacteristically silent. Evalene was impressed. This woman demanded respect.

As dusk settled over the camp, Mae left to speak with the council. Olive brought Evalene to a bonfire near the council tent that was surrounded by a large group of people. Only an hour or two later, Luc and Jeremiah wandered in to sit on the other side of the fire, deep in conversation, and Evalene understood why they'd been waiting there. Olive, like a magnet, found her way to Luc's side not long afterward. While she attempted banter with Luc, Jeremiah was approached by one refugee after another, in constant dialogue with someone.

Comfortable in her silence, Evalene enjoyed staring into the flames. The darkness fell quickly, cooling the air around them until the breeze was chilly and everyone scooted closer to the fire. The twinkling flames rose high as logs were added. The fiery orange blaze showed hints of blue.

From their vantage point on top of a hill, Evalene saw the light of similar bonfires throughout the camp. She could get used to nights spent like this. Eavesdropping on bits and pieces of conversations around her, Evalene smiled behind her hands as Olive bothered Luc into leaving. When he stood to go, Olive stood as well, asking him to walk her to her tent. That made him stretch and sit back down, deciding to "stay a while longer." But Olive was nothing if not persistent, and eventually Luc gave in.

The clusters of people around the fire grew smaller. Sometime past midnight, Evalene found she was the only one left on her side. Jeremiah said his goodbyes to the man he'd been talking to, coming around the fire to sit on the log next to her. They were the only ones still out. It must be late. But Evalene was wide awake.

"Hey, Hiccups." The nickname endeared him to her. She smiled and nodded hello.

The fire flickered, casting a warm reddish-orange glow across his face. He looked tired. Distracted. Not wanting to interrupt his thoughts, she sat with him in quiet support.

He finally spoke. "I saw you and Olive with Magnolia – Grandma Mae – earlier. Did she tell you about her dream?"

Mae had mentioned a message for the council, but no dream. Evalene shook her head.

"What do you think would happen if I sent every frightened person home?"

Evalene was confused. "Didn't you already do that when you gave people the option to join you or stay on the island?"

Jeremiah nodded. "Yes, but God spoke to Magnolia in a dream that if we went into battle with the men and women we have now, we would lose. But if we told every person who was afraid and having second thoughts about the fight to stay behind, we would win."

Evalene laughed a little. "But... it's just a dream?" she said, turning it into a question at the end when she realized he was serious.

"Not in Magnolia's case." Jeremiah shook his head. "Over the years, God has spoken to her through her dreams more times than we can count." There was that idea again, that God could speak to someone other than the priests or the Number One. Evalene felt the urge to look around, to make sure no one was listening. But maybe it wasn't heresy on the island?

Jeremiah's eyes were steady and sincere as they gazed into her own. "Magnolia was the one who advised the people on Hofyn that we were coming a whole year before Welder and I even arrived on our scouting mission." He laughed, shaking his head in wonder. "I'll never forget stepping onto the island and being greeted by a welcoming committee who brought us to the tents, already set up to hold thousands. Not everyone in Hofyn believes in God, but those who do saved for an entire year to buy this land where we sit and the tents we sleep and work in so that we could have a place to stay and prepare for the revolution."

Evalene tried to picture that. "How did Mae convince them?" It was hard to fathom anyone listening to a dream like that before there was even a hint that the refugees were coming. But it was equally hard to declare it a coincidence.

"You should ask her sometime to tell you some of her stories. I think the one that caused people to start listening was about twenty years ago, before Olive was born. Olive's parents were barren, just like most people on the island, though they tried for almost fifteen years to have children. They had given up, and were in line for some of the BioGrading surgeries, which would've lowered their chances of conception to less than one in a million. But Mae had a dream that they would have a daughter. So they withdrew their names from the operations, and they waited. It was three long years before Olive was born. She is one of the island's rare miracle babies."

"Wow." Evalene didn't know what to say. She found herself wanting to believe it was true. Had Mae seen the future somehow? Was it possible God really spoke to people?

Jeremiah shifted to face her again. "It's okay if you don't believe in it."

Unable to help herself, Evalene met his gaze. "But you do?"

Instead of immediately answering yes or no, Jeremiah closed his eyes, frowning in concentration. After a moment he opened them, and his brown eyes were clear and focused. "I do." He smiled to himself, staring into the fire. Turning to her, his eyes were sincere. "Thank you. You've helped more than you know." Staring into the fire, he said, "I talked to Luc and the council all day, and we didn't get anywhere. But you just reminded me how simple it is."

Evalene opened her mouth, struggling to form the right words. "What are you going to do?"

He turned his focus back to her. "I'm going to obey." And he smiled confidently, as if he expected to have ten thousand more men instead of the opposite.

How could he have more conviction in this one moment than Evalene had ever had in her entire life? She found herself wanting to believe that he could do it. That maybe God really did promise them a victory. It just made her wish even more that she was brave enough to join them.

Was this how her mother had felt? Evalene wanted to be more like Pearl, but instead, she favored her father and his inability to act or stand up for himself. She regretted judging him so harshly.

Jeremiah took a deep breath, pulling her out of her musings. "I need to go talk to the council immediately. We have to make a decision tonight." Always so direct. He stood.

Clearing her throat, Evalene wished she had time to talk to him more. She had so many questions. "Aren't you afraid?"

Jeremiah took her question seriously, not answering right away. He stared into the fire, shifting his feet as he did. Though it brought him closer to Evalene, she still felt safe. Somewhere in the last few days, she'd decided to trust him.

"If you think about it," he finally answered, "I would only be afraid if I didn't believe that God was with us."

"But you do."

She heard a hint of a smile in his voice as Jeremiah agreed. "Yes."

"How?"

Again, he took her seriously, not just throwing out a nice-sounding answer, but considering her question. "You know how back home all the priests talk about how faith is a feeling?"

Evalene thought of the way Numbers came to priests as impressions, a feeling from God that they could sense. "Mmmhmm."

"That never made sense to me. Especially when my parents died. If faith was a feeling, then it would disappear whenever bad things – whenever life – happened. Whenever you needed it most." His voice was low, full of emotion. "It wasn't until I met a wise woman a few years ago that I realized faith is the exact opposite."

"What do you mean?" Evalene frowned in confusion, distracted by the mention of a woman. Did he mean Mae? He would've said her name if he'd meant her. Maybe he had a girlfriend back in Eden? Was that the reason he chose to fight?

Jeremiah sat back down, angling to face her. "Well, who gave you your Number?"

"God did." Evalene repeated the answer she'd heard her whole life.

"Well, that's what they tell you. But who actually did your tattoo?"

"One of the priests…"

"Right. And you decided, because everyone else did, that it was from God." Jeremiah's gaze was intense. Evalene didn't know what to say.

"So, let me ask you this: what do you think is your Number?" Jeremiah continued as the fire flickered.

"You know what it is." Evalene felt herself shrink at the reminder of how little she was worth.

But Jeremiah shook his head. "I know what your tattoo says, but what do *you* think your Number is?"

"It doesn't matter what I think it is," her voice cracked. "I'm a twenty-nine."

His voice was gentle. "Are you? Or did you decide that was your Number because everyone else said it was?" Jeremiah pointed to her neck, where the tattoo lay underneath the blue scarf. "You're still choosing to believe that Number is yours. That people have Numbers at all."

"But it's who I am," she whispered, tears filling her eyes.

"We're not even in Eden anymore." Passion filled his voice. "Numbers don't exist here. Don't you see? You're making a choice to believe that it's who you are." He lowered his voice, trying to be quiet for the sake of those sleeping nearby. "It's the same way for faith."

Maybe because it was so late or maybe it was her emotions getting in the way, but she didn't understand. "What do you mean?"

"I'm saying believing you have a Number is a choice, and so is faith in God."

A choice?

Had the priests back home ever said anything like that? Not one came to mind. The idea of him choosing to believe in God – no, more than that – choosing to believe that God cared enough to fight for him, mystified her.

"I'm sorry I need to go call an emergency council meeting,"

Jeremiah said, moving away from the fire. "But we can talk more tomorrow if you'd like?"

Evalene nodded, wanting to hear more, wanting to spend more time with him, wanting to believe that the dream would come true so she could come with him. But she only said, "I understand. Goodnight."

"Goodnight," he replied, turning and disappearing into the darkness. Evalene sat alone at the fire staring in the direction he'd gone and fighting the urge to chase after him. The more she tried not to think about the revolution, the more she thought of home, of her father, and Violet, and Fleur, and even Daeva, still living in the world that she'd fled. She tried to remember the library job, to tell herself she would enjoy it, that she could find a way to move past her Number. Without joining this fight. But all she could think about was doing exactly that.

28

Day Three: The Announcement

T HE NEXT MORNING, THEY stood in line for the second breakfast shift. The line stretched all the way around the cook tent, making a full circle. Olive, Evalene, and Grandma Mae were all the way in the back, only a few feet from where the front of the line started. Normally the breakfast rush was staggered, creating a smooth flow of people, but today they'd closed the tent doors so that everyone would gather.

A rusty blue pickup truck created a makeshift stage in front of the cook tent. Evalene had noticed the antique before, with its cement blocks in place of wheels, but now they'd added speakers and a sound system attached to a nearby generator. Jeremiah and a few others, who Evalene guessed to be council members stood in the bed of the truck. They looked ready to give a speech, and Evalene's nerves tingled in anticipation.

"Welcome everyone," Jeremiah spoke into the microphone. "We have an announcement for you all." He began by introducing himself for the benefit of those on the opposite side of the tent who couldn't see him.

As he described Mae's dream, Evalene barely listened.

Instead, she heard his words the night before. *Faith is a choice.*

He kept it short and simple, telling everyone who had second thoughts to stay on the island. Standing there in a camp full of thousands of people, with no doubt in her mind that most of them were scared out of their minds, Evalene wondered what they thought of the dream. She studied the people around her. Everyone reminded her of her mother. The woman who held her little daughter's hand tightly. The man a few groups ahead who wore ragged clothing and had a thick, gray beard just like the low-Number homeless man Pearl used to give money to once a week. All were here to fight. But would they stay?

Murmurs came from all around them in line. As Jeremiah finished speaking, the buzz grew louder. Luc stood on the side, frowning. Had he voted against the dream? Maybe he didn't believe in it? But when he stepped up to speak next, he was his usual confident self. "One way or another, we are going to win this battle against the Number system!" People in line cheered at that. "No matter what happens, we will fight for justice!"

Luc stepped back, and another man took his place at the microphone. "My name is Adri," he introduced himself as a council member, just like Jeremiah and Luc, "and we want to encourage all of you to think about your decision over the next day and determine what is right for you. If you are dealing with second thoughts, then by all means, stay behind."

A few people broke from the line to leave right then and there. Most stayed, but who could say whether or not they just wanted breakfast before taking their leave?

"I'm not afraid," Olive declared, scowling at those around

them and staring them down. Though it was the first the girl was hearing of the dream, she immediately knew what she believed.

But Mae frowned at Olive. "You're not going. You're needed here." Now that Evalene knew the history behind Olive's birth, she was amazed they'd allowed her off the island at all, even if it was only for the low risk submarine missions.

Evalene felt conflicted. In Eden, she'd always been focused on herself. First as an assumed high Number, ignorant of the rest of the world, then later on as a low Number, focused on survival and making it safely through each day. But how selfish was that, to only think of herself? The desire to join the revolution stirred in her again. She was eligible since she didn't feel afraid, although that was likely just because the decision wasn't made yet. But how could she let go of her freedom and the opportunity to work in a library? To find out if she was better than a Number 29? Or maybe that was exactly why she needed to join them. Because unless she stood up to the Number system, she would always wonder if they were right about who she was.

Even in the midst of the crowd's anxiety, Jeremiah's voice was sure as he stepped up to the microphone again. "Whatever you decide, we will meet at the harbor immediately after the breakfast shifts end tomorrow morning. Please pray over your decision, and do what you think is best."

He stepped down from the truck bed, and a silence reigned briefly as everyone processed the news, but a hum of voices grew louder and louder as people began discussing the announcement. The kitchen tent flaps swung open. Breakfast began. The noise of the crowd swelled until it was hard to hear each other.

When Mae left to go speak with the council again, she raised her voice to be heard over the crowd. "Meet me at the exit in fifteen minutes." The girls nodded, picking up toast for breakfast so they could take it to go, making their way back to their tent where it was quieter.

"Can you imagine?" Olive said, unaware that the dream was all Evalene had been able to think about since the night before. "I don't think that many people will leave, do you?"

Evalene considered it for a moment. "I'm not sure," she admitted. "It's not an easy decision. It might mean torture, or even death... Why do you want to go so badly?"

"Why do people always ask me that?" Olive snapped, surprising Evalene. "I want to help, to make a difference! I wasn't born to have tests run on me, to just be special genetically. I want to fight for what's right and make a real difference!"

They reached their tent, and Evalene sat on her bed while Olive threw her clothes into her suitcase angrily. "I would be on that boat tomorrow, but Grandma Mae says I can't go." Evalene watched her wide-eyed. She'd never witnessed Olive upset before. "Luc and the captain and everyone else respects Grandma too much to let me."

Olive sighed. She shook her head and changed the subject abruptly. "I need to give you your dress back." She began to remove the layers of the blue clothing disguise she'd borrowed from Evalene again.

"Do you want to trade permanently?" Evalene offered hopefully. She didn't want the reminder of her old life.

Olive agreed instantly. "I would love to, thank you! It's my favorite." She pulled out the first dress Evalene had borrowed and fallen in love with. "You can have this one, I know how much you liked it." Evalene smiled as she accepted it, laying the dress on her cot. She eyed Olive's little brown bag full of clothes. Evalene didn't even own a suitcase. Just one more thing to buy, if she stayed. But she was having trouble imagining her life here past tomorrow.

She and Olive made their way to the camp exit. The dirt and gravel path leading away from the camp was surrounded by tall green grass on either side, and the wide-open blue sky added to the feeling of freedom. How could Evalene give this up? She wanted to talk to Olive about it, but she couldn't find the words.

Before she could, they'd reached the exit, where Mae stood waiting. "Grandma, can I please stay?" Olive begged one more time. "It's only one more day. What if they need extra help? What if I'm supposed to join them and fight?"

Grandma Mae placed a comforting hand on her granddaughter's shoulder. "That's not an option, and you know it. Now come, you've already said your goodbyes to your young man. The rest is in God's hands."

Olive gasped. "Grandma Mae!"

Mae just chuckled. "You think I didn't notice?"

Evalene felt a smile tugging at the corners of her lips. Olive swung around and hugged Evalene. She didn't release her until Evalene hugged her back. Once she did let go, Grandma Mae surprised Evalene by embracing her as well.

Evalene stepped back and cleared her throat. "How far is your farm?"

"Oh, it's about an hour and a half walk down this road," Olive said. "It'd be a lot less if we drove. But the truck broke down again and Grandma refuses to buy a new car."

Mae shook her head. "No need to waste money when we can fix what we have. I just haven't had time yet." She smiled at Evalene. "May God bless whatever you choose to do. I'll go on ahead and let you two say your goodbyes." She nodded to Evalene, raising a stern brow at Olive. "Don't be long."

Evalene stood rooted to the ground, watching Mae leave. Would she ever see her and Olive again? Especially if she made the foolish choice she was considering? She wanted to ask Olive more about the revolution, but instead she just said, "Do you come to town often?"

Olive shrugged. "Well, we do when we sell crops and milk, and I have weekly appointments. I could come visit you each week… once you decide where you're staying?"

"Well…" Evalene hesitated, she couldn't believe the words on her lips, but if there was anyone she could talk to, it was Olive. "I'm not sure yet, but… I might go with Jeremiah."

"No way!" Olive squealed in excitement. "I wish I could go with you!"

"It's not a vacation." Evalene crossed her arms, hugging herself at the thought of going back. She might not feel afraid at that exact moment, but she wasn't excited either. "Haven't you ever been to Eden?"

"No…" Olive tempered her enthusiasm. "I know it's serious. It's just… I really do want to help."

"Yeah," Evalene murmured, "I guess I do too."

Olive glanced down the road, where her grandmother was growing smaller in the distance. "This is horrible. I mean, I'm glad you want to go... but I guess I won't see you in Hofyn after all..." She hugged Evalene again, sniffing. "Goodbye, Evie. I'll swing by the tent next week just in case you do stay."

"Okay," Evalene said, sad to see her go. "Bye, Olive." She added, "I'm glad I met you." And she meant it.

Watching Olive jog to catch up to her grandmother, Evalene felt aimless, unsure of the future. As much as she wanted to stay for that library job, it didn't feel right. Not only was it not guaranteed, but she might never see her father again. And if she stayed, she would always know she could've helped and didn't. But most of all, if she joined the revolution and fought against the Number system then maybe, just maybe, she might finally, truly escape this Number. Because it had followed her to Hofyn. And she desperately wanted to believe Jeremiah that it wasn't real.

It's a choice. She wasn't sure how she felt about God, but she had faith in a man named Jeremiah. She could choose to follow him. Maybe they could win. Somehow she couldn't picture herself on the island past tomorrow. She made her decision. It felt good to take control of her life. Evalene felt surprised that instead of fear, she felt excitement, hope. She turned to go back into camp. Why wait until tomorrow morning? She wanted to tell Jeremiah now!

Half jogging through the sand, she reached the camp out of breath. The line was dwindling at the breakfast tent. The third shift was almost over. That meant he'd already given his final speech. Probably had been over for a while now.

Evalene wasn't sure where his tent was located. He'd always

come to find her. But she thought she could find the council tent. Traveling down row after row, she rehearsed how she would tell him as she went.

She was about to give up when she heard Jeremiah's voice. Listening intently, she tried to detect where it was coming from. Narrowing in on it, she came up on the council tent from the back, but hesitated. If they were in the middle of a meeting, she didn't want to intrude.

Luc's loud voice reached her easily. "Jer, at least consider it. The people need a leader to take the Number One's place. Someone to look up to until everything settles down."

Intrigued, Evalene bit her lip at eavesdropping, but she stayed put. She even crept a little closer.

"No," said Jeremiah's quieter voice, "we need a democracy. If I accept a leadership position, even temporarily, the country will fall right back into its old ways. Nothing will change. All our work would be for nothing!"

No one else spoke. Was it just the two of them? Luc's voice was confident, persuasive. "But what better way to change their worldview than to give them a low Number leader? To prove to them that a low Number is just as capable of leadership?"

Who was Luc was talking about? She started backing away. This sounded like a secret. But Luc's voice carried. "Imagine, Jer! A Number 28 in charge of the whole country! It has to be you!

She froze.

Had he just called Jeremiah, the captain, a Number 28? That didn't make any sense...

But Jeremiah didn't correct Luc. Evalene held her breath,

waiting for him to argue, but nothing. She stepped up to the edge of the tent, pressing her ear up to the fabric.

She heard a sigh, and Jeremiah finally spoke. "Luc, you know higher Numbers wouldn't respect my leadership. Even low Numbers, as indoctrinated as they are, may not want change. They might even be swayed into thinking I'm not fit to lead. The people need a council of leaders that they elect from all areas of life. Our fight is fragile enough without my adding more doubt to people's minds."

Evalene's lungs froze and she couldn't breathe. Her mind raced. She must have heard wrong. Jeremiah couldn't be a Number 28. A low Number. She ripped her face away from the tent, backing away in shock.

He'd lied to her?

29

Day Three: The Truth

STANDING THERE BEHIND THE council tent, Evalene heard the rustle of someone exiting the other side. Luc walked down the road, and she glimpsed him between the gaps in the tents. Right before he saw her, she whirled and ran.

She didn't know where she was going. She just wanted to get as far away as she could from yet another person who had lied to her. She had trusted Jeremiah.

Running towards the camp exit, she reached the spot where she'd said goodbye to Olive and Grandma Mae just a half hour earlier, and sprinted past it.

Not many cars or people were on the road, but those she passed, she ignored. Hot tears blurred her vision. But she ignored them, refusing to let them fall, and ran on, tripping occasionally over bumps in the road. Finally, a hitch in her side forced her to stop and catch her breath. No one was around. She dropped to the side of the road to rest, pulling her knees up to her chest. She was sick of crying. Anger sparked, roaring loudly over the hurt.

After all she'd been through, she should have known better than to trust him.

Evalene buried her head in her arms, crossing them tightly over her legs, and stayed that way, trying to think. Now what could she do? If his Number wasn't what he'd led people to believe, then was anything about the revolution true? How could she still join his cause if she couldn't trust him? She felt lost. A hand on her shoulder made her jump.

It was Sanidine, the woman who'd worked with her, Jeremiah, and Trona, her first night on the island. Evalene hadn't seen her since. She carefully rearranged her face into the old mask of indifference she always wore at home. It was harder than it used to be.

"Are you alright?" Sanidine asked, forehead creased in concern.

"Fine, thank you." Evalene stood, straightening out the tangled cloth of the pantsuit around her legs.

Sanidine cleared her throat at the obvious lie. She tried again. "Did... something happen?"

Evalene brushed the dust off her back and legs. Instead of answering the woman, she asked, "Have you come far on this road? Passed anyone recently?"

Sanidine's brow wrinkled, but she shrugged. "Been walking this way about twenty minutes. Passed a few women, one family,"

"Thank you." Evalene started walking.

"Oh, I remember how I know you!" Sanidine said. "You spent time with the captain! Had all the ladies gossiping!"

"Waste of their time," Evalene told her, struggling to keep her face calm, "Jeremiah – the captain – means nothing to me."

Immediately she regretted her words. At Jeremiah's given

name, Sanidine's eyebrows skyrocketed and her eyes lit up with curiosity.

Evalene began walking down the long dirt road, calling back over her shoulder, "I'm sorry, I've got to get going. Good to see you again."

Sanidine's voice caught up to her after a long pause. "You too... be seeing you?" Her farewell twisted into a question at the end and hung in the air, unanswered.

Evalene unclenched her fists five minutes further down the road. Without planning to, she'd started chasing after Olive and Grandma Mae.

She stared at the trees on all sides, trying to think rationally enough to make a plan, to force her thoughts away from Jeremiah. Maybe Mae would let her stay with them for a few days. At least until she could go back to the city to check on her job applications. Especially the library. Thinking of the library led to thoughts of Jeremiah, which just left her more confused. As she drew further away from the city, she crossed paths with fewer people.

Evalene wished she'd asked for a landmark. Not knowing where the farm was, she needed to catch up to Olive and Mae while they were still on the road. If she didn't, she could easily pass by their home without even knowing it. She glanced at the sun, trying to estimate how much time she had left. Not long.

Evalene took off running. She tired quickly, forced to alternate between a walk and a jog. The sun was high in the sky, beating down on her. When she slowed her pace for what felt like the millionth time, she was panting hard, gulping in air. Sweat dripped down her back. She focused on a step at a time.

Coming to the top of a hill, Evalene finally glimpsed two figures at the bottom. She recognized Olive's golden blonde hair and Mae's silvery-white tresses. She breathed a sigh of relief. Jolting into a run once more, muscles screaming, she tore down the hill towards them as they disappeared again around a bend in the road.

"Hey!" she called as she got closer. "Wait for me!"

Her legs felt like jelly as they came back into sight. They stopped to face her, confusion wrinkling their brows.

"Evie, what're you doing here?" Olive raced forward to meet her halfway. "This is so exciting and unexpected! Did you decide to come to the farm after all? Wait, what about..." she dropped her voice to a whisper. "What about joining Jeremiah? And the revolution?"

Breathless, Evalene shook her head, pressing her lips together firmly. "Changed my mind."

For once, Olive didn't question her. Instead she looped Evalene's elbow in her own, and swung them both around to face her grandmother. "Grandma Mae, Evie's coming to the farm with us!"

Evalene produced her best smile, but Mae weighed her with her eyes before responding. "You are always welcome," was all she said as she turned back to the road ahead and began walking. "Come."

Letting out the breath she'd been holding, Evalene yielded to Olive's tugging and together they followed Mae.

"Oh, I'm so happy you decided to come with! You'll love Mr. Carrots and Mr. Beets – we named the goats after their favorite foods – they'll do tricks if they're in the mood or if you have treats," Olive chattered on, not asking Evalene to explain herself. Thankful for the trust, Evalene willed herself to listen and forget everything for a while.

Once they arrived, Olive's tour of the farm, mixed with Mae reminding them to take care of the chores, kept them busy during the day. But when they sat down to dinner that night, Mae lifted her fork, pausing to look at Evalene. "What made you choose to come work on the farm, Evie?" The older lady took a bite of ham, her brown eyes sharp and savvy.

Unsure where to start, Evalene hesitantly asked, "Has Jeremiah ever told you his Number?"

"Can't say that he has," Mae answered. Blowing on her next bite to cool it, she glanced at her granddaughter. "What about you, love?"

"Nope," Olive responded around a mouthful. She shoveled in another bite. "That doesn't mean a whole lot here, sorry to tell you. Is it good or bad… or, um, average?"

Evalene's brows rose. "It's definitely bad." How did Olive still not understand low versus high Numbers? "He's a 28."

"Okay," Olive replied. "Hold on… that's towards the bottom, right?"

"Yes."

"Well that's good! The lower the better. It proves to everyone that Numbers don't matter, since he's obviously a great leader. I'm sure it's working already!"

"But he's not proving anything to anyone," Evalene argued. "It's a secret."

"Oh..." Olive frowned.

"Exactly. He's lying to everyone."

Olive turned to Grandma Mae. "Why would he do that?"

Mae thought for a moment. "It's possible that he doesn't want anyone to doubt his leadership." Evalene's fork sat on her plate, food forgotten. That was fair. She hadn't considered the fact that no one would listen to a low Number. But couldn't he have told her? The questions were giving her a headache.

Mae set her silverware down, tenting her fingers on the table thoughtfully. "I know you feel lied to. But did Jeremiah tell you a different Number? Or give a false Number to someone else?"

"No... not exactly." Evalene frowned at the realization. He'd never outright lied to her. "But he wore the blue of a high Number when we met."

"Ah yes," Mae touched her cloth napkin to her lips before tucking it back in her lap. "I've heard of the color laws. My favorite color is green like the trees. I'd have a hard time giving that up."

Olive nodded. "Me too. I love my yellow dress."

The deception was clear to Evalene, she couldn't figure out why they didn't see it. "As far as anyone from Eden is concerned, it's dishonest!"

"Aren't you a Number 29?" Olive piped up with unfortunate timing, as she remembered Evalene's tattoo. "And you came onto the ship dressed in high Number clothes?"

Frustrated, Evalene frowned at her. "Yes. I lied too. But he knew my Number and so did you. And I'm not the one leading a revolution." The excuses rang false even in her own ears. Though it hurt that Jeremiah hadn't told her, it made sense that he kept his Number a secret.

"Evie, help me understand." Mae's voice was gentle but firm. "If the captain is, and always has been, extremely clear about his desire to rid the world of these awful 'numbers,' then why do you feel that the number he was given in the past would even still be relevant today?"

Evalene blinked, shrugging at the obvious answer. "Your Number is who you are."

"I disagree," Mae replied. "You don't need anyone else to tell you who you are." The words reminded Evalene of her mother. She knew what came next.

"You're saying I have to decide who I am," she quoted Pearl, "choose my own Number."

"No. Definitely not," Mae set her fork down with a full bite on it, her clear brown eyes meeting Evalene's squarely. "You would get it just as wrong as anyone else."

Olive took a bite, the crunching of the sausage in her mouth the only sound in the room. She swallowed loudly.

Evalene had never felt more confused in her entire life. "But then how am I supposed to find out my Number?"

"Who says you have a number?"

Mae wasn't making sense. "You know what I mean, how am I supposed to find out *who I am*?"

"You ask the One who made you." Mae's fiery eyes burned bright as she smiled. "You ask your Creator."

Ah yes. Evalene should have expected that answer. God. Were Jeremiah's God and Mae's God the same? It seemed so. Their faith was extremely different from the priests back home. Evalene contemplated the idea of asking God, but she'd never spoken to him herself. People didn't pray in Eden. She tucked the idea away to consider later, when she was alone.

They ate in silence for a few minutes, but Evalene finally broke it. "Even if I believe that Numbers aren't real," her worldview felt like it might shatter at the thought, "it still doesn't change the fact that I can't trust Jeremiah anymore. I can't trust anyone."

Mae set her fork down carefully, giving Evalene her full attention. "Why do you say that?"

The only way to explain was to tell them what happened. She described her road trip with Kevra, surviving the escape and each checkpoint only to be betrayed by her best friend. She clenched her fists underneath the table, trying to keep her voice even, though it wobbled as she described that moment when she'd woken up, without hope, abandoned. "That's where Jeremiah found me."

And he'd saved her.

She remembered waking up to his concerned eyes.

Not only had he rescued her and cleaned her wounds, but he'd also offered her safe passage on his ship. He'd known her Number all along, known she was a runaway, desperate to escape. Known she was trapped.

"He told me that he didn't care what my Number was, that Numbers meant nothing to him," she whispered, more to herself than to the women.

"That sounds like the captain," Olive ventured.

"But how do I know that he's different from Kevra? Kevra

282

lied to me too." She paused, feeling bad comparing him to her old friend. His kindness to her cast a spotlight on how inferior Kevra had always treated her. "Maybe Jeremiah didn't lie… but he didn't tell me the truth either."

Mae nodded thoughtfully. "I can tell that it matters a great deal to you."

Evalene nodded.

Mae stood up, moving to the window to view their crops. "We planted seeds over a week ago. Many still haven't grown. If you dug them up right now because they failed you, that would be the end of them." Mae turned back to face Evalene and Olive. "If you cut people out of your life when they break your trust, you will certainly end that friendship as well."

"But if instead," Mae continued, "you work through the pain and forgive them, in time the roots may grow strong and create a new thing much more valuable that what it was in the beginning. The little seed will bloom into a powerful friendship."

The simple analogy made Evalene feel like Mae was correcting a little girl. Maybe she had been acting childish. "You think I should talk to him."

Mae smiled at Evalene, eyes twinkling. "I do." She and Olive began collecting the empty plates, cleaning up dinner and waving Evalene away when she offered to help.

"Maybe you'd feel better if you did talk to him," Olive said as she took Evalene's plate. "We could go now – they don't leave until morning!" The idea made Evalene nervous, and at the same time, she hated the thought of not getting a chance to hear what he had to say.

But Mae shook her head. "It's late. Sleep on it, and you can decide what to do tomorrow."

They gave Evalene their spare cot, and she lay awake well past when they'd gone to bed, covered in an extra blanket and using her arm for a pillow. She struggled to get comfortable. Her mind didn't know where to settle, whether to think about God, or Jeremiah, or the revolution, or what she was going to do. Though it still stung that Jeremiah covered up his true Number, she understood. She even felt a little embarrassed at her reaction. Why did she care so much? It wasn't as if she meant anything to him. But could she still join the revolution or would he think her leaving meant she'd made her decision?

It was a long time before she drifted off to sleep.

The first soft light of the sun gently touching her face woke her. The tiny one room farmhouse threw her for a moment before she remembered why she was there. All the questions from the night before flooded her mind.

Staying in the warmth of her blanket on the little cot, Evalene tried to decide what to do as she listened to Olive and Grandma Mae quietly rise and make breakfast. Finally, she made her choice. Stretching, she sat up. "What smells so delicious?"

"Oh, good morning!" Olive perked up, coming over to plop down on the cot next to Evalene. "That's probably the eggs and bacon. But we also have fresh coffee brewing. I love coffee so much. Have you ever had it?" Evalene had, but Olive brought her a full cup before she could answer.

"I've been thinking..." Evalene began, and both women looked over, waiting. "I guess it would be fair to talk to Jeremiah."

She found herself wanting to hear his side. And to join the fight, if he still wanted her.

"You'll need help finding your way back," Olive said. "There's a few turns that could get tricky. I'll go! But the car's not fixed yet, so it's a long walk – we need to go right now, or we might miss him!"

Olive glanced at her grandmother as if expecting her to disagree, but Mae just nodded. "Go ahead." Olive squealed and hugged Mae before running to the door. Mae held out her arms to hug Evalene as well, and for a moment Evalene didn't want to leave the safety of the farmhouse and these new friends. But she let go, and turned towards the door, determined.

Within moments, they were sprinting down the road back to the camp. Evalene's muscles felt like rubber. She rarely ran anywhere, and now she was running for the second day in a row. Her legs weren't responding well. They felt distant, like someone else's legs that she was operating from far away. Soon she couldn't run anymore, and they slowed to a walk.

Olive pushed her on at a fast walk. Watching the sun, Olive frowned and eventually asked Evalene if she could run again. They did, and Evalene kept going until her lungs were on fire. Gasping for breath, she nearly fell over. She bent down, planning to rest her hands on her knees, but kept going until she hit the ground.

Olive didn't notice for a few more seconds, and had to run back a dozen feet.

When Olive held out a hand to help her up, Evalene took it. They jogged on. Then walked again for Evalene's sake. She hoped they would make it in time.

30

Day Four: The Departure

JEREMIAH'S EYES FELT SWOLLEN shut as he listened to the camp wake. Juno licked his fingers where his hand hung off the bed. He ignored it all for as long as he could. He needed to get up, dress, prepare. They set sail in just a few short hours. But his head ached and eyes itched from lack of sleep. The back of his throat burned from arguing all day with the council up until the decision yesterday. And then again the moment he'd stepped down from the makeshift pickup truck stage, surrounded by the refugees, full of questions.

"What if I'm scared but still want to come?"

"Will you still go back to Eden if everyone leaves?"

"Why did you spend the last few years forming an army if you were just going to send everyone away at the last minute? I'm not going to fight if we don't have enough men!"

"Will there be anyone left tomorrow?"

And, his least favorite, "Don't be a fool. This isn't from God. Why would He tell you to do something so stupid? You're all going to die if you do this."

Over and over. Person after person.

He'd shifted on his feet as he stood in the same place throughout the morning, missing lunch and dinner, repeating himself to each new frowning face.

"Pray about your decision."

"Yes, we're going no matter what."

And most of the time, "Thank you for your concern. But I have to do what I believe is right."

He rubbed his face and sighed.

Time to face the music once more.

It felt like he hadn't slept in weeks.

He dragged himself to a sitting position, absently petting Juno, whose tail wagged in appreciation. His head pounded, hinting at the beginnings of a migraine. That and the lack of sleep felt like a fog clouding his mind.

After the crowds yesterday, it had been the council once more all night. Finalizing decisions. Strategizing how to use a smaller army. Long past when everyone else slept, he'd been berated by red-faced council members. He could still picture Adri, one of his friends on the council, trying to calm Flint. "We all voted on this decision. It's not soley the captain's responsibility."

And there was Flint's frustration as he yelled back, "I know what I voted, but the camp is nearly empty! How do we know the dream didn't come from the devil himself?" Jeremiah could count on one hand the people who still considered him sane. But the decision had been made. They would fight.

He strode towards the cook tent, swerving away from the line to go through the back. Pushing through the tent flap, he silently prayed no one would notice him. But he barely made it to the back table.

"What is that blasted dog doing in my kitchen?"

Hand hovering over a sandwich, Jeremiah turned to where Trona's finger pointed. Juno's head poked through the tent flap, and she was ever so slowly placing her first paw inside the tent as Trona yelled.

"Juno, out." Jeremiah's reaction was slow, but the dog obeyed, huffing as her head disappeared through the flap. Turning back to the table, he picked up the sandwich he'd been eyeing and stuffed almost half of it in his mouth before anyone else could stop him. He closed his eyes in relief, swallowing the bite nearly whole, and took another.

"I've been meaning to talk to you," Trona's voice said behind him. Still chewing, Jeremiah faced Trona, and took another bite. "Sanidine ran into that newer gal from the last boatload you brought from Eden? The jumpy one?"

"Evie?" Jeremiah lowered what was left of his sandwich. "What about her?"

Trona fidgeted. That was odd. "Sanidine said she passed her on the road yesterday. Dead set on leaving camp and mighty upset about something." The cook turned and waved. "Sanidine, come tell the captain what you told me."

One of the young women left the prep tables to join them, clearing her throat and wiping her hands on her apron. "Yes, um, well… it seemed to me that she was unusually upset with you, Captain. But I might have been imagining things. In fact, I'm sure I did."

Jeremiah looked from Trona to Sanidine, trying to understand.

He shook his head, trying to clear out the cobwebs, but the movement sent stabs of pain shooting into his skull. After a moment's pause, where both women shifted nervously, Jeremiah asked, "What did she say exactly?"

"Oh, um... well, it's hard to remember the exact words." Sanidine blushed, and wouldn't meet his eye. "Um... I just mentioned how I'd seen her with you a few times recently, and... well, she seemed a bit angry about it..." Sanidine cleared her throat. "I could be wrong, but I got the impression that there was something personal."

Nodding, Jeremiah thanked her. He knew Evie had planned to stay on the island. But it was strange that she'd left the camp so soon. She couldn't possibly have a place to stay yet. He didn't have any answers for the women. Sanidine returned to her table, but Trona still stared him down. "What did you do?"

Luc entered the tent as Jeremiah protested, "I didn't do anything! Evie already told me she was going to leave. I completely understand."

His friend joined them at the table, also picking up a sandwich. Through a mouthful, he said, "Your new girl didn't say goodbye? I saw her yesterday morning at the council tent. Maybe she chickened out." Jeremiah raised his brows at that. She'd come to the tent?

Luc clapped a hand on Jeremiah's shoulder as he took another bite. "Don't worry, man. We're gonna win this thing. You'll come back to her in no time."

But Trona interrupted him. "Doesn't matter if he comes back or not if he upset her." She crossed her arms, standing up for all womankind, and making sure Jeremiah knew it.

"Trona, I swear to you, I didn't do any – " He stopped at a thought. "Luc, what time did you say you saw Evie?"

"We'd just finished that talk after breakfast." Luc skirted around the topic of their discussion since the women were listening, but Jeremiah remembered the conversation clearly. His gut told him he knew why she'd left. Luc had been telling him a Number 28 should lead the country. Had Evie overheard that Luc meant him?

Turning back to the women, Jeremiah looked past Trona to Sanidine. "What time did you run into Evie on the road?"

"About a half hour after breakfast ended, Captain," the young woman answered.

The timing confirmed his instincts.

Jeremiah nodded his thanks to Sanidine, then to the cook. "Thank you, Trona, for bringing it to my attention."

The cook frowned and opened her mouth, but he spoke first. "I'll make sure to look into it further. Right now, I'm needed at the pier. Are you prepared to run the camp with whoever is left until we return?"

Not a question he usually asked her when leaving, but they both heard the unspoken question behind it: *Are you prepared to run the camp if we don't return?*

Nodding, Trona uncrossed her arms and dropped the matter, huffing as she returned to her worktable and dismissing him from her kitchen with a wave of the arm.

Luc stole a sandwich on his way out and Jeremiah followed suit. As they strode towards the pier, they passed refugees and soldiers, some headed to the pier as well, others leaving camp in the direction of Hofyn with guilty expressions, not meeting his eyes. Jeremiah pitched his voice low so only Luc would hear. "How bad is it?"

Luc didn't answer immediately. That never bode well. "Let's see..." he scratched the dark stubble forming on his chin in thought. "The good news is we've rescued over 20,000 people from Eden."

Jeremiah nodded. He knew the stats. Great news any other day. But the reminder didn't make him feel better today.

"And nearly 10,000 stayed here in camp, planning to join us..." Luc trailed off.

Again, Jeremiah nodded. Luc was only stating what he already knew, avoiding the question. They crested the hill, finally able to see the harbor that should've been full of men, and Luc didn't need to say another word. Only a small fraction of the beach and surrounding area, which should've been packed shoulder to shoulder with people, was full.

Luc took a deep breath. "We have under a thousand men."

The air flew out of Jeremiah's lungs as if he'd been punched.

Hundreds.

How they would ever succeed with less than a thousand – with less than five thousand even – it would have to be a miracle. *Well Lord, I guess that's the point, right?* He sighed.

He felt Luc's eyes on the back of his neck. His friend had always felt that people should believe whatever they wanted. He'd never had any interest in God, although he liked the way Jeremiah and Beryl saw God more than the way the church of Eden did.

When the council had first voted on the dream, Luc had been one of the votes against it. But once the decision was made, Luc supported the choice, unlike a few others on the council.

"You could still stop it," Luc said lightly.

Turning, Jeremiah met Luc's eyes. "No."

"It's only a few years of planning gone to waste. We could sail to the FreeLands. Make a living hauling stuff. Lots of ships work trade routes."

"No," Jeremiah said again, shaking his head firmly. "I can't."

Luc rolled his eyes at Jeremiah. "Okay, I know God wants us to do this and all. I hear you. But if we didn't do it, he could probably find somebody else, right? I mean, does God want us dead?"

Frustration boiled in Jeremiah at his friend's doubts. He stopped in his tracks, forcing Luc to stop too. "You sound like everyone else, asking me to take the easy way, telling me to be selfish, to run away." His fists clenched as he tried to find the words. "You know what I don't understand?" He didn't wait for Luc to respond. "Why do people think life is so great outside of God's plan? Do you think that we would live forever if we abandoned Eden and went somewhere else?"

Jeremiah pressed a hand to his temple where the pain was the worst, struggling to speak past the blinding headache. "We could die in the FreeLands just as easily as we could die in Eden. And would our success drown out the news of our friends suffering back home? Is your 'easier way' really that much easier in the end?"

"Absolutely," Luc snorted. "Not dying is a hundred percent

better as far as I'm concerned."

Jeremiah dropped his hand to look Luc directly in the eyes. "We are all going to die someday." He held Luc's gaze, daring him to argue. "There's no guarantee any of us will live longer if we play it safe."

Luc turned away, toward the pier and the men. He shrugged. Jeremiah pushed further. "Whether we live to be ninety or die tomorrow, only God knows, but at least while I'm living I can do what's right."

Luc nodded thoughtfully, not saying anything for a moment. When he looked up finally, his face was serious, but he deadpanned. "Guess we're doing it then." And he saluted Jeremiah. "Lead on, Captain."

The corner of Jeremiah's mouth lifted in a smile, and he nodded his acceptance as they descended towards the pier. "We need to leave as soon as possible."

"Eh," Luc said, slapping the air away, back to his casual self. "I've got tons of time. It's gonna take you hours to sort everybody out and get all the supplies on board."

"Me?" Jeremiah mock lifted his eyebrows. "Oh no, I won't be alone. I have a first mate to do all the dirty work."

His first mate frowned back at him.

"Besides," Jeremiah continued, "there's no need to load supplies. We never unloaded, just left them on the ship for a week. Trona and her kitchen staff restocked the fresh food per the council's request. All that's left is to get the crew on board."

"That'll still take hours," Luc shrugged.

"Technically, yes." Jeremiah tucked his hands in his pockets as they walked. "But again, I have my first mate to take care of that. I'll be taking the first full ship, and we'll set off as soon as they're aboard."

Now Luc's frown was real. "You're leaving me behind? I thought we were in this together?"

"We are," Jeremiah reassured him, clapping a hand on his friend's back. "You know we had to downsize the original plan. We were already short on good sailors before this started. I need you to captain a ship."

"Jer –," Luc interrupted.

"Don't worry! You and I will still have the same rendezvous point when we land."

"Jer," Luc tried again, "I don't like it. The fighting could start before I get there –"

But Jeremiah cut him off. "Look." He gestured widely to small groups of men they were approaching. "We don't have the options we used to have. I need people I can trust to make sure everything goes smoothly on the other ships. Luc, I need you to do this."

Luc didn't like it, but he understood. He frowned, nodding his acceptance.

Reaching the men, he and Luc became all business, quickly assembling the first full ship, Jeremiah's submarine. As the men assigned to Old Victorious loaded up, Jeremiah, Luc, and the council members bent their heads together, sorting out last minute details. The last dozen men boarded.

"Hold on," Jeremiah said to Luc, searching his pockets. "Do you have any paper?"

They scrounged up a piece of paper and a short, worn pencil. Holding it against his leg, he wrote quickly, then folded the paper carefully. Returning the pencil to its owner, he held the folded paper out to Luc. "I need you to do me a favor."

"Mmmhmm," Luc accepted it, reading the name on the front. He tucked it into his right breast pocket. "I don't want to ruin the moment or anything, but… you know I'll only be a few hours behind you."

"Right," Jeremiah said. "Um, give it to Trona before you go."

"Ok, and then I'll tell her to bury it somewhere special that only you two lovebirds have ever been." Luc scrunched up the entire left side of his face in an exaggerated wink.

"Sure, great idea," Jeremiah muttered back, ignoring the jab. It was useless to argue with Luc, to explain that he didn't have feelings. And what if he did? It still wasn't the right time to act on them. He needed to focus on the revolution.

He held out a hand, and Luc clasped it. They held for a moment, then let go. Without another word, Jeremiah strode across the long levee dock. He climbed aboard his submarine, entering the hatch, and traveled down deep into the belly of his ship.

31

Is It Too Late?

I DON'T KNOW IF we'll get there in time," Evalene said, gasping. Her legs were trembling and her lungs were on fire.

Olive looped her arm through Evalene's in support. "You see that hill up ahead with the big boulder?" She pointed to a distant spot down the path.

All Evalene saw was green. Green grass and trees for miles to the left and to the right. But when she squinted, she thought she glimpsed a large rock. She nodded.

"That's the camp entrance," Olive said, tugging at Evalene. "C'mon, just a little further!"

Evalene's muscles felt shaky and weak. But she put one foot in front of the other, and finally they reached the top of the hill, entering the camp.

"Where is everyone?" Evalene wondered out loud. The camp was deserted.

"I'm sure they're all down at the harbor," Olive said, not slowing. "They're scheduled to depart today."

Evalene bit her lip, worrying they'd left already.

"Let's hurry to the pier," Olive took off down the path through the tents, "We can still make it!"

The sun was almost directly above them, well past the end of the breakfast shifts when the boats were scheduled to leave. But Evalene forced her feet to move, jogging after Olive, nearly tripping a few times when she didn't lift her feet high enough.

They crested the hill on the opposite side and the water came into view. A ship was sailing off into the distance.

"No!" Olive wailed. "That's one of our ships!"

Evalene sagged, slowing down.

But Olive didn't stop. She waved Evalene on. "There's still a small group down in the harbor, hurry!"

Dragging herself forward, Evalene ignored the blisters on her feet, finding the strength for a wobbly jog down the hill to the waterfront. What if Jeremiah was leaving right that second? Olive stayed with her until the last stretch, when she caught sight of Luc. Squealing, she ran ahead, waving to him.

Luc frowned. "What are you doing here? Is Mae hurt?"

"No silly, Grandma's fine," Olive smacked him lightly on the arm. "Is the captain still here?"

Luc shook his head, "No, he took the first ship. They left right after breakfast."

The ship they'd seen earlier was now just a tiny dot in the distance. "That wasn't the first ship?" Olive asked.

"No, that was the fourth," Luc told them. "Mine will be the last one."

"You're kidding," Olive said. "But that means there's only…"

"A little over 900," Luc confirmed her thoughts. "The ships are at full capacity, except for this last one. I'd say we boarded roughly 150-200 on each of them, depending on their size."

As Evalene listened, the grim twist of Luc's mouth as he relayed the numbers told her they weren't good. Olive's rare lack of optimism spoke even louder.

"Oh, Evie," Luc patted his front breast pocket, "Jeremiah asked me to give this to you. I didn't expect to see you..." He trailed off, handing a small, folded piece of paper to her. Evalene took it. Jeremiah had left her a message? That was above and beyond charity. Her heart beat faster, hopeful.

Unfolding the note, she felt both Luc and Olive's eyes on her. "I'll be over here." She pointed to a nearby log, hobbling over to it for some privacy, kicking off her shoes to free the blisters as she sat.

Jeremiah's script was hastily scrawled across the paper, his handwriting bold and confident, just like him.

"Dear Evie,

I can't stop thinking about you since we met. You are destined for great things, once you realize how valuable you are. I think you overheard my Number, but even if you didn't, I want to tell you. It was a 28. It's not who I am and means nothing to me. But if I hurt you by keeping it in the past, please forgive me. I hope to come back here after the fight to see you. I would like to get to know you better.

Sincerely yours,

Jeremiah."

Evalene's heart agreed with the note immediately. He wasn't a 28. He was so much more than that. He was loyal, kind, and an amazing leader... his Number didn't fit him at all. But what stood out to her most was that he thought she was valuable too. No one had called her that in years. Could it be true?

She reread the letter.

I can't stop thinking about you… I hope to come back to see you. And the way he signed it, *yours.* He wanted to see her again. He didn't know about her decision to join them.

Olive's bare feet appeared in her blurred vision. "What's going on? What did he say?" She plopped down on the log beside Evalene. "It's a love note, isn't it? That would be so romantic…" Olive stared over at Luc. He was oblivious.

Holding a clipboard, Luc was checking off supplies as the men loaded the ship, coming from a large tent at the edge of camp.

"Evie, you're killing me," Olive said when Evalene didn't answer. "Did he ask you to come with him? I wish Luc would ignore Grandma Mae and ask me to come with."

Evalene folded the paper. She didn't want to show it to Olive just yet. She wasn't sure what it meant. And it felt too special to share. But she could tell Olive part of it. "He told me his real Number."

"Oh wow," Olive breathed the words on a sigh. "How perfect."

"Not really," Evalene rubbed her fingers along the creases of the paper folds. "I didn't get a chance to talk to him. Or ask if I was still welcome to join them." She placed the paper in her pocket for safekeeping.

"Of course you're still welcome!" Olive swiveled on the log to face Evalene. "Do you still want to go?"

Evalene frowned and nodded once, firmly. "I do." She'd

known she wanted to for a while now. She stood. Watching the line of men and women boarding the ships, she gathered her courage to ask Luc if she could board.

"Grandma's going to be so mad," Olive whispered before saying to Evalene louder, "I'm coming too." She stood, adding, "I just need to figure out how to get past Luc. And everyone else."

The idea of Olive coming with made Evalene feel so much better. Studying Luc and the assembly line, Evalene thought for a minute. "I have an idea. Follow me." As they approached Luc and the men carrying supplies, she whispered her plan to Olive.

The girl immediately agreed to it. "I can handle Luc," she whispered. As soon as they were within earshot, she raised her voice. "Luc, give us some boxes, we're helping!"

"No way," he replied, running an anxious hand through his short-cropped hair. "We have enough to do without having to babysit you two." He waved another man on towards the gangplank for the ship, checking another item off his list.

But Olive wasn't taking no for an answer. "We don't need supervision carrying boxes from one place to the next. You're not letting me fight, you're not even letting me go with – the *least* you can let do is let me help!"

Luc had clearly heard the argument before. He was stuck in a hard place between grandmother and granddaughter. Sighing, he gave in. Waving towards the line coming down the hill from camp, he said, "Don't break your back trying to be a hero. Just bring whatever you can carry. Don't make me regret this."

With a quick "Thanks Luc!" Olive and Evalene headed in the direction of the supply tent. Once there, they searched for boxes that would be easy to carry.

Lifting a case the size of a large pillow off the table, Olive whirled to leave. Evalene hoisted a smaller box and hurried to keep up. It was heavier than she'd thought.

They lugged their load down the hill towards the docks, pausing as they passed Luc so he could check their choices off his list. He didn't say a word, just nodded them on.

Marching along the pier with the other sailors loading up, they passed the smaller docks and continued to the levee wall where the submarine and other larger ships anchored outside of the bay. The line of men trailed like ants along the pier, across the plank and onto the ship.

This ship was shorter than the submarine, but much wider, made of metal painted white and blue, a cheerful mix that contradicted the boat's purpose. Together the girls crossed the plank, walking with purpose, as if on a mission. They passed a group of men tying down a pile of boxes at the front of the ship with a tarp. In the middle of the ship, by the captain's cabin, there was another pile of supplies. Olive glanced at Evalene, prepared to stop, but Evalene shook her head.

The muscles in Evalene's arms strained from carrying the heavy cargo so far. At the opposite end of the ship, they reached the last supply pile, also covered with a big blue tarp, tied down. It was quieter here. This would work.

Evalene set her box on the ground, untying one side of the tarp. By the time Olive imitated her, stood, and shook out the kinks in her arms, Evalene had slipped underneath, shoving boxes to the left and the right, lightning quick.

With just a few pushes, she created a tiny cave, with boxes for walls and the blue tarp for a roof. It was tight, but they could squeeze in. The perfect hiding place.

Ducking under the tarp, Evalene waved for Olive to join her. Together they slid the two boxes they'd carried up to the opening, placing one on top of the other. The final touch was to fling the tarp up and over the new boxes, effectively adding them to the pile and completely concealing their hiding place.

They knelt to sit on the hard metal deck. Though Olive pushed the boxes out a little further so she could stretch her legs, it was cramped. The space was so tight their legs were touching. Evalene leaned against the box behind her and crossed her legs, reevaluating her plan. There was no way they could sit like this for two days. But they just had to smuggle Olive far enough out to sea that they wouldn't turn around.

The sounds of the waves and the men hollering as they loaded the ship had faded with the barrier of the boxes, creating a peaceful bubble of quiet. But they kept silent, just in case.

It was hard to tell how much time passed like this before the rocking of the boat grew stronger. Olive whispered, "I think we've left the harbor." Evalene nodded, but she didn't respond. If she opened her mouth to answer, she might throw up.

The motion sickness was far worse above the water than deep below the surface on the submarine. Pressing against the boxes, struggling not to crowd Olive in the tiny space, Evalene curled up on her side, closing her eyes and breathing shallowly through her nose. The only sound in the small space was her shuffling to get comfortable on the hard floor.

Evalene wished she had a bucket. The rest of the morning and afternoon looked the same from their hiding place. Evalene lay still on the ground of their tiny shelter, enduring the rocking of the waves. Barely. Olive's stomach, on the other hand, growled loudly as time passed. She complained in a hushed voice, growing bored. But Evalene ignored her, too nauseous to make conversation. Night fell, and their tiny cave grew pitch black. Olive's complaints grew louder until Evalene thought she wanted someone to hear her.

When footsteps sounded near their stack of boxes, Evalene felt relief. Boxes were pulled away, revealing the self-made entrance. Olive stood, as if prepared to kick and scream until they allowed them to stay. Evalene was far less worried. Still lying on the deck, she didn't move, just blinked at the bright light of a flashlight shining in her eyes.

"Who's this?" said a man's voice.

Another said, "Stowaways! Bring them to the captain!"

Olive shook one of them off when they grabbed her elbow. "I can walk by myself!"

But Evalene gratefully accepted their help to stand, leaning into the arm of the stranger so fully that another arm materialized on the opposite side. Too sick to pay attention, she focused on breathing. On not throwing up all over the men's shoes.

They were dragged to the captain's cabin. Light spilled out of the doorway into the darkness. Knocking on the open door, the men entered with Olive and Evalene. Luc stood at the heavy desk in the center of the room, meeting with a few other men seated around the table.

His jaw dropped when he saw them. "Hey Luc." Olive grinned

at him, unashamed.

"Olive? What were you thinking? Magnolia made it extremely clear you weren't allowed on this trip," Luc groaned, and addressed the men who'd brought them. "Where did you find them?"

"They were holed up in one of the supply piles," said the man still holding Evalene upright.

"Ah," Luc nodded. He crossed his arms, shaking his head at Olive with a slight lift of the brow. "That explains why you suddenly wanted to help."

That upset Olive. "That's not fair! I always wanted to be involved, you just wouldn't let me!"

"Your grandmother made the rule," Luc said. "I'm just enforcing it."

"But Captain," the man next to Olive spoke up for the first time, "we can't turn back now, we'll lose too much time."

Luc's fist clenched. "I know." He sighed and shrugged, and spoke to Evalene as well as Olive. "We'll have to figure out what to do with you two. You can't fight, that's for sure. Testimonials were supposed to go with Jeremiah or the second ship so they would be at the news station for the broadcast. As it is, we've had so many delays, we might be hours behind them at this point. Maybe more." He looked worried. Muttering to himself, he added, "We should have left at the same time."

"Jeremiah wants to take the harbor during the night," said one of the men sitting at the table in the room. He'd been quiet up to this point, but when he spoke up, Evalene studied him. His face was familiar. He'd been one of the council members standing in the truck giving the announcement the day before. "We'll still get there before dawn, and the harbor will be secured for our arrival."

"I know, that's all true in theory," Luc said, pulling out a chair across from the man. "But things can always go wrong. Take these two for example." He waved a hand at the girls. "Get them settled into the bunks for now – and make sure they stay out of trouble." He bent over the map spread out across the desk, done with them.

The sailors who'd found them ushered the girls out and brought them below decks. Evalene dropped into a tiny bunk and closed her eyes, ignoring everything around her, fighting seasickness. She huddled there in misery until someone handed her a bucket, just in time. She kept it within arm's reach, needing it again shortly.

Between bouts of sickness, she slept. Each time she woke, she wondered how long it had been. Each time, Olive said only a few hours. It was a two-day trip. In retrospect, the submarine voyage with all those encounters with Talc seemed like a pleasant vacation. Evalene clutched her stomach, heaving again. Nothing but bile. The room spun, and her stomach didn't relent, trying to throw up food that wasn't there.

How far were they behind Jeremiah's ship? What would happen when he and his men arrived? She wondered if they would still be alive when she got there. Another thought struck her. If they didn't win, would she live through the week?

32

The Fight

JEREMIAH STOOD ON THE end of the long dock, watching the dark waves hit the shores of Eden. The buildings along the pier crowded together, rising in many places like a wall, blocking his view of the rest of the city. It was just past three a.m. A sliver of the moon cast pale light on the men, but kept them mostly in shadows. Each man wore black, adding to their invisibility. The color of the Regs, meant to confuse their enemy from a distance. So far, it had worked.

They'd taken the harbor easily, just a small guard station, only manned by three Regs at night. Hopefully by sunrise, the Regs would be needed elsewhere.

The rebels' third ship radioed their approach. Jeremiah could make out its silhouette if he squinted. They'd be docking within a few minutes.

It was the darkest part of the night. The city was at its most vulnerable.

It was time to strike.

Just a few soft words set the plan into motion. Everyone moved swiftly, hand signals used to communicate whenever possible. Silent feet left the dock and harbor in carefully planned groups. Jeremiah's supervision was strictly for morale; each man knew his role by heart.

Three companies of men and women would target three specific areas of the city. With only a fraction of the soldiers they'd expected, they had to be even more strategic than they'd originally planned. He hoped it would work.

When the third ship docked, that whole group would form one company. They would move on foot towards the Number One's home, only an hour's walk from the harbor. Best time to take that fortress was the middle of the night. The second largest company would target the Regulator Headquarters in the heart of the city, arriving around sunrise. Jeremiah would lead the third and smallest company to the News Station. Located all the way on the other side of the city, it would be the longest walk, nearly six hours. But he had a short cut.

The silent jog to the abandoned store he'd used so many times before, reminded him of the last time he'd traversed this path, with Evie. The thought distracted him. Would she ever get his note? He shook his head. Focus.

He and his soldiers reached his hiding place in just under an hour. Rounding the corner to enter the parking lot he found, as promised, seven classic cars.

Every single vehicle Lady Beryl owned, minus one for her to leave town, was parked in the abandoned lot, keys strategically hidden inside the store. She'd demanded to help. This had been their compromise. Jeremiah double-checked that she'd removed the plates like he'd asked. Even with this step though, Regulators could still track down the vehicle's owner if the revolution failed.

Just one more reason it couldn't fail.

He let Welder, his second in command, pass out the keys to the previously selected drivers. Every single one of the cars was an old-world sports car. Lady Beryl's first husband had a fondness for the way they'd been made, and money to burn. He'd spent the last few years of his short life chasing down the flashy cars. Even when they'd been brand new, Jeremiah knew they'd been designed to impress, but the history was what fascinated him. He regretted giving in to Beryl. Not one of these beautiful antiques was even remotely designed for combat. But at least they would have speed. Jeremiah took the closest.

There weren't enough cars to fit his whole company. A little over half would stay behind and make the rest of the long, six-hour walk. Although if anything went wrong, they were prepared to run or potentially steal transportation.

No one spoke.

Those chosen for the car ride squeezed into each of the small vehicles, only five or six in most, until not an inch of space was left. The nods and salutes between the two groups spoke volumes. *See you if we make it.*

The tiny sports car soon smelled like sweat and anxiety. Engine roaring, Jeremiah gunned it to a reckless speed. If a Regulator on patrol saw them, they would assume a high Number was out for a joy ride. Hopefully.

Driving transformed the six-hour trip into less than a half-hour, though they still took the long way around, slowing to travel the back roads. It was worth it to avoid the Regulator

Headquarters. The dark streets were empty. Curfew was strict here.

Pulling up to the news station, the sky was just starting to lighten, although sunrise was still an hour off. The square, cement building, like all the other surrounding homes and businesses, had few windows, a leftover habit from the war. At first glance, the station was dark and silent, but around the corner, light spilled out of a tiny window. Someone was already at work. Or maybe just finishing?

Jeremiah pulled his car up to the building, parking so close the bumper touched the ugly gray cement, the beginning of a makeshift barricade. His team followed suit. The cars formed a half moon barrier in front of the building, parked bumper to bumper. They didn't leave a single opening. The city streets were narrow enough that the line of defense also effectively blocked the street. But more importantly, the roadblock protected their position, a defensive measure, providing a shield to hide behind if shots were fired. They needed to take this building and keep it long enough to broadcast their message. The entire outcome of the war depended on it.

The men and women climbed out of their vehicles into the semi-circle, or if they exited into the street, they climbed over the cars to get inside the barrier. Jeremiah stepped out the driver's side, intending to climb over the hood of his car as well. Out of the corner of his eye, as he closed his car door, he caught a flicker of light by the station. Muscles tight, he tensed to face a potential attacker.

A young man stood in the propped open door of the station, with a half-burned cigarette hanging out of his open mouth. At the sight of 40-plus men pouring out of the cars, he fumbled and dropped his cigarette. The butt fell to the ground.

Showing up in sports cars instead of Regulation vehicles, Jeremiah knew their Regulator disguise was tenuous at best, but nonetheless he held up a hand, palm out. "Halt." He was on the wrong side of the barricade. Physically climbing over the car might be the last straw to convince the young man they weren't true Regulators, so Jeremiah motioned for Welder, who stood half a dozen feet away inside the circle, to move instead.

But one of their newest recruits, a huge bald man with an angry face who'd volunteered to give his testimony, pulled out a gun, pointing it at the station employee. How had he gotten a gun? This made the young man in the doorway screech in fright. His scrawny legs kicked the doorstop out and he hurled himself through the closing door, yanking hard on the handle and slamming it shut, even as Jeremiah's men sprinted towards it. The loud click of the lock sounded in the night air. Welder jumped up the concrete steps and reached the door just moments before Jeremiah, grabbing the handle and pulling with all his might. It didn't budge.

Jeremiah cursed. What should have been a quick take-over had just become much more complicated. He rounded on the big man. "Who gave you a gun?" he yelled, nearly punching the car next to him.

Welder stepped up next to them, a voice of reason. "I'll take care of Talc, sir." He held out his hand for the man's gun.

The man, Talc, tried to defend himself. "What's the big deal? We can just blow down the door." He swung the strap of the gun over his shoulder, but was reluctant to hand it to Welder. "I didn't come here to just watch. I want to fight!"

Jeremiah met his glare with his own until the man let go of the weapon. "We can't blow it up. We need to be able to lock ourselves in later." Jeremiah paced away from them. He didn't waste time explaining further. Welder would take care of it. His men stood spread out inside the half circle of the barricade. They looked worried enough without him mentioning how the loose employee was likely calling the Regs as they stood there.

The upside of Jeremiah's small force was that they'd likely only send one or two Regulator vehicles out to make arrests at first. That they could handle. But if they brought reinforcements... "Where's my lock picker?" Jeremiah called out.

Ferris pushed through from the back of the group to stand in front of Jeremiah. "Here sir."

"We'll need to hurry," Jeremiah told him, clapping a hand on the young man's shoulder, leading him towards the front door of the station. Ferris was by far the most skilled at lock picking, and even he was slow on a good day. They had expected to have more time.

Ferris scurried up the concrete steps and set to work, laying out his tools, poking them into the lock at different angles. Jeremiah stood on the corner of the steps, watching the road from this vantage point, praying Ferris would be faster than ever before. His men took up defensive positions behind the cars at Welder's orders. Jeremiah stayed focused on Ferris's work, available if he was needed. The sky continued to grow lighter as the sun rose. Soon, too soon, they heard the roar of engines coming their way.

"How's it going?" Jeremiah pitched his voice to a casual tone.

Ferris was sweating. He clearly knew the stakes now. Everyone did. Ears cocked across the company as the thundering grew closer. The lock picker wiped his brow with one hand, while the other never stopped jiggling and working with the tools. He shook his head without looking up. "It's more resistant than an average lock. It has at least five cylinders…"

Jeremiah jumped off the steps. They had less than a minute before the Regs arrived. He ran towards his car, hauling himself in through the passenger side onto the driver's seat, turning the key in the ignition, and jerking the car into gear. He hit the gas and drove just a half dozen feet past the building before slamming on the brakes. Leaning across the passenger seat, he opened the door and pushed it hard until it fell open as wide as it would go. With one quick look in the rearview mirror, and a few twists of the wheel, he punched the car into reverse. The crash of the passenger door against the heavy cement building was deafening, but it worked. With a squeal of metal tearing from metal, the passenger door ripped off and fell onto the pavement in front of the car.

Maneuvering the little sports car back into its original position, Jeremiah leapt out, running towards the severed car door where it now lay on the ground. Welder appeared at his side as he lifted it, and together, they dragged it up and over the cars, inside the barricade. Others joined them, and with their help, they quickly dragged it up the stairs of the building, setting it in front of Ferris. A crude shield. Jeremiah knelt behind it, hoping it would be enough.

Just seconds later, two Regulator vehicles came into sight.

Shots fired instantly. Jeremiah ducked behind the car door, shouting at his men, "Hold your fire!" They didn't have bullets to waste. "Wait until they're closer! Aim!" They stopped firing. But now the Regs, alerted to the fact that they had weapons, were firing back, filling the air with loud volleys. As their cars came within reach of his men's bullets, Jeremiah yelled, "Now!"

Pulling his crude defense closer to the door, Jeremiah tried his best to shield Ferris. "Don't stop!" he yelled at the boy over the shooting. "Get us in!" Voices yelled on both sides. The gunshots were deafening.

A bullet clipped Jeremiah's finger where he held the edge of the door. He hissed in pain. Finding a grip along the handle on the inside of the door, he held his place. The wound stung, but he forced himself to hold on with his injured hand while he moved to pull his gun out with the other. The blood made his grip slippery.

He peeked out from behind the shield and took a shot as they closed in. A Regulator fired back. They had the advantage of years of training for this. Their aim was too good. With Jeremiah's dominant hand injured, he was forced to shoot with the weaker, and wished he'd spent more time shooting with both hands. More time shooting in general.

"I've almost got it!" Ferris yelled as Jeremiah leaned out to shoot again. Jeremiah got off a shot that hit one of the Regulator's cars, making the man duck back inside his vehicle, but that only drew the Regs attention to him. A bullet shattered the window of the car and hit Jeremiah in the shoulder.

Clenching his teeth at the pain, Jeremiah pulled back, gun dropping to his side. He thought for a moment the bullet had only grazed his shoulder, but one glance showed a hole that bled profusely. He could still move the arm, barely. Holding the door with fingers that struggled to keep their grip, he felt with his other hand for an exit wound. There wasn't one.

Kneeling behind the shield, he made himself as small as possible, needing to use his good hand to hold the door now. As much as he wanted to shoot, the priority was getting the news station door open. If he dropped the shield, they would hit Ferris. His shoulder wound burned, drowning out the pain in his fingers.

As Jeremiah shifted his position, another bullet hit his toe where his boot peeked out. Yelling in pain, nearly dropping the car door, he dragged his foot in just before another bullet hit the concrete where it had been. He sucked in a breath. It stung. But he didn't have time to inspect the damage. He focused on holding the shield up.

Jeremiah's company all wore the armored vests created by Hofyn's brightest, so he didn't understand why Welder had most of the men hidden behind the cars, not firing, until the Regs stopped their vehicles at the barricade and climbed out, and the man shouted, "Now!" The entire company jumped out in ambush, except one young soldier, Ion, who lay on the ground.

The four Regulators were taken by surprise at how many of the rebels there were. They got off a few hits before they were shot down. Since the Regs were trained to shoot at the heart, most of Jeremiah's soldiers were simply winded, thanks to the vests. The low Number healers, the best medical training their army had, immediately turned to aid the wounded.

They'd bought themselves a little more time. How much,

Jeremiah didn't know. It depended on if the Regs had radioed their headquarters or not. Ferris still struggled with the lock. Minutes ticked by. Everyone stood tense, waiting. Too soon, they heard the roar of more cars headed in their direction. Jeremiah held his position, ignoring the sting of his wounds, while Welder reorganized the group to execute the same maneuver once more.

The fight began anew. Shots fired, and another soldier clutched her arm where the bullet hit. Jeremiah tensed behind the car door, waiting to be spotted. Though it felt like hours, the fight had barely lasted a minute before Ferris hollered, "I've got it! We're in!"

Jeremiah felt Ferris disappear behind him. Half standing, still behind the car door, he backed up inside after the boy until the car door forced him to stop at the door frame, too large to pass through without turning it sideways. Calling out to his soldiers from where he stood in the threshold, Jeremiah only had time to yell half a command to Welder before he felt something sharp hit him in the back near his shoulder, hitting right where his own protective vest ended.

He came to lying on his back on the ground somewhere indoors. He couldn't make out any details about the room except the white ceiling and the faces of his men staring down at him. A piercing white light streaked through his vision on and off, matching the throbbing in his back. They yelled for a healer. It must be bad. Gunshots had stopped outside. They must have successfully stopped the second assault. But there would be more.

He saw Larimar at the edge of his vision. "Where's Welder?" he managed to ask.

"He's hurt bad, not waking up," Larimar replied, eyes squinting in worry. "We've lost two men, and nine wounded, including yourself, sir." His eyes landed on someone else in the room as he yelled, "Somebody get that gun and hold him!" In his haze, Jeremiah saw one of the station employees, who stood shaking over a smoking gun on the floor. He was pale, hands over his mouth like he might vomit. Well. That explained the searing pain exploding across Jeremiah's upper-back and shoulder. He'd been attacked from behind.

The employee was quickly apprehended and dragged out of Jeremiah's line of sight. He closed his eyes. It was hard to focus on anything past the pain. His back was on fire. It was absolute agony. He prayed to pass out, but continued to feel every piercing red-hot poker. "We need to roll him over. Check if there's an exit wound," a new voice told Larimar.

His friend agreed. Jeremiah floated on a cloud of pain as hands gripped his sides, preparing to move him. He tried to speak, to tell them no, but the energy evaded him. As they rolled him, the pain assaulted him so heavily he gratefully felt himself blacking out once more.

But it didn't last. The nerves and muscle around the wounds were screaming even as he woke. Why couldn't he focus? This newest injury must be serious. Jeremiah forced his eyes open, but couldn't see anything while lying on his stomach. Someone's crumpled shirt was under his head acting as a pillow, cushioning his face from the hard cement floor. It smelled like sweat. The fire in his back raged.

"We need to dig it out," said a voice behind him.

"No!" His stern yell came out in a whisper. He couldn't pass out again. Rational thought was returning, and he knew with Welder down, the men needed a leader.

The face belonging to the voice bent down so that he could see the man in his line of sight – one of his healers. He'd brought the man along as a backup. Never expected to need his services himself.

"You're very lucky," the healer was saying. "You could have died. You still might. Now shut up and be still, or you still will."

"Wait!" Jeremiah's command still held some authority. "Larimar!"

Larimar's face replaced the healer's in his vision. His friend was frowning in concern. "Yes, Captain. We're still holding, but we don't have enough men to last much longer."

The healer began to clean Jeremiah's shoulder wound. He sucked in a breath at the cleaning, closing his eyes to the pain. "You're in charge now," he told the man, who'd worked under Welder for years now. Though Larimar was anxious at the unexpected authority, he would lead well. "Radio the rest of our company. Tell them to run or steal transportation, but to get here as fast as they can." His voice was ragged, but he forced himself to continue. "Radio Flint's company to send some men as well. The news station is more important than Regulator Headquarters." He choked as the healer wrapped a bandage around his arm. "And find out how far Luc and the other ship have to go. They should have arrived by now."

"I need to get that bullet out," he heard the healer saying to Larimar.

They spoke over him, but Jeremiah repeated himself as loudly as he could, straining against the intense heat in his back. "We can't lose the station!"

Larimar's face came back into his line of sight once more, and he nodded. "I know. I'll do what I can. You focus on staying alive." He disappeared, already calling out orders for men to radio backup. But Jeremiah didn't think they would get there in time.

The healer dug into his back. A scream of pain ripped out of Jeremiah. Everything flashed light and dark. He begged the healer to stop, fighting to stay conscious, as a sharp instrument tortured the open wound on his back. Shredded muscles and broken skin screamed in pain, his body refusing to endure it any longer. There was nothing he could do to stop himself from passing out.

33

Coming Back to Eden

EVIE, WE'RE HERE!" *EVALENE* opened her eyes to find Olive standing over her. Her field of vision was still narrowed to the bunk in front of her and the wall behind it, ignoring the rest of the room, and she pulled the bucket closer out of habit, but she didn't need it. The rocking wasn't as bad now.

"What time is it? We made it?" Evalene stretched a little, blinking awake.

Olive bounced nervously onto the springy mattress across from her. "We got in at dawn, but they had to leave right away. Something's happening at the news station. They wouldn't tell me what. All Luc would say was, 'we don't have time to watch over two defenseless girls. We need everyone who can fight. We'll come back and get you.'" Olive's imitation of Luc wasn't nearly as flattering as it would've been a few days ago. Maybe his allure was finally wearing thin.

At first, staying on the ship sounded like great news. They wouldn't have to fight. But as Evalene's stomach squeezed sharply, she closed her eyes and groaned. They couldn't get off the boat? How long would the fighting last? A day? A week? Maybe even a couple weeks?

"It should be calmer now that we've docked," Olive said, trying to comfort her. She hopped from her bunk onto Evalene's to pat her on the shoulder, unwittingly bumping the bed and disturbing Evalene's stomach more.

It was true. The rocking motion of the boat was less now than out on the open sea. Evalene groaned, but pulled herself up to sitting. The room spun.

"Hey, you feel better!" Olive said, jumping up, rocking the little bed all over again.

"Sort of," Evalene said, although it wasn't much different. She moved slowly, dizzy, setting her feet on the floor. "How long have they been gone? Can we go up to the top deck? I think that would help."

"Just an hour or so," Olive said and stood. "Sure, let's go." Leading the way on light feet, she passed the bunks, through the galley, and up the steps. Evalene wobbled after her. The floor felt slightly crooked, but the urge to empty her stomach lessened as she gulped deep breaths of ocean air.

Evalene stared out at the crowded city of Delmare. The walls built up throughout the city blocked her view of the streets. But far away, in the heart of the city, orange flames flickered, swallowing up one of the wall towers, smoke billowing out around it and the nearby buildings. "What's happening?" Evalene whispered.

Olive came to stand next to her at the railing, leaning against it and staring out at the nearby city. "I think that's the Regulator Headquarters," she said. "Luc was supposed to send half his company there when we landed, but at the last minute, something came up and they all headed for the news station."

Evalene tore her eyes away from the chaos to look at Olive. "That doesn't sound good."

Olive frowned. "I know. I wish there was something we could do to help. They're headed there now, but I don't know if they'll make it in time unless they find a faster way than walking."

Neither of the girls moved for a few minutes. They were anchored far enough out to feel separate from the awful scene. The deep blue waves peacefully lapped at the bottom of the ship. Evalene felt a twinge of relief that she didn't yet have to step foot back in Eden. Suddenly Olive ducked below the railing, jerking hard on Evalene's arm. "Get down!"

Evalene let Olive pull her to the ground, scanning the docks as she did. "Why? What's going on?"

"There's a Regulator on the shore! He was looking right at us!" Olive sounded more afraid than Evalene had ever heard her. "Luc told me to stay below, but I didn't think it was a big deal because I thought they'd taken the docks. I'm sorry Evie…"

Her words hit Evalene squarely in the chest, taking away her breath. They'd been discovered? Already?

Maybe Olive was seeing things. Steeling herself, Evalene crawled to the left, away from Olive about a dozen feet. Cautiously, she peeked over the railing.

Sure enough, there was a man wearing black. Not only was he staring directly at their ship, but he was waving to someone behind him. More men in black uniforms poured out of an alleyway into the harbor. A few were already running towards a smaller motorboat. It would take them less than a minute to reach the ship.

Evalene gasped and ducked below the railing again.

"What did you see?" Olive hissed.

Shaking her head, Evalene just said, "They're coming."

"We can hide!" Olive said, copying Evalene's crawl and scuttling over to her. "We can stack the boxes again! Or we could go down to the galley, find some place deep in the bottom of the ship where it's dark—"

"No," Evalene said, searching for an escape. "They saw us. They won't give up –" An idea struck her. "Olive, are there any lifeboats left?" Ships like this had dozens, enough to carry every passenger on the vessel if necessary. But had the rebels taken all of them?

The girls rushed together across the deck to the side of the ship that faced the ocean. Hanging above the water, tied tightly to the ship, were two small boats.

Thinking quickly, Evalene took the ties holding the closest boat against the ship and frantically started pulling them loose. Waving to Olive, she hissed "Help me lower it!" Olive imitated her, unravelling the ties on the opposite side. As soon as it was loose, they climbed into the boat where it hung midair, and spun the wheels that lowered the boat onto the ocean until the shore was out of sight.

Evalene struggled to find her balance, feeling queasy. It was a long shot, but the tangle of boats along the shoreline might offer enough cover if they could reach another ship. Maybe. The lifeboats weren't powered with an engine, but that would've just given away their position anyway, and they had only seconds before the Regulators reached this side of the ship in their boat.

"Grab a paddle," Evalene said, lifting one herself and thrusting it into the water. "This will only work if we're out of sight before they reach this side of the ship."

They dug into the waves on both sides.

Breathless, Evalene glanced back as they rounded the front of the ship. No other boat had appeared yet. Whipping back to face the front, Evalene forced her burning arms to paddle harder, faster. They passed in front of the ship, and Evalene breathed a sigh of relief. But it was short lived. Only some of the Regulators were in pursuit, and those left on shore spotted them immediately.

Evalene and Olive froze as weapons were trained on them. Hands in the air, they sat in the boat as it bobbed up and down in the water, drifting closer and closer to shore with the current.

Four men in pursuit appeared on a motorboat. One of them yelled, and Evalene flinched, expecting to feel the shot any second. But nothing hit them.

The metal side of the Regulator's motorboat thunked into the wood of their little lifeboat. Two of the men boarded their craft. Evalene gritted her teeth against the pain as her arms were wrenched behind her back. She felt the harsh sting of a rope around her wrists, tying her hands together.

If they spoke to her, she didn't hear. Her ears were ringing and her heartbeat muffled all sound, tears blurring her vision.

She pictured herself hanging from a rope by the end of the day.

Why had she agreed to come?

"Evie. Evie!" Olive's voice broke through. "Evie, what's going to happen?"

Their captors were dragging them by their elbows into the Regulator motorboat, not caring if they stumbled. Thrown onto the bottom of the boat, Evalene curled up, closing her eyes and her ears to Olive's pleading, and begged God to let her die right then.

It would be better here than what they would do to her.

She could throw herself into the sea... she peeked one eye open. The water wasn't even visible from her vantage point in the bottom of the boat. She'd never make it. She felt bruises forming on her shins from being hauled over the metal sides.

Olive's voice reached her ears.

"It'll be okay," Olive was saying. "Evie, we're going to be ok–" she yelped as one of the Regulators struck her across the face. His gloves were rough. Evalene watched as her friend's left cheek grew red and swollen.

The numbness receded. Evalene felt a surge of anger.

She stared at the sour-mouthed man who had hit her friend.

Through her anger, she made a choice. Evalene angled her body to the side, leaning awkwardly on her hands where they were tied behind her back, pushing herself up until she was sitting tall. She glared at the man with the puckered mouth.

What more could they do to her, that wasn't already going to happen?

The hostile Regulator who'd hit Olive was stocky, built wide and short. His cropped hair was bleached a platinum blonde underneath his heavy helmet. He cradled his gun as if hoping to use it.

As the boat neared the docks, he barked a command to the waiting men. There were only six or seven of them, but it was enough. Evalene didn't have the skills to fight even one, and she doubted Olive could take more than one or two. While the men on the docks leapt to secure the boats, their leader moved out of Evalene's line of sight.

Only then did Evalene notice the Regulator behind him, who'd been steering. His olive skin, though darker than her own, seemed light against his thick black hair. His forehead and eyes were stern, his fists clenched, but his frown was directed at the leader, rather than at the girls. His grip on the weapon at his side was so tense, his fingertips were turning white.

When Evalene met his eyes, he looked away.

She didn't have time to wonder about it. A vicious pair of hands yanked her to her feet so hard her arm nearly popped out of its socket. She could guess without looking who hauled her roughly over the side of the boat onto the dock.

The younger man moved away from the wheel, still not meeting her gaze, and helped Olive stand. Behind her, Evalene's captor snorted at the gentler treatment as he jerked her around to face the city. Evalene twisted her neck back, worried they were separating her and Olive. But the young Regulator who held her friend was lifting the girl – much less roughly – over the side of the boat as well.

Evalene's bad-tempered guard was almost wrenching her arm out of its socket. She struggled in the vise-like grip of her jailor, digging in her heels. They'd come here to fight, hadn't they? She twisted in his grasp, succeeding in pulling away mostly due to surprise. Before she had a chance to run or somehow attack with her arms behind her back, a sharp crack sounded, knocking her off her feet.

Off balance with her arms tied, she dropped hard and the impact knocked the air out of her lungs. The slap stung but she ignored the pain. Instead of attempting to stand, she stayed on the ground, knowing it would irritate him more if she was harder to move.

When he reached down to haul her up, she kicked. Hard. All the years of frustration with Daeva when she couldn't fight back were thrown into the kick. She aimed for his groin, but missed, hitting his knee instead. It was still a good blow. She enjoyed a small, tight smile of victory before his boots laid into her side. Each blow of his heavy boots left her gasping, certain that he'd broken at least one of her ribs, and the kick to her stomach made her vomit up the little bit of bile left in her stomach after the long voyage.

Someone stopped him, and Evalene lay in the dirt, eyes closed, mentally assessing the damage. Everything hurt. Arms hauled her up on both sides. She'd been reassigned to two new Regulators who dragged her along, following in the wake of their leader.

Olive was ahead of her now, the younger, dark haired Regulator pressing a hand to her forehead to lower it as he loaded her into the backseat of a Regulator vehicle. Picking up her feet, Evalene tried to meet Olive's eyes as they passed, but the men blocked her view, and she was deposited in the backseat of a second vehicle.

Isolated in the backseat, the men in front didn't say a word. Where were they taking them? She was left alone with her thoughts as they traveled through the city, stopping briefly at check points, waved through quickly. Would she ever see Olive again?

34

Regulator Headquarters

S HE DIDN'T KNOW THE city well enough to recognize where they were going until they were just blocks away from Regulator Headquarters. Evalene heard shots fired by the front of the building, but they turned down a side road before the combat was visible, and pulled up to the back of the enormous building instead. It didn't matter. None of the rebels would know to rescue them.

Staring at the headquarters looming over them as the vehicle pulled up to the building, Evalene felt dread fill her. But her newly found courage rose along with it.

There was still hope.

They dragged the girls inside the building. Evalene was only able to take in the tall ceiling, the desks on one side, and the cells on the other, before she was tossed head first into the closest cell. With her hands still shackled tightly behind her back, Evalene tucked herself inward to break the fall this time, bending her knees and twisting her body so that her right hip and shoulder hit first, hard, resulting in a shooting pain, but thankfully she avoided smashing into the ground with her face. Olive, who came in directly behind her, was not so lucky.

Her friend landed face first on the floor directly in front of her. Evalene winced.

"Olive," she whispered. "Olive, are you okay?"

No answer.

Blood trickled from Olive's forehead onto the concrete floor where it had hit. Her body angled in a way that couldn't be comfortable, yet Olive didn't move.

Behind them, the metal door to their cell swung shut.

A key turned in the lock.

Glancing at Olive in concern, Evalene rolled over onto her back. Olive needed medical attention. Evalene pushed herself up awkwardly on one bound hand until she was sitting. She would beg them for help.

But when she turned towards the room, the first man she saw was the angry Regulator who'd struck them both earlier. Evalene shrunk back instinctively. Her mouth was dry.

"We don't have time to deal with them right now," said the man with the puckered lips. He was moving across the room towards the front of the building. "I want every man with me. We've got them with their tails tucked between their legs. Time to blast them before they get away!" Were the rebels really losing or was he bluffing?

He stopped at the door, waving all his men through, but stepped in front of the young Regulator who had held Olive, effectively blocking the man's path. "You're staying here to guard them. I'll take care of them, and you, when I get back."

The young one's frown deepened, but he nodded.

This time when the sour-faced man took the last few steps to the door, the younger man stayed put. As the angry Regulator swung the door open wide, he chuckled, a sharp, hacking sound. "When we crush this uprising, I look forward to your punishment."

He left cackling. Evalene couldn't tell if he'd been talking to them or the younger Regulator.

The sound faded as the door swung shut behind him.

Evalene leaned over until she was resting against the bars of their prison, pushing off the floor, forcing her tired legs to lift her and using the bars to keep herself upright. Once standing, a wave of dizziness, leftover from the voyage, threatened to knock her back onto the ground.

Deep breaths.

Focus.

It took a moment to find the young Regulator where he now sat in the middle of the large room, with his feet up on a desk, arms crossed, leaning back in his chair. He was frowning at the door.

"Please sir," Evalene called, wishing she could recall the correct Regulator titles. She guessed. "Control Leader, sir, my friend is hurt. Please, we need help!"

After a moment of indecision, the young man swung his feet off the desk to the floor. Strolling towards them, he stopped a half dozen feet away from the bars of their cell. His face was unreadable, other than the permanent brooding stare.

"Grausum is the Control Leader," he said, crossing his arms again and tipping his head the slightest bit toward the door where the hostile blonde Regulator had vanished. "I'm just a Watchman."

"Of course." Evalene leaned into the bars to keep her balance. She tilted her head towards Olive since her hands were unavailable to point. "My friend is hurt Mr. Watchman –" she peeked at the badge on his uniform that said C. Solomon. "Watchman Solomon."

"Sol," he corrected her, dark eyes expressionless.

"Watchman Sol," she repeated the name he gave her, trying to be agreeable. "Please, can you do something? Even if you just untied my hands, at least then I could help her."

He scratched his nose and shifted his feet, but didn't come any closer. He glanced towards the door.

"I won't tell the Control Leader that you helped," Evalene bargained. "He can think I got free on my own."

When he still didn't move, she pressed herself up against the bars and yelled in frustration and desperation. "Are you deaf? She's hurt! Do you want her to die before your stupid hanging? Get a med kit!"

Evalene didn't know who was more startled, him or her, when he jumped into action.

Bringing over the med kit from the wall, he twisted to take the ring of keys off his belt. Instead of untying her hands and passing the kit to her, he unlocked the cell door and surprised Evalene by entering.

Stepping away from him, Evalene backed into the far corner, feeling vulnerable with her hands tied. But he ignored her, and bent down beside Olive. First he removed the restraints on the girl's wrists. Once her hands were free, he gently rolled her over onto her back.

Olive moaned.

Evalene watched her friend's eyes flutter and close again. Blood dripped down the side of Olive's forehead, not slowing much since her fall. But this Regulator – what was his name again? Sol? He wiped away the worst of it with some gauze. Cleaning the wound with something that smelled strongly alcoholic, blood continued to gush from the cut, and finally he pressed the gauze against it, in an effort to stop the bleeding. Digging in the med kit for more supplies, he came up empty-handed.

Eyes catching on her purple pantsuit, Evalene had an idea. "I can help if you remove my restraints?"

Watchman Sol's eyebrow twitched in skepticism at the idea, the only sign that he'd heard her. But after a moment, he stood. Approaching her, he spun his finger in a circular motion, indicating she should turn around. She did, uneasily. The moment her hands were freed, she yanked them in front of her, even as she whirled to face him.

He simply raised his eyebrows at her and crossed his arms, waiting.

Evalene hesitated, not wanting to take her eyes off him any more than he did her. But a moan from Olive reminded her they didn't have time to waste. She stepped around the Regulator toward her friend, coming to stand on the opposite side of Olive, hunkering down next to the girl.

Testing the bottom of her pant leg, Evalene exhaled sadly, and ripped. The fabric tore easily. Pulling slowly, carefully, she ripped off a long, winding strip from the bottom of the pant leg, circling a few times and stopping halfway before she reached her knee. She offered it to the Regulator.

Standing on the other side of Olive, he reached across and took it. Kneeling as well, he set the fabric on the floor beside him, removing the gauze he'd pressed into Olive's wound, which was now soaked with blood. Seconds after he lifted it, blood pooled underneath. Evalene frowned.

He picked up the fabric and placed it on Olive's forehead carefully. Lifting her head with gentle hands, he wrapped the cloth around the back of her head, and back up to where her golden hair was stained red near her forehead. One full wrap around Olive's head, pulled tight, was immediately followed by a second wrap, covering the first. On the fourth wrap around Olive's head, he ran out of fabric right by Olive's ear, and lowered her head back to the floor.

Evalene watched Sol fish a safety pin out of the med-kit, securing the makeshift head wrap. A sigh of relief escaped Evalene's lips. But then he shifted to pick Olive up, this time her whole body instead of only her head.

Evalene protested. "Don't move her! Leave her here with me!"

But he wasn't separating them. He laid Olive on the hard cot against the back wall. The thin mattress was a slight improvement from the concrete floor.

His face, so expressionless before, now showed a hint of concern in his frown as he stared at the unconscious girl. "I'll get you some water."

He locked the cell door behind him and disappeared down a hallway.

"Olive," Evalene whispered, coming over to the cot, kneeling on the cold floor and leaning close to her friend's ear. "Olive, I need you to wake up. Please. I can't do this on my own…"

Stirring, Olive's eyelids trembled, but didn't open. Head tilting to the side, she could've easily been napping if not for the tiny spot of blood leaking through the purple fabric wrapped around her head, growing larger. Evalene slumped on the floor next to the cot, leaning against the wall.

They were going to die here.

She regretted so much. "I'm sorry, Olive," she whispered, staring at the bars of their cell. "This is my fault. If I had come with Jeremiah, you would still be home right now with Mae."

Olive's hand touched her shoulder, startling her. Evalene hadn't thought she was awake. "It's okay," Olive said. She was so pale. "I wanted to come. And you don't have to be afraid. God will take care of us." She smiled, but her hand dropped back to the cot weakly.

The girl with the bloody head, lying on a prison cot, recently captured and beaten, and quite aware they might soon die, smiled peacefully. How was it that she could have more peace in a moment such as this than Evalene had known in her entire lifetime?

Evalene didn't have a chance to ask.

Sol's boots echoed loudly in the hallway as he re-entered the large room. He held a small cup. Striding towards their cell, he handed the cup to Evalene, and she immediately brought it to Olive, setting it on the floor to help her friend sit up.

But pain scrunched up Olive's face before she was even fully upright, and she sank back down. "I'm feeling better," she whispered, refusing to sit up, her eyes closing.

"You should drink something," Evalene argued. She lightly shook her arm, trying to wake her, but Olive didn't answer. Evalene didn't know what to do. *God,* she found herself praying through her fear, *if you're really the God that Olive believes in... can you save us?*

"You should keep her awake in case she has a concussion," a voice said behind her.

Evalene jumped.

Watchman Sol still stood where he'd handed her the cup. She'd forgotten he was there. But his gaze was on Olive, forehead furrowed. "I mean it," he said. "You can't leave someone with a concussion, they need to be kept awake, monitored..."

"What do you care?" Evalene heard the defiance in her voice. It surprised her.

Arms crossed casually, he continued to stare at Olive the way someone might look at a zoo animal. "How did she get to the age she is without being Numbered?"

Evalene blinked in surprise. Vaguely a memory of hands on her neck when they were first captured came back to her. It made sense they'd checked Olive's neck too. Bare skin. Evalene smiled. It felt like a small triumph.

"She's not from Eden." She crossed her arms as well, although it didn't hold as much punch while sitting cross-legged on the concrete floor, with one pant leg ripped half off.

She knew all the questions flooding his mind. They'd been her own. How did they know their Number? What to do in life? Who they were? Their value? Their role in society?

"Numbers aren't real," she told him, standing, quoting Jeremiah to him as if she believed the words herself. "They're not who we are." Did she actually believe that? She realized she was starting to.

He surprised her by nodding thoughtfully. "You hear whispers," he said, still staring at Olive, "families who bribe the priests for higher Numbers. Or those who fall out of favor with the Number One, and their children just 'happen' to receive unusually low Numbers." This was the most he'd spoken since they'd met. Evalene's eyebrows rose. She hadn't heard those rumors, but his last example made her wonder if she wasn't the only one?

Olive twitched and stirred. Both Evalene and the Regulator paused their conversation to examine the girl.

"You really should wake her," he said again.

"Mmm, I'm up, I'm up," Olive mumbled, eyes closed.

"No you're not," Evalene argued.

It worked.

"Yes I am!" Olive's eyes flew open. She struggled to sit up and Evalene helped her. Evalene didn't know anything about concussions, and against her better judgement, she found herself trusting the Regulator's recommendations. Holding the cup for Olive, she helped her friend drink. Her throat was parched, but she ignored it, letting Olive have the entire glass.

Sitting on the cot next to Olive, she held her friend upright with an arm around her shoulders, wincing at the bloody head-wrap. Olive reached a hand up to touch it at Evalene's expression. When she pulled her hand down and saw the blood on her fingertips, she paled visibly. "Oh… That's not good…"

Sol's keys jangled as he unlocked the door once more. He stepped into the cell, holding out his hands, "Give me the cup. You need to drink more water."

Olive smiled at him gratefully. He looked away, taking the cup, and disappeared down the hallway again.

He left the cell door wide open.

What was he doing?

Evalene wondered if Olive could make it if she asked her to run. Olive swayed a little to the left, blinking away dizziness. No. They wouldn't even make it to the door.

When Watchman Sol reappeared though, Evalene lifted her chin. "We could have escaped."

His smile was so small and quick she almost didn't catch it. He shook his head as he handed her the cup of water. "You wouldn't get far. There's fighting out front and guards out back." He shrugged, crossing his arms and leaning against the cell doorway. "Believe it or not, this is the safest place for you two right now."

Olive smiled up at Sol. "Well then, I'm glad you caught us!"

Evalene frowned at Olive. "We would have been just fine on our own. And the safest place is with our friends, *not* locked up, waiting to be hanged.

Sol grunted.

He fiddled with the keys on his belt. Stared at a spot on the wall. Then, as if making a decision, he finally said, "Maybe you won't be here much longer." That was cryptic. Was he offering to help them escape?

Olive brightened and smiled, immediately reading into his

words. "You're going to let us go?"

Evalene couldn't believe it when Sol nodded, still scowling. She scowled back, not trusting him. She wasn't sure if his permanently dark expression was directed at them or the situation.

"God sent an angel to help us even here." Olive's smile was huge as she got to say her favorite words. "I told you."

Evalene didn't answer. She stared at Sol, unconvinced. He looked uncomfortable at being called an angel.

"Oh! I know," Olive turned to Sol. "You should come with us!" She clapped her hands at the idea, but weakly, her energy fading quickly. "If you're changing sides, there's no point in staying."

Sol started shaking his head before she'd even finished. "I can't."

"Yes you can!" Olive argued. "If you change your mind later, you can just come back and say we took you hostage." She grinned at the idea.

He didn't say anything for a moment, staring at her in thought.

Olive drew a deep breath to argue further. Evalene knew from experience that her friend could hound him all day. Evalene held out a hand, interrupting. "Whatever you do is fine. Just let us go."

Sol nodded, swinging the cell door further open, leading them out. "Where are you headed? I can at least point you in the right direction."

"The city news station," Olive said, leaning forward to stand.

"Why should we trust you?" Evalene said at the same time, as she helped Olive up. She flung her free hand out in frustration. "Olive! This could be a trap! He could send Regulators!"

They entered the main room and stopped outside the cell in front of Sol.

"He won't," Olive said confidently.

"I won't," Sol said at the same time.

Olive swayed a little.

"Here," Sol pulled out the closest chair. "Rest. You're not ready to travel yet."

Wanting to argue, Evalene glanced once at Olive's pale face and the thin line of sweat on her lip, and held her tongue.

Once Olive was seated, Evalene assessed the rest of the room, wishing they had more options. She could try to roll Olive out on a chair with wheels when Watchman Sol wasn't looking. But the city roads were filled with potholes. Dragging Olive might not be physically possible for more than a few blocks.

She crossed her arms and leaned against the closest desk, eyeing Sol. The young Regulator made her nervous. She couldn't read him.

He met her gaze without a word. Neither of them looked away. It could have gone on indefinitely if Olive hadn't broken the silence.

"Would you be terribly offended if I asked who was winning the fight?" Olive bit her lip as she asked Sol.

He shook his head, expressionless, and spoke as if giving a report. "Shortly before dawn, we received a call to the local news station. We sent men to respond, and more men when they needed backup. That left us shorthanded when they attacked here around six a.m. before our day shift started. They began to retreat about an hour ago, but we're not sure why. We don't have enough men to crush the rebellion entirely until reinforcements arrive from other cities."

"Has anyone else been captured?" Evalene asked.

Sol gestured to the empty room. "Our orders are shoot to kill."

Olive gasped.

"Why didn't you shoot us then?" Evalene demanded.

He ignored the question, looking at the door where Control Leader Grausum had vanished. "The city news station isn't too far from here. I could drive you."

"Oh yes! Please!" Olive accepted his offer immediately.

Evalene squinted at him. Had he stopped the Control Leader from shooting? Someone had yelled. It might've been him. That would explain why the leader had mentioned a punishment. But she was still skeptical. "What's in it for you?"

"Evie!" Olive chastised, tsking at the question, waving her hand as if to effectively wave the words away. "Sol is a gentleman. I can tell. Why are you so quick to judge him based on his Number? What if he doesn't want his Number any more than you want yours?"

Now it was Evalene's turn to look away.

Sol lifted his chin. "I never had a choice before." He shut his mouth, pressing his lips together tightly. Evalene thought that was all he was going to say. She turned to Olive and took a breath to ask if her friend could walk instead, when Sol surprised her by adding, "I'd like to come."

"You're willing to risk a hanging?" Evalene frowned at him in suspicion. "If the revolution doesn't succeed?"

"Yes." Sol shrugged, giving them no further insight into his decision. It didn't feel like enough. But he clearly wasn't going to share any further. His gaze met Evalene's as she considered him. After another long pause, he gestured to the blood-soaked fabric around Olive's head. "Whatever you do, decide quickly. She needs a doctor."

Olive touched her forehead, wincing in agreement.

"'She' has a name," Evalene shot back. But she nodded. The sooner they left this prison, the better. "You can drive us."

"It's Olive." Her blonde friend beamed up at Sol. She held out her hand. "Nice to meet you." And he shook it, humoring her.

"You too." He strode towards the door they'd come in. "This way."

Evalene helped Olive out of the chair, and they slowly followed. At the exit, Sol stood waiting for them. "Stay here." His jaw was set in determination, serious gaze unwavering. "I'll pull the car around and pick you up." A hint of worry as his gaze touched Olive again briefly was the only change in his expression. He hesitated, hand on the doorknob. "There's fighting breaking out all over the city. It will be dangerous…"

"We'll be okay," Evalene told him, unflinching. He didn't say another word. Opening the door, he vanished from sight as it swung shut behind him.

"Olive, you can't tell him anything else," Evalene whispered to her friend while they were waiting. "We don't know if he's really going to help us." She refused to be fooled again. "He could be manipulating us for information, or maybe when we reach everyone else, he'll put a gun to our heads and try to use us as hostages. We can't trust him."

Olive was blinking as if the light hurt her eyes. She turned her head slightly towards Evalene, then winced at the movement, putting a hand up to the bandages on her head. "I understand," Olive's voice was weak, un-Olive-like, "but we can't stay here either."

Evalene didn't have an argument for that. If they stayed, they could be killed within the hour. Olive added, "He's our only option." And Evalene knew it was true.

35

Injured

"HOW IS HE?" *JEREMIAH* recognized Larimar's voice above him. He floated for a moment, but sharp arrows were hitting him in his back, his shoulder, his hand, his foot… He scowled in anger at whoever was shooting him. Slowly he woke up, blinking at the white ceiling in confusion. Where was he? Why did everything hurt?

"We're still holding the station, Captain." Jeremiah's eyes found Larimar. The man was standing over him with two others. Why was he lying down? Jeremiah moved to sit up. Immediately the men forced him back down. White spots danced in Jeremiah's vision. He didn't have any strength to fight, and let them ease him back down. The pain came rushing back in its full intensity. He groaned.

"Just relax," Larimar's voice said again. The screech of metal on the floor sounded, and Jeremiah carefully opened his eyes to find Larimar pulling up a chair. The man sat, gesturing to the other two men to leave.

One of them frowned as he left. "Don't let him get up. He'll pull out all my stitches." Jeremiah recognized the healer from earlier.

But the moment the door closed, he ignored the command. "Help me up."

Larimar started to shake his head, but Jeremiah's glare stopped him. "At least rest a minute before you do," Larimar suggested.

Still frowning, Jeremiah allowed it. He couldn't get up without help anyway. "Report."

"The Regs were minutes from taking the station," Larimar obeyed, leaning forward, "maybe less. We held the front door, and blew up the back door. If we didn't have the vests and the barricade, we would've lost for sure. But each time they climbed on top of a car, they made a perfect target. We lost a lot of men. Too many. They figured out the weak spots in Hofyn's armor." When body shots didn't work, the Regs would've aimed elsewhere. It made sense.

Larimar leaned back in exhaustion. "Your plan worked. We stalled while the rest of our company ran the last quarter of the way here, and Flint's company stole some vehicles to make it here too. They arrived just in time." Larimar stopped there. But he was frowning, and wouldn't meet Jeremiah's eyes.

"What's wrong?" Jeremiah demanded, struggling to sit up on his own. This time Larimar helped him. Once in a sitting position, Jeremiah rested, breathing hard. The healer had been right about his stitches breaking open. "Tell me."

"We had the advantage for a bit. Took most of the street once the other men got here. And for a little while, we were picking off Regulator reinforcements before they realized we weren't on the same side." Jeremiah found himself more grateful than ever that Adri had thought to have the men wear black like the Regulator uniforms. "But we're losing ground again. It's a matter of time before their reinforcements get here. We don't have enough men. We're going to lose the station."

"Where's Luc?" Jeremiah ignored the prediction.

"No word yet," Larimar shook his head. "We spoke on the radio earlier. Told them not to give away their position. But it might be too late for that, if the Regs guessed they were in the harbor."

That worried Jeremiah. How much time had passed? His eyes found the clock on the wall. It was already 7 a.m. They were behind on their plan. "Tell Flint to leave the Regs HQ entirely. We need them here. As soon as possible. And we need to broadcast immediately. It might be our only chance." Jeremiah didn't expect Luc until noon. That meant Flint's men were their only hope. Them, and the people of Eden if he could convince them in time.

Larimar helped him stand. Jeremiah leaned heavily on the man as he hobbled out of the small room and down a short hallway. Irregular shots fired outside, but he ignored them. The broadcast was his mission now. He had to let the men outside take care of the Regulators.

They entered the large newsroom, filled with desks in rows, rolling chairs, and computer screens cluttering every surface. Though Eden was still lagging behind the rest of the world in their technology, the equipment in this room was highly advanced compared to the rest of Eden, excluding the Number One's home.

A small group of Jeremiah's men stood along the wall, ready

to do whatever was needed. Three station employees were tied up, sitting on the floor against the wall. The man who'd shot him was one of them, and he started shaking again when he saw Jeremiah.

"Bring them," Jeremiah waved towards the captives, ignoring the sting of his bandaged fingers. He was dizzy. But he hid it from them. "Hurry. There's not much time."

They made their way through the large room, past the desks and computers into the adjoining smaller room, where the filming was done. "Set up the emergency broadcast," Jeremiah commanded the news station employees as they were untied. His request would turn on every television in the country that wasn't already on, airing the broadcast on every single channel.

Surrounded by Jeremiah's men, the three employees thankfully didn't argue. Watching closely, Jeremiah made sure they used the special frequency the Number One had set up that couldn't be interrupted. He'd done his homework on that portion.

"No," Jeremiah said as they made a valiant effort to use the wrong channel, thinking he wouldn't catch them. "Not that one." He pointed out to Larimar and the other men in the room which frequency they needed to use, making it clear to the station employees at the same time that he wouldn't be fooled. Hopefully this would prevent further defiance. They didn't know it, but this was the extent of his knowledge.

Turning, Jeremiah stepped up on the short stage in front of the green screen. The stage had a long, curved desk for typical nightly news, with two chairs for the anchors. "Radio Adri's company at the Number One's home," he said, sinking into the nearest chair in relief. "Let them know to be ready to go on air."

Every part of him hurt as if he was being repeatedly stabbed, especially the wound on his back, which felt wet and likely had opened just like the healer said it would. But he kept a calm front. None of that mattered right now.

He nodded for the broadcast to begin.

Shooting began again in earnest outside just as the cameramen started their countdown. Three, two, one. On air. Screams in the background. "Citizens of Eden," Jeremiah began quietly, "my name is Jeremiah Bloom. My parents were Eben and Tarsa Bloom. You might recognize their names from nearly ten years ago, when we all lived through the Bloom Rebellion." The dozen or so people in the room gasped, including the cameramen.

Jeremiah ignored them and continued. "They died fighting for you. But their dream lives on in me. A dream of a world without Numbers. Though the Number One has kept it hidden, there have been frequent uprisings throughout Eden since that day. People just like you have recognized the injustice. I'm proud to say that not just hundreds, but thousands of people have stood up to the Number System in some form. But we have never been unified enough to coordinate a full-scale attack. Until now."

He held out a hand for the radio. Larimar stepped up to place it in his hand. Jeremiah pressed the button and spoke into the device. "Status at the Number One's home, confirm."

Static crackled as the men on the other side responded, "We've taken the Number One's home. He's confined to his living quarters. His guards are in custody. We wait for your command."

The crackling stopped as the radio conversation ended. Jeremiah set it on the desk.

Speaking once again to the camera, he continued. "The Number One does not deserve to lead this country. We are not going to let him." Some of his men shouted their agreement in the background, unable to help themselves. Sporadic shooting continued outside, often followed by cries of pain. It was now or never.

"We need your help," Jeremiah spoke through the pain, pleading with the camera. He would beg them if he had to. "Please, if you have ever felt that our country needed to change, now is the time." Jeremiah felt dizzy. He wanted to speak further, to tell them more about riots and insurrections the Number One had buried. But if he lost consciousness on live television, it would be a huge blow to the citizen's trust. He couldn't risk it.

Instead he wrapped up quickly with a simple call to action, "Come to the news station, to the Number One's home, or to the Regulator Headquarters. We will bring change by standing together. Join us. Fight with us! With your help, we can win!" He nodded to Larimar, signaling his talk was finished.

As Larimar stepped on stage to begin the next portion, Jeremiah forced himself to stand tall, to stride off stage and off camera as if in full health.

He stumbled at one point, but thankfully, the monitors showed he was off the screen by then. He lurched over to sit in a chair along the wall.

"Join us at the news station, at the Number One's home, or at the Regs' Headquarters," Larimar repeated to the camera now, making sure the locations were clear. Urgency underlined his tone, but he didn't give away just how badly they needed help. The

Regulators could watch this channel as easily as anyone else.

Jeremiah gestured to one of the soldiers in the room that he recognized. "Dross, it's time for testimonies. Can you gather a few people to get that started?" The man nodded, quietly exiting the room. Had Larimar said the rest of their company had arrived? He wasn't sure. They'd brought a few men and women with them for this exact purpose, but most had been in the group walking here, and he wasn't sure what had happened to them. Thanks to his injuries, he didn't have a clear grasp of where anyone was or how the fight was going outside.

But they needed to use the broadcast while they had it. Anyone would do at this point. Larimar was still speaking when Dross returned with a small line-up of two men and one woman. "Only three?" Jeremiah said softly, so they wouldn't overhear.

"We couldn't spare anymore," Dross replied in a whisper as well. "The barricade is the only thing between us and the Regs right now, and we're running low on ammo." He glanced towards the station employees, operating the cameras willingly now, and at the three soldiers preparing to speak on camera. "I don't know if we'll make it past these three. But if we do, we can swap them out for others."

Jeremiah nodded his acceptance. While he sat, unable to move even if he wanted to, the men took their turns speaking on camera, pleading with the country to listen. Their words blurred together in the background for Jeremiah, as he tried to think of a solution. Larimar took over without needing to be asked, bringing in a fourth and fifth man as the first and second ran back out to fight.

After a half hour, he felt rested enough to hobble out of the camera room, through the newsroom, and down the hall towards the front door. Jeremiah watched his men fighting from the doorway. They were unable to go outside, but not letting the Regulators get any closer either. The lack of windows made the building well protected, but hard to defend, since only so many men could fit around the doorway. The rest were forced to fight outside from behind the barrier of cars, more exposed.

"I'm out!" The shout came from a woman outside. She ducked down against a car, dropping the useless weapon. "Me too," a man said from inside by the door. But two more soldiers stepped forward, kneeling and taking their place. They fired only when necessary, to save ammunition. Where were the citizens? Had he been wrong to believe that many were dying to fight back?

"Radio Luc again," Jeremiah started to say, not willing to give up, when a cry rose outside. He stopped and moved closer to the door to peer out. More of his men began to yell. It was a triumphant sound. From where Jeremiah stood, he couldn't tell what was happening to cause their excitement, but the Regulators on the other side of the barrier stopped shooting, turning around to face whatever it was. After a moment, Jeremiah risked stepping up to the front door to get a better look.

Citizens of Eden were flowing down the streets towards them. Not many at first, but enough to distract the Regulators. That was all the rebels needed to get the upper hand. The fight began to turn as the Regulators were surrounded. Unarmed citizens were shot down. But more appeared to take their place. As the minutes ticked by, the Regulators began to be overwhelmed by sheer numbers.

People streamed towards them from all directions until there were more than Jeremiah could count. A sea of people from all sides, rallying, moving steadily down the streets towards the fight. Some of the Regulators began shooting into the crowd to deter them. But it only made them angry. With a growing roar, the mass of people began to run at the Regulators. No matter how many shots they got off, the people just kept coming. They were going to trample them.

Jeremiah's men still wore the black uniforms that had served them well earlier when they'd wanted to appear as Regulators. But now as the frenzied crowd drew closer it became dangerous. "Take off the black! Take off the black!" Jeremiah screamed out at his men, ignoring the pain streaking from his back through his side and into his limbs as he tugged at his own black shirt, trying to rip it off.

A second after he began screaming, Dross and Larimar caught the hint, and joined his cries, pulling their black jackets off as well to reveal their gray and blue ship uniforms underneath. "Take off the black, men! Take it off!" They shouted, and after a moment of confusion, men began to respond, ripping the dark clothing off. Some had shirts underneath, others just stripped down to bare skin. They cheered the people on as the Regulators were completely overpowered and defeated.

Jeremiah felt something wet trickling down his back. He wiped at it with his good hand. Lifting the hand to his face, he found it covered in blood. He recognized the blackout as it came this time, but not quick enough to sit or kneel or do anything except hope that one of the men nearby would catch him before he hit the cold, hard concrete.

36

The News Station

WATCHMAN *SOL DROVE EVALENE* and Olive in the caged backseat of his Regulator jeep all the way to the news station. Though Sol took the long way around to be safe, driving all the way to the outskirts of the city before turning towards the station, each time they turned back into the city, they couldn't make any headway. Roads were blocked by crowds of people filling the streets, forcing them to turn around.

The crowds stunned Evalene. There were so many people. And from what she could tell, there weren't even any rebels, just regular citizens of all Number ranges. With only tiny hints of blue, black, or white in the crowd, it was mostly made up of the middle and lower classes with brown and gray featured much more heavily than the red of the merchant class.

More than once, Sol was forced to exit in reverse as the crowd spied the black Regulator symbols on the vehicle and began to chase them. Some were riled up to the point they even kept chase for a few city blocks.

Sol was in more danger than either of the girls. For Evalene and Olive, this mode of transportation was by far the safest passage in the entire city. Protected from other Regulators because they appeared to be already captured, yet safe from the rebel group as well, as their cage in the backseat showed they were on the rebel's side.

It took almost four hours to make what would normally be just a half hour drive. By the time they reached the station, it was past noon.

Evalene recognized the street they were on as Sol took some older backroads, getting them as close to the news station as he could. "We're going to need to walk from here," he said as they saw crowds forming in the distance once more. Stepping out of the jeep, he helped Olive step down. Evalene jumped out before he could give her a hand too.

Then he startled the girls by pulling his black uniform shirt off. Olive looked like she might faint again. He caught them staring and shrugged, gesturing towards the throngs of people swarming down the road. "I don't think this crowd will give me time to explain." He dug through the back of his jeep, pulling out a piece of brown fabric and tying it around his neck. "Better safe than sorry." Evalene nodded in understanding. Though it was a serious moment, she bit her lip to keep from smiling at the way Olive stared at the man. He was extremely fit, which made sense given his line of work, and even as serious as he was, Sol was still handsome. Maybe Olive's crush on Luc finally had a rival.

They slowly walked the last few blocks to the news station building, pressing through the crowds. Sol paused for Olive to rest a few times, but eventually they reached their goal. Though the ugly concrete station was new, built after the war, a couple nearby brick buildings were still standing, a remnant from the old world. Evalene would never forget driving by them daily when she was young, staring at the posters of soldiers who'd fought in the last world war, the Number One's reminder that they needed him, needed their Numbers. She suddenly had the urge to tear them down.

Two rebels stood outside on the steps of the news station, guarding the door. There was a strange barrier of twisted metal that almost looked like cars. Other soldiers stood inside this barrier, spaced out evenly, watching the crowd. All of them had guns. Every face was set in determination.

When they stepped up to the cars and Sol placed his hands on one in preparation to climb over it, guns lowered, pointing directly at him.

"Cooley!" Olive shouted, leaning in front of Sol and waving wildly, then wincing, as she put a hand to her bandaged head. Evalene grabbed her before she fell, putting Olive's arm over her shoulder to better support her. But it worked. Every soldier recognized Olive's face. The men brightened, giving the girls friendly smiles as they lowered their weapons.

"What are you doing here?" Cooley called as Sol helped Olive onto the hood of the nearest car first, then Evalene. Now that she was up next to the barricade she was certain they were cars. Unusual, horribly damaged cars. Were those bullet holes? Evalene's eyes grew wide at the sight.

Cooley stepped up to help Olive down, but Sol got there first, having leapt up and over the trunk of the car next to them, already inside the barricade. Olive let him pick her up and set her on the ground.

"Who's this?" Cooley said, slowing as he approached, eyeing Sol and not bothering to hide his suspicion. Evalene hovered above the tense triangle, waiting for them to move so she could get down too. She shouldn't be worried for Sol. She barely knew him. But she held her breath.

Olive stood shakily in front of Sol, as if trying to protect the bigger man. "This is Sol," she told Cooley. "He's with us."

But Sol took off the brown bandana around his neck, not saying a word as he revealed his tattoo. "You'll find out sooner or later," was all he said.

Cooley took one glance at his Number 11 tattoo, then scrunched up his face in disgust and spit. The spittle landed at Sol's feet, but the challenge hung in the air for less than a second. Sol ignored the man completely, turning to help Evalene down.

Accepting his hand, Evalene jumped off the hood of the car. Once more, there was a strained silence. "Can we go inside?" Olive asked. "I think I need a doctor." That jump-started Cooley into action.

He jogged ahead of them while Sol and Olive shuffled towards the news station at a slower pace, and Evalene trailed after them.

As they reached the concrete steps, Evalene's steps slowed.

Jeremiah was here.

Olive swayed a little in the doorway after climbing the steps, paling, and Watchman Sol took her elbow once more, encouraging her to lean on him. Cooley was barely containing his hatred of the Regulator. Only Olive's condition kept him silent as he and

Evalene followed them inside.

The building, much larger on the inside than the exterior had let on, was filled with empty rooms and hallways. Muffled voices floated towards them from double doors at the end of the long hall. Cooley thrust the doors open, letting them swing shut behind him and leaving Sol to open them for Olive. Evalene dawdled in the hallway, letting them go on ahead. She felt unexpectedly nervous about seeing Jeremiah.

But yells from the room a second later roused her into action. She ran up to the door and into the room. It was chock-full of desks covered in computers – she'd never seen so many in her entire life. But they faded into the background as she took in the scene.

Luc knelt on the ground, cradling Olive's unconscious head. She must have fainted. Sol stood to the side, held back by two rebels Evalene didn't recognize. Sol's nose was dripping blood. "What in the Number One's name happened?" Evalene asked.

"I punched him," Luc said flatly. Then his voice rose. "I told you two to wait on the ship!"

"It's not our fault!" Evalene yelled back, gesturing to Sol. "The Regulators came to the harbor. If he hadn't rescued us, we'd still be in headquarters right now, waiting for our hanging!"

Luc glared at Sol, hearing only what he wanted to hear. "We'll take their headquarters. It's just a matter of time. Did he do this to her?"

Sol glowered back, not saying a word.

Olive's eyes fluttered open. Evalene answered for Sol when it was clear he wasn't going to. "No. I told you, he *helped* us."

"He did more than help," Olive spoke up, joining the argument before she even knew the details, struggling to sit. "He's the only reason we're still alive."

Luc helped Olive sit upright, but he didn't answer her, and he didn't look at Evalene. "Rest for a minute," he said to Olive. He stood and faced Sol. Both men were the same average height and lightweight build, but something made Evalene think that if Sol decided to fight back, he would win. Luc glared at the Regulator as he said, "You're not needed anymore. Go back to where you came from."

"Luc!" Olive gasped. "Shame on you! Sol's here to help!"

Evalene turned so that she was standing side by side with Sol in silent support, and agreed with Olive. "We need all the help we can get."

"Actually, we don't," Luc replied, stubbornly. He helped Olive stand, turning his back on them entirely, leading Olive towards a nearby chair. "Let's get you cleaned up." He asked one of the men nearby to fetch a healer.

But Evalene gritted her teeth, feeling that surge of anger that made her brave. "You're not in charge to make that decision. Where is Jeremiah?" Evalene glared at the men holding Sol's arms and they let go, backing off.

Luc's back was turned and he didn't argue, but he didn't answer either. What did that mean? The healer arrived and began to untie the makeshift fabric bandage around Olive's head while Luc pulled a med kit off the wall and dug out fresh gauze. As the healer worked, Luc frowned at Olive's wound, finally answering Evalene's question. "Jeremiah's recovering from some injuries. He can't be disturbed right now."

Evalene frowned in concern, working up the nerve to argue with Luc again and demand to see him anyway, when Olive spoke first. "How is the revolution going? Are we winning?"

"I think we finally are," Luc replied, as the healer wrapped a fresh bandage around Olive's head. "It may take a few days to know for sure. A lot of cities are less certain than Delmare, and a few were taken back. We're running low on people willing to make a statement, unfortunately. I sent runners out to meet citizens and ask them to share their stories. But most don't want to share on live television and risk a hanging until they're sure we've won."

"I can give my story," Olive said.

"You're injured," Evalene argued. "You're not up to it."

"No, it's the perfect time!" Olive argued. "It will be inspiring for people to see others outside of Eden, nobly fighting for their cause!"

With the fresh white bandage, she didn't look like the warrior she described, just a pale, blonde girl wearing a headscarf. But Luc's expression brightened. "I don't need to know the details. Here, let's tie the bloody wrap over the new one... just for a few minutes. It's not like we're faking it. It is your blood after all."

He made quick work of adding the blood-soaked purple fabric back to her ensemble. "That's perfect. Okay, follow me and I'll get you in line. They'll need someone within the next five minutes."

Helping Olive stand, Luc led her past all the computers to the door at the opposite side of the room. Evalene's eye caught the screens all along the top of the room as she glanced up, and her jaw dropped as she recognized the man on the television as Talc.

Luc and Olive disappeared through the door on the other side, leaving Evalene and Sol to fend for themselves.

This was the broadcast Jeremiah had described, the one where people would tell their stories and influence citizens to join the revolution. Evalene didn't know if they were allowed in to watch, but after a pause, she decided to try. She strode across the room, and Sol followed, ignoring those who turned to glare.

Evalene tested the door handle to the next room. It opened easily. She entered with Sol right behind her. This was a much smaller, brighter room. Compared to the chatter of different conversations in the computer room, this room was hushed, all attention focused on the speaker on stage.

The stage itself was only a couple inches off the ground, but it spanned the length of the entire right wall and was a bright, vivid green. This same green paint covered the wall behind the stage as well. She'd never seen anything like it. But the desk looked familiar. The color wood and the way it curved to hold the chairs reminded Evalene of the nightly news with Sterling and Opal, but this couldn't be their desk, could it? They'd always had a serene neutral background behind them, not this neon green. The array of cameras and lighting spread out around the stage in orderly chaos, all pointing towards Talc as he spoke. The monitors held the same image that was playing in the room behind them. They were broadcasting live.

Chairs lined the walls at the back of the room, and Sol and Evalene found seats. As they did, those nearby stared at the shirtless man, and once they read his tattoo, they stood and moved away, unwilling to sit near him.

Talc was wrapping up his statement, but he made Evalene too nervous to listen. She found herself oddly grateful for Sol's presence. Luc took the stage. Stepping up onto the tiny platform, he placed a hand on Talc's shoulder, but directed his grin at the camera. As he thanked the big man for speaking, he waved for Olive to come up, beginning to introduce her.

As Olive stepped up next to him, Luc made a show of helping her, asking if she was sure she felt up to it. Olive waved him off, annoyed. But as she walked around the table to sit, she tripped slightly, and Sol stood unconsciously, moving towards the stage in concern. He stopped halfway. Staying put in the middle of the room behind the cameramen, he crossed his arms.

Olive recovered from her trip, lowering herself into a chair. The bright light fixated on her, exaggerating the bloody bandages even more. She began to tell the camera of life outside of Eden, the island and all its technological advances they'd never been allowed to have here. She described how well they functioned without Numbers. Talking had never been a problem for Olive. She enjoyed the attention, not even a concussion could stop that, and she dramatically told the cameras and everyone in the room the story of when she first learned about Eden.

As Olive spoke, Evalene watched the large optical screen that displayed the camera's focus, what was broadcasting to the rest of the country at that moment. It caught her attention because as Olive spoke, they zoomed in on her bare neck, where her hair, snagged by the bandage, was pulled back enough to reveal perfect, smooth skin, untouched by a tattoo.

Evalene struggled to listen to her friend's story. Talc's

presence in the room, where he sat in a chair on the opposite side, drove her to distraction. Thankfully, Sol sat back down next to her. She felt slightly relieved.

Luc made his way around the room as Olive spoke, whispering to people here and there. He found a seat next to Evalene and leaned towards her, ignoring Sol. "We still need someone to go next. You'd be perfect."

Evalene peeked at him out of the corner of her eye. Perfect, as a supposed high Number? Or did he guess her true Number?

"I couldn't," she whispered back. "I always say the wrong thing."

"We desperately need someone to speak to the higher Numbers," Luc argued, "to help them understand our cause. Someone like you could explain to them why change is necessary, even though they personally might be comfortable, for the sake of those who aren't treated well and deserve better." So he did think she was a high Number. Jeremiah had kept her secret as promised.

Sol spoke for the first time since they'd entered the room. "You should do it." Evalene squinted at Sol in confusion. He knew from their capture that she was a low Number. But he just shrugged, as if to say, *what could it hurt?*

"You don't have to say much," Luc continued to petition her. "It doesn't even have to be good. I just need everyone in Eden to recognize this is real, get off their soft couches, and join us!"

Nervous, Evalene considered it. This was what Jeremiah had asked her to do only a few days ago, though it felt like years. And she reminded herself that this was why she had come, though now she definitely felt afraid. Finally, she whispered, "Okay."

"Wonderful." Luc vacated his seat as soon as she agreed, not giving her a chance to change her mind. He made his way to the video team, bending to speak in their ears.

Evalene's pulse sped up, pounding in her ears, making it impossible to hear Olive now. She had no idea what she was going to say. Her palms felt sweaty. She wiped them on her pantsuit, which just reminded her of the horrible rip along the bottom of the pant leg where she'd torn off the bandage for Olive. How embarrassing to go on live TV in such a state. She touched her hair, trying to comb out tangles with her fingers.

But she didn't have a chance to do anything else – Olive was finishing. Luc ran up from the back and hopped onto the short platform.

"Thank you, Olive," he said, resting a hand on her shoulder like he had with Talc. But unlike Talc, Olive beamed at the gesture. As usual, Luc was oblivious.

"Our next guest, will be Miss Evie – er –" he faltered at her last name, realizing he didn't know it. Evalene ignored him, still sitting in the plastic chair. She was shaking. She tried to swallow, but her throat was closing. Why had she agreed to this?

Was it too late to back down?

Luc waved a hand in her direction, his eyes bugging out at her in silent communication that said, "Get up here right now!" But to the camera, he stalled. "A young lady who grew up here in Eden, who managed to *escape*," he paused for dramatic effect, knowing this would shock the audience, "and even more amazing, chose to come back and fight with us. With all of you. For justice!"

As he spoke, his hand waved more and more wildly in her

direction, motioning for her to move. But she couldn't. Her feet felt glued to the floor. Luc clapped his hands loudly. The rest of the room joined in belatedly, and people were staring at her now, wondering why she wasn't getting up.

"But enough from me! I'll let her tell you all about it!" Now Luc's look said if he had to drag her to the stage himself, he would.

Sol nudged Evalene, startling her.

Standing, she took one small step, then another. Forcing herself to breathe, she reached the stage just as Luc helped Olive step off the other side. Evalene's face felt flaming hot. She was certain it was bright red.

Mounting the couple inches onto the platform felt like climbing a mountain.

Her hands shook visibly.

The room was silent.

Evalene scanned the room. Olive stood to her right with Luc where they'd dismounted while Luc signaled with his hands to hurry up. But Talc's presence behind them erased all thought as he scowled at her, especially when she saw his hands clamped around a huge gun.

The silence stretched unbearably long. Ten seconds turned into fifteen, then twenty. She didn't know what to say to the watching world. Overwhelmed.

Finally, Luc broke all television protocol and called a reminder to her from where he stood off camera, "Just tell your story, Evie!" The urgency in his voice was unmistakable. Her mind cleared a little at the nickname – technically the false name – and a starting place finally came to mind. She gathered up her courage, wringing her hands together, and began.

"First of all," Evalene said, not looking at the camera, but at Olive and Luc, "it's time I told you the truth." She bit her lip, wishing this were an intimate conversation instead of one that involved the entire country.

Averting her eyes from their faces to focus on the camera, she continued. "My name isn't Evie... It's Evalene Vandereth, daughter of Byron Vandereth, Number 4, and Pearl Vandereth, Number 6. I was born in Eden, right here in Delmare."

She swallowed. Hard.

The room had fallen so silent everyone could hear her gulp. Taking a shaky breath, she paused, not sure what to say next. She looked around the room, at all their anxious faces. So much brown clothing. She needed to help them understand what she'd learned, what she was still learning.

"I knew the way Numbers worked even before I knew the words *freedom* or *human rights*." She licked her lips. Her mouth felt dry.

"When I was nine years old, my mother was killed in the Bloom Rebellion. Her crime? Being in the wrong place. Possibly, being in the wrong place on purpose, standing up for those who couldn't stand up for themselves."

She felt tears forming at the back of her eyes, not at the memory of her mother, but at the idea of Pearl seeing her now. "I will never know for sure. But one thing I do know, my father was never the same." Evalene paused, imagining him watching on the television at home. Was he still ashamed of her? Probably.

But she had to tell the truth.

"Despite my mother's choices, we *never* expected my Numbering Day to turn out the way it did." Evalene looked down at her purple pantsuit which gave nothing away. But then she touched the scarf she'd retied around her neck, hiding her tattoo. It was blue, misleading those watching now into thinking she was a high Number. She started to slowly untie it.

"Someone wanted to silence my family." The pretty bow over the knots came undone. "Someone wanted to punish us." The first knot gave her some trouble. "So someone decided that I should be given a low Number." The connotation that someone other than God doled out the Numbers didn't escape those in the room. She hoped those watching on television caught the innuendo as well.

With a yank, the first knot came loose, and she set into the second. She'd gone to a lot of trouble to make sure the scarf wouldn't come off on its own. "And not just any low Number."

The last knot came loose and she ripped the scarf off her neck.

Against all her instincts, she pulled her hair back and the collar of her shirt down, so the left side of her neck was clearly visible. So that her tattoo was visible. She held still, allowing the cameraman to zoom in on it as they had with Olive.

She forced herself to say it aloud. "A Number 29."

The entire room stared at the image, at her tattoo. Having viewed her first as a high Number, they were confused. The only people who had known her true Number were Olive, and of course Sol who'd seen it during their capture. But as she met their eyes, she saw tears streaming down Olive's face, and even Sol's were suspiciously moist. She was afraid to look in Talc's direction, so she turned back to the camera.

Her voice shook. "For a long time, I thought, maybe... maybe this really is who I am." She swallowed, hard. Her chest felt tight.

"But a friend told me something that I think, if we admit it, we already know... That it's not *God* who gives us our Numbers. It's selfish, cruel men." Her hands tightened into fists at her sides.

"I am not a 29. But what I didn't understand," she stepped closer to the camera, right up to the edge of the stage, "what I have struggled to understand, is that I am not a Number 10 or higher either." The cameramen adjusted, zooming in on her face. No one moved. Evalene lifted her chin, looking directly into the camera, wanting to make her next words exceptionally clear.

"I am not a Number," she enunciated every word, carefully, "at all."

She pointed a finger at the camera.

"Neither are you."

Stepping back, Evalene gazed around the room now, pointing at those around her. "Neither are you." She pointed at another man, and another. "Or you." The cameramen were happy enough to oblige her, panning the faces of those crowded into the newsroom, revealing the captivated audience, before returning to Evalene.

Her finger stopped on Talc, whose weapon was lowered now. She choked out the words, in a strangled voice. "Or you." And she nodded to him. He no longer appeared angry, just confused, dropping his gun to his side and leaving the room.

Evalene watched him leave, and felt confident that she wouldn't have to deal with him again. That relief mixed with the joy of finally letting go of her Number threatened to overwhelm her and make her cry on stage. Her chest hurt at the sobs held back.

"If a high Numbers daughter could be treated so poorly, so could anyone's children. No one in Eden is safe. We need change. Please, fight with us." A couple tears leaked out, despite her efforts not to cry. "Thank you for listening to my story," she sniffed, swallowing once, then twice to clear the lump out of her throat. "Thank you for caring." She hoped she'd said enough, that she'd helped motivate the people the way Luc said they needed to. She struggled to get the words out. "Please, for me, and for the people you love… Help us. You know what you need to do."

She took two steps to the edge of the short little stage, and stepped down.

The room was silent.

37

Jeremiah's Decision

JEREMIAH WATCHED EVIE ON the little screen in front of him as the entire room collectively took a breath and then broke out into applause at the end of her speech. He felt so proud of her. He'd been right to think her story was important. It might have even sealed the revolution's success.

He was back in the side room where they'd placed him before, out of the way. No one else was with him.

His muscles weren't responding, and he was fading in and out of alertness, but he struggled to get up. His efforts just made the room spin. He was too weak.

But he needed to get up. Just an hour before, Luc had arrived at the station and entered Jeremiah's room, giving orders as he went. "Keep an eye on the broadcast and don't let the line get too short. Make sure the men outside take shifts; they need to stay fresh." Through the doorway, Larimar had nodded and disappeared to do Luc's bidding.

"Hey man," Luc said when he saw Jeremiah's eyes were open. "You look awful."

A weak chuckle escaped Jeremiah's lips. "Where've you

been? What time is it?"

"It's after noon. We tried to get here as soon as we could, but we were barely a half hour out of the harbor before the Regs found us," Luc said, dropping to sit by Jeremiah on the floor. Resting his arms on his knees, he continued. "Nobody was getting anywhere, and we didn't know if we would get here at all. But then the people showed up. Big swarms! They just came running!"

"Same here," Jeremiah said in awe as the scene right before he'd blacked out returned to him. "I didn't know if it would work..."

"What? You're telling me that now?" Luc joked, smacking him on the arm right below the bandage. Jeremiah winced.

"I figured I wouldn't see you if it didn't," Jeremiah teased back, wheezing. He tried to hit Luc back, but his aim was off, and he only slapped at air. He was so tired. Maybe he would close his eyes and rest a minute...

"I sent a team with those camera guys to get the Number One's home on film," Luc said.

That made Jeremiah blink awake. "Who's running the cameras here?"

"Don't worry, I know what I'm doing." Luc rolled his eyes. "I had them teach our guys how to run things here while they're gone. The basics at least. We'll be fine."

Jeremiah frowned, but Luc did seem to have things under control. "I even got them to set up a live feed on the screens in the news room so everyone can watch," Luc added when Jeremiah still seemed worried. Luc turned towards a tiny television screen in the small room where Jeremiah lay. "You know what, they're probably all connected. Let's see if we can't get it in here too."

The screen winked on, and sure enough, it showed the small stage, with the desk, chairs, and green screen background. Luc had everything taken care of. Jeremiah felt himself starting to relax.

"Rest up," Luc said, patting him on the shoulder before he stood. "We're finally winning. Regulators are surrendering. We have Delmare and most other large cities. It's just a few outliers now. That and getting the high Numbers on board." He turned at the door. "Everyone agrees it's just a matter of time before we're crowning the new Number One." He winked at Jeremiah. And as the door swung shut behind him, Jeremiah realized that despite all his arguing with Luc, his friend had never let go of the idea of Jeremiah as the new leader. He might never.

As Jeremiah watched each testimony on the little screen, he grew more and more convinced. Luc would argue and persuade, get the council on his side, convince the people, until finally Jeremiah would find himself giving in. Temporarily, Luc would say. Just temporarily. And instead of forming a council and system of voting that Jeremiah had studied for years and worked so hard to create, they would fall right back into the Number system he detested.

He watched all the way up to Evie's speech, but as soon as she finished, he knew what he had to do. If he stayed, he would be tempted to do exactly what Luc asked. It would be so much easier to enforce changes with sole leadership of the country.

He couldn't let that happen.

It was the easiest and hardest decision he'd ever made.

He had to leave.

It took him forever to stand and get dressed. After many breaks to rest, he opened the door, panting. They'd given him something for the pain, but it wasn't enough. Little needles were stabbing him in each of the locations he'd been shot. The needles sticking him in the nastiest wound on his back shoulder felt more like six-inch knives.

Once in the hallway, he turned reluctantly away from the newsroom, where they were still broadcasting. He wished he could see Evie again. He knew she was right on the other side of those double doors. But so was Luc.

Jeremiah walked towards the front door. Every step hurt. But he continued outside, down the concrete steps.

His men posted on guard duty outside nodded to him in respect. They assumed he was on a mission. In a way, he was.

He doubted they knew the extent of his injuries, and he tried to stand tall to avoid looking weak. They watched him pass but didn't say a word.

The classic cars were riddled with bullet holes. At the back, where the fighting had been the worst, they were shredded into unrecognizable piles of metal, as if the Regulators had tried to drive their vehicles over them, smashing them into pieces.

Striding towards the car he'd initially driven up to the building, Jeremiah climbed in through the gaping hole where the passenger door used to be, clumsily sliding over to the driver's side. He knew his men were still watching, but he moved agonizingly slow, unable to put on a show, thankful that his back was turned as he winced in pain. His stitches ripped open again in his back and shoulder. His foot and hand throbbed, but the pain in his back was so intense he had to pause a moment before continuing.

His men frowned in concern, but watched without comment. Jeremiah turned the key in the ignition, but nothing happened. The car wouldn't start. The fighting must've damaged the engine.

Outside the half circle of cars, multiple Regulator vehicles stood, abandoned. If their owners had all been gunned down during the fight, he supposed it was worth a shot. Holding back a groan, he climbed out of the driver's side of the car, and made his way to the closest Regulator jeep.

The keys were dangling from the ignition, never removed. He dragged his hurting body inside and once settled, turned the keys. The engine roared to life. Jeremiah sighed in relief.

It took some maneuvering with his hurt shoulder to turn the jeep around, but finally he managed to pull away from the blockade.

Blinking back white spots in his vision, he refused to lose consciousness again. He put the vehicle in drive and floored it. Beryl's summer home was a full day's drive from here. Could he drive that far in his condition? He didn't know.

He watched the news station and his men in the rearview mirror until he rounded a corner, and they disappeared.

38

The Necklace

PPLAUSE. ROARING APPLAUSE, CHEERS, and shouts of her name. The camera panned to follow Evalene into the crowd, and she shied away. Her face pleaded with Luc to save her. She wasn't used to being in the spotlight this long. Or at all.

He directed the next person in line onto the stage, guiding the camera-crew's focus away from Evalene, but not before she'd grown bright red and embarrassed. She'd just cried on television. How awful.

But no one seemed to mind. Instead, as she tried to escape the cameras, some people in the camera room followed her out into the larger newsroom with all the computer screens. Those sitting or standing throughout the newsroom began to clap as well. Evalene hurried to close the door behind her to block out the noise.

A woman approached her and gave her an unexpected hug. A man nearby reached out to shake her hand. Their kindness made her uncomfortable but she thanked them until the crowd dispersed.

Evalene sank into one of the desk chairs in front of a computer. Watching the screens as the next speaker finished, she blinked in surprise when her face appeared on the screen again. They were replaying it? Watching her revelation of the tattoo felt like watching someone else.

As she watched, a weight lifted off her shoulders. She'd denied her Number in front of thousands, maybe hundreds of thousands. And she'd survived. Not only that, but people had listened. Each time she said the words, they felt a little more real. She had value. She was worthwhile. The speech had changed her forever. But had it made any difference in the fighting?

The broadcasts continued to go on in the tiny camera room, and Evalene watched with bated breath along with the rest of the room as they filmed walking into the Number One's private chambers on live television, where the Number One sat, tied and gagged, to a chair, stripped of his fine clothes, wearing only his pajamas. He was just a shriveled, weak old man. His power and hold over people suddenly seemed foolish.

Olive looked especially pale and exhausted. The healer had told her she needed to stay awake for at least 12 hours, just to be safe. Evalene recalled how she'd felt after Kevra had knocked her out. She sympathized with Olive's pounding head, remembering the feeling well.

Olive stretched out along the floor against the back wall where it was quietest, while Evalene and Sol sat nearby, helping to keep her awake. Someone had found Sol a shirt, although Evalene almost thought it'd be easier to keep Olive awake if they hadn't.

Keeping an eye on her, they continued to watch the broadcast. Sol propped his dirty boots on the clean newsroom desk. After a moment of consideration, Evalene followed suit.

Throughout the room, the rebels huddled in whispering groups, flowing in and out on errands, while others pulled out chairs to watch the story unfold as well. Luc was doing a fabulous job of pacing the story and narrating in-between, painting the rebels as triumphant heroes.

A little while later, shots fired outside, and everyone tensed. It continued for less than a minute, then nothing. Waiting another five minutes, then ten, everyone was getting antsy when Luc rushed through the room. An older woman, thin but strong, grabbed his arm. "Tell us what's happening! We heard gunshots!"

"It's nothing to be concerned about." Luc tried to keep going, but the woman wouldn't let him. He sighed, and spoke up so the whole room could hear. "The Regs were outside with reinforcements. They tried to take the station, but the citizens helped us fight. We're fine. We will likely deal with resistance for the next couple days. Just sit tight and let us handle it."

He pried the woman's fingers off when she didn't let go, moving towards the camera room. Olive was sitting up, watching Luc, and when Evalene tilted her head towards where he'd disappeared, she nodded. Evalene helped Olive up and together they followed Luc. Sol trailed after them.

"Radio the Number One's home," Luc was saying in a hushed tone near the doorway as they entered the camera room. "Tell them we need to shut down the grid. Let's use his helicopter and get some footage of the fighting around the city." The men leapt into action.

When Luc left the camera room to reenter the newsroom, Evalene, Olive, and Sol shadowed him until finally he turned around, annoyed. "I promise if I have any news, I'll let you know."

Evalene cleared her throat. "Is Jeremiah doing okay?" She hadn't seen him since they'd arrived hours ago, and Luc hadn't elaborated on his injuries. She was beginning to worry.

Luc stared at the screens anxiously, waiting for the live feed of the helicopter to come online, though the Number One's Grid couldn't possibly be shut down so quickly. Staring blankly at the monitors, which currently held the testimonials going on in the next room, his response was delayed, but he finally turned to face her. "Uh, yeah. I haven't spoken to him in a few hours. He's been resting. He's probably wondering what's going on. I'll go talk to him and let you know if he wants any visitors."

It was almost fifteen minutes before the view from the helicopter blinked onto the screen. The entire room gasped. The streets outside the Number One's home and the news station were flooded with an ocean of people, their movements rippling like waves. Evalene had never seen so many people in her entire life. Some carried signs that she couldn't make out from the distance.

In awe of the crowds, Evalene wondered if this was what Jeremiah had imagined. So many people had responded to the revolutionaries. Evalene wanted to tell him she'd given her testimony, like he'd asked. Or maybe he'd seen it already?

In the background, Evalene listened to Luc speaking softly with the revolutionaries' best technicians. "Can you reverse the Number One's observation equipment?" He was asking about the equipment everyone knew the Number One had developed to watch people in their homes through their televisions.

"Sure, no problem," one of them said, and set to work.

Evalene had no idea what Luc meant by "reversing" it. Were the people going to watch them? Talk to them?

Evening fell with talk of victory. Though it would take a few more days for the dust to settle, it felt certain now. They'd won. In the news station, someone discovered a bottle of wine and popped it open to celebrate, passing it around them room. Everyone felt encouraged and relieved.

Almost the entire city was in the streets, and when the rebels figured out how to use the observation equipment, they discovered this was the case across the entire country. The Regulators weren't prepared for this level of rioting. They were losing due to the sheer numbers of the people. Regulators ran from the crowds. Rioters pursued. It was becoming a bloodbath.

At 8pm, their message appeared on every station.

And the message was simple.

We. Have. Won.

But few people were in their homes to see it, and the fighting in the streets continued. Regulators refused to admit defeat, though a few more were joining the revolutionaries besides Sol. Evalene's message had swayed many higher Numbers, but others detested the idea of losing their status, standing against the rebels instead and fighting anyone who came near their home. It didn't matter to them that the vast majority of the country wanted change. They liked their lives the way they were.

Luc radioed the base where the Number One was held hostage in his home. "We need air communication. Send every plane he owns up with the message." The planes flew simple flags with the same message as the broadcast. *We have won.* The population saw it in the air as the sun was setting, and cheers could be heard throughout the city.

Evalene overheard Luc asking if anyone had seen Jeremiah. Quietly, she stood without disturbing Olive or Sol, who were glued to the screens, and followed Luc down the hallway, where he stopped at the door to speak to the guards on rotation.

It was hard to hear what he was saying without getting too close. She didn't want them to notice her eavesdropping. But then Luc yelled, "What do you mean he left?"

"That's what Zuriel told me. He took the North Road," the other man's voice rose too as he replied.

"But that's going *away* from the city! He wouldn't –" Luc cut off mid-sentence. He stepped to the side with the radio, asking to speak with the rebels at the Number One's home. "I need to speak with the captain. Is Jeremiah there?" The rebels at the Number One's home said no. Luc didn't notice Evalene as she crept closer.

Luc radioed the company that had taken the Regulator Headquarters, the last to fall, just hours before. "No, he's not here," the radio crackled.

A thought came over Luc that made him close his eyes and sigh. When his eyes opened, he wiped his face clean of all expression.

Evalene stepped forward. "Did he really leave the city? I thought you said he was injured? You have to send someone after him!"

Luc's simmering gaze met hers. His eyes were hooded and furious. Evalene had never seen him like this before. He glanced around to make sure no one was listening. "Jeremiah is just one man. The plan doesn't change. We move forward."

"But Luc –" Evalene tried to argue.

He cut her off. "The plan doesn't change," he repeated. "We move forward." In a quieter tone, he added, "This is not the time for people to find out their leader is gone. Keep it to yourself, do you understand?"

Luc strode away from Evalene, calling out commands as he went. "Prepare for the Transition Stage. We'll need the council members on deck for the 9 o'clock broadcast." People jumped into action.

Trailing after Luc, Evalene was still trying to process that Jeremiah was gone as Luc paused in the doorway before entering the filming room. His voice rose above the murmurs, allowing anyone who wanted to know the plan to listen in. "We'll discuss immediate changes first, followed by more long term plans for Eden. We'll need to mention the Number One's trial." He snapped his fingers in the direction of the tech guys. "Let's get that Media Response tech up and running – we need this done yesterday! We need to hear from the people –" Was he talking about the reversed observation equipment from earlier?

Evalene stopped listening.

Jeremiah had left. By choice?

Those four words through the radio kept echoing through her head. *Took the North Road. Took the North Road.*

Not "was taken." Not "forced" to take. But took it of his own free will. Abandoned them.

Why would he do that? Exhausted, Evalene slipped away from the chaos in the newsroom, where Luc continued to give orders, and rejoined Olive and Sol on the far side of the room, reclaiming her chair. They sat silently watching the monitors, eating up the news, while Evalene pondered what her future looked like now.

She pulled out the necklace her father had given her, playing with it absently. Would he welcome her home or would she be forbidden to return? Sol saw the necklace and gave a low whistle. "Where did you get a protection charm? I've only ever seen 3s and above with those! Never any lower, much less a Number 29." Olive swiveled to stare at the object, forgetting the television.

Evalene's gut instinct was to shush Sol before she remembered everyone knew her Number now. She'd told the entire world. Unhooking the little necklace, she pulled the round charm with the inscription in front of her. "This? My father gave it me. It doesn't mean anything." She handed it to Olive, who'd already seen it, but still took a moment to admire the delicate leaves on the tree before offering it to Sol.

But Sol shook his head, refusing to touch it. He stared at the simple jewelry as if it was worth his weight in gold. "It means everything. *Deus et natua non nocere,*" he quoted the inscription along the side even though it was too small and far away for him to read it. "God and nature, do no harm. A Regulator can't even *touch* someone wearing the tree of life." He gave a short laugh. "Wish we'd seen that when we caught you. Would've gotten Control Leader Grausum off my back."

Evalene thought she'd never heard Sol speak so many words at once. Was it true? She stared at the simple jewelry. Her father had been looking out for her all along? She thought back to the moment he'd given it to her. He'd been about to tell her what it meant when they'd been interrupted. And then she'd left before he had another opportunity to speak to her. She felt her eyes fill, happy tears for once. It was hard to swallow.

Olive handed the necklace back to her, and Evalene carefully hooked it back around her neck. She pulled it over the top of her clothes instead of underneath, to display it proudly, wishing she'd been more grateful. For the first time since she'd left, Evalene wanted to go home.

"Maybe Kevra was right," she murmured, more to herself than to the others. "Maybe I would've been fine after all."

Sol leaned over to peer around Olive again at the mention of Kevra's name. "Brunette? Green eyes? Lot of attitude?"

Evalene frowned, about to say no, Kevra's hair was red. Then she recalled how Kevra had dyed it brown. She perked up. "You saw her? Is she okay?" She found herself hoping she was.

But Sol's face didn't match her excitement. He slowly leaned back. "Yeah, I saw her last week. She was apprehended trying to flee the country with a stolen ID that didn't match her Number. Captains are required to check every passenger. I saw her with a noose around her neck."

Olive gasped, clapping both hands over her mouth. She didn't even know Kevra, but tears sprung to her eyes. Evalene stared at Sol as he watched the television. His lips flattened in an unhappy line.

Wiping at the tears flowing down her face, Olive said, "That's horrible." Evalene agreed, but she wasn't as surprised as she'd thought she would be. She and Sol both knew what Olive didn't: that's just how life worked in Eden. Or, how it *had* worked.

Hopefully things were about to change.

A thought hit Evalene. "It could've been me."

Olive and Sol both looked over at her words. Evalene stared into space as she said, "If Kevra hadn't stolen the ID, it could've been me they caught. Me with a noose. I doubt even something as powerful as this," she touched the necklace, "could protect a fugitive."

Sol confirmed it with a nod. "And impersonating a high Number," he reminded her.

As they turned back to the monitors, Evalene felt chills run up and down her arms. Had God allowed the pain in order to save her?

She closed her eyes. There at the computer, with Olive and Sol next to her, Evalene chose to pray, really pray, for the first time in her entire life. She hesitated, not sure where to start.

She decided to keep it simple. *Thank you.*

EPILOGUE

Six Months Later

L UC HAD ASKED EVALENE to read a "quick memorandum" on live television, just a week after the revolutionaries had won.

"I accept my nomination to be a council mem-" halting immediately, Evalene read the rest to herself, jaw dropping. Whipping her eyes up to find Luc in the audience, she glared at him.

He frantically waved for her to continue. Lifting the script, Evalene reminded herself this was live TV. She ground out the rest of the sentence, "...a council member for Eden, in our new government system, speaking up for my fellow citizens, and helping to create our new, Number-free world."

She'd stormed off the air, feeling manipulated. Luc had argued with her for hours. "No other council member voted in had anywhere *near* your popularity. Everyone wanted the girl in purple. You understand both high and low Numbers – no one else is more qualified." He spoke in percentages. Annoyed, Evalene thought he was a born politician. But Olive sided with Luc, and when she reminded Evalene that "this was the system of leadership

Jeremiah always wanted," Evalene had been persuaded.

Now, six months had passed since the revolution ended.

Since the world started over.

Since being catapulted into a new life – one she hadn't necessarily asked for.

Evalene stepped outside of her new apartment that she shared with Olive, heading in to work. She missed her home and her father, but Ruby was furious with Evalene and all the rebels. As far as Ruby was concerned, some people were more special than others, and this equality business, getting rid of Numbers, was ridiculous. Though Evalene's father had begged her to come home, Ruby had loudly expressed that she was far from welcome.

Olive said it would take a while for the higher Numbers to adjust to the changes, to give up certain privileges, and earn others. And truth be told, it would be so much harder to re-learn who she was if she stayed home, with Daeva and Ruby and the others around, constantly reminding her of her past.

Entering the Capitol building, the previous Number One's home, Evalene quietly made her way to her office. The idea still boggled her as much as it had on her first day. She, Evalene Vandereth, had an office. She was a council member.

Though people nodded as she passed, with friendly smiles, she didn't stop, preferring solitude. That was one of her absolute favorite things about her office. She smiled as she entered her sanctuary – she was in charge of who entered, who spoke to her, and who she worked with. Well, mostly.

Settling into her desk chair, she touched the letter hidden in her pocket, out of habit. It was wrinkled and soft from carrying it with her everywhere. Jeremiah had never come back. Never even sent word. Had he gone back to the island like he'd said he would, only to find she wasn't there? She was such a different person now, was it really worth wondering what might have been?

A knock sounded on the door. Her first meeting.

"Come in," she called.

A short, balding man entered. He wore multi-colored clothes, and his tattoo was covered, yet his entire demeanor, hands folded, head bowed as if in prayer, screamed that he'd been a Priest prior to the revolution. He bowed slightly, honoring her.

Evalene waved it away immediately, uncomfortable no matter how many times she experienced this. "Please, sit. There's no need for ceremony. What can I do for you today?"

He came to sit in the chair across from her desk. "Actually," he pitched his voice to almost a whisper, the way people had in the past when they were near a television or a potential eavesdropper, "I've come with a bit of information, that I believe will help *you*."

Unable to help herself, Evalene leaned in. She had no idea what he was referring to.

"By all means, go ahead."

He leaned in as well, whispering in earnest now. "I knew your mother years ago, during the Bloom Rebellion."

Evalene stopped breathing. Her chest tightened. This man had known her mother? Taking a deep breath, she said, "Do you have any information on her death? On where they put her body?" It was almost too much to hope, that she might finally be able to bury her mother, after all these years.

"I can give you better than that," he said, smiling now.

"During the Bloom Rebellion, we were able to help many refugees escape. Pearl was one of them." Evalene blinked at him trying to understand what he was saying. Her heartbeat was erratic, blood flowing to her ears, and she almost didn't hear him as he confirmed what she had never thought was possible. "Your mother is alive."

END OF BOOK ONE.

Acknowledgments

I'm thankful above all to God for the inspiration of this story. Equally thankful that He blessed me with my sweet husband who has supported my dream, frequently tells me not to give up, and endures having ideas bounced off him regularly. And speaking of bouncing ideas off people, I am beyond grateful for my beta reading group who read the entire book before it was anywhere near the final product: Alissa Jones, Allisa White, Amy M. Olson, Brenda Patik, Carolyn, Danielle Gibson, Jennifer Dehn, Katherine Ley, Kris Cox, Lia Anderson, Mackenzie Claypool, M. L. Everidge, Meghan Morrison, Mike Batty, and Valerie Wheeler. Each one of you impacted this story in a unique, helpful way - thank you! Also, I want to give a huge shout out to everyone who supported me via the Kickstarter that launched this book into reality. Thanks to all of you, this book is now out in the real world instead of just an enormous word document on my computer. THANK YOU a million times, you are amazing! And finally, to YOU, my reader: I appreciate you more than you know and sincerely hope you've enjoyed this story. I can't wait to entertain you with many more in the future!

EVALENE'S STORY CONTINUES IN BOOK TWO:

PEARL'S NUMBER

Ten years ago, when Pearl Vandereth's life was in danger during the Bloom Rebellion, the rebels helped her fake her death and flee to the FreeLands. A country known to the natives as the Divided States.

But while she escaped the horror of life in Eden, where everyone has a Number for their station in life, her daughter Evalene was left behind to an unfortunate and unexpected fate. Now, though Pearl doesn't know it, Evalene has risen above her circumstances, discovered her mother is alive, and is on her way to the Divided States to find her.

Will they meet? Will Pearl even want to be found? And will Evalene like what she finds?

FOR MORE INFO, VISIT:
WWW.BETHANYATAZADEH.COM

"Are not five sparrows sold for two pennies? Yet not one of them is forgotten by God. Indeed, the very hairs of your head are all numbered. Don't be afraid, you are worth more than many sparrows."

-Luke 12:6-7

Bethany Atazadeh is a Minnesota-based author and avid reader. She graduated from Northwestern College in 2008 with a Bachelor of Arts degree in English with a Writing Emphasis. After graduation, she pursued songwriting, recording, and performing with her band, and writing was no longer a priority. But in 2016, she was inspired by the NaNoWriMo challenge to write a novel in 30 days, and since then she hasn't stopped. She is passionate about God, her husband, writing, painting, music, and dogs, specifically her Corgi puppy, Penny.

CONNECT WITH BETHANY ON:

Website: www.bethanyatazadeh.com

Instagram: @authorbethanyatazadeh

Facebook: www.facebook.com/authorbethanyatazadeh

Twitter: @bethanyatazadeh